"JUST DON'T TRY IT AGAIN, DO YOU HEAR ME?"

Kohl said, throwing up his hands in exasperation and stomping about the room. "If you hadn't insisted on going back alone, this never would have happened."

"You make it sound as if I sneaked out!" Carson retorted.

He narrowed her a glare. "If the shoe fits . . ."

In a flash of anger, she ripped off one of her shoes and hurled it at the exasperating man. "Why, you!"

Kohl dodged it. "Don't ever do that again either."

Without thinking, she sent the other shoe spinning at him. He ducked, but it smashed into his shoulder.

"You little hellcat! I warned you."

With deliberate steps he stalked her. Carson scrambled to the far side of the bed, but wasn't quick enough.

Kohl pounced.

The wind was momentarily knocked out of her. She glowered up at him. But the sensation of his hard body lying the length of hers caused her scowl to fade and be replaced with a flourish of mesmerizing excitement.

Kohl had been angry when he'd launched himself. That vanished the instant he gazed down into those blue depths with the urge to capture those full pouting lips not more than an inch from his. His breath mingled with hers. Her chest began to rise and fall at a faster pace against his.

"Oh God, Carson," he murmured, his lips swooping down on hers.

"Ms. Cleary is marvelous at combining humor, action, and a lot of sensuality." —*Romantic Times*

GWEN CLEARY

NEVADA TEMPTATION

ZEBRA BOOKS
KENSINGTON PUBLISHING CORP.

For Don

ZEBRA BOOKS

are published by

Kensington Publishing Corp.
475 Park Avenue South
New York, NY 10016

First printing: February, 1992

Printed in the United States of America

Chapter One

1880 San Francisco

Startled by the crash at the rear of the church, Carson swung around as the other four girls in the group fled toward the altar. Adding to Carson's quandary, Annette rushed back to her and thrust a cigarette into her hand before fleeing again.

"Where are you going?" Carson called out to Annette's retreating back. The only answer Carson received was a round of adolescent giggles before the door slammed behind the girl.

It was then Carson heard the pounding footfalls of the rotund Mother Superior barreling down on her. Her heart doing a drum roll signaling forthcoming cataclysm, she quickly swung her hands behind her back.

Mother Jude's sly eyes raked the girl. "Carson Mueller, what are you doing in church at this hour?"

"Would you believe I came to pray?" Carson offered in a small, sheepish voice.

"Not for a moment. You never come to church without first being called. What are you up to this time?

That mischievous twinkle in your eyes—" Mother Jude's voice broke off when she spied the swirling ring of smoke drifting up behind the nervous girl. "What do you have behind your back?" she demanded.

Carson swallowed hard and tried to appear calm. "Nothing."

"Humph! Let me see your hand."

Immediately repentant, Carson's sight caught at the votive lights. She wished she had time to light a few of them. A few? No. She'd need the entire rack of candles burning in silent prayer, she was in such trouble. Slowly, she brought her right hand forward.

"Now the other one, young lady."

Carson sucked in her cheeks. She was caught!

Equally as slow, Carson brought her other hand to the forefront, the offending cigarette smoldering between her fingers.

Mother Jude's hands flew to her cheeks. "Blessed Lord!" she gasped when her eyes fastened on the cigarette. "Your dear departed parents must have had an inkling how unruly you would turn out when they named you after the wild town Carson City was at the time of your birth." She shook her head, swinging her gaze to the rack of candles flickering near the girl.

The soft yellow light framed Carson's red hair like a halo and made her appear angelic with those sparkling blue eyes set wide in that innocent round face, but the nun knew better. Carson Mueller was anything but! The girl had been in and out of trouble due to her impetuous acts since her arrival at the convent as a small child fifteen years ago.

Then the realization hit the nun: The Mueller girl must have lit that cigarette on the votive candles!

Mother Jude immediately fell to her knees in front of the statue of the Virgin Mary and crossed herself.

A numb feeling descended over Carson. In a panic, she frantically looked for somewhere to stash the evidence. Trying to appear as nonchalant as possible, she inched her toward the coin slot at the flickering candles.

"Stop right there!" the nun practically shouted before she remembered where she was. You did not raise your voice in the house of God. More softly, she commanded with a hiss, "Do not take another step, young lady!"

Carson fought down the lump in her throat. She was in for it now!

"Just exactly what were you trying to do?"

Carson swallowed hard. "Me?"

"You are the only one here," the nun sputtered. "And put out that cigarette! Such sacrilege I have never before witnessed until you came to this convent. All those pranks you girls have played are one thing. But this!" — she motioned toward the cigarette which now lay crushed on the floor — "this is beyond redemption!"

Carson stood inside the old church studying the offending bit of tobacco while the Mother Superior's tongue lashed her for a full ten minutes.

"What kind of young lady are you?" berated the aging nun with the face of a bulldog. "What kind of person would light a cigarette on the church candles? I can't believe you would do such a thing!"

"I didn't . . ."

The nun cocked a brow, narrowing her eyes. "If you didn't, who did?"

Carson bit her lower lip. There was a code among the girls at the convent and Carson had pledged not to break it.

"It is my fault," she said and hung her head, but continued to sneak peeks at the furious nun.

The nun sighed and shook her head. Disappointment settled over her features. "I thought as much. Although I shall never understand why you insist on shouldering all the blame alone, since I have no doubt that there were others involved." Mother Jude huffed out a groan. "But since it is apparent that you have no intention of naming your accomplices, you are going to be the one to bear the punishment . . ."

Carson continued to listen to the nun's tirade as the woman paced back and forth in front of her, wringing her hands as the cross around her neck swayed side to side over her huge bosom, and the rosary at her waist swung back and forth like a pendulum of doom.

Carson pressed her lips together and quietly prayed for a miracle of salvation. Despite Mother Superior's brusque treatment and outrage, the old nun had always had a soft spot in her heart for her.

"I am afraid this deviant behavior and your escapades can no longer be ignored. I cannot protect you this time; your sin has been too great. Pity you don't stop and think before you act. At the rate you are going"—she crossed herself—"only our Savior knows what dreadful end will befall you within the next five years! You are much too impetuous. I have never known a girl on the brink of young womanhood to remain so impulsive.

"I am afraid you have outsmarted yourself this time with your antics. I warned you that one day it would happen. I am sure that Father O'Clanahan is going to write your guardian about this unforgivable infraction against the Church."

Carson's head snapped up and she gave the nun a beseeching entreaty. "Oh, please, you can't let him do that. My guardian will be very upset."

"Well, you should have thought about that before you went ahead and lit that cigarette!"

"But I—"

"Clean up that tobacco, then go to your room. I shall let you know what your penance will be. But I fear that such a stunt will cause your expulsion this time."

At that, the Mother Superior shook her head, silencing Carson's attempts to seek further interview. The nun then swung around, her black habit flying out around her like a black storm cloud portending ruination, and marched toward the rectory to consult the priest.

For ten days Carson spent the majority of the time on her knees while she waited for a response from her guardian to the priest's letter. Her knees ached from the innumerable Hail Marys and Our Fathers she'd recited on the kneelers. When she wasn't in church atoning for her sin, the priest had seen to it that she was responsible for every chore she had ever detested. She mopped floors, swept and raked the grounds, and cleaned the kitchen. Except during church, they kept her separated from the other girls who giggled and winked whenever they passed her.

"I'm sorry you got caught," Annette Singleton whispered during prayers. "I heard Father O'Clanahan tell Mother Jude that he not only wrote your guardian, but he also notified your fiancé's family."

Horrified, Carson forgot herself and turned full on toward the pretty blonde. "You know you were the one who smuggled that cigarette into the church."

Annette raised her chin ever so slightly. "Perhaps. But you were the one caught with it." Her sympathetic expression changed to a sly grin. "Besides, even if you did confess now no one would believe you; you've waited too long. Incidentally, I overheard that a letter just arrived from your guardian in reply to Father O'Clanahan's letter."

"And I suppose you also know the contents of the letter," Carson shot back, chagrined with her tenuous position.

"Shh!" Mother Jude hushed and cast Carson a frown meant to freeze the devil in hades.

Annette gave Carson a smug smile and returned to her prayers. Carson Mueller had been a thorn in her side since childhood. Prettier and more personable, Carson had lured Sinclair Westland away from her two years ago, and since that time Annette had tried to think up ways to get him back. She smiled to herself. Sinclair's prominent mother would never stand for Carson's latest infraction. Annette was sure of it. Annette waited until prayers were over, then filed out of the pews and followed Carson from the church.

Outside, Mother Jude dismissed the girls. Then the nun hailed Carson. "A reply came from your guardian, and Father O'Clanahan wishes to speak with you about it."

Annette shot Carson a vainglorious grin and

flounced off. Carson watched the girl join a group of their peers before she dragged her attention back to what Mother Jude was saying.

"Come along, Carson. You might as well get this over with."

"Did he say what was in the letter?" Carson asked, dreading the reply.

"I am not at liberty to divulge the contents. But I fear you are not going to be pleased."

The nun clasped her hands, swung around, and headed toward the rectory, Carson following close behind. Her mind worked furiously as she tried to think up something to say in her own defense to forestall the feared inevitable. Nothing clever came to mind.

Mother Jude directed Carson to take a seat before she shook her head in disappointment and left. Carson settled on the hard chair outside the priest's office and waited until the forbidding wooden door creaked open and the lilliputian figure of Father O'Clanahan stood before her.

"My child, come into my office. There is much we have to discuss."

With great trepidation Carson rose. "Yes, Father," she said and followed him into the austere room.

"Please, child, sit down." He motioned to the high-back chair directly in front of his desk and took up his position before the huge walnut retable. He clasped his hands on the shiny surface and leaned forward. "As I am sure you are aware, I have written to your guardian of your misadventures and, although he is not in agreement, it is felt that we here at Saint Francis have provided all the guidance and direction we can for you and it is time you return home."

"No!" Then in a softer voice filled with panic. "No, I can't leave San Francisco. What will Sinclair's mother say?"

"I have already advised your fiancé's mother of the situation and she is in complete accord. Sending you home to allow people time to forget your misdeeds is the wisest course of action." To Carson's crestfallen look, the priest added, "She has agreed to accompany Sinclair to Carson City in three months time. At that time, if you have proved that you can conduct yourself like a lady, and if the gossip has died down, Mrs. Westland stated she would sponsor your return to the city. Then you will reside with her until your marriage, so she can properly present you to society. Therefore, as soon as arrangements for your transportation are made you will be leaving for Carson City."

The priest cleared his throat. "I am afraid that your guardian did not send adequate funds for train travel. Consequently, you will be traveling by stage." Carson opened her mouth to protest, but he raised a hand and shook his head. "No argument now. Go pack your things, then return to the chapel and pray that you have learned your lesson so you can prove to your fiancé's mother that you have changed."

Carson thought of protesting further, but from the look on the priest's face it was obvious that there would be no changing his mind. She silently nodded. "Yes, Father. Thank you, Father."

She started toward the door, but his harsh voice halted her exit.

"Carson, I hope you will use the next three months in Carson City wisely and stay out of trouble. It would be unseemly if you got yourself involved in any more calamities, since it may force your future mother-in-law to have a change of heart. She is already teetering on putting an end to this recent engagement of yours. So I suggest you make every effort to show her how you have matured."

"Yes, Father. I promise you, I shall stay out of trouble. I shall prove to everyone that I can be a proper lady. And the next time I encounter Sinclair's mother, she will be able to see just exactly what kind of lady I have become."

Chapter Two

Carson stood outside the stage depot, her red curls kinking up around her hat in the morning misty fog. Despite a valiant, last minute effort she was being sent to a home she had not seen since she was five years old and her guardian had decided that she should be reared in a convent. Since he was a bachelor and was busy building the brewery business he had started with Carson's father back in 1860, he had announced it would be in her best interests to be sent away.

Remembrances of her parents' deaths at the hands of Indians at Pyramid Lake and her subsequent youth without a mother's love saddened her, and she wiped at her eyes. It was a bitter memory. Her mother had so loved her father that she had followed him when he'd ridden out with Major Ormsby to punish the Indians for attacking Williams Station and taking back their squaws after white men had abducted them. Thinking it more of a lark and ill-prepared, they had been slaughtered.

Carson sniffled and forced the reminiscence aside

before Sinclair rejoined her. He would not approve of such an open display of emotion over something that could not be changed.

Waving the ticket in hand, Sinclair cut a dandy figure in his finery coming toward her through the fog, and Carson could not help but lose her downtrodden lamenting. She was not one to remain glum in the face of adversity for long. She had always recovered quickly and got on with her life, and she would not let this mere setback to her plans for a happy marriage with Sinclair daunt her.

Sinclair was considered a prime catch among the girls at the convent with his blond good looks and impeccable manners. He was in demand at all the most important social functions the girls longed to attend. And they all whispered about the social position his wife would enjoy residing in the Westland mansion.

"Here you are, Carson, dear," Sinclair said. He leaned close and motioned toward three people standing not far from them. "Pity your guardian refused to send adequate funds so you could take the train and save such an uncivilized trip with the likes of those people. They certainly do not look to be of proper social standing, and I do not want you associating with their kind."

Suppressing the urge to inquire why he had not stepped forward to provide the additional funds for train travel, Carson gave a quick glance. She could not understand how Sinclair could so easily judge them lacking, since the two men wore heavy coats and had their backs toward her. The only female, a girl barely twelve clutching a small, worn box, looked perfectly presentable to Carson. But, of course, Sinclair was a man of the world and knew such things.

She also had noted the forbidding height of the man who was sporting a bulge in his fine coat where she had seen guns strapped to unsavory characters during her outings from the convent. Thinking about the width of the man's back, Carson vowed, "You needn't worry, Sinclair, I intend to follow all your instructions to the letter."

"Good. Now repeat them to me one last time, so Mother will be pleased when we arrive to fetch you back where you belong . . . at my side."

Carson swallowed and looked about her to make sure she was not observed being asked to recite a lesson like a silly schoolgirl.

"Don't hesitate, Carson, when I make a request. You know that is not proper comport expected of a Westland lady."

Carson pinched her lips to keep from retorting. Instead she took a breath and looked into Sinclair's amber eyes. "You needn't worry, Sinclair. When you and your mother arrive in Carson City I shall be the perfectly proper lady, demure and retiring. I shall speak softly and only when spoken to; I shall not speak my mind unless we are in private; my dress shall be impeccable; my manners above reproach; I shall have prepared a proper home to demonstrate my wifely skills; and I shall have made friends with only the best circles of people on the appropriate social level. Did I leave anything out?"

A frown curled his upper lip, detracting from his handsome face. "Yes, Carson, you did. When my mother and I arrive you will have arranged a proper welcoming committee of the town's finest citizenry."

"Of course. I shan't forget again."

"Good girl. Now, I am truly sorry I cannot tarry here any longer to see you off, but you know I am expected at the Appleton's promptly at nine."

Carson forced a brave smile for Sinclair's sake. "Of course," she repeated again as if by rote. "I shall be anxiously waiting for you."

He took her hand and gave it a peck. "Naturally you shall."

Sinclair looked about, then gave Carson a quick buss on the forehead. Carson was such an abstruse young girl. He had difficulty understanding why his mother insisted she would make a proper wife and meet his familial obligations. And despite her beauty the girl did not make his blood boil. Inwardly he sighed. His mother was always right. Carson Mueller was the best choice under the circumstances. Keeping his face placid he turned from her and headed toward the convent to escort Annette to her parents' home where his mother was expecting him.

Carson watched Sinclair saunter from her, then turned her attention to the stagecoach. The driver was bellowing for them to board. Her chin high with determination to fulfill all of Sinclair's expectations, Carson moved over to take her place in line.

"Excuse me!" she snapped with all due outrage as the tall man with broad shoulders stepped in front of her. "I have been patiently waiting to board and I suggest that you do the same . . . behind me, since I was here first."

For the first time the man turned full on toward

17

her and her breath caught. He was the most danger-ous-looking man she had ever seen. Inky curls waved thickly over his forehead in a lazy fashion. He pinned her with a penetrating blue gaze as icy as the worst winters in Virginia City, except his eyes were forested with a wealth of curling black lashes. Just the hint of a beard surrounded full, unsmiling lips. He was nearly twice Sinclair's size. Huge shoulders anchored arms and hands that she was sure could crush her if he had a mind to.

"You were not here first," was all the resonantly deep voice answered.

Carson was tempted to retort, but she had to re-member that she was practicing to be the lady Sin-clair expected to find when he came for her, so she gave her chin a haughty lilt, looked down her nose the best she could, since he was so tall, and replied, "A gentleman always allows a lady to precede him."

To her chagrin he cocked one straight, black brow. "So a gentleman does, does he?"

"That is what I said, sir."

"So it is," he said and continued to block her entry into the coach.

"Well, then either step aside and allow me to board, or offer your arm like a gentleman and assist me."

"Those my only two choices?"

Offended, Carson bristled up to her full five-foot, two-inch height barely reaching his collarbones. "They can hardly be considered choices; they are proper social behavior."

He chuckled at that. "Oh, social behavior."

At the full-bodied hardiness of his laughter, Carson decided that there was plenty of time to practice being a lady later—after she set the man straight! "Since you so obviously have no social graces, just move," she barked out and attempted to give him a good shove, merely shifting their positions.

To her shock, her efforts did not yield the desired results and he further infuriated her with, "And I suppose that is the way a 'lady' conducts herself?"

"Only when she is in the presence of someone who so obviously is not a gentleman."

To her disgust her rejoinder seemed to have had no effect on him. He was giving her a perfect white-toothed grin all the way to his eyes "Did you ever think that a man knows how to be a gentleman in the presence of a lady?"

At that, she crossed her arms over her chest since he had so openly allowed his gaze to roll over her as if she were no more than one of those loose painted women Mother Jude had instructed her to cross the street to avoid. She wasn't certain whether it was an act of agitation or defense of her person. "And just what are you implying?" she demanded, outraged.

"Look, if the corset fits, wear it, darlin'."

"How dare you refer to such an intimate piece of apparel in my presence!" she gasped. Unconsciously, her hands smoothed at the waist of the trim beige traveling suit.

"Thought you might learn something, since you so obviously are trussed up tighter than a Christmas turkey." To her snort, he added with an appreciative smile of assessment, "Can't say that it isn't becoming though."

"You know nothing of the subject, since I am not

19

wearing one," she burst forth before she realized what she had said. A lady would never discuss such a topic in the presence of the opposite gender.

"My compliments to nature then," he observed with a cocked brow.

Before she could halt her wayward tongue, she blurted, "Well, nature did not do such a bad job with you either."

He burst forth with a robust laugh to Carson's horror. In an attempt to redeem such a blunder, she quickly added, "Pity Mother Nature neglected to give you some manners. You are rude beyond deliverance."

"In that case, step aside so I can take my place in the coach," he announced and promptly picked her up by her arms and set her aside as if she were no more than an annoying barrier easily breached.

Well, she was not going to stand still for such ill-treatment at the hands of such a scoundrel! Quick as light, Carson ducked in front of him and blocked his efforts to enter the coach.

The other passengers were hanging out the windows, enjoying the tiff as Carson and the man stood, nose to nose, exchanging another round of barbs. Disgusted and impatient to get underway, the grizzled driver shouted, "Look yous, I don't give a jackass's tail who puts their behind in the coach first, but if you two don't want to have to start hoofin' it to Sacramento and points east, get in the damned stagecoach before me and my girls" — he shot a glance at the restive roans — "leave the both of yous here to duke it out."

Carson's stubborn streak moved to the forefront

of her reasoning. Planting herself firmly in line with the open door, so the driver would be unable to move the stagecoach without first climbing down and helping her inside, she gave the runty man her most daunting stare. "I am not moving from this position until . . . oh!" she gasped in shock as she found herself being bodily raised in warm, strong arms and then coldly tossed inside the coach without ceremony.

She struggled to right herself and regain a portion of her dignity as a masculine body, as hard as a rock and smelling from the fresh scent of soap, plunked down practically on top of her. Fighting with her askewed hat, she managed, "How could you be so utterly ungentlemanly?"

"Guess you bring out the gentler side in me. Now, move over and give me some room before I'm forced to sit on your lap."

Carson let out a squeal, brushed off her skirt, and plastered herself against the far side of the coach, huddling in the corner in disgust and horror. Sinclair had not been gone more than five minutes and already she was having difficulty living up to his expectations.

"Now, that is much better, don't you think so, *lady?*"

Carson's mortified expression caused the older male passenger to comment. "What you lookin' so dismayed for? Didn't you want to be called a lady?"

These were the people she was going to be forced to travel with, she realized. So she decided to graciously relent and put an end to such a travesty. "Yes, but—"

"But, hell, you got what you wanted," he observed with an open grin. "So why don't we all introduce ourselves and get acquainted since we're going to be traveling companions? My name is Mortimer South, but most folks just call me Pots 'cause I sell 'em and because my gut looks like one." He patted the enormous overhanging bulge. "Yessiree, I'm the best pot salesman in the West."

Pots hesitated to take a breath and studied the pair for a moment. "Say, how would you two like to save time and buy what you need to set up housekeeping now? I can give you a good discount?"

Carson's gasp of horrified disbelief reverberated around the coach. "Why, the very notion is so repulsive that I shall not attempt to make further reply," Carson spat, but continued just the same. "This man and I are total strangers and shall be so when we depart this stagecoach!"

Pots looked to the man despite his trepidation at his menacing appearance. The big man held up his hands. "Don't look to me. I have no desire even to learn her name. As far as I'm concerned there needn't be any further conversation." With his piece said, the man shoved his hat over his eyes and crossed his arms over his chest, effectively shutting everyone else out.

Carson cast a glance at the young girl sitting next to Mr. South for support, but the mousy little girl dressed in worn calico merely shrugged and directed her attention out the window. Carson looked to Mr. South, but he made a big display of shuddering at the cool reception his suggestion had received and turned his attention to a dime novel

22

he had pulled out of his bag.

Left to her own company in the dusty coach, Carson made every attempt to analyze how her behavior had disintegrated from being the lady Sinclair expected to the harridan adaptation she had displayed. She considered it over and over in her mind until she finally concluded that she had not been at fault in the slightest. The blame was to be laid at the shiny boots of the ruffian sitting next to her.

Thank heaven once this trip was over she could set the egregious incident aside and get on with practicing proper behavior. And she would never have to be bothered by that antagonizing degenerate again!

Chapter Three

By the time the stage stopped for the night Carson was exhausted. She had been jarred and shoved, jostled and forced to remain seated much too close to that insufferable ruffian. And to make matters worse, neither man had offered to help her alight from the stage. Taking a deep, fortifying breath, Carson climbed down and stood perfectly still.

Before her was little more than a run-down shack out in the middle of nowhere!

To her added shock, once she entered the way station, she was totally chagrined. The grimy little place had only one room! Attempting to remain calm, Carson moved about the small, dingy room. It appeared that its inhabitant had an aversion to cleaning by the draping spider webs, dust, and accompanying odors of rancid food.

"Is this where we shall be spending the night?" she asked to no one in particular.

"Unless you'd prefer to sleep in the coach," that same intolerable man answered with a grin, leaning arrogantly against the wall watching her.

"Is that where you intend to sleep?" she queried before she realized the implication of her words. The expression on the man's face told her that he had not missed her faux pas.

His smile was slow and lazy as he said, "You asking to join me?"

"Don't be absurd!" she sputtered. "Sleeping with you would be a horrifying thought."

"Oh, I don't know, you might find that you enjoy it," he retorted to a round of smirks and suppressed laughter from the others nearby. To add further insult, he added, "But you needn't worry, darlin', I like my women warm and willing, not cold and disagreeable as a spinster-in-learning."

Fighting to keep from parrying further words with the man, Carson showed him her back and took a seat at the opposite end of the long table, which nearly ran the length of the small, stuffy room.

"Pay him no mind," the young girl said, joining Carson.

Carson's head snapped up from her own murderous thoughts. For an instant Carson thought the girl's eyes held a strange light, but she decided that it was merely a reflection of her own feelings she saw there. "I keep trying, but that horrible man is making it difficult."

"Heard tell he's a gunslinger named Kohl Baron who's tryin' to get respectability by buyin' some business," the girl said, her fingers wrapped tightly around a worn box.

"Well, Mr. Kohl Baron certainly cannot 'buy' respectability. No doubt he intends to run a house of ill repute."

The girl did not smile at Carson's attempt at humor. "Heard that he hires out his gun to the highest bidder—that's his business."

Carson's eyes rounded. "He kills people?"

"That's what his kind does."

"He is dressed like a gentleman," Carson observed, sneaking a glance at the man attired in San Francisco's latest fashion. He had turned his attention from her and was now engaged in a conversation with the stage driver and way-station keeper as the bearded man dished up supper. Her pulse sped up and she settled on the explanation that it was because she feared for her safety in the presence of such a man.

"Looks can be deceivin' but Kohl Baron don't fool me none. And if I was you I'd be careful."

"Don't worry, I shall. By the way, my name is Carson."

"I'm Addeline . . . ah . . . Addie." At Carson's bemused expression, the girl quickly said, "Only my pa called me by my God-given name."

"Addie's a nice name. I hope we can be friends during this trip. I'm afraid it is going to be a long journey."

Addie's attention shifted to the man and back again to her new friend. "It ain't gonna be too bad. You'll see."

"Are you going to be meeting your family?" Carson asked.

Addie blinked. "Naw. Just goin' where the stage takes me until I can find me work. Ain't got a permanent home."

"You don't have any family either?" Carson surmised, feeling a sudden bond with the girl.

"My kin's all gone," Addie said and hung her head,

but she watched her traveling companion from beneath her sparse lashes as her hands tightened around her box.

Carson reached out and patted the girl's hand; it was ice-cold and the girl pulled the box closer toward herself. Carson thought it strange how glacial the girl's hand was since it was a warm day, but realized that the girl must be nervous traveling all alone. She wondered about the box the girl always carried with her and had the urge to inquire about it. But she decided to leave the girl her privacy since the box probably contained all the childhood things that were important to a young girl.

"It must be Fate that brought us together, Addie, because I am also an orphan."

"Fate," Addie echoed in a low voice.

"If you don't have any particular town in mind you might consider coming to Carson City with me. I'm sure I can help you find employment."

Addie furrowed her brows. "You named after that place, Carson City?"

"My mother and father were German immigrants. They settled in Carson City to start a new life in America and were so happy after they arrived in the fledgling town that when my mother gave birth to me it seemed the natural thing to do."

"What happened to them?"

It seemed a rather intrusive question, but Carson chalked it up to the girl's own circumstance. "They were killed during an Indian uprising at Pyramid Lake. What about your family?"

The girl fidgeted. "After Pa died, Ma just sorta withered away with grief till she died, too."

Carson understood the girl's unease. Losing your family was a tragedy difficult to share with strangers, and the raw pain was still evident in the girl's voice. Before Carson had the opportunity to offer her commiseration the brusque voice of the way-station keeper intruded into their conversation.

"Grubb's on. Come 'n' get it before I feed this here slop to the hogs," announced the grimy man who ran the way-station.

Feeling that now she had at least one ally during such a disagreeable trip, Carson picked up a bowl, wiped out the specs of dust, and got in line for supper. If she weren't so famished she would have foregone the meal, but she had to keep up her strength.

It was her misfortune that the gunslinger took up a place in front of her. Carson thought about what kind of man Kohl Baron was before she decided that regardless of his unsavory profession, she could not allow him to use his size to squeeze in front of her a second time.

She tapped him on the shoulder, then stepped back. "Do you intend to make a habit out of infringing on my rights?"

Kohl shoved his Stetson back on his head. "Didn't know womenfolk had 'rights.' "

Carson ignored his observation. The fact that women did not enjoy all the freedoms afforded to men galled her, but she was not going to let him see it. "I was in line first . . . once again."

Slowly, the man pivoted around, amusement in those blue eyes. "If I'm not mistaken, you were across the room when Bundy called out supper."

"Well, yes, but —"

"But since you finally are able to admit the error is yours, I suppose I can be generous this time and allow you to have my place since you seem to be so anxious to eat Bundy's cooking."

He stepped aside and swung out his arm with a flourish.

Carson was so startled by the man's sudden change in behavior that the bowl tumbled out of her hands and clattered to the floor.

Carson bent down to pick up the bowl.

The gunslinger also bent down.

A stab of pain seared through Carson's temples as their heads collided and she shot back up straight, grasping her forehead. She sent him a scorching look. "What are you trying to do, make sure that this trip is as unpleasant as possible for me?"

Her bowl in hand, he rubbed the rising bump on his head. "Lady, first you try to use that body of yours to keep me out of the stagecoach, when that failed you try to knock me over the head. One would think that you don't like my company," he said to male snickers.

"Oh, if only I had the ten cents a mile it took to ride the train I wouldn't have to be subjected to the likes of you," she hissed.

"Looks like we are being 'subjected' to the likes of each other." He hesitated for a moment before a calculating grin captured those full lips of his. He rubbed his chin. "Of course, if you're interested, we might be able to work out some kind of arrangement for you to earn your ten cents a mile."

Carson was not so sheltered that she did not realize what he was implying. She bristled and ignored the men as they cast the gunslinger envious glances. "You obviously know nothing of culture, let alone dealing with those who do not welcome your intensely crude, unwelcome ways. There is absolutely no kind of 'arrangement' we could work out now or *ever* together, sir."

Not bothered by her attempts to harangue him with her highfalutin ways, he gave a shrug. "Then why don't we try to make the best of the time we are going to share together, darlin'?"

Carson grabbed the bowl from his hand and held it out to the way-station keeper, then dealt the gunslinger her most blistering look. "I have no intention of attempting 'to make the best' of your company regardless of the situation. Just stay away from me!"

She was so furious that she hastily grabbed the bowl of stew. To her horror, it promptly splashed down the front of her beige jacket. She frantically attempted to wipe at the spreading brown stains.

"Allow me," said the gunslinger with a grin in his voice.

Carson's attention snapped up. The ruffian was standing in front of her, casually holding out a handkerchief. Carson slammed the bowl down on the table, ripped the handkerchief out of the grinning man's hand, and wiped at the stains.

"Don't you think a 'thank-you' for the use of my handkerchief is in order?" Kohl suggested in a lazy voice.

"Hardly!" she gasped and tossed the white scrap of material back at him. She caught sight of the others who were standing clear, watching the scene with suppressed amusement. She was about to turn her wrath on her fellow passengers, but the gunslinger cast them a look of warning and the others immediately seemed to shrink back and move off.

Carson was astounded at the power the gunslinger seemed to have over the others, and she wondered if they were aware of something about the man that must have escaped her. Her gaze shot back to Kohl Baron. He was now busy dishing up a bowl of stew. Even such a simple action displayed his physical strength in the bulge of muscles.

He was so different from the men she had been exposed to during her tenure at the convent. Carson could not help but wonder if his kind was the norm outside polite society. If so, she had to make sure that she wasted no time surrounding herself with only the best people once she reached her destination despite the pique of curiosity assailing her.

After managing to get through that first awful night, Carson forced herself to make the best of the trip. The excursion by stage settled into a jarring routine of dry, hot, dusty days, punctuated by crude accommodations at night and food that made the convent cuisine seem gourmet upon reflection.

Carson made every effort to maintain a distance between herself and Kohl Baron, but every time she glanced in his direction he seemed to be staring at her. Even at odd times, when the other passengers were dosing or sharing conversations over a meal, he sat removed from the others watching her.

On the next to the last day of the journey Lake Tahoe came into view. Carson's breath caught at the sheer beauty of the shimmering azure water, which glistened in the sun and was surrounded by immense pines. The pine scent managed to break through the dust kicked up by the stage and Carson closed her eyes to revel in the serenity offered by the mountains.

Gun shots broke Carson's musings as the stage team broke into a mad pace. Holding her hat, Carson stuck her head out the window to assess the sudden change in events. Her breath failed her when she saw the coach careening down the steep road. A bullet whizzed past her head and she screamed.

Carson was immediately yanked back inside the coach and tossed onto the floor, Kohl Baron on top of her pinning her beneath him.

"Stay down!" Kohl shouted and shoved her back when she tried to push him off and rise. All the while he held her down, he was shooting out the window with his free hand, the sun glinting off the simple gold ring he wore on his little finger. Her heart hammered against her chest, and despite her fright she could not help but experience the hard feel of him.

In the next few minutes chaos reigned inside and outside the coach. Addie cried, "We're all gonna be killed!"

Pots grabbed the money belt around his ample waist. All the money he had in this world was on his person. Hysterical, he snatched at the gunslinger and Carson scrambled back onto the seat. "You got to save us, Baron. You're a gunfighter. You got to know what to do."

Kohl gave Pots a shove, his attention momentarily taken away from the window. It was just long enough to give one of the highwaymen time to leap onto the stage. Carson saw the masked face appear in the window and screamed.

Kohl swung toward the window, the gun still smoking in his hand. But the outlaw was already pointing his gun at him and pulled the trigger just as the stage lurched over a rock.

The power of the blast knocked Kohl back on top of Carson, sending them both sprawling sideways. Carson landed on her back with the gunslinger's head settled on her chest. She was horrified at the sudden intimacy, but at the same time her breast filled with a tingling sensation which radiated throughout her body. Once she recovered, she tried to shove him off her, but he was unconscious and his life's blood was flowing over her white blouse.

As the outlaws overpowered the driver and reined in the stage to a halt, Carson was sure they were all about to be murdered.

Chapter Four

It seemed like an eternity once the stage was stopped near the top of the Kingsbury Grade before the highwaymen swung open the door and ordered them from the coach. While the others meekly followed the outlaws' directives and disembarked, Carson frantically tried to rouse the gunslinger.

"Ya comin' outta there, sweet thing?" one of the highwaymen snickered.

Carson looked up and her gaze fastened on a huge black dusty form with hard green eyes above a mask, hiding his identity. She should have been frightened, but she was furious. She had been forced to endure an uncivilized stage trip, starved by near inedible food, given a hard time by Kohl Baron, and now she was being put in this frustrating position.

Without thinking through the consequences of her actions, she reached out and ripped the kerchief from the man's face.

A look of sheer disbelief spread over his unshaven countenance. "Fiery little thing, ain't ya?" the man said with a laugh.

He reached in to take her. Carson grabbed her parasol and smacked his hand away, then hit him over the head, causing him to back out of the way with his hands crossed protectively over his head.

"What's the matter, Bart, the little spitfire more'n you can manage?" The enormous man who was the obvious leader laughed. He slid from his horse and waved a gun menacingly at the other passengers trembling together off to the side.

"Yeah, maybe I ought to take her on fer you," the smallest of the three said a safe distance from the coach. The man dressed in a long duster laughed so hard, he nearly fell from the saddle.

"Shut your puss, Jake! Or I might just up and make you et them words," the unmasked outlaw bellowed. Then he swung back to the wildcat cowering over the unconscious man in the coach. "Protective little thing, ain't ya? That there man in there yours?"

"I do not even know him," Carson retorted. As she watched the outlaw like a cornered rabbit she chided herself for not simply complying with their orders as the others had done. Why couldn't she control her hasty behavior? If only she had, she would not be in such a precarious position now.

The outlaw narrowed hard eyes. "Well, ya seem mighty friendly for being strangers." He pointed a gun at her head. "Now ya get that pretty little tail of yours outta that coach. I ain't got me no more time to pussy-foot around with ya."

Carson swallowed back the urge to launch herself out of the coach at the man and offered the outlaw a gloved hand. When he just stood there, she settled him an indignant look. "Well, since you are forcing this stage to make an unscheduled stop, the least you can do is help me down."

The outlaws threw back their heads and chuckled, then the one who had tried to grab her holstered his gun, presented Carson with a formal bow, and offered his hand.

The outlaws' gazes were focused on Carson, which gave Kohl the opening he had been waiting for while he had been playing possum. With slow precision Kohl slid his gun from beneath him in readiness to spring once the lady was out of the coach.

As Carson took the outlaw's hand, her heel caught, propelling her forward against the man and sending them both flying backward. Kohl leaped from the coach, guns blazing. He winged the leader, shoving the man back against the dirt with a thud, and got the drop on the skinny one before the man had a chance to unholster his gun.

Keeping his gun trained on the one still in the saddle, Kohl said with a lazy smile. "Now, I think that you might be best advised to toss your gun down and get off that horse before I blow you off it."

As the outlaw complied without an argument and slid from his horse Kohl waved him over to his companion. He picked up the gun and handed it to the driver. "Keep 'em covered, Shorty."

"Don't worry 'bout me. If one of 'em moves as much as a horse's hoof, I'll blow a hole through his gut."

While the other passengers relaxed their stances, Kohl went over to Carson. She appeared dazed, lying on top of the third outlaw who had been knocked out when he hit his head as they landed on the ground. Kohl thrust out his hand. "Need a hand up, lady?"

Carson looked up at the gunslinger, her hat askew and covering one eye. She glared at the man who looked ten feet tall from her position on top of the out-law. "I can manage, thank you."

Carson crawled to her feet and brushed off her sim-ple fawn-colored skirt. She surveyed the scene, then with pride in her voice she announced, "Well, I guess we showed them they picked the wrong stage to rob."

A look of disbelief came over Kohl's face. "We?"

"Why yes, you and I."

To her irritation, the gunslinger shook his head. "You little fool, you could have gotten everyone killed. Men like those"—he motioned toward the outlaws— "kill without provocation. Instead of offering you a help out of the coach, the bastard could have filled you with lead."

Carson bridled. "Well, I saved your person. No doubt they would have shot you first—"

"They did shoot me first," he growled, ignoring the pain in his shoulder.

Carson's eyes trailed to his arm and the bright red stain seeping through his shirt. "Considering your pro-fession, you would be the best target." She turned to the outlaw who was still on the ground and now rub-bing his head. "Isn't that right, sir?"

"Yeah, that's right," the outlaw agreed in a grudging snarl.

Kohl narrowed his eyes. "What about my profes-sion?"

Carson slapped her hands on her hips. "You are a gunslinger, a hired gun, aren't you, Mr. Baron?"

All eyes swung to Kohl. The passenger's expressions showed awe and wonder at the girl's nerve, the outlaws

37

quirked their lips and whispered, "not *the* Kohl Baron" among themselves.

Kohl stared at her without answer, stretching the sudden silence which had fallen over the group.

Careful to keep the anger from his face, Kohl ground his teeth. If she weren't so damned innocent with her unthinking comments he might have been tempted to show her exactly what kind of gunslinger he used to be. But Kohl was trying to put that image behind him. Silently, he could have wrung her neck for announcing a profession he was attempting to put into the past, but he had to admit that she had gumption and admired it despite his agitation.

More minutes ticked off the clock and Carson began to fret that she had said the wrong thing. Unable to endure the silence any longer, she offered, "Well, you are a gunslinger, aren't you?"

Kohl ignored her, climbed up on the stage, and threw the driver a rope. "Tie them up, then let's get this damned stage rolling."

He jumped down, ripped a strip of cloth from his shirt, and wrapped his arm. Carson stepped up behind him and placed a hand on his shoulder.

"How is your arm? Let me have a look at it."

Kohl pivoted around and his blazing eyes caught with her guileless blue ones; they were the colors of Lake Tahoe, pure, sparkling cerulean. He had to catch himself from getting lost in those inculpable depths.

"In my profession, I've had worse," he answered and walked away before the urge to touch her rosy cheek got the better of him. He stopped and threw back over his shoulder, "If you really want to be of help, get those people inside so we can get the hell out of here."

Carson nodded and went to the other passengers. Pots was holding his middle with white knuckles. Addie stood, clutching the box to her breast, staring at the gunslinger as if in a beleaguered trance. "Addie, it's all right. You don't have to be frightened anymore."

Addie swung her attention to Carson. "I wasn't scared," she snapped.

"I thought we were done for." Pots took out a hankie and wiped his forehead. "Did you see how Baron handled those three outlaws? Why, he is the fastest man with a gun I've ever seen."

"Yes, I suppose he is," Carson answered absently. "I think he wants us to get back in the coach."

"Yes, yes, of course." Pots patted his money belt. "We all owe Baron a debt of gratitude. He not only saved our hides, but all the money I have in the world. I got it on me, you know."

"Perhaps you should put it in a bank," Carson suggested, considering that Mr. Baron had truly saved their lives as they climbed back inside.

Pots plunked down beside Carson. "Don't trust banks. No sirree, I keep my money with me. Only from now on I'm gonna find a better place."

Kohl shoved the three trussed-up highwaymen across the seat from Carson, Addie, and Pots and climbed in, squeezing next to Carson. Holding his gun pointed at the men, Kohl hollered to the driver. "Move 'em out, Shorty."

Carson's face grew hot, his leg was pushed so tight up against hers. And she had to wonder why he elicited such a response from her when Pots was pressed as close on the other side of her and she felt nothing toward him. She glanced over at Addie. The girl was staring blankly out the window. Carson leaned back and tried to ignore the outlaws who were glaring at her.

"Why would such a pretty little thing like you want to protect someone like Baron?" the outlaw who had tried to drag her out of the coach asked.

Ordinarily Kohl would have silenced the man, but he wanted to hear the lady's answer.

"Why should Mr. Baron be any different than any other human being?" Carson said, confused by such a question and not sure why she had acted as she had.

A sarcastic grin curved the outlaw's lips. "Baron's got one hell of a reputation, that's why. Men's been comin' up against him for well over ten years. Nobody's faster."

Carson turned to the gunslinger. "Is that true?"

"Maybe is. Maybe isn't," he grunted.

"I don't know about the others, but I for one sure would like to hear how you came to be so fast," Pots said in awe of the man who had to be at least ten years younger than his near forty years.

"I ain't so different than a whole passel of others. Just better, is all."

"That's obvious," Pots said. "But how did you come to get that way?"

"Heard he used to ride with the Beauregard Brothers. Before the governor pardoned him, that is, and he went straight," the outlaw sneered with contempt.

Carson's eyes rounded. "You were an outlaw?"

Usually, Kohl didn't bother to answer those kind of questions one way or another. He gave the lady a lengthy perusal, then ran long, slender fingers through his hair. "I rode with a number of men when I was a

40

wild kid. Didn't mean I went astray of the law."

"Guilt by association," Pots blurted out. He picked his dime novel off the floor and patted it. "Bet your story would make a good book."

"Have lots of killin's in it," the leader added. "Wouldn't it, Baron?"

Kohl was not about to qualify the highwayman's snide remark. "You'd be best to hold your tongue before I add another notch to my gun."

Carson's eyes immediately went to Mr. Baron's gun. "I don't see any notches," she announced to a round of amused snickers.

"Chrissake, lady, what's wrong with you? One would think you were brought up in a convent, you're so damned naive."

"I was."

"What do you know, she's one of them altar girlies. Too bad Baron was on board, little lady, 'cause if he wasn't, we mighta teached you a thing or two."

As quick as a flash, Kohl leaned forward, swung out his fist, and knocked the highwayman out cold. He slumped against his companions, the corner of his mouth trickling with a stream of blood.

"How could you?" Carson demanded, horrified by the violence.

Kohl furrowed his brows. "You rather I let them talk to you that way?"

"No, but I—"

"You don't have to thank me. I'd do the same for any female."

"I was not going to thank you. I abhor violence and I certainly would never condone such behavior, even if it was in my honor."

41

"Your honor? Lady, you know nothing about honor. Why don't you go back to your convent. You'll be totally protected there, shielded from 'such behavior' as you put it."

Carson pinched her lips to keep from trying to explain that she hadn't meant anything personal. But the vehemence in his voice caused her to keep to her silence. Feeling self-conscious and awkward, she directed her attention out the window.

The coach was descending down the steep grade and she could see the Carson Valley below them. It was a magnificent basin. A wide plain with a meandering river, sprinkled with dark green dots of sage and scrub trees, bordered by dry pinioned hills. Her vision caught on a wild herd of mustang below. They were running free across an open expanse.

Silently, she breathed a sigh of relief. There, before her was her home. And now when she gazed at the landscape, the word "home" associated with Nevada no longer seemed so foreign. Soon she would leave the stagecoach and Mr. Kohl Baron, notorious gunslinger, behind forever and get on with preparing herself for the day that Sinclair and his mother would arrive to fetch her back to San Francisco.

Chapter Five

It was late afternoon and the sun shone gold on the buildings in the bustling capital which was Carson City as the stage entered the outskirts. Carson peered out the window, marveling how Abraham Curry, the founder of Carson City, had held fast to his dream of making it the capital city of Nevada and had persevered even when his partners had given up.

Carson and the other passengers waited while Kohl got the highwaymen off the stage. She watched in awe at the way the gunslinger handled himself and the men. He had an easy fluid motion despite the tenseness surrounding him.

"Bye, sweet thing," one of the highwaymen called back to her. "Hope we'll have the pleasure of meetin' again real soon." He gave her a lewd examination and she turned away to catch sight of the sheriff heading toward them.

For a moment she was afraid that the sheriff was going to arrest Mr. Baron and she carefully sneaked a peek back in his direction.

"Well, Baron, what do you have for me this time?" the gangly sheriff asked.

"Just three incompetent bumblers who tried to rob the stage."

"My God, the Babbitt brothers," he announced and fixed a triumphant grin on the three. "You three fools are lucky to still be alive. Do you know who you just tangled with?" Before one could open his mouth, the sheriff continued. "None other than Kohl Baron, one of the most celebrated gunslingers in the West."

"Why don't you quit wasting breath on these three and get them hauled off to jail where they belong," Kohl suggested when it appeared the sheriff was going to stand there all afternoon telling tales of Kohl's past.

The sheriff hailed his deputy and they cuffed the men before the deputy led them away. Then the sheriff turned back on the gunslinger. "Don't suppose you're gettin' back on the stage and leavin' town, are you?"

Kohl shrugged and declined to answer.

"Well, just see that you don't start no trouble. Problems usually follow your kind around like a tail on a mangy dog and I don't want no trouble in my town."

"I don't start trouble. I end it."

The sheriff frowned. "Well, just see that you keep your nose clean."

Carson quickly tried to appear busy checking her reticule when Mr. Baron turned back toward the stage. She did not want him to know that she had been eavesdropping. Attempting to seem as unaffected as possible after such an eventful trip, she stepped out of the coach with her head high. Unfortunately, her hat was immediately taken up by a Washoe Zephyr, a strong

44

gusty wind with a reputation for blowing down flimsy houses.

As she fought to retrieve her hat, she had to chuckle about the tradition her guardian had written her about. He had described in amusing detail that the reason Carson City had so many bald people was that the wind blew the hair right off their heads while they were looking skyward for their hats. At that moment Pots's bowler hat was sent swirling off his head to display a pate as denuded of foliage as a burned-out forest. She could not help herself; she let out a howl of most unladylike laughter.

"What's so amusing?" Kohl asked as he picked up his bag the driver had tossed down.

All laughter immediately fled her. "You aren't remaining in Carson City, too, are you?"

"What if I am?"

She tried to smile sweetly, but for some strange reason the thought of his continued presence unnerved her. "Curious, is all."

"Just keep that curiosity away from me," he said but wasn't sure he really meant it. "Your kind of inquisitive intruding could get a man killed."

Stung by what seemed to be an indictment against her, Carson retorted, "You needn't concern yourself, Mr. Baron. I seriously doubt that we shall be moving in the same social spheres."

Kohl barely quirked his lips at her comment. He was used to the "good" ladies of a town shunning him, although he was the one who had cleaned up the messes created by their bumbling husbands. He tipped his hat, picked up his bag, and sauntered toward the nearest saloon.

"Mr. Baron, oh, Mr. Baron," called out Pots, who had reclaimed his hat and was rushing after the gunslinger. "I've got a great idea if you and the young lady truly are not interested in my wares at the moment." Kohl glared at the man, but he just kept talking. "Why don't you let me sell you a starter set any unencumbered man would envy?"

Carson watched Mr. Baron and Pots disappear behind the swinging doors of the Red Dog Saloon before Addie's high-pitched voice drew her attention back to the stage.

"Miss Mueller . . . ah . . . Carson, I think I'd like to take you up on your offer of hospitality, if you don't mind none," Addie ventured, stepping forward with her worn carpetbag in one hand, the box in the other, after the gunslinger had left.

"I'm so glad." Carson put her arm around the girl's bony shoulders. "I haven't seen it since I was five, but my parents had a very nice home. They built it from native sandstone."

"Sounds nice. Me and my folks never had much. Lived in tents mostly."

"Then you'll love making your home with me," Carson said and hailed a carriage.

Once they and their bags were settled in the coach and were underway, the driver asked, "Where to, ladies?"

"108 North Minnesota Street," Carson instructed and sat back.

Addie seemed awed by the size of the city as they headed north along Carson, past the U.S. Mint and other government buildings and turned right on to Caroline. Carson herself couldn't help but feel awe for

46

Carson City. It was no longer the mining boomtown she vaguely recalled as a child. The city had matured and was alive with an energy all its own.

Once she had paid the driver and they stood before the single-story house adorned with dormer windows surrounded by a white picket fence, Carson pinched her lips. This was her childhood home and she felt a strange communion with the house, although she had not seen it for fifteen years.

"Gosh, it looks like a real home," enthused Addie in a rare display of emotion.

"It is a real home."

"How does it feel to be home?" the girl asked.

"A little strange, I guess. You see, my guardian has lived in it since he sent me to a convent in San Francisco when I was five years old. Until this minute I have felt that San Francisco was my home. But you know, seeing this place after so long somehow gives me the feeling that Nevada is somehow more than just my birthplace." Then as if she caught herself, Carson, blurted out, "Of course, in three months my fiancé and his family are coming to take me back to San Francisco where I truly belong."

Addie gave Carson a strange look. "You don't make sense."

Feeling awkward and confused herself by the newly awakened feelings, Carson hurriedly said, "Come on, let's go inside. My guardian is expecting me."

The door was ajar and there was no answer when Carson called out to her guardian. They entered and Carson looked around. "Everything is just as I remembered. The horsehair couch, the velvet chairs, the rug my mother braided out of old clothes." Then her vision caught at the mantel and she went over there and ran her hand over the gilded picture frame. "Strange, I don't recognize anyone in these photographs."

"And why should you?" a gruff voice said from behind her.

Carson twirled around, expecting to see her guardian. Instead there was a strange man with suspenders, holding a shotgun aimed directly at her. Two dirty-faced children stood behind the man, clinging to his legs. "You aren't my guardian," she squeaked out at the sight of the gun.

The man narrowed his eyes and kept the gun pointed at Carson. "Name's Spokes."

"Well, Mr. Spokes, what are you doing in this house?" Carson demanded, ignoring her better judgment to remain cowed.

"What are you doing in this house?" Spokes demanded.

Addie stood as still as a statue, her eyes fastened on the gun. "Maybe we ought to leave, Carson, and get this all straightened out later when everybody is in a talkin' mood," she suggested when she found her voice.

Carson crossed her arms over her chest. "Absolutely not! I am not going anywhere until Mr. Spokes explains himself." She turned on the man. "I demand that you put down that gun before you accidently shoot someone with it!"

"Damned if you ain't got guts for an intruder," he said and lowered the shotgun.

"That is much better. Now, what are you doing in my house?" Carson questioned, ignoring his remark.

"I don't rightly know who you are, but this here's my

48

house. I got the papers from Mr. Farley to prove it."

"Farley? Gideon Farley?" Carson interrogated.

Suspicion filled his black eyes. "Yes."

Carson breathed out a breath of relief and plunked down on the horsehair sofa, ignoring the man's assertion over ownership. "Well, that explains it. I am so relieved."

"Nothing's explained, lady."

"Of course it is. Mr. Gideon Farley is my guardian. This was my parents' home and it now belongs to me. Mr. Farley must have let the house to you since he is a bachelor and did not have need for such sizeable accommodations. I fear, Mr. Spokes, that since I have now returned you and your family are going to be forced to seek other living arrangements. I will, naturally, give you time to locate another home."

He raised the shotgun again. "Me and my family ain't going nowhere. It's you and that girl with you who are leavin', if you know what's good for you."

"Since you put it so eloquently, I think that I should locate Uncle Gideon and have him straighten this confusion out," Carson said with all the hauteur she could maintain under the circumstances.

"Farley's been livin' at the Ormsby. But it ain't gonna do you no good." He waved the gun toward the door and held it aimed at the females until they had backed outside onto the porch. Then he slammed the door and threw the bolt.

Standing out in the yard, Addie picked up her carpetbag. "You sure you got the right house?"

"Of course I'm sure. Once we locate Uncle Gideon everything will be straightened out." Carson snatched up her bag and began walking back toward town. "I

49

was going to give that man and his family a reasonable amount of time to vacate, but after the way he threatened us with that shotgun, I am going to demand that he move immediately."

Addie shook her head and trailed after Carson.

It was after dark by the time they reached the Ormsby House. It was an elegant hotel with the reputation as the lodging place of solons and nabobs. Addie couldn't believe she was standing in the lobby with a fourteen-foot ceiling decorated with Brussels carpets and lace curtains.

Carson marched up to the desk. "Which is Mr. Gideon Farley's room?"

The clerk looked down his long nose at Carson and she wanted to shrink. She swallowed and held her ground. "It is not the policy of this establishment to divulge that information, miss."

Kohl Baron was just leaving the dining room with a woman on his arm and noticed the female from the stage seemed to be in trouble again. "Excuse me, darlin', I'll be right back." He disengaged himself from the fancy blond woman, ambled over to the desk, and leaned his elbows on the counter. Putting a toothpick between his teeth, he inquired, "You givin' the lady trouble?"

The clerk knew of Baron's reputation. "No sir, Mr. Baron. No trouble." Without another word, his nerves were so on edge, the clerk reached for the key to Mr. Farley's room and thrust it on the counter.

"That's better," Kohl said. He tripped his hat toward Carson, then rejoined his lady friend and strolled from the hotel.

Carson took the key and watched the gunslinger amble from the hotel with a woman who looked to be at least ten years his senior. A twinge of jealousy grasped her, although she could not understand why she should feel rivalry toward the woman.

"Mr. Farley is not in," the clerk said, breaking into Carson's thoughts.

"It doesn't matter. We'll wait in his room."

"Suit yourself." He rang for a bellboy to take their bags. It was none of his business if Farley had decided to entertain such young females.

Carson and Addie followed the bellboy upstairs. They were shown into a regal suite, and Carson's breath caught at the very opulence of the rooms. Addie waited for the bellboy to leave then explored the spacious rooms.

"Gosh! I ain't never seed anything so grand in my entire life! There's even a inside tub! The bed's got brocade and velvet on it. Oh Carson, come see."

Carson went into the bedroom and was quite overwhelmed by the grandeur herself. "I guess the brewery business must be doing better than I imagined."

Addie crinkled her nose. "Brewery business?"

"Uncle Gideon was my father's partner in the Sierra Brewery. They started it together shortly before my parents were killed."

"Gosh, then you must be rich."

"If this room is any indication, I suppose I am."

"Think Mr. Farley'd mind if I took a nap on his bed. I'm mighty done in after the trip."

"I'm sure he wouldn't. As a matter of fact, I'm rather exhausted myself. Why don't we both take a nap. Then we'll be refreshed when he returns and we can all go down to supper together."

Both girls slipped out of their dusty traveling clothes and washed up before they settled on the bed and were soon fast asleep.

It was past midnight when the click of the door startled Carson awake. She quickly slipped into a robe and went into the parlor room prepared to greet the guardian she had not seen in years. To her utter shock, Gideon was half undressed, red-eyed, and was leaning heavily against the very same painted woman who had left the hotel with Kohl Baron earlier in the evening.

Chapter Six

Carson was flabbergasted when she recognized the fancy woman who was supporting Uncle Gideon's generous weight. She could not understand how he could come to be involved with the same woman who had been with Mr. Baron earlier.

Still speechless, Carson marched over to the lamp and turned up the light.

Gideon squinted at the beautiful young lady, wearing little more than a flimsy robe, her bare feet peeking out at the hemline. He rubbed his eyes. He could hardly believe his good luck. Two women in one night! Fortune was truly smiling on him, since most nights he went wanting. Then a thought hit his fuzzy mind. "I didn't engage your services too this evening, did I?"

Carson grasped her robe tighter around her neck. The years had not been kind to Gideon Farley. He appeared to have been accosted by the cruel gravity of nature, the way his jowls hung down alongside his double chin, pointing to a belly every bit as large as Mr. South's.

"Well, did I?" Gideon demanded when the little dove just stood there mute.

"Did you what?" Carson sputtered, not wanting to believe the implication of what he had said.

"Pay you for the evening?"

"I do not want to understand what you are talking about, Uncle Gideon. You were expecting me, don't you recall?" Carson inquired.

Gideon immediately sobered upon hearing the girl call him uncle. He took another long look before he realized that before him stood Carson Mueller. She certainly had changed from the last time he had seen her eight years ago.

He removed his arm from around the woman's shoulders and pushed her aside. "Carson, you weren't supposed to be here until next week," he sputtered.

"Sinclair managed to get me on an earlier stage. Aren't you glad to see me?" she questioned at his strange tone.

"Of course. I'm surprised, that's all."

He opened his arms and Carson stepped into them. But she did not like the familiarity of the hug at all. She withdrew from his embrace and her line of vision trailed to the fancy woman with the frizzy blond hair. "Why are you with the same woman who was with Mr. Baron earlier this evening?"

Gideon frowned at the woman who merely grinned through her heavily painted red lips.

"Baron? Who is this Baron?" he demanded of the woman.

Carson noticed the strange look she gave Gideon

54

before she relaxed her stance and fiddled with the fringe on her red satin shawl. "Sorry, Giddy, you know a girl's got to make a living."

A triumphant look on his face, Gideon rationed Carson a sheepish grin. "There. That's settled." He took Carson's arm and ushered her toward a green striped chair. "Why don't I get rid of Lily so you can tell me all about your trip."

Carson glanced at the clock. It was nearly 2 A.M. "It is rather late. If you don't mind me staying here with you, since there seems to be some mix-up over at the house, we can talk in the morning."

Gideon fidgeted with his fingers. "Don't worry about the house. I'll take care of it for you. After all, haven't I always taken care of everything? But I am afraid that we'll have to wait to have our little talk until Monday afternoon. You see, Carson, there is a pressing matter in Genoa which concerns the brewery and requires my immediate attention. So I am afraid I shall be out of town for a few days."

"If it is concerning the family business, why don't I accompany you?" she set out. "Now that I am back, I want to learn all there is to know about the financial matters, since the business will become half my responsibility soon."

Gideon looked to the fancy woman and dismissed her before returning his attention to Carson. His face was flushed but, of course, that was one of the sins of drinking, Carson recalled from the time she had been caught imbibing at the convent. "What time do you wish to leave in the morning?"

"I must get an early start. I'm sure a young lady

such as yourself would much rather remain here in comfort until I return."

"Nonsense. I want to learn about the family business. Just tell me what time to meet you in the lobby and I shall be there."

The little chit was kicking him out of his own room!

Gideon scratched the thinning strands of gray hair left on his head. He was careful to keep his face impassive, although she was being most difficult. "Well, let me see, would 4:30 be suitable?"

Carson thought about the early hour; she would not get much sleep. "In the morning?"

"I am making allowances since you just arrived," he offered shrewdly.

"4:30 will be fine," she announced to his chagrin. "I shall meet you in the lobby."

"But are you sure you can rise so early?"

"I often rose early at the convent." What she didn't say was that she was forced to rise early because she had spent so much time doing penitence for all her childhood misadventures. Of course, that was all behind her now.

His dead partner's daughter rose and when she did, Gideon was able to take a really good look at her. She was quite a nicely rounded woman for such a small thing. He heaved a sigh at the thought that he had to seek sleeping arrangements elsewhere tonight. Bedding the likes of Carson Mueller would undoubtedly be a most pleasurable experience.

Gideon leaned over and brushed his lips across her

forehead. Her skin was baby soft and she smelled of roses. "Goodnight, Carson."

Carson walked him to the door, aware that his meaty hand seemed to remain on her waist just a trifle long.

"Oh. Uncle Gideon, I wonder if you might advance me some money against my allowance. I seem to have run out of funds."

He fumbled through his pocket and handed her two dollars and a key. "That is all I have on me. Here is the key to your safe deposit box at the bank. It contains ample funds and all the legal documents to your holdings and the investments I have made in your name over the years. I realize you won't be able to get into it until Monday. But I trust the two dollars will tide you over. It is time you started handling some of your financial needs."

Carson swelled with pride despite the moment of disappointment she had experienced when he'd offered her so little money. She was being treated like an adult. "Thank you. Goodnight, Uncle Gideon. See you in the morning."

Carson watched him weave his way down the hall until he was out of sight before she shut the door.

"He was a strange sort," Addie announced from the open bedroom doorway.

"Yes, he was," Carson agreed absently and followed the girl back to bed.

It took the longest time for Carson to fall asleep. In her mind she relived her parting from Sinclair and the trip to Carson City on the stage. The vision that kept coming into her mind was of the gunslinger

Kohl Baron. He was a dangerous man to be reckoned with. But for some reason the thought of him awakened her senses and she found herself wondering how his kiss would compare to Sinclair's.

Carson put a hand to her lips. She was being foolish, she thought as she turned over and punched the pillow. Such thoughts were just silly schoolgirl pastimes. She was an engaged lady now.

After what seemed as if she had gotten only fifteen minutes sleep, Carson slipped from the bed and hurried to get ready to meet Gideon on time. Before she left she glanced at Addie. The girl was sound asleep. Attired in a smart cinnamon day dress, Carson slipped from the suite and headed down the stairs.

The hotel seemed vacant as she descended the last steps to the lobby. The lights flickered dimly and a sleepy clerk dozed at the desk. Carson looked around. Gideon was nowhere in sight yet so she took up a position on a nearby settee to wait. Her eyelids were heavy and the flicker of light mesmerizing as she laid her head down on her arm and drifted off to sleep.

"Miss? Miss?"

Carson started and opened her eyes. Sunlight streamed in through the small-paned windows. She sat up straight and focused on a young boy's narrow face. "What time is it?"

"Nearly nine, miss. The lobby is filling up, so you cannot continue to sleep here."

"Nine o'clock?" she said in disbelief.

"Yes, miss."

"But Gideon Farley was supposed to meet me here at 4:30. It can't be nine o'clock."

" 'Fraid it is. Mr. Farley did leave a message for you. Took it myself."

Dismayed, Carson jumped to her feet. "Where is it?"

"At the desk."

The boy fetched the note and handed it to her. "You best move along now before the manager gives me whatfor."

Carson nodded and started back upstairs before she stopped to read Gideon's message:

Carson dear,
Sorry I could not wait, but I am sure you will understand. I did not want you subjected to the crudities of what may be the unpleasant side of the brewery business. Remain in my suite at the hotel until I return. We shall discuss everything then.

Gideon Farley

Carson returned to the room where Addie was sitting at the dressing table in the bedroom, brushing her mousy brown hair. "Isn't that my pink blouse?" Carson questioned, surprised that the girl had gone through her things.

Addie put the brush down slowly and swiveled to face Carson. "Didn't think you'd mind."

"I suppose it is all right," Carson relented.

"Thought you were goin' out of town with that Farley fellow? That's what your note said."

"I thought I was, too. But he left without me. I'm to wait here until he returns. He mentioned that he would be back Monday, so we have the whole weekend to explore the city. And why don't we start with breakfast down in the dining room?"

"I got things to do," Addie said.

"Like look for a job?"

"Yeah," the girl answered too quickly.

"Well, then look no further. When Uncle Gideon returns I'm sure he will offer you employment. Meantime you can keep me company."

Addie looked at her sideways, then hesitantly nodded. She gathered her hair into a tail and clasped a threadbare bow around it before she gathered up her box, stood, and followed Carson from the room.

They were shown to a table in the corner of the dining room. They ordered and were waiting for their meal when Carson suddenly dropped the spoon she had been toying with.

Kohl Baron and that same fancy woman were being shown into the dining room across the room from them!

Addie craned her neck. "You staring at the gunslinger and that woman?"

"No, no, of course not! I was just wondering what he is doing here, and with the same woman that Uncle Gideon was with last night." Then another thought leaped into mind.

Over Addie's objections, Carson rose and weaved her way around the diners to stand directly in front of the gunslinger's table. Kohl looked up from his conversation with Lily.

"Well, well, you certainly do get around. What's the matter? You miss my company?"

The fancy woman laughed and clung to Mr. Baron's arm, making Carson long to peal her fingers off him. "I thought you were my uncle's female friend," Carson said.

The woman shrugged her indifference. "Your uncle?"

"He's not actually my uncle, but you were with him last night."

"Honey, I'm many men's female friend," Lily cooed, unaffected by the girl's apparent jealousy. "You got a claim on Kohl?"

"No, of course not!"

"Then why do you have your back up like a spitting cat, honey?"

"I don't," Carson insisted. She was horrified that her actions had been misconstrued. Then she had to wonder if they had been.

Lily's full, hearty laughter broke the growing tension. "Sure you don't, child. Why—"

"I am not a child."

Lily looked to Kohl. His expression was hooded, but he was staring at the little lady awfully hard. " 'Course you're not, honey, anybody can see that. Now, why don't you pull up a chair and tell us what's on your mind?"

Feeling awkward and foolish for so impetuously coming over to Kohl Baron's table, Carson secretly wished she were back in the hotel suite. But she wasn't, so she took a buoying breath and sat down.

"What can I do for you, lady?"

"Kohl, don't you know her name?" Lily inquired, surprised since it was obvious to her there was a spark igniting between them.

Mr. Baron's shrug of seeming indifference wounded Carson. The man had not bothered to learn her name, even though they had been passengers on the same stage. "My name is Carson."

"After the city?" Kohl said.

"My parents came to this country from Germany. They loved this town."

"No doubt."

"They are dead," Carson said with sadness in her voice.

Kohl did not say a word. But again he had to admire her for her spunk. Most "nice" women would have turned tail and run from him already, since he was being a little rough on her.

Lily leaned forward. "No last name, honey?"

"It is not important for this discussion. I am here, Mr. Baron—"

"Since we seem to keep running into each other you might as well refer to me as Kohl," he said without emotion.

"All right, Kohl. Well—"

"Not that anyone's interested, but you may call me Lily," interjected the fancy woman who held out a long-nailed hand in greeting.

"Lily," Carson returned with a hesitant nod. She felt awkward in such a woman's presence. Sinclair would never condone her knowing *that* kind of woman.

"Well, you gonna give my hand a shake or just stare at it, honey?"

"Sorry. Of course." Carson shook the woman's hand before returning her attention to Kohl Baron. "Well, as I started to say, I actually came over to your table to ask a favor of you."

Chapter Seven

Kohl leaned forward and rested his elbows on the table. Carson glanced at Lily. She was also leaning forward with anticipation. Carson shifted uneasily in her seat. She was still not used to being in the presence of a soiled dove. Her thoughts shifted to what Uncle Gideon had been doing with such a woman.

"You were saying, Carson?"

Carson's attention snapped back to Kohl. "Oh, yes. I have a favor to ask."

"Then ask. Don't keep us in suspense."

"Oh. Oh yes, my favor." Carson felt her cheeks grow hot. Her idea seemed suddenly very foolish. "It is nothing, really. I should be getting back to Addie, the girl who traveled on the stage with me. She is waiting for me, quite anxiously, I'm sure."

Carson started to rise. Her nerve had failed her and she chided herself for coming over to the gunslinger's table before thinking the whole idea through.

Kohl placed a staying hand on Carson's. The

warmth surprised him. "Don't run away, darlin'."

Carson looked down at the bronzed hand with long slender fingers covering hers. His palm was rough, calloused, and sunburned, not soft and white like Sinclair's.

Kohl rubbed his thumb along the back of her hand. "You can't lose your nerve now, little lady. What's the favor you wanted to ask?"

Carson snatched her hand back and cradled it with the other one, rubbing it where his thumb had touched, leaving raw sensations still tingling. She stared down at the hand.

"Honey, you ain't got to be afraid of Kohl. He's really just a big lover," Lily cooed.

The whore's comment about their relationship snapped Carson back to reality. She dropped her hands to her sides and pinched her lips. "I am not afraid! And you needn't share the nature of your relationship with me!"

" 'Course you ain't afraid, honey."

"My friendship with Lily causing you problems?" Kohl declared.

The amusement in the tone of Kohl's remark made her furious. She was going to show him that she was not disquieted by him or his association with the woman. She raised her chin and looked down her nose at the grinning gunslinger. "I can see that I made a mistake coming over here. I came to ask for your help in taking me to Genoa to join my guardian, but it now is obvious that I should have known you would be otherwise engaged. Good day to you, sir."

Carson swung around and kept her head high as she weaved her way back toward her table. But inside she felt she had just made another ill-considered adventure.

"Kohl," Lily said and laid a hand on his arm to draw his attention from the girl back to her. "You just gonna let her up and walk away like she done? She did have the gumption to come over here and talk to you. Not many men, let alone females, has got what it takes to stand up to you like she just done. Her kind's led a sheltered life; they don't know nothin' about friendships like ours. Kohl, you always been on the side what needs you. Go help the little lady."

Kohl dragged his eyes from Carson and stared at Lily for a moment. "I'm not in the trade anymore. I told you I bought a business with intentions of settling down."

"She don't need your guns."

"Ah hell, Lily, one would think you're trying to play matchmaker."

"Get on with you. You know I'm saving you for myself. Go'n help her."

Shaking his head in defeat, Kohl ambled toward Carson and the young girl with her.

"He's coming over!" Addie hissed to Carson, her expression dark. "Wonder why."

Carson looked in the gunslinger's direction. All eyes were on him. The women patrons gazed with appreciation at his muscled figure, and the men with jealousy and awe.

"Addie, would you mind going back to the room

66

and fetching my gloves?"

"Your gloves? What you need them for?"

Carson glared at the girl. "Just go!"

"Humph," Addie grunted and flounced from the table. As she passed Kohl Baron, she sent him a look of hatred.

"What's got gravel in her gut?" Kohl asked Carson when he reached her.

"Addie's just out of sorts because she wanted to remain and listen to whatever you have to say to me."

Without asking, Kohl straddled the chair next to Carson. "When do you want to leave?"

Carson had had time to reconsider her nonsensical actions. She was in Carson City to cultivate only the cream of society, although she had to admit that riding out of the city with the gunslinger excited her in a most unladylike fashion.

Kohl grew impatient waiting for an answer. "If you've had a change of heart, tell me. I've got business to tend to and you're wasting my time."

"As a matter of fact, I have decided to remain in Carson City and await my guardian's return," she forced herself to say.

"Suit yourself," Kohl replied stiffly and left without further comment.

Carson watched him return to Lily and immediately regretted having to be a lady.

After Addie refused to accompany her, Carson rented a buggy and after receiving directions to

Genoa she headed south to locate Gideon. It was a glorious day. Hawks soared overhead. A pesky magpie alighted on the horse's rump and screeched at her before taking flight. Jeffrey pines gave the desert landscape a green swath and she inhaled their refreshing scent.

Carson was pleased that she'd made the trip with such ease as she entered Nevada's first town of Genoa and stopped the buggy outside the J. R. Johnson Store to inquire after Gideon.

Kohl waited atop the stallion he had purchased and watched Carson go inside the building. He had seen to it that she had not been accosted by any unsavory characters, since he'd had the gut feeling she was going to make the trip anyway. Why he had taken his valuable time to shadow the girl was a mystery to him. He just hoped she would conclude her business in short order so he could return to Carson City and start running his new enterprise.

Carson was discouraged as she walked back out to the buggy. Gideon had stopped at the store earlier but had mentioned heading on to another town. Of course, the clerk could not recall if Gideon had mentioned the town's name.

Carson stood at the rail trying to decide whether to explore the town of Genoa before returning to Carson City. It seemed to be a prosperous town, and the fact that it was Nevada's first settlement intrigued her.

"Oh, miss," hailed the stout clerk who had rushed from the store.

"Yes?"

"You mind givin' this order to Farley when he returns? Nelson over at Hansen's Saloon missed Farley when he was here. Folks has been drinkin' more beer'n usual. And there ain't enough to last till the next scheduled shipment. Nelson says he'll need twice more than was brung out last trip."

Carson gladly took the order. It was her first official duty in the family business. She beamed at the clerk. "The brewery was started by my father and I intend to take an active role in its operation. So anytime there is anything that can be done to add to Mr. Nelson's order or anyone else's in town, please tell them to let me know."

The clerk scratched his head. "I'll be. I ain't never heared of no woman in the beer business in Washoe."

"Well, you have now."

Carson was so excited about the order that she forgot all about exploring the town and headed back to Carson City. Gideon was going to be so pleased when she showed him the additional requisition on Monday.

Kohl was pleased when the girl reined the buggy back toward the city. At least he didn't have to wait out in the hot sun all day while she dallied in Genoa.

The remainder of the weekend Carson spent in anticipation of Monday when she would demonstrate to Gideon how capable she was. He would straighten out the muddle over her house, and she could begin getting to know Carson City's finest citizens so she would be received in the finest social circles for Sinclair's sake.

Monday morning Carson awoke early and as she was dressing she looked over at Addie. She was a strange girl and seemed so secretive, but Carson liked her. They had both lost their parents and Carson understood why it was difficult for the girl to trust.

"What are you doin' up so early?" Addie asked, sat up, and rubbed her eyes. She tucked the box she always carried with her under the pillow when she was sure Carson was not looking.

"I told you that I am going to the brewery today to meet Uncle Gideon and get everything with the house straightened out so we can move out of this hotel room. I also have the additional order from Hansen's Saloon to give him. And as I told you last night, he can help introduce me to polite society so Sinclair's family will be proud of me when they arrive."

"Humph! Don't know why you need to do that. His kin ought to be proud of you just the way you are," the girl said.

"Thank you, Addie. You are a sweet girl."

"No, I ain't," the girl blustered and started for the bathroom.

"Addie, you forgot to take your box," Carson called out.

Addie sent her a suspicious look, rushed back, and snatched up the precious container. Pinning it against her heart, she frowned at Carson before she shut the door behind her.

"See you later in the day, Addie," Carson said through the door and left to meet her guardian at the brewery on King Street.

"Good morning, Miss Mueller. You are up quite early," the hotel clerk said as she passed his station in the lobby.

"Good morning," she returned with a cheery smile. Then she continued on her way until his voice halted her progress.

"Miss Mueller, may I speak with you for a moment?"

She went over to the desk. "Yes?"

The clerk cleared his throat and straightened his bow tie as if it had suddenly begun to choke him. "It is about the bothersome matter of your bill, miss, and how you wish to pay it."

"My bill? Need I remind you that I am residing in Gideon Farley's suite?"

"Mr. Farley has not . . . he has not paid for a guest to remain in the room, miss."

"If you charge an additional amount for guests, I am certain Mr. Farley will reimburse you when he returns. Have a pleasant day, sir," she said and left the man staring after her.

"But, miss," he called out, "Mr. Farley no longer—" The young lady swung through the doors, cutting off his explanation. The clerk shook his head and deemed to turn the matter over to the manager for resolution.

Carson knew she had been rude for not listening to what the clerk was saying as she left the Ormsby

71

House, but Gideon had always handled the finances and whatever the problem seemed to be she knew Gideon would resolve it later in the day.

She opened her parasol against the bright morning sun and strolled north along Carson Street toward King. She hummed to herself with thoughts of how well her life was falling into place. And for the first time she actually felt like a real lady without having to make such a conscious effort.

Carson turned on to King Street and stopped across the street from the large brick, two-storied building. She read the enormous sign painted on the face of the building.

SIERRA BEER

FAMOUS SINCE 1860

The nuns at the convent had taught her that drinking spirits was wrong, and she had read in the newspapers about the temperance movement spreading in the east. She recalled overhearing two ladies in the dining room last night discussing a sermon they'd heard in church yesterday, condemning Satan's brew, which had been delivered by a fiery preacher arrived from some small town in Kansas. But across the street was the business her father had started and she was proud of it!

Carson's excitement faded when she walked through the office door of the brewery only to discover Kohl Baron leaning back in the chair behind the battered cherrywood desk with his boots propped on it.

"What do you think you are doing here?" she demanded.

Kohl leaned back farther and crossed his arms behind his head. He gave her a long, slow perusal. "I might ask you the same thing. What's the matter? You afraid the good folk of Carson City might find out you like to tip a few? So you came to buy your liquor directly from the source?"

Carson was scandalized at such a notion. "I've never drunk alcoholic spirits." She hesitated before blurting out, "Except once or twice when I got caught trying a taste of wine at the convent."

She expected him to laugh at her, but he just sat there staring, amusement in his usually icy eyes. "At least you had the good taste not to comment on my youthful forays."

"Hell, I tipped a few when I was a young'un, too. Got my hide tanned for it. Only thing that taught me was to be sneakier."

Carson could hardly believe the camaraderie in his confession. And she had to fight down the urge to smile. Then she grew serious. Sinclair would never have done such a thing. "It is a part of my life I have put behind me."

"We were all young and foolish once," he said and returned to staring at her.

"I find it difficult to believe you were once an innocent child."

He grinned at that. "Nobody said anything about my ever being innocent."

She forced herself to ignore his banter and redirect her attention back to her original thought when she'd entered the brewery and found him. "Well?" she said, crossing her arms over her chest.

"Well?" he echoed.

"Are you going to explain yourself? I demand to know what you are doing behind that desk!"

Chapter Eight

Carson gasped in a startled breath and backed away from the counter when Kohl began to unfold from the chair, rise, and start toward her. She was not sure what he had in mind since his eyes were hooded, but she did not take her eyes off him.

She had backed against the wall and he was not more than two feet in front of her when he stopped. She watched his hand go toward his gun belt and her breath nearly failed.

He was going to shoot her!

Kohl took a pouch from his hip pocket, withdrew a match, and stuck it between his teeth.

"What's wrong with you, lady? Afraid the notorious gunslinger is going to shoot you where you stand?"

"No. Of course not!"

To her surprise he took her arm and sat her down on the bench lining the wall. He disappeared and an instant later returned with a bottle of beer. "Here, have a swig of this. It'll put the color back in your cheeks."

Carson's hand went to her cheek. She was sure they must be flaming instead of pale. She remained speechless, losing sight of her original question.

To her chagrin, he shrugged. "If you don't want to join me, guess I'll just have to drink alone."

"Drinking is the root of all evil," she blurted out Mother Jude's words.

"And all these years I thought evil started with a woman in the Garden of Eden." He looked her over. "If Eve looked anything like you I can understand why."

Not about to be docile and take such an outrageous notion without retort, Carson took a deep breath. "And if Adam looked anything like you I can understand why Eve got into trouble with the apple in the first place."

Kohl cocked a brow. "Oh?"

"Adam probably offered her a beer."

"Would you prefer I go fetch you an apple?"

"I should say not!"

"Don't say I didn't offer."

By the time Kohl had uncapped the bottle and finished guzzling down the beer, Carson had regained her composure. She thrust out her hand, palm up. "That will be five cents."

It was his turn to look surprised. "You are trying to charge *me* for the beer?"

"I am charging you for the beer, yes."

"And is that how you hope to make a living?" He grinned and took out a bill.

"As a matter of fact, yes, it is," she said through tight lips. "If you need change I am certain I can

76

manage to accommodate you."

A self-satisfied grin split his lips. "What if I let you have the change and take it out in trade?"

"I shall pretend to ignore that. If you intend to continue drinking, I suggest you locate the nearest saloon. I am certain they must carry Sierra beer and you can purchase it there."

"Why would I want to go to some saloon and buy beer there when I can get all I want here for free?"

A horrifying thought entered her mind. "You didn't come here to rob the place, did you?"

"That wasn't my intention," he answered, keeping the grin off his face.

Suddenly her original question reentered her mind. "Then, as I asked you before you managed so ably to sidetrack me, what are you doing here?"

"I might ask you the same question."

Her nerve returned and she came off the bench to stand directly in front of the gunslinger. "I happen to own this establishment."

All amusement left his face and was replaced with a deep frown. "I don't know what you are trying to pull. But *I* happen to own this place and have the legal papers to prove it."

"You? You can't own this brewery."

"Look, I not only can but I do."

"My father started the Sierra Brewery with Uncle Gideon—"

"Gideon? That wouldn't be Gideon Farley, would it?"

"Why, yes. How do you know Uncle Gideon?

Other than that you two seem to share the affections of a certain *lady*."

"Be careful what you say about Lily; there's none finer." Carson was immediately ashamed; it was not charitable to speak of others in such a manner. "As for Gideon Farley, he's the bastard who sold me the business, lock, stock, and beer bottle."

Her dander returned. "Don't you dare refer to my guardian in such vile terms."

"However you want me to refer to him, he still sold this business to me."

Carson felt numb and sat back down on the bench before her legs failed her. Shaking her head, she said, "I don't believe you. He did not mention anything about this to me. He couldn't have sold you this business."

"Afraid he did." A grin came to Kohl's face. "Look, I am willing to be charitable. I'll allow you to stay on and work here."

Carson shot to her feet. "What! You will allow me to work for you when I own this business! This is absurd! You cannot own my family's business!"

Kohl crossed his arms over his chest. "Afraid I do."

He had invested his hard-earned money in this brewery and he was not going to let some pretty little lady stroll in here and try to wrench it from him.

"Where are these legal papers you were talking about?"

"In the bank." At that moment Kohl wondered why he had decided to keep the papers in a bank. He wanted to fling them in her face. Maybe Pots had the right idea after all.

"Well, my ownership papers are also in the bank. And I have the key with me." She dug in her reticule, thankful that Gideon had given her a key. Kohl's face turned dark when she waved the key in front of him.

"I ought to throw you out of here. But since I don't have nothin' to lose, I'm willing to waste a little time in the company of a pretty lady. Why don't we go have a look-see at that claim of yours? That should settle it once and for all."

"If seeing that I hold proper title does not satisfy you, my guardian and the sheriff will," she said and swung out of the brewery office.

Kohl grabbed his hat and followed her. He liked the gentle sway of her hips as she walked ahead of him. And the flaming color of her hair reminded him of her red hot temper. He had always thrived on a challenge and found that the little lady seemed to be trying to present him with a formidable one—in more ways than one.

Carson stomped around the corner to Carson Street and down to the bank without missing a step. She approached the manager, not wasting time on the teller behind the cage. She looked at the name on the desk. "Good day, Mr. Stanley. Let me introduce myself. My name is Carson Mueller and I have urgent business with your bank this morning."

Stanley rose from his chair and adjusted his vest. He perused the handsome young woman. Pity he was so busy this morning. He would have dismissed her, but the big gunslinger standing behind her vanished that inclination. "What can we do for you, Miss Mueller?"

"Mr. Baron and I both maintain safe deposit boxes in your bank and we need to examine the contents immediately." She thrust out her key and the manager looked down at it.

Suspicious, the manager gave the young woman a closer examination. "This is Mr. Farley's box, miss."

"Mr. Farley is my guardian."

The manager assigned her a strange expression and immediately hollered for the clerk to fetch the sheriff.

Instantly pandemonium broke out in the bank. Female customers ran screaming from the building, clerks dove for the floor, and several male customers and one guard rushed over and grabbed Carson and tried to wrestle Kohl to the ground.

Carson screamed and struggled, biting Stanley's hand as he tried to restrain her. He yelped and grabbed her again. "You little wildcat. You are not going to get away with trying to rob one of the bank's customers in my bank," he spat as they continued to grapple.

Kohl easily threw the men off who had tried to restrain him and pulled his gun. "Nobody moves until I find out what the hell is going on." The half dozen people inside the bank froze. Kohl turned the gun on Stanley. "Release the lady."

Stanley immediately complied and held his wounded hand. He instantly became a quivering mass and Carson groaned inside as she straightened

80

her hat and went to stand next to Kohl Baron, notorious gunslinger.

Mr. Stanley had to be one of Carson City's leading citizens. She certainly had not made a very good first impression on him in her quest to be the lady Sinclair expected to find when he arrived. Yet standing next to Kohl made her senses heighten.

"You got some explainin' to do, Stanley," Kohl said in his most threatening voice.

"I don't know what you two are trying to pull, but Mr. Farley was in earlier this morning and did not mention anything about sharing the box with anyone. Nor has he ever mentioned being anyone's guardian."

Carson immediately gulped in a breath. She had to straighten this out. "Mr. Stanley, this has all got to be a dreadful mistake. Mr. Farley is my guardian. He gave me the key. Mr. Baron and I merely are engaged in a dispute over ownership of the Sierra Brewery and I need to get into the box to demonstrate to Mr. Baron that he is mistaken.

"If you continue to have doubts concerning my claims, won't you accompany us to examine the contents of the boxes, and I shall be able to prove to you that what I am saying is true."

Stanley listened to the gunslinger explain his side and then grudgingly agreed to accompany the pair after putting the customers' minds to rest and reassuring the sheriff, who had made a sudden appearance rather belatedly.

Stanley obtained both boxes and set them down on a large oval table next to his desk. His line of vision

81

caught with the sheriff's and he was grateful the man had decided to remain in case he was needed.

Kohl took out his documents first. "Let me see," she said with skepticism.

"Darlin', I only agreed to come here to humor you. You aren't touchin' these papers until I've had a chance to have a look-see at your so-called claim."

"This is ridiculous," Carson hissed and opened the box. Her smug expression faded and was replaced by one of shock. The only item in the box was a folded slip of paper, lying in the bottom. She looked to Mr. Stanley. "I don't understand."

He shrugged and watched her reach into the box and remove the plain white sheet. Disbelief mirrored in her eyes as she read. Then she dropped the paper and sat staring at the box.

"Mind if I have a look-see at it?" Kohl asked at her distress.

She nodded, holding her forehead as he read aloud.

My dear Carson,

You have always been so trusting that it almost hurts to have used your inheritance money for my own needs all these years. But since you will be marrying into such a wealthy family I am sure you will understand why I have been forced to leave you with nothing.

Gideon Farley

P.S. I had to sell the house, too.

When Kohl finished reading and looked at Carson

82

her eyes were bleak. If he could have gotten his hands around Farley's neck he would have squeezed the girl's inheritance out of the man.

With all the dignity she could maintain, Carson managed to rise. "I beg your pardon, gentlemen. It seems I have caused a terrible scene for nothing. I apologize. Now, if you'll excuse me, I shall take my leave."

Kohl watched the girl's shoulders slump as she started toward the exit, then they suddenly stiffened and she turned back and marched toward them. "Kohl, earlier you said that Gideon *sold* you the Sierra Brewery, is that correct?"

"Yeah, that's right." He didn't like the gleam in her eyes and wondered what she was up to this time.

"Mr. Stanley, as banker, did you handle the transaction for Gideon, per chance?"

"As a matter of fact, my bank did handle the sale," he said, not understanding what the girl could be carrying on about.

"Kohl, do you mind if I look at your bill of sale?"

Kohl shrugged. "Suit yourself."

Carson settled back down in the chair and studied the legal document. Finally she looked up. "Mr. Stanley, this document states that Gideon sold *his* interest in the Sierra Brewery."

"That is correct."

"Well, then I still own half of it, since Gideon and my father were partners and the brewery was part of my inheritance." At their two blank expressions, she added, "Don't you see he sold *his* interest, not mine. So he did not sell the entire business, which means that I—"

Kohl shot to his feet. "Wait just a goddamned minute, Stanley. I did not buy half a business. Nor did I buy into a business to have a partner who is barely dry behind the ears and a female to boot; a disagreeable one at that!"

Stanley took the document and studied it before he looked up. "I am not a lawyer, Baron . . . ah . . . Mr. Baron, but it looks as if the little lady is correct. You own the portion of the brewery that Gideon Farley sold to you. But since it seems he did not indeed own the entire business, then that does truly make Miss Mueller half owner and . . . your partner."

"I'm not responsible for the bastard skipping out on her," Kohl bellowed with outrage. "I've never had a partner before and I'm not going to start now, do you hear me? I'm not going to share my business with a sassy female partner! I've never kept anything in a bank before. I never should have gone through a damned bank this time. Probably wouldn't have been cheated . . ."

Carson let the man wear himself out with his rantings and ravings. She leaned back in her seat with a pleased complacent smile. She had her own ideas in the matter.

Chapter Nine

Carson trailed behind Kohl as he stormed from the bank and stomped along Carson Street. His wide strides made it difficult to keep up, but she was determined not to let him get away.

"You are not going to ignore me," she hissed. "I own half of the brewery and you are just going to have to accept it!"

Kohl stopped dead in his tracks, and Carson ran into the back of him. The collision sent her sidestepping off the boardwalk and right into the middle of a freshly laid pile of horse dung. One impaled itself on her heel.

"Ugh!" she squealed and tried to disengage her heel from the nasty bit on the edge of the wooden walk.

His fists clenched, his face as glacial as the highest peaks in the Sierras he turned to glower at her.

Carson swallowed to keep from shrinking under the foreboding weight of his anger. Even in the distress of her situation, he did not seem to have any appreciation for it.

"Get caught with another apple, did you, Eve?" he snickered at her heel.

"I beg your pardon?"

He motioned to the bit stuck on her heel. "Road apple, lady. Horse shi—"

"I get the message. You needn't finish your crudity. The least you can do is offer your assistance, even if you are upset with me."

"Upset is putting it mildly, don't you think?" he said and roughly scraped her heel. "There. Now go away and leave me and my business alone!"

He swung away from her and started walking.

"Kohl! Kohl Baron! If you do not come back and listen to me I am going to scream that you tried to accost me!"

There was murder in his eyes when he returned to her. "You try screaming anything like that and I promise you, the mood I'm in, you just might have cause."

Carson swallowed down the urge to flee under his furious gaze. She was part owner in her own brewery and she was not going to be set aside! "Kohl, I do not like sharing ownership of the brewery with you any more than you like sharing it with me. It seems that Gideon has cheated us both. And because of it we are stuck with each other. So since we seem to be partners . . . unwilling partners, don't you think we should try to make the best of it?"

"I don't intend to make the best of any partnership with you," he gritted out and moved off again.

"Where are you going?"

"To the hotel to check out," he hollered back and was immediately sorry he had bothered to answer the annoying female when she promptly joined him. "What do you think you're doing now? Didn't I make it clear I don't want your company?"

"You did indeed. But since I am staying at the hotel and am also headed in that direction, we might as well walk together."

"Why?"

"So we can talk about the brewery."

"How many times do I have to tell you, there is nothing to talk about?" he snapped.

He stepped up the pace to the point that Carson practically had to run to keep up. People on the street stopped to stare and whisper to their companions. Carson noticed the scene she seemed to be creating with the gunslinger, but she did not have time to worry about her image at the moment. She had more important things to concern herself with now.

She followed Kohl into the lobby of the Ormsby House and to the desk. As she tried to catch her breath, Kohl pounded on the bell.

The clerk hesitantly came forward. "Yes, sir, Mr. Baron, what can we do for you?"

"Get my bill ready, I'm checking out."

"Of course, sir, right away," the man said meekly, cowed by the gunslinger's anger. Then he caught sight of the lady standing behind the gunslinger, holding her side as she gulped in big breaths of air. He wondered what had made her so winded and the gunslinger look so downright pissed. Whatever it was, it would make a good tidbit of gossip to sell to the reporter from the newspaper that hung around the hotel hoping for a juicy story. "Miss Mueller, do you wish your bill as well?"

Carson stepped up to the desk next to Kohl. The only money she had was what was left of the two dollars Gideon had given her before he'd absconded with all her inheritance. "No. I am not prepared to settle the amount today. Since I shall be remaining in the hotel for a while longer, we can discuss the matter when it is closer to my departure date."

"I am sorry, miss, but the manager instructed me to inform you that since Mr. Farley checked out and did not make arrangements to engage the suite past last Friday, you will be required to make arrangements with the hotel for your bill before I can allow you to reenter the rooms."

"But my bags are upstairs. And what about the girl I was with?"

"The girl left shortly after you did this morning. As for your bags, we shall be happy to hold your luggage until the account is settled and once it is, move your things to another room for you."

"Look, I don't have all day!" Kohl interjected.

"Sorry, sir, I shall prepare your bill immediately,"

the clerk said and turned from Carson.

Kohl dug into his pocket and threw a wad of bills on the counter. "Take what I owe you out of this. I'll pick up the change on my way out. Oh, and have breakfast sent up to my room."

Carson watched Kohl disappear up the stairs, then swung back around to the clerk. Her eyes fastened on the money and an idea flashed into her head. If she wasn't so desperate she would never consider what she was about to do. But the twists of life sometimes called for desperate measures. Not giving her plan another thought, she gave the clerk her haughtiest smile.

"Well, since Mr. Baron has given you money to pay for both our bills, I shall insist upon my key. I, too, shall be checking out."

"But Mr. Baron said nothing about paying for your bill, Miss Mueller," the clerk sputtered.

She sent him a look of outrage she hoped would still him from seeking Kohl to verify her fabrication. "You saw us come in together, did you not?"

"Well, yes, but—"

"But? But what, sir? Do you wish that I hail Mr. Baron back? He will tell you the same thing, although I would not want to be the one to face him, considering the mood Mr. Baron was in when he left."

She held her breath as she watched the clerk's indecision. He was wavering and she had to get her bags out of the hotel before Kohl returned. "I can see that it is necessary to call Mr. Baron," she announced. In a bold move, she turned her back on the man, pinched her lips in silent prayer, and headed toward the stairs, hoping that he would halt her progress.

"Miss Mueller?"

Carson stopped and gazed at the ceiling as she exhaled a breath of relief before turning to face the clerk with a look of triumph carefully hidden on her face.

"Yes, sir?" she said with all due innocence.

"Here is your key. I'll get your bags."

"You have made the most expeditious decision. I am sure Mr. Baron will be most pleased that you chose not to disturb him. Oh, and would you hail a coach?"

"Don't you want to go up to the suite and wait to depart with Mr. Baron?"

"Mr. Baron will be meeting me later," she said sweetly.

Carson held her breath while the clerk instructed someone to see to Mr. Baron's breakfast and then fetch her bags and load them on a coach. All she had to do was figure out where to go and then locate Addie. Carson felt a responsibility toward the girl. As if Fate was in her corner, Carson saw Addie through the window.

"Sir, I shall be waiting outside. Do not dawdle with my bags. You wouldn't want Mr. Baron unhappy if I'm forced to inform him that I did not receive quality service?"

Through tight lips, the clerk said, "Yes, miss."

Feeling quite pleased with herself, Carson sauntered from the hotel. Outside, she hailed Addie. "Where have you been?"

Addie frowned. "What's it to you?"

"I'm not trying to pry, truly. I was merely concerned about you."

The girl pouted. "Had business." She started to swing past Carson and into the hotel.

"We can't go back inside, Addie."

Addie took an impatient stance. "Why not?"

"I am afraid my guardian has absconded with my inheritance and left me without funds. I've managed to get our bags out, but we are going to have to find somewhere else to live."

"You got any ideas?"

"Not at the moment, but I'll think of something."

"I got a job this morning. Maybe we can stay in the back room. I'll go check it out."

So that was where the girl had gone, Carson thought. "Why don't I come with you?"

"No. You meet me in front of the stage depot this afternoon," Addie announced and flounced off before Carson could stop her. She was such a secretive girl, but Carson thought of some of the other girls at the convent and how they had kept to themselves, much like Addie. Carson decided it must have come from being on her own at such a tender age.

Carson tried to appear patient as the man took his time loading the bags, but inside she wanted to scream at him to hurry before Kohl Baron made an appearance and wrung her neck!

Once the bags were loaded, Carson settled in the coach and heaved a sigh of relief. She had managed to pull it off. She had managed to outwit that annoying hotel clerk and had her bags.

"Driver, take me to the stagecoach station," she instructed and leaned back as the coach gave a jerk and rumbled down Carson Street. They must have been halfway to her destination when another thought flashed into her mind. "Driver. Stop. Turn this coach around. I have had a change of heart . . ."

Kohl could have taken on a bear and won, he was so mad by the time he left the hotel. Of course, the clerk was probably even more upset after he had finished with him, Kohl thought with little satisfaction as he toted his saddlebags toward the brewery. Hell, at least he was rid of Miss Carson Mueller, even if it had cost him the few bucks it took to pay the hotel bill she'd stuck him with. Yet he had to admit that if he had not been so inclined, no one on earth could have forced him to pay the bill.

That infuriating schemer would never again be able to show her face to him after what she'd pulled! Although deep inside he had to admit her grit; he'd probably done the same thing in her situation.

Kohl was hot and crankier than ever by the time he reached the rear of the brewery and trudged up the stairs toward the apartment he'd spied yesterday while inspecting the place. He walked through the door and tossed his saddlebags down on the old worn couch. Dust immediately billowed up in a hazy cloud and Kohl waved it away.

It made his throat dry, so he went down to the brewery, retrieved a beer, and returned to the apartment with the intention of making a home out of the place until he learned more about the business that Lily had suggested he purchase.

He popped the top and took a swig.

"Oh, I see you are already depleting the profits. That beer will cost you two and one half cents," Carson announced from the doorway to the bedroom.

"You!" he bellowed and started toward her with his arms outstretched, ready to wring her neck. "I'm going to wring your neck, you little criminal."

Carson ran back into the bedroom behind a chair. She brought her palm up to ward off his advance. "Now, wait just a moment. I realize you may be a little upset—"

"Upset! First you weasel your way into my business, then you manage to hoodwink that stupid hotel clerk into thinking I intended to pay your bill. That bastard threatened to call the sheriff and have me arrested for what you owed. Do you hear me? *Me!* They were going to arrest me for what you did. People like you make me wonder why I am trying to settle down and lead a respectable life."

Carson gulped and gave him a weak smile. "Since you are starting a respectable life, as you so aptly put it, I'm sure you could have explained the mistake to the sheriff, and he would have let you go."

"Well, I am not going to let you go until I have wrung the hotel bill out of you."

Carson backed away, holding the chair between them. "Then I am afraid you are going to be disappointed. You read Gideon's note. He left me with nothing."

Kohl ran a hand through his hair. "I should have known you'd come up with a way to get out of paying me."

He seemed to have calmed, so Carson stepped from behind the chair. "Well, I certainly am glad that you finally see reason."

"Reason?" he echoed, his fingers itching to unholster his gun and force her from his place once and for all.

"Yes. Since it is obvious that I have no money or no where to go, it should be self-evident that the first place I would come was here."

"Here," he repeated, his temper near exploding again.

"Why, yes," she went on calmly in spite of his rising ire. "This is the perfect place for me to live since I own half of this establishment."

"You are not living here!" he bellowed. In his anger he picked up her bag and threw it down the

94

stairs. Then slapped his hands on his hips. "Now that I have been kind enough to remove your luggage, you can be on your way."

Carson crossed her arms over her chest. "You might as well quit being so obstinate. I am staying." She gave him a smug grin. "Furthermore, you threw Addie's bag out. Not mine."

He started toward her again and she ran to the bed, jumped onto it, and sat in a position which dared him to try to remove her.

The girl sitting in the middle of the bed stopped him, and a different sort of vision flickered into mind before he beat it down. A sly grin came to his lips. There was more than one way to rout the pretty little interloper. "Never had a lady so literally jump into my bed before, but I guess there's always a first time."

Chapter Ten

Carson grabbed the dusty quilt in front of her when he started toward her with that gleam in his eyes. The dust formed a cloud about her, and she immediately went into a choking spasm until tears ran from her eyes. Through the blur, she could tell he had stopped and was watching her.

"There. See what you have done? You've made me cry." She made a big production of sniffling for effect. "I hope you are happy now. I have been cheated out of every penny I have in this entire world and have nowhere to go, and now you make lurid suggestions after trying to throw me out into the cold."

She hesitated to take a breath. She was on a roll now and was sure he would relent before she was through with him. "Why I could very well freeze to death if forced out into the cold, dark, cruel world, a poor, defenseless young lady such as myself . . ."

Kohl rubbed his nose as he waited patiently for the girl to cease such carryings on, although she seemed nowhere near ready to wind down. He waited another couple of minutes until he could no longer stand the sound of that whiny voice she was trying to ply him with. "For God's sake, shut up before I'm forced to gag you."

Carson immediately clamped her lips together and stared at him with her most innocent gaze.

"Hell, will you quit looking at me like that!" he growled.

"Like what?"

"Like I am some sort of monster, that's what."

"Well, what other kind of man would toss a poor, innocent, young—"

"Stop it! Dammit! You've made your point. I won't toss you out . . . for the time being."

She had the upper hand now. Despite all his blustering and his reputation as a hardened bitter gunslinger he was proving to be quite a gentleman, actually. Although she was not about to admit it, she was starting to feel quite secure in her position and beginning to look at him in a most different light. And she was beginning to realize that the tripping of her heart when she was near him might very well store other meaning than trepidation.

She pulled the quilt up closer around her neck for good measure. "You aren't going to try to take advantage of me, are you?"

"Hell, lady—"

"Carson. You might as well quit calling me lady and call me Carson."

Kohl rolled his eyes. "Hell, *Carson—*"

Must you continue to use such profanity? I was

reared in a convent, you know. And I am not at all used to hearing such language."

He was getting exasperated and had to fight to keep from letting go with a whole string of profanity, as she put it. He ran a hand over his face. "Let me try this one more time. And this time, don't interrupt me!"

He paused, expecting her to be unable to keep her tongue. The little troublemaker just sat there, on his bed, as big as she pleased. "Anyway, as I was trying to say . . . oh hell, now I don't remember what I was trying to say."

"Something on the topic of taking advantage of me, I believe," she supplied, feeling most comfortable now.

He silently counted to ten. She was trying to goad him, and he was not going to let her get away with it. "Oh, yeah, now I remember. I was going to say that such a scrawny little thing like you couldn't interest me if you tried." To her indignant gasp, he added, "So you needn't worry about your virtue, darlin'. I like my women to be the weaker sex, warm, willing, and soft. You, darlin', are as prickly as a porcupine."

"Not to my fiancé," she retorted without thinking.

"Oh, yes, the fiancé your guardian's letter referred to. Why don't you simply have him send you money? Then you can get out of my hair, so I won't have to put up with you!"

"I can't do that," she cried, feeling her grasp on the upper hand begin to slip.

"All right, I'll bite. Just why can't you contact your fiancé's family?"

She stared at the big gunslinger. His expression had transformed into one of boredom. Real tears threatened her and she quickly wiped at them. He would never believe she was truly crying after the act she had just put on. "If you must know, I was sent here to prove I could be a proper lady when Sinclair and his mother come in three months to take me back to San Francisco."

To her dismay, he threw back his head and laughed. "Then I suggest you write and break your engagement immediately, because from what I've seen you'll never pass inspection."

"It is not funny! My situation is serious! Sinclair's mother has to accept me; she simply has to." He did not look moved. An idea flashed into her mind and before she stopped to think it through, she blurted out, "I'll make a deal with you."

He looked suspicious. "A deal?"

"Yes. I'll remain here . . . since I do not have anywhere else to live . . . and participate in the brewery business while I establish my proper social position in the community—"

"That ought to take you not more than . . . say . . . ten to thirty years."

She crawled off the bed and slapped her hands on her hips. "Will you hear me out before you make further comment? Your remarks are not the least amusing."

He raised his palms. "Such that I should interrupt a budding lady."

She sent him her most vinegary frown. "I will make it worth your while."

She had pricked his interest. "How worth my while?"

"What if when Sinclair and his mother come to Carson City and approve of me that I turn full ownership to the brewery over to you?"

Kohl cocked a brow. She really had his attention now. "No strings and we make it legal?"

"Agreed."

"Only one thing. I get full ownership of the brewery whether they approve of you or not if I am to put up with you for three months until they arrive."

"That's not fair. If they don't approve of me, I shall be left a poor orphan with no worldly means of support, forced out into the cold, dark—"

"Enough! You've already tried that on me, re-member? It isn't going to work a second time, darlin'."

Carson immediately ceased. "All right. But you really have nothing to lose. I shall succeed in being the proper lady for Sinclair."

"If you're so sure, then why are you so afraid to grant me full ownership in the brewery unless they approve of you?"

She glared at him. He had her and he knew it. If she didn't agree to his stipulation, she was ad-mitting that she didn't think she could prove to Sinclair that she had become a proper lady when he came for her. Of course she would have no fur-ther trouble becoming a proper lady. So why was she so upset at the prospects of turning the brewery over to the gunslinger in three months?

Her father had started the business, but she had to admit to herself that she wanted to return to San Francisco. There was nothing left here in Carson City for her.

Without further consideration, she blurted, "All right. Deal." She thrust out her hand and waited. "Aren't we going to shake on it?" she said when he merely stood there.

He cocked a brow and held out a hand.

Her hand was velvety soft and warm, and fit in his like it had been made to go there; like the feel of a gun butt hand crafted specially for him. He pulled his hand back as if he had been burnt.

"What's the matter? Have a change of heart?" she inquired at his sudden withdrawal. "You act as if you had just been burnt."

He shook his head, the twinkle in his eyes aglow. "As a matter of fact, I'm not sure that I haven't."

Ignoring the strange inflection in his voice, she walked over to her bag and began unpacking it. "You needn't worry about our deal. As soon as I get settled, we'll seek out an attorney and have the appropriate legal papers drawn up."

"I wasn't worried about our deal," he mumbled under his breath and went out to the parlor and plunked down on the horsehair couch.

"What are you doing?"

"Making myself comfortable. What does it look like?"

"It looks as if you are making yourself comfortable in my apartment."

"Our apartment, darlin'. Our apartment. For now, I am half owner of this brewery, which means half these premises belong to me, which means half this apartment is half mine. Isn't that true, Miss Mueller?"

"Well, yes, but—"

"If that's true, then what is your problem?"

"The problem is that you can't stay here! How will it look to polite society?"

"Becoming a so-called lady is your problem, darlin'. Not mine. You forced this situation."

"Me? This is not my idea! No. You simply can't stay here!" she cried, aghast at the very thought of such an arrangement.

"This arrangement is your doing, since I ended up paying your hotel bill."

"What does that have to do with this present unworkable situation?"

"This present 'unworkable situation' as you put it came about because I had to use the last of my cash to keep the sheriff off your tail. Guess you owe me more than the brewery; you owe me for saving your neck during the hold up of the stage, as well as keeping that pretty little neck out of jail."

"Then you are penniless?"

He pulled his pockets inside out. "Not a penny." What he did not say was that he had amassed quite a fortune during the years he spent hiring out his gun, and had only spent the last of the cash he'd had on him. The rest was stashed safely out of her reach in San Francisco.

Carson walked over to the window and parted the frayed curtains. The glass was so dirty she had to take her hand and rub it in order to look out. Down below her the town's inhabitants were going about their business unencumbered by the demands some gunslinger she had only known for a short time was making on her.

She turned back to him. "No. I cannot agree to such a living arrangement. The Masonic Lodge has rented a portion of the second floor since 1864. I cannot live here with you and have the lodge members see me here. No. The living arrangement just will not do."

To her chagrin he stretched out his long legs and crossed them at the ankle, his arms spread out across the back of the couch. "Suit yourself. Guess you are just going to have to find other accommodations then, because I'm not going anywhere."

She opened her mouth to protest further, but heard the faint call of her name and quickly looked back out the window to see Addie below, waving up at her. "Well, you can just stay. It seems I may have found other accommodations after all."

She stuck her nose up and rushed from the apartment, only to trip on the stairs on her way down. How all those other ladies managed to walk around with their noses held so high was a mystery to Carson, but in the next three months she would master the skill.

Joining the girl, Carson asked, "Addie, oh Addie, how did you find me?"

The girl frowned. "Didn't make it easy. When you wasn't at the stage depot, I figured you didn't have no place else to light, so you'd come here. Just asked where the Carson Brewery was and followed directions."

Carson gave the girl a big hug; the girl did not respond. "Thank heaven you're here. Now we shall be able to go to that room you mentioned earlier."

The girl's face tightened. "Afraid there ain't no room no more. The shopkeeper tried to get friendly so I belted him one. Guess we'll have to stay here."

"But we can't do that!" Carson cried.

"Why not? Looks like it'd suit."

"Because Kohl Baron is staying in the only apartment, and we certainly cannot live with him!"

Carson watched a strange play of emotions cross the girl's face before she blanked them out. "Guess he's just as good as the next one. And with me stayin' with you, he wouldn't dare try nothin'."

"Oh, I'm not worried about him trying anything. He gave me his word he had no interest in me."

Addie looked unconvinced, but asked, "Then what's wrong? We gotta stay somewhere and up there's"—she motioned to the second floor apartment—"better than sleeping in the streets. Unless you got other ideas."

Carson thought about it for a moment. Fact was she had been counting on Addie. She looked at the girl; she had an expectant look on her young face.

Carson could not let her down. And truth was, Carson was not streetwise and hadn't the faintest notion how to go about sleeping on the street if she had to. Then she considered Sinclair. What would his mother think if the socially prominent woman ever discovered she had slept on the street? She would never approve her for her only son.

Trying to firm her resolve, Carson's gaze absently wandered up along the brewery wall as she contemplated her position when she caught sight of Kohl passing the window.

Even through the dirty streaks in the window she could see that he had removed his shirt. He passed again and she noticed how muscled his bronzed torso was. Unbidden thoughts flickered into her consciousness and she had to force them back. Surely nice ladies did not speculate what it would feel like to run their fingers down such a muscular chest. She brushed her fingertips together, marveling at their heightened sensitivity all of a sudden, and questioned whether it had anything to do with her thoughts about how Kohl's skin would feel.

She dragged her attention back from the window to Addie and put such fanciful notions out of her mind. She was a lady with a mission.

"All right, we'll go back inside and work out some kind of living arrangements with Kohl Baron," she said, wondering what the next three months were going to bring.

Chapter Eleven

Kohl stood with his hand around the butt of his gun, trying to keep his temper under control as he glared at Carson and now an additional intrusion into his life: A young girl, who had sullenly stared at him all the way from San Francisco.

"No. And that is final. I am not running a boarding house. The girl goes," he stated.

"Addie stays," Carson retorted flatly. "Need I remind you that for the next three months I am half owner of this building and she can stay in my half. Furthermore, I have hired her to help out where needed in my half of the brewery," she added without first thinking it through.

Kohl swung toward Addie. He expected the girl to make a meek pose and throw herself on his mercy. Instead she stood rigid, glaring at him, daring him to remove her. There was also something else, which he could not quite discern and it troubled him. He had seen that same stance in men he had faced before. "You got a problem, girl?" he asked.

A strange grin barely lifted the corners of her lips. "No problem that my stayin' here won't take care of."

Kohl rubbed the back of his neck. Hell, he was outnumbered. He ought to take his saddlebags and mosey on to another hotel before it was too late, but he had an investment to protect.

"All right, she stays—"

"I knew you would see reason," Carson said and hugged Addie. The girl continued to stand like an Indian totem, still and staring, cold to the touch.

"On one condition," Kohl added after being cut off by Carson's enthusiasm.

Suspicion came to Carson's eyes. "Condition?"

"You are responsible for the cookin' and cleanin' around here for the next three months."

"But I don't know how to cook," Carson protested and looked to Addie.

"Don't go lookin' at me. I ain't gonna be nobody's maid." Addie rolled her eyes and started snooping around the apartment.

Carson gave Kohl her best beseeching look that used to work on Mother Superior at the convent. "Won't you reconsider?"

He crossed his arms over his chest. "That's the deal. Take it or leave it."

"Oh, very well, you win," she huffed out. "But only if you promise to eat what I set before you without complaining."

There wasn't that much to cooking, Kohl thought. He was used to simple fare. How could she ruin fried potatoes and ham? "Okay, but I take the bed."

"Agreed," Carson said and thrust out her hand.

Kohl stared at it, remembering the uninvited

thoughts that her touch had evoked last time. Everything inside him cried out to take her hand and revel in the sensations. He held himself in check. "Once was enough," he announced and headed toward the stairs.

Confused by his reticence, Carson called out, "Where are you going?"

"To take a cold shower."

Once he was gone Carson turned to Addie. "I wonder what brought that on?"

Addie rolled her eyes. "Chrissakes. You really was brought up in a convent, wasn't you?"

After Carson had set a grumbling Addie to cleaning the apartment, she went downstairs to inspect the brewery. It had been fifteen years since she had walked among the bags of barley and hops. The scent of malt being soaked in water to germinate reminded her of her father. She fingered the wood-fired kiln, then the tarnished copper brew kettle drew her attention. Keeping it polished had been her mother's pride over her father's objections that it was a waste of time. And she had to smile at the thought of their bickering, since they had loved as fiercely as they'd fought.

She was almost over to the metal floater filled with ice to cool down the beer when a crotchety male voice halted her.

"What in all tarnation is ya doin' in here?"

Carson swung around. Kohl was coming toward her behind a stooped old man toting what looked to be a miniature spittoon with latticework covering the flared opening and a curved open-ended tube for a handle. The pair stopped in front of her and to her surprise the old white-haired man funneled the tube into his ear.

"I didn't hear your answer, missy. How'd ya get in here?"

She realized the spittoon was a hearing device, an ear trumpet. Carson assigned the wrinkled face a closer perusal. Then she broke into a huge smile. "Horace? Horace Krause? My father's brewmaster? Is that you?"

The man squinted and scratched his ear with gnarled fingers. "Dadblamed thing makes my ear itch." He took a closer look, hobbling around her to come back and stand before her. "You look a mite like the little missy whose pa started this here brewery."

"I am the little missy, Horace. I am Carson Mueller. Don't you remember me?" she cried with delight. "You used to shoo me out of here regularly."

"You that little toddler full of sass who used to get into trouble every time I turned my back?"

"She's still full of sass and hasn't quit getting into trouble," Kohl interjected with a grin.

To Carson's chagrin, Horace let out a hearty chuckle. "Well, I'll be. Little Sunny Mueller."

"Sunny? Summer thunderstorm would be a more appropriate label," Kohl muttered, causing the old man to laugh all the harder.

Carson dealt Kohl a daunting look, but he ignored her.

"You should have seen the ruckus she caused at the Ormsby House. She—"

"I don't think Horace cares to hear about my mis-adventure right now. Do you, Horace?"

The old man's wrinkles deepened into a frown and he shook his head, dislodging the ear trumpet. "Horace? When you was a young'un, you called me Horse 'cause I used to give you horseback rides, remember?"

"Yes, of course I do, Horse."

"Horse?" Kohl said, staring directly at Carson with a knowing grin. "As in road apple?"

She glanced down at her heel before returning to glare at Kohl. "Very amusing, Kohl."

Horse put the ear trumpet back to his ear. "Eh? I miss something?"

"No," Carson hollered into the ear trumpet. "Kohl was just trying to dredge up an old joke at my expense.

"You two a pair?" he asked.

Carson's hand flew to her chest. "No. Of course not!"

"Eh?"

"I said no. Kohl and I are partners in the brewery. Nothing more."

"Your ma and pa used to act just like the pair of you. So I thought—"

Carson was looking into Kohl's hooded eyes when she answered the old man. "You thought wrong, Horse. Now, why don't you show us around the rest of the brewery?"

Horse leaned toward Carson, the ear trumpet pressed to his ear. "Eh?"

Kohl took Carson and Horse's arms. "Come on, let's get on with the tour of my new business."

"It is still our business," she retorted and withdrew her arm. "And unlike some people, I have already begun work. I have an additional order from an establishment in Genoa."

"Baron, there you are. Thank God I found you!" Pots headed toward them at a fast clip, Addie trailing after him.

"Tried to stop him, but he was a persistent cuss," Addie said to Carson.

"It is all right. Why don't you go back to your cleaning now?"

"Humph. Cleaning," she grumbled and headed back to her chores. But once she was out of sight, she returned to eavesdrop.

Kohl watched the girl disappear, then turned on Pots. "What are you doing here?"

Pots thrust out his hand, a rolled newspaper in it. Waving it at Baron, his words rushed out. "When I got this newspaper and read what some two-bit newspaper gossip columnist wrote about you, I thought you'd want to know."

Kohl ripped the paper out of the hysterical man's hand and snapped it open. "What the hell are you jabbering about?"

Pots immediately calmed and stepped back. He did not want to become the next notch on the gunslinger's gun. "Look for yourself. Front page. Right next to the story about a speedy trial promised to those highwaymen who robbed the stage we came in on."

Kohl rustled through the pages until he came to the headline:

"A new series based on the true adventures of two of the city's newest entrepreneurs," Kohl read before Carson grabbed the newspaper out of his hands.

"Let me see that! 'Today your reporter learned that Kohl Baron, the notorious gunslinger, and Miss Carson Mueller, whose father started the Carson Brewery, seemed to have formed a new partnership. But, you may be asking, what kind of a partnership is it? It has just come to my attention from an unimpeachable source that the pair has been staying at the Ormsby House and the gunslinger paid the lady's hotel bill . . .'

"This is trash!" Carson wailed. "How can they twist things to make it sound like we were engaged in something less than innocent? Who could be responsible for giving that dreadful reporter such information?"

Kohl kept the grin from his face when he remembered the confrontation he'd had with the hotel clerk. For some unbeknown reason, the article did not bother him. As a matter of fact, he found the title greatly amusing, if not strangely endearing.

"Now Baron." Pots shrunk under the scathing look Kohl gave him. "I mean Mr. Baron. I thought you would want to know that someone gave such a story to the newspaper. It does not reflect kindly on the lady. If I were you I'd—"

"You're not me!" Kohl barked out. "Look Pots, no one gave that story to the newspaper."

"Then there won't be any more?"

Carson slapped her palms to her cheeks. "Oh,

dear Lord, I hope not! What if this gets to Sinclair?"

"Quit worrying, Carson. How is one little article going to make its way all the way to San Francisco?"

"But it states that it is the beginning of a series," Carson complained.

"About me. Not you. Furthermore, there won't be a series unless someone feeds the reporter additional information, and who is going to do that with neither one of us living under the public's eye? There's nothing further to concern yourself about. This will all die down long before your precious fiancé comes to claim you. Hell, this is already yesterday's news." Kohl crumpled up the newspaper and tossed it on the floor.

"Eh? Eh? I didn't get half of what you said, son," Horse hollered. "What's that about you and Sunny?"

Carson shot Kohl a quelling look before she circled Horse's stooped shoulders. "Nothing, Horse, truly. The newspaper simply made an incorrect remark about Kohl and I."

"It did what with yous?"

Carson took a deep breath, put the trumpet in the old man's ear, and hollered, "The newspaper wrote something that was wrong, is all."

Pots grabbed Kohl's arm. "What about buying that starter set of cookware we talked about?"

Kohl glared down at Pots's hand and the man immediately removed it. "What about it?"

"Guess you haven't thought on it much yet?"

"Exactly."

"Well, you will let me know, won't you? Because I'm going to have to go back on the road. And well, truth is, I'd sure like to see you get set up before I leave." Kohl merely cocked a brow toward the hefty pot salesman, causing him to decide a hasty departure would be expedient. "Well, I guess I'd best be getting back to my hotel."

"Sounds like a good plan to me."

"Ah . . . you will get back to me when you decide?" Baron ignored him. He tipped his hat to the lady. "Good day, Miss Mueller."

"Mr. South."

"Come on, Horse," Kohl hollered into the ear trumpet. "Let's get a look-see at the rest of the brewery."

"Okay, son. But the way you're bellowin' your lungs out at me, you'd think I was deef or somethin'."

Carson and Kohl both suppressed smiles as they followed the old man toward the west building where the beer was brewed.

All the while they toured the remainder of the brewery, Carson could not take her mind off the article in the newspaper. If Sinclair ever linked her name together with Kohl Baron's, his mother would immediately find her wanting.

She had built up the article so much in her mind that she was waiting for the first opportunity to excuse herself from Kohl and Horse to go back and reread it.

"Carson, you daydreamin'?"

Kohl's voice snapped her thoughts from the newspaper article. "Pardon?"

"Horse and I are getting hungry."

"So?"

"*So*, remember our deal? You are to do the cooking for the next three months. *So,* you had best go see how Addie is coming with the cleaning, *so* you can have supper ready by the time we finish going over the last few details."

If she hadn't been trying to think of a way to excuse herself so she could retrieve the newspaper, she might have been out of sorts with the way he accented the word "so" so many times. "You'll have your supper. But don't forget your part of our deal. You can't complain about my culinary skills."

She hurried back into the main building to where Kohl had tossed the crumpled newspaper on the floor.

It was gone.

Chapter Twelve

By the time Carson entered the second-story apartment, she was pleasantly surprised. Addie had worked a miracle. She inspected the three rooms and could hardly believe Addie had been able to make such short work of what Carson had thought of as a major job, and then disappear. The girl always seemed to be disappearing, but it was the girl's prerogative.

Carson went to the kitchen. All the boxes on the shelves looked to be quite old. But Kohl wanted supper, so supper he was going to get!

An hour later Kohl appeared unaccompanied and announced that Horse had begged off. "What smells so . . . so interesting?"

Frazzled, she wiped the flour from her cheeks. "Supper," she declared with sarcasm.

He kept his face placid despite a growing concern that he was about to get the meal of his life if the curious odors barraging him were any indication. "Let's eat."

Kohl managed to consume little of whatever it was that she had thrown into the pot and heated to a crusty black. He heaved a sigh of relief when she set a huge square of gingerbread before him.

"This looks good."

"You don't have to compliment me. Just keep to our bargain." She leaned forward and watched him take a corner with his fork, popping the gingerbread into his mouth.

He choked out the entire mouthful. "My God, what did you put in that?" he demanded and rushed to the sink to pump a glass of water. He downed the entire glass before turning on Carson with flashing eyes.

"What did you put in that?" he demanded when his throat finally quit burning.

"Just a good dose of ginger from that box over there on the top shelf."

"I haven't had anything so hot since I was in Mexico." Kohl reached up and pulled the unlabeled box off the shelf and peeked inside. One whiff was all he needed. "My God, this is cayenne pepper!"

She shrugged. "I told you I couldn't cook."

Fighting down the urge to demand if she had tried to burn out the lining of his throat on purpose, he questioned, "Didn't they teach you how to cook at the convent?"

She gave him a sheepish grin. "Don't laugh. But I spent most of my time there on my knees."

"Your knees?"

"Doing penance."

"What for?" he asked before he thought better of it.

"If you must know, for doing a lot of stupid, childish things. Nothing serious . . . except maybe the last thing I got caught for."

Keeping the urge to smile at her confession at bay, he ventured, "And that was?"

"Lighting a cigarette on the votive candles. Except I wasn't the one who actually did it. I just happened to be in the wrong place at the wrong time . . . for once."

Kohl barely hid a grin at her open confession. Not many women would have been as honest. He was used to women trying to hide things from him; Carson Mueller was a refreshing change.

"You still hungry?"

Carson looked up from underneath her lashes. "Actually, I am."

"Good." Kohl untied her apron. She opened her mouth to protest; he put a finger to her lips. "Hush." He took the corner of her apron and dabbed at the remaining flour dusting her cheeks. "Now you are presentable enough to take out to supper. We'll eat out tonight and tomorrow I am going to get Lily to teach you how to cook."

Carson drew back. "But Lily is a—"

"Whore. She's a whore."

"Yes, she is."

Kohl narrowed his eyes. "Don't even think of looking down your nose at Lily. Lily is what she is. But she is the salt of the earth. The 'good' ladies of the town may snub her, but she is better than all of them put together. She would give you the shirt off her back if you needed it. She has brought food to the miners and nursed them when they were ill and they

118

all love her. So don't ever even think of saying anything against Lily to me."

Carson forced a smile as a surge of guilt over her
disapproval of Lily washed over her. "Lily is fortunate to have found such a defender in you."

"I'm the lucky one to have Lily as a friend."

Carson bit her lip to keep from asking just what
he meant by "friend." She thought about Kohl's suggestion and decided that as long as no one saw her
and Lily together, their acquaintance couldn't cause
any harm or get in her way of becoming a proper
lady.

"Is the offer of supper still open?" she inquired,
feeling quite ashamed of herself for automatically
thinking she was superior without getting to know
the woman. She had been taught to be charitable; it
was good manners.

"As long as you're paying. You do have some
money, don't you?"

"Only what is left of what Unc . . . ah . . .
Gideon gave me." She had ceased referring to
Gideon as uncle after she'd discovered his deceit.
"Isn't the gentleman suppose to pay?"

"I see you did learn a few things at that convent."
He pulled out his pockets. "No money, remember?"

"All right, I'll pay. But I am going to deduct the
cost of your dinner from your portion of our first
profits."

Kohl rolled his eyes. "I'd say, you are well on your
way to becoming one of those first-class society matrons."

She ignored his sarcasm. "Do you really think so?"

"I know so." Kohl tossed her her reticule. "What

are you standing there for? Let's go."

Carson awoke with a stiff back. She was sure that no society lady ever had to sleep on the hard floor with nothing more than two blankets. Carson sat up and looked over at Addie. The girl was lightly snoring and looked as comfortable as ever curled up on the couch.

Carson crawled to her feet and rubbed her back. At least Kohl was sleeping quietly in the bedroom, she thought as she folded the blankets. Although he could have relented and offered her the private room. She sneaked a peek through the opened door as she passed and discovered that Kohl had already gone. No wonder he hadn't been snoring!

She went to the window and looked west toward the snow-covered Sierras. She was trying to figure out a more equitable sleeping arrangement when she caught sight of Pots, a newspaper tucked under his arm, his belly bouncing as he scurried toward the west building of the brewery.

She stood there for a moment and stared at the man until it hit her; he seemed to be upset and he was carrying a newspaper. A newspaper! "Oh, no! Not another article!" she cried, wondering about the missing newspaper she could not ask Kohl about since he had not wanted her to see it. She darted from the window and was flying into her clothes as Addie rose up on her elbow and rubbed her eyes.

"Why you in such a all-fired rush?"

"I always dress this fast. Go back to sleep." Addie shook her head and lay back on the pillow.

Carson charged down the stairs to intercept Pots as he was disappearing inside the brewery.

Kohl sat in Lily's little plank house on the edge of town with his arms crossed, waiting for Lily to make herself presentable. Her parlor was neatly decked out with crocheted doilies and embroidered platitudes.

Lily appeared in a ruffled wrapper, her generous breasts barely restrained by the filmy fabric. She took a seat near Kohl. "Thanks for waitin', honey. What brings you out my way so early? You know I don't usually get up at this hour, since I keep late nights, an' all. Don't get me wrong, I'm awful glad you came by. Always appreciate your company."

"Actually, Lily, I came to ask a favor."

"You know I'd grant you anything in my power, Kohl. Just name it, sweetie."

"I need you to teach Carson Mueller how to cook."

"Giddy's Carson? The sweet little thing that came over to our table at the hotel?"

"She's the one."

"Well, I'll be. 'Bout time you decided to get hooked up with her kind of lady. She's the kind that's for keeps, you know."

"Lily, I ain't interested in her that way." At her raised brow of disbelief, he added, "Look Lily, Gideon Farley made off with her inheritance. She owns half the brewery, so we're partners, nothing more." She still looked unconvinced. "Furthermore, she's engaged to some rich dandy back in San Francisco."

"Then why do you want me to teach her how to cook?"

"We have this arrangement . . ."

Lily listened patiently while Kohl explained his relationship with the lady.

". . . so you see, Lily, she has to show the fool's mother that she has become the lady they expect her to be. So her learning to cook will serve a twofold purpose: I won't have to starve and she'll be able to show her fiancé's mother what great culinary talents she has."

Lily crossed her arms over her ample chest and leaned back in her chair. "I see."

"Well, will you do it?"

"You know I'd do anything for you, Kohl. But what if she don't want the likes of me near her?"

"She's not like that," he insisted. He didn't bother to tell Lily that he had made certain that Carson would not act scandalized in front of Lily.

"You defendin' her now, too?"

Kohl bristled at the implication and stood up. "Seems I took you from your beauty sleep. See you around, Lily," he announced and was at the door before Lily could hail him back.

"Don't go away mad, Kohl." She patted the arm of the chair. "Come back here and tell Lily when you want me to pay the lady a little visit."

By the time Kohl entered the brewery, Carson was waiting for him. "Have you seen today's newspaper?" She waved it at him.

The second article written by the same reporter was titled OR SHOULD IT BE LADY'S GUNSLINGER? Kohl

122

hid his amusement and read the article.

"Your reporter has it on good authority that the lady in yesterday's column was seen last night paying the gunslinger's supper bill after they had had a very cozy supper. Therefore, the series title is in question, and it has been decided to put it to a reader vote. Once you have read the pair's latest escapade, send in your vote as to which title is the more appropriate . . ."

Kohl looked up from finishing the story. "What do you think? Which title gets your vote?"

"Kohl, this is serious! My future is at stake. You have got to stop that reporter from writing those articles or I'll never be able to become a proper member of society before Sinclair arrives."

"What do you propose I do?"

"You're the gunslinger, stop him!"

"You want me to call him out into the street at high noon and gun him down? That would stop him cold."

"Of course not!" Carson cried. Then she gave him a sheepish grin. "Perhaps you could shoot him in the foot?"

"Wouldn't the hand be better? He wouldn't be able to write then."

Her sense of amusement shriveled and she snapped, "Just get him to stop printing those articles!"

"Anything else you'd like me to do? Walk on water possibly?"

Carson ignored him and turned back to the brewing kettle. She had already added water to the malt and hops and now the brew was ready to be cooked before she would draw it off into a metal ship to be cooled. She tried to reel the kettle up over the fire, but the pulley caught.

"What are you doing?"

"I am finishing up this batch of beer, of course."

"Where's Horse? That is his job; it isn't a job for a 'lady.' "

"Horse is in the cellar adding yeast to the barrels. And if this brewery doesn't continue to make a profit, I won't be able to become a proper lady because there won't be enough money for me to repurchase my family home so I can entertain properly."

Kohl pinched his lips. He was getting a little tired of her constant harping about being a lady. As far as he was concerned she was fine just the way she was—except for her cooking. "Move aside and let me take care of it."

Carson stepped aside and watched with a smug grin as he managed to raise the kettle halfway before the ropes got hung up. He tried to free the ropes to no avail.

"What's the matter, is it stuck?"

Feeling frustrated by her complacent comment, he waved toward the ladder leading up to a catwalk from where the brew could be stirred while cooking. "Climb up there and work the kink in the knot free."

"I'm not going up there; I'll fall," she protested.

"Someone has to stay down here and hold the ropes, and there's only two of us present."

"You go up; I'll remain and hold the ropes."

"Carson, you aren't strong enough. Furthermore,

I'm too big, I wouldn't fit up on that ladder. Now get going. We have a profit to make, remember?"

Carson shot him her most daunting look, but it didn't seem to faze him. She'd teach him to send her up that ladder without regard for her safety! Keeping one eye on Kohl, she tied her skirts, then started up the ladder.

"What's the matter, darlin'? Afraid I might get a look at those slender ankles?" he taunted when she was four rungs up.

"I am saving my 'slender ankles,' as you put it, for Sinclair. So will you be kind enough to look away."

Kohl laughed and shifted his line of vision. Hell, he liked parrying words with her, he realized. "Hurry up, will you? These ropes are straining my muscles."

"I certainly would not want to strain those precious muscles of yours . . . Yeeowwww!" Her scream pierced the room, just as the contents in the kettle splashed over the sides, drenching Kohl.

Chapter Thirteen

Kohl's heart nearly stopped with fear for Carson as he frantically looked for her. She was nowhere to be seen on the catwalk and the big kettle was swaying precariously above his head.

"My God, Carson!" he yelled and worked furiously to tie off the ropes so the kettle would not come crashing to the floor. "Carson!"

She did not answer and Kohl managed to squeeze his big frame up the ladder to rescue her before she drowned. When he reached the catwalk, he stopped.

Carson was sitting, her legs crossed, her hands drumming on her arms. "I knew you could fit up the ladder," she said smugly.

"That was a dumb prank!" he roared and reached for her.

Carson scrambled to her feet. But as she attempted to dodge under his grasp she lost her balance, teetered perilously for a moment before she made a grab for Kohl, and sent them both plunging into the kettle.

Kohl came up first, sputtering. Carson was nowhere in sight. He reached down through the mixture, grabbed her up, and held her limp body against him, smoothing back the wet strands of red hair which streamed down her face. When she did not respond, he started kissing her face. "Come on, baby. Wake up."

Still half conscious and only partially aware of the welcoming sensations, Carson lifted her lips to his.

Kohl looked down at those full, sensuous lips and couldn't help himself.

He kissed her.

Carson was swimming through constituent consciousness and automatically parted her lips when something soft, warm, and inviting pressed against her mouth. She moaned and felt the pressure against her lips increase. She put her tongue out and tasted something sweet along with malt and hops.

Kohl could not believe her response, and his tongue danced with hers as he held her tighter against him. He could feel the hardening buds of her breasts crushed against his chest, reckoning him with overpowering force. Responding, he deepened the kiss.

Carson's eyes suddenly flew open as full consciousness returned and she shoved against his chest.

Gasping for air, she accused, "What do you think you were doing?"

"Trying to revive you, darlin'," he offered.

She considered his explanation, then stopped struggling against him. "Oh. It is okay then, I guess." She gazed up into his face. "Where did you learn how to do that?"

Kohl had to fight to keep from smiling at her naïveté. "Guess it comes natural."

He was still holding her, and she ran her hands along the rough edges of his collar. "Well, it certainly works. Quite well, as a matter of fact. If I am ever in danger of drowning again I hope you won't hesitate to use such a maneuver on me."

"Such a maneuver. Don't worry, Carson, I won't hesitate if the opportunity ever presents itself again."

Feeling awkward, although she did not understand why, Carson nodded. "Good."

Beneath them, Horse tossed another log on the woodpile beneath the kettle and lit a fire.

Kohl looked over the edge and hollered at the old man, but he didn't even look up, and kept tossing more wood on the growing fire. "That deaf old man is going to cook us if we don't get out of here right quick."

Kohl helped Carson out of the kettle and they climbed back down the ladder. Horse's head snapped up.

"What the devil you two up to up there? And how'd you both get all wet?"

"We were inspecting the kettle," Carson offered lamely.

"Eh?"

Kohl grabbed Horse's ear trumpet and put it to his ear, yelling into it. "We fell in the kettle!"

Horse glared at the two of them. "How'd you manage to do that when it ain't even on the ground?"

"I'll explain it to you later after I've changed

128

clothes. Get this mess cleaned up." Kohl took Carson's arm.

Horse gave them a blank look. "Why don't you two go get out of them wet duds while I clean up this mess." He waited a moment while the two young'uns just stared at each other with strange grins on their faces. "What you standin' there for? Get goin' before you catch your deaths. Young'uns these days ain't got the sense God gived 'em."

Carson was leaning over the sink, trying to wash the malt out of her hair without help since Addie had disappeared again, when Kohl entered the kitchen. Still bent over, she glanced back at him. He was naked from the waist up and he looked even better than when she had seen him pass by the window.

"Having trouble?" he inquired.

She was immediately jolted out of her reverie. "You'd have trouble, too, if your hair was waist length and full of malt."

Carson returned to trying to clean the long strands until she felt his fingers slide over hers. She started. "What are you doing?"

"Hush up and remain still," he instructed and began gently washing each strand.

Carson stood still, her heart the only thing moving and it was racing as Kohl washed her hair for her. He was gentle as his fingers massaged her scalp while he worked. He stroked the back of her neck and Carson felt as if a lightning bolt had struck her, his touch was so electrifying.

The heat from his fingers brought back the vision of him partially undressed, and she had to hold her hands to keep from turning around and running her fingers through his hair. With each stroke, she wanted to moan with pleasure. Thoughts of those sensuous fingers moving down from her head, along her neck and over her shoulders to drift lower caused her to close her eyes in anticipation, until he dumped a pan of cold water on her head.

"What do you think you're doing?" she yelped at the sudden sobering shock.

"I might ask the same question myself," Lily cooed.

Kohl swung around. Lily was leaning against the door frame, her ankles crossed, two bags in her hands. "My, my, this is a rather domestic scene. Hope I'm not interruptin' nothin'."

Carson groped for a towel and wrapped it around her hair. Embarrassment heated her cheeks at standing, bare-footed, in nothing more than a robe before the fancy woman all gussied up in lavender-blue silk with black lace. And she was ashamed at the unbidden thoughts she had been having about Kohl.

"We had an accident at the brewery, and Kohl was just helping me to get the malt out of my hair," Carson explained in a rush.

Lily gave her a patronizing smile. "Of course he was. Anyone can see that. Kohl's always been a big help."

Carson forced a smile. "I'm sure he has."

Lily plunked the bags down on the table and gave Kohl a suggestive once-over. "Well, Kohl, honey, you goin' to stand around here all day half-naked or you goin' to get dressed and leave us ladies to get on with this here little gal's cookin' lessons?"

"Cooking lessons?" Carson repeated weakly.

"Why, yes. Didn't Kohl tell you? He paid me a visit earlier and asked that I come over and give you a little instruction." At Carson's horrified look, Lily added, "In cookin', my dear girl. Cookin'. Unless, of course, you're interested in learnin' about what else I'm well versed in, honey. I'm a willin' teacher."

Carson shot Kohl a shocked glance. His amused expression indicated he had no intention of rescuing her. "I think cooking will be quite sufficient," she announced, recalling her earlier conversation with Kohl.

Lily shrugged and leaned against the table. "Your loss. All right, Kohl, you go put some clothes on and mosey on out of here before you make me forget what I come for."

"Thanks, Lily." He chuckled and strolled into the bedroom to return buttoning a shirt. "See you ladies for supper."

Carson watched him disappear down the stairs, feeling awkward in the presence of such a woman and more than a little disappointed that Lily had interrupted them.

A sudden disturbing thought flashed into her mind, and she blurted out without thinking, "If you wanted to be alone with Kohl, I could have been the one to leave."

Lily studied the girl. "Honey, I have wanted to be *alone* with that man for years." She heaved a long sigh. "But he ain't never paid for it, and I ain't never gave it away." A wicked grin tipped her generous mouth. "So I hope that puts to bed any questions you've got about my friendship with him."

Relief highlighted Carson's features. "Then you two are truly just friends?"

"For well on ten years now."

"Do you think you could tell me about him?" Carson ventured.

"After you get back from changin', I'll tell you anything your little heart desires to know about Kohl Baron. Now, you run along, put on something practical for gettin' messy, and then get right back here. We've got some cookin' to do."

Carson felt sheepish and just a little wicked, and forgot all about her vow to Sinclair to stay away from Lily's kind as she quickly dressed and rejoined her in the kitchen.

Lily had unpacked the bags and was putting the staples she had brought on the shelves. "Here, honey, sit down at the table and take a look at this while I finish puttin' everything away."

Carson took the *Fanny Farmer Cookbook* and flipped through the pages with little interest.

"There. We're all ready to begi—" Lily started to say as she swung around, but stopped. "You ain't got much domestic interest, do you, honey?"

Carson closed the book. "Not a lot. But if we are going to work together, I wish you would call me Carson."

"Sure, hon . . . Carson." Lily pulled out a chair and plunked down next to the girl, laying a hand on

132

her arm. "Before we get this lesson started, why don't we get whatever is on your mind out into the open."

The woman was very perceptive, not to mention direct; Carson did have something else on her mind—Kohl Baron. "Can we keep it between us?"

"Young lady, if I spilled the beans then sold 'em on just half of what my customers tell me, I'd be a mighty rich woman. But I ain't let out their secrets and I ain't goin' to let out yours."

"It's not a secret. I just thought that since Kohl and I are partners I should know what kind of man he is." She furrowed her brow. "I just don't want him to know that I asked, is all."

Lily watched the girl's eyes light up when she mentioned Kohl's name and she wondered if the girl realized just how interested she really was in the gunslinger. She had to smile inside. She had seen it before. Two people starting to get close before either one of them knew it; Kohl and Carson were a classic case of it.

"Here." Lily handed Carson a bowl. "Pour some flour in that bowl. Ain't no reason not to work as we talk."

Carson dumped the flour into the bowl, causing a white cloud to rise around her. She waved it away. "What's next?"

Lily batted at the dust cloud. "I can see that we're goin' to have to start from scratch. Didn't they learn you nothin' at that convent?"

Carson gave Lily the same explanation she had to Kohl, telling Lily all about her parents and life at the

133

convent. Soon Lily was sharing her own childhood tales, and the two women were laughing as Lily guided Carson's cooking lesson.

Carson waited patiently as they worked for Lily to broach the subject of Kohl. But Lily had seemed to have gotten sidetracked with her own boisterous tales.

Lily had had a difficult childhood with a drunken father who had tried to take advantage of her after her mother had taken ill. Lily had run away and made her own way in the world from the time she was twelve.

Carson felt sympathy toward the woman at how she had come to be in such a business due to a man. Lily's tale reminded Carson of Addie's behavior, always sneaking off, and she silently vowed to keep anything like the tragedy that had happened to Lily from happening to Addie.

"Well, that is the story of my life," Lily said as Carson used the glass to cut the last of the biscuits they had made and put it in the pan. "It was a man who done me wrong. I learned never to love any of 'em after Harvey sold me to that first cathouse. Hmmph! And I thought the fool loved me, too."

Lily noticed the alarmed expression come over Carson's face and laid a comforting hand on the girl's shoulder. "I hope you don't think that Kohl would ever try to cheat you out of everything and then leave you like Harvey did with me."

Finally. Lily had finally brought up the subject Carson had been waiting for. She was going to hear about Kohl.

"I hope not!" Carson did not bother to inform Lily about Sinclair, although she had to wonder why she suddenly did not want to share her engagement with Lily.

"You can put your mind to rest. Kohl is twenty-four carats through 'n' through. The salt of the earth. The crust of the bread."

Carson smiled at that. "He said the same about you."

"He would. But I'll tell you, that man has helped me out a time or two. We met when he stopped some drunk from pistol-whippin' me 'cause I don't sleep with drunks. Nearly got himself killed protectin' me. Then he gave me money to move here so I could start fresh. We've been friends ever since." A distant light glinted in her eyes for an instant. " 'Course, a girl's got to do what a girl's got to do." She blinked three times, then waved her hand. "Yes sir, Kohl's special."

"But he's a gunslinger."

"He *was* a gunslinger. Now, I'm not sayin' that he ain't a hard man when he's got to be. He's lived a hard life and he's had to live by his wits. But he never went lookin' for trouble. Ranchers or business-men hired him on to stop it. So it seems natural that trouble would come lookin' for him. He never shied away from it either, though. But he's turned over a new leaf. Bought a business and plans to settle down, if others'll leave him be."

"He is not a gentleman though," Carson said, perplexed by feelings so new she did not begin to comprehend them.

"Hell, girl, if he ain't no gentleman, then I don't

135

know who is. He's never mistreated a lady. And there's been a few what deserves it, too. Why, he's the most gentle man I know to those he cares about." Lily watched the wavering emotions in the girl's eyes. "Honey, to my way of thinkin' Kohl is the same as your papa."

"How can he be the same as my father?" Carson cried, feeling another strange emotion bombard her that she could not name at the comparison.

"Honey, your papa owned the Carson Brewery, and now Kohl owns the same brewery. To my way of thinkin' that puts them as both being brewers. The same, you know."

Lily's blunt observations caused Carson to start thinking even more about Kohl Baron as they finished up the day's cooking lesson. Only now she found that she was thinking about him in an entirely different light, and such foreign thoughts surrounded her with an unnerving persistence.

Chapter Fourteen

Warm fingers of sunlight settled on her face and Carson fluttered her eyes open. She gazed up at the freshly cleaned window, then stretched and turned over. Kohl had surprised her last night after complimenting her on the supper she'd served by hauling up a pallet for her to sleep on.

"Don't you think it is time you got out of bed? If I had known that you were going to try to sleep the day away, I never would have got you something soft to lay on."

Kohl's deep voice squelched all warm thoughts of his thoughtful gesture last night and consideration of going back to sleep now. She rubbed her eyes and looked about for him. To her surprise he was sitting on the horsehair couch, the morning newspaper resting on his lap.

"You were watching me while I slept," she accused and burrowed farther under the covers.

"Why would I want to watch you? I have better things to do with my time," he lied, not wanting her to feel ill at ease around him. Fact was, since he had sent Addie down to the brewery to start cleaning under Horse's direction, he had been sitting there, studying the way her red hair seemed to flame in the sunlight, the gentle curve of her lips and the slow rise and fall of her breasts beneath the covers.

"Oh," she said, not sure whether to be disappointed or relieved. "May I see the newspaper if you are done with it?"

To her chagrin he stood up, tucking the newspaper under his arm. "I haven't finished reading it. Now, get going. You have work to do in the brewery. We're partners, so whatever work needs to be done, I've decided we're going to share it."

"When you're done with the newspaper, I want to see it."

Concern glistened on her face, and Kohl was aware why she was so persistent to see the damned newspaper. He had already read the latest article and she was going to be upset when she read the latest story, describing his purchase of the pallet she was sitting on, and raising the question of what it might be used for. Luckily, the reporter had not yet mentioned anything about their living arrangement.

"Where are you going?" she demanded when he headed toward the stairs.

"To work."

As he passed her, she lunged and grabbed the newspaper. Before he could retrieve it, she snapped it open and read the title.

"Oh, no. Another story," she said with a sigh, looking up at him.

She looked beautiful with her tousled hair flowing over the shoulders of her embroidered lawn nightdress. "Carson, forget about the newspaper stories."

"I can't," she cried. "Don't you see, if those stories don't stop I'll never be able to live up to Sinclair's expectations."

"Sinclair's expectations," he echoed through tight lips.

"Of course. Have you forgotten why I am here in Carson City?"

"You won't let me," he muttered under his breath.

She held her head. "Right after work I am going to go to that newspaper office and give that reporter a piece of my mind."

"Don't be foolish. You'll only give the man more fuel for the fire." She just stared at him with a look he had come to read that meant she intended to ignore him and barge ahead in her usual impetuous manner. "Carson, I promise you, there won't be any more articles."

She crossed her arms over her chest, belatedly remembering that she was still in her nightgown and he had seemed totally unaffected by it, which made her even angrier and she called out to his back. "That is what you said once before."

Carson entered the brewery a half hour later,

wearing an old tan sprigged skirt and plain white shirt, rolled up at the elbows. Beer bubbled in the kettle, lending the room a strong aroma. She glanced around. Only Addie was apparent, a pout on her lips, sweeping with a vengeance.

"Morning, Addie. I can see that Kohl's given you a job."

"Hmmph! Child slave labor," she sneered and went back to sweeping.

"So you finally realized you are not a society matron who can sit on her butt, spending the day eating bonbons," Kohl said from the doorway.

"I may not be a society matron yet," she raised her chin "but once I marry Sinclair, I shall be the most sought-after society matron in San Francisco."

"That's really important to you?"

"Yes. More than anything," Carson said with conviction.

His lip twitched. It annoyed him that she wanted to live such a frivolous life. He grabbed the one-gallon copper measure pitcher off the counter. "Then you can start practicing to be a society matron with this." He thrust the pitcher in her hand. "While you're down in the cellar you can practice your tea service etiquette by pouring the yeast in the barrels."

Carson's eyes flashed at his attempts at humor at her expense. "You can make all the jokes you want. But I am going to be a lady Sinclair will be proud of."

Kohl watched her swish her skirt and couldn't help himself. He admired her spunk. Then his expression grew serious. "Horse, take over the deliveries for today, I have to go out."

Addie glared at Kohl as he passed her. Once he was gone, she threw down the broom. "Horse, I'll be back."

Horse shook his head. Folks sure didn't know what it meant to put in a full day's work these days. He propped the broom in the corner and began loading the barrels ready for delivery.

"I'm finished with the yeast. What do you want me—" Carson stopped. "Where's Kohl?"

Horse's head snapped up. "We don't use coal under the kettle; we use wood."

Carson smiled at the old dear and set the ear trumpet to his ear. "Where is Kohl?"

"Kohl?"

"Yes, Kohl Baron. My partner?"

"You mean that young whippersnapper what now owns this here place?"

"Yes," she hollered into the ear trumpet. "But he only owns half of the business."

"Gone."

"Pardon?"

"Said, he's gone. I don't know how he thinks he's goin' to earn a profit if he runs off whenever the spirit moves him. And that girl. Addie. She took off right after he did. Oh, for the good old days. Folks knew how to give a day's work for a day's pay back then. Yes, they did. They—"

She cut him off. "Thanks, Horse."

He grabbed her arm. "You ain't thinkin' of runnin' out on your chores, too, now are you?"

"No." She sighed. She could not leave the old man to shoulder all the work alone. "What needs to be done?" Carson had wanted to go after Kohl. After he had insisted she do her share of work, she was not going to let him simply run out on his responsibilities whenever he felt the urge!

"You drive a team?"

"I can drive a buggy."

He repositioned his ear trumpet. "Eh?"

She put her hands to her mouth. "Yes!"

"Good. Then you can make today's deliveries. Go get them leather gloves off that glass case in the office while I hitch up Sarah Mae . . . What you standin' there for? Get on with you, girl. We got a business to run."

Kohl smacked the newspaper down on the reporter's desk. "I want this nonsense stopped!" he snarled.

Klaus Millard drew back. His source had told him that his series of articles might cause the gunslinger's trigger finger to itch. He looked past the huge ruffian; the staff was huddled outside the glassed office watching. "Now look here, Baron," he blustered, "I have a duty to my readers to write the news. My very right to print such a recital is guaranteed by the Constitution."

Kohl's reach was as quick as his draw. He grabbed the overstuffed buffoon by the collar, plucked him out of his chair, and smashed his face against his desk. "This is my guarantee, Millard," Kohl growled, holding the man's face down. "Quit writing those articles unless you want to face the business end of a gun, you hear me?" Kohl righted the man, who promptly took out his handkerchief and mopped his brow.

"I can't just stop the series. My publisher—"

"Where's your publisher?"

Klaus's eyes grew to twice their beady size. "He's upstairs in the corner office. But I don't think—"

"That's what I've been telling you, you haven't been thinking." Kohl slammed out of the office, breaking the glass in the door.

"You can't get away with this, Baron. This isn't the uncivilized Old West anymore!" he said softly enough so only the staff would hear and not Baron.

It was not twenty minutes and workers were still clearing away the splintered wreckage when Kohl reappeared, crunching across the floor into Millard's office. The reporter put his hands up. "I'm unarmed, Baron."

A triumphant look on Kohl's face, he leaned over the desk. "And unemployed." He gave Millard a benign smile. "You're fired."

"What gives you the right to try to get me fired? You can't come in here and—"

"I not only can, but as new owner of this rag, I

did. Now get out before I have you tossed out with the garbage."

A murderous expression on his face, the reporter gathered up the papers on his desk, stuffed them into a case, and stormed from the building.

"Psst. Psst. Come here," came a voice from around the corner in the alley.

"Want more dirt on the gunslinger?"

"You! Thanks to you I no longer work for the paper. And I suggest you don't try peddling your information to anyone else at the paper. Seems that Kohl Baron is no ordinary gunslinger. The bastard just bought the newspaper lock, stock, and printing press, and kicked me off it."

"Can't you get a job at another newspaper and sell the story to them?"

"I will get another job. But there is no way I am going to touch that story again. I got a family to support."

He stared at the young girl. There was a strange gleam in her hard eyes. "What's this Kohl Baron to you? And why are you so hell-bent on exposing his life?"

Addie sent the man a look filled with pure hatred. "That's my business."

The girl started off; he halted her with a hand on her shoulder. She threw it off and glared at him with such hatred that he removed his hand. "Maybe I ought to dig into your background," the reporter threatened.

"Go on ahead. You ain't gonna find nothin'."

"Nothing to connect you to Baron?" She merely shot daggers of loathing so intense that he shrank back. "Don't worry, as far as I'm concerned our relationship is over."

Addie's lips twisted as she watched him scurrying away, then she turned her attention back to the front door of the newspaper building and waited for Kohl Baron to come out.

Kohl was feeling victorious in a way he never had after a gunfight. Although he had used more force than he had intended, he hadn't resorted to guns to solve a problem. He had seen to it that there would be no further articles about Carson and he had also paved the way for entrance into her precious society.

He was whistling as he stuffed the bill of sale into his pocket. All he had to do was head on over to the bank and have the necessary funds transferred from San Francisco.

The air stuck in his throat when he caught sight of Carson. She was sitting, as big as you please, atop a beer delivery wagon!

"Stop the wagon!" he hollered and ran across the street, dodging a carriage, to where she had stopped in front of a saloon. "What the hell do you think you're doing?" he demanded.

Carson put the reins down and scowled down at the big man. "I am making *your* beer deliveries," she hissed.

"Why are you so out of sorts, darlin'?"

"Unlike some others I have had the misfortune to be stuck with for the time being, I am forced to work for my living."

"Well, you are not going to work by delivering beer to unsavory types in saloons. Get down from there. I'll finish the deliveries," he said.

She held her position. "I can handle myself. And furthermore, I am not a schoolgirl in a convent any longer. I need to make these deliveries so I can buy some new clothes which will be presentable in proper society!"

"You'll never be presentable in proper society if one of those precious society matrons of yours spots you delivering beer."

"No! I have plenty of time to impress society once I have made these deliveries."

"Dammit, you're getting off there," he growled and dragged her off the box, only to be set upon by three men who were coming out of the saloon.

"Nooo! Stop!" Carson screamed. She jumped down from the wagon and joined the fray. She tried to pull one of the men off. "Stop it! Leave him alone! Get off him! Get off . . . Ooof!" she screamed as she found herself flung backward against the wagon.

Kohl let out a roar like a lion and proceeded to take on all three. Carson scooted under the wagon. From behind the wheel she struck out at an imaginary foe, all the while yelling her support of Kohl despite the growing numbers of spectators.

"Get 'em," she yelled. "Punch him in the nose, gouge his eyes out. Kick him in the—"

Carson broke off at the sudden intake of breath coming from the crowd. She glanced up and saw two apparently wealthy society matrons by their fine dress, their hands pressed to their bosoms, staring directly at her with horror in their eyes.

Chapter Fifteen

Without giving a second thought to how the spectators had perceived her part in the ruckus, Carson climbed out from under the wagon and, ignoring the fight and her disheveled appearance, proceeded over to the two women to introduce herself.

She thrust out her hand, still encased in Horse's old leather work gloves. "How do you do? I would like to introduce myself. I am Miss Carson Mueller, late of San Francisco."

Agnes Maplewitz gasped that such a person would dare to approach her. The girl's skirt was marbled with dirt and grease and the flower on her hat drooped to the left side, not to mention the filthy gloves she wore. Agnes clasped a fine gloved finger to her lips, and looked aghast at her companion.

Beatrice Heimerman looked down her long nose at the young woman, who so obviously must have come from the seedier side of town. "No doubt, young woman, you have no idea to whom you are speaking. My husband is the owner of the *Tribune*," she announced with acid superiority and pushed past Carson.

Her bearing regal, she strutted past the three men who now lay prone and battered on the boardwalk and ignored the big gunslinger she had recognized from the articles in her husband's newspaper. "Come Agnes, fine ladies of our breeding and position in the community should not have to be subjected to such sights on the streets in broad daylight."

Carson swallowed hard at the apparent snub. She withdrew her hand, which had been left dangling in midair and watched the middle-aged matrons hurry about their way.

"Show's over, folks. Move along," Kohl announced and brushed himself off. He took a threatening step toward the three men he had bloodied because they found the beer delivery girl lewdly appealing, and they scrambled back into the saloon. If Carson hadn't looked so forlorn he would have given her a good talking to, but he let the thought drop, finished brushing himself off, and joined her.

"You okay, Sunny?" But he could see that Carson's expression was anything but sunny. She stood, staring after the disappearing, overfed figures of the women. Her lip was trembling, and she was wringing her hands. "They're not worth it, darlin'," he said in a comforting voice.

Carson tried to smile at his use of her nickname, but she felt nothing like smiling. "Although you're probably right, they are the very people I was sent to Carson City to make an impression on." Her shoulders slumped and she let out a breath of self-disappointment. "I guess I made quite an impression on them, didn't I?"

"You truly want to associate yourself with their kind?" Kohl motioned toward the pair of aging biddies. He had a devil of a hard time understanding how any man worth his weight would want to mold Carson into some old gorgon such as those two had become.

Carson did not look up at him when she answered. "I want to be a lady of quality. Sinclair expects it. Do you think I should go after them and try to explain?"

He lifted her chin with the crook of his finger and stared into her face. If she only knew that she already had more *quality* than those two ever would, she'd—He broke off such thoughts. What the hell had he been thinking? Carson Mueller was more trouble than a peck of rustlers holed up in their own hideout. Then it suddenly hit him and he turned her chin.

"You won't be going anywhere for a while." His fingers touched her puffy cheek just below her eye and she flinched. "Looks like you've got quite a shiner starting."

Carson's hand flew to her face and she realized she had been wearing Horse's work gloves when she'd introduced herself to the women. "Oh, no!" she cried.

Some odd urge caused Kohl to gather her into his embrace, despite the warning bell in his head. "Don't worry, the fight wasn't your fault. We'll get some cold meat on that eye so the swelling won't be so bad."

Carson pulled out of the circle of his arms. "I know it wasn't my fault," she said flatly, surprising the hell out of him. "And I'm not worried about the black eye." She held up her hands. "I had Horse's work gloves on when I introduced myself to those two ladies."

Kohl rubbed his face. Women! They worried about the damnedest things! "Come on, let's get you back to the brewery."

She stood her ground. "We'll make the deliveries first and collect the money owed us."

He took her elbow roughly and practically loaded her in the wagon as if she were a beer keg, he felt such bald exasperation over her stubbornness. "I am not going to argue any longer. If you want to go around looking like some pugilist who lost, why should I care."

Carson didn't know what a *pugilist* was, but she was sure she would not like it if she did. "The least you can do is stop at the butcher shop."

"Good idea. I'll get a nice big steak that you can keep on your eye while we deliver the kegs. Since it'll be so close to your brain, let's hope you've absorbed some of Lily's teachings so you can cook it for supper tonight."

She shot him a look of disdain and refused to respond to such a rude attempt at humor at her expense. "Delaney's is the next stop."

It was late afternoon by the time Kohl dropped her off at the apartment and announced that he was going to see to the horse. Carson was proud that all the deliveries had been made and their first profits collected.

As she climbed the stairs, she was pleased that she had managed to ignore the men's strange looks when she had insisted on helping roll the kegs into the back of the saloons. She even had managed to ignore one man's attempt at humor at her expense with a coarse comment about the beer barrel polka.

Perhaps Mother Jude was wrong after all. Despite the incident causing her black eye, she had conducted herself like a lady the rest of the day. She thought about a lady delivering beer, then had to amend her thoughts. She had not let her tongue rule her brain, at least. It was a start, she ruminated, placing the cash box on the kitchen table and laying the steak next to it.

"Where you been all day?" Carson's attention snapped up, expecting to see Addie. Instead, Lily was sitting at the kitchen table in all her red satin glory. "I thought we had a cookin' lesson today, honey."

"Lily, I'm sorry. I was so busy making deliveries that I completely forgot."

Carson watched in horror as Lily picked up the steak and gave it a thorough perusal. All Carson's contemplations about starting to become a lady vanished at Lily's spreading grin.

"This what you had in mind to fix for supper?" she asked, swinging the hunk of meat between her fingers. "Or is this what the best dressed ladies are wearin' to accompany their black eyes these days?"

Carson grabbed the meat. "Oh, Lily, don't make jokes. The fight wasn't my fault."

"Maybe not, but I hope the other guy don't look no better." Lily rose and examined Carson's eye.

Carson smiled despite the pain as Lily probed the sensitive skin. "You should have seen Kohl. He beat the three of them—"

"Three?"

"Yes. They were advancing toward me and Kohl out in front of one of the saloons while I was attempting to deliver beer, and Kohl just jumped in and—"

"And defended your honor."

"Well, yes. I suppose he did."

Lily pumped cool water over a cloth and handed it to Carson. "Put this on that eye. Maybe now you'll start believin' that Kohl's more like your pa than just some 'gunslinger,' as you put it." A glint Carson could not comprehend entered Lily's eyes. "I'll lay you odds that that guardian of yours, Giddy, would've never even thought to come to your rescue. Hell, honey, look what he did to you, takin' all your money . . ."

Carson listened patiently to the woman praising Kohl's virtues, wondering if Lily was ever going to remember to stop calling her "honey" as she'd requested. "I suppose you're right."

" 'Course I'm right."

"Oh Lily, I acted terribly foolish in front of two ladies today."

"What did you do that was so foolish?"

"Without thinking about the fight and how I must have appeared crawling out from under the wagon, I tried to introduce myself. Oh, Lily, they were scandalized by me. I don't know why I can't seem to stay out of trouble. What will people ever think of me if I can't quit acting so rashly?"

"Their kind really so important to you?" Lily inquired, not understanding why anyone would aspire to become so high and mighty as to forget that all folks were put on this here earth the same way, and all folks ended up six feet under the same way too.

"You need some lessons with learnin' to be a lady?"

Carson just stared at the woman in disbelief. How could Lily know anything about being a true lady? "Ah . . . I . . ."

"Lily could probably teach you more about parlor conduct than those two shriveled up old biddies ever could," Kohl answered from the doorway, his hands bracing the frame. "Lily has entertained more gentlemen in the last two years than most *ladies* do in a lifetime."

Carson cleared her throat. "I am sure she has, but I am more interested in how to present myself properly at teas and charity balls."

"Then you got nothin' to worry about, honey. Me and my girls between us know more about such stuff than you can shake a hickory stick at."

Lily ignored the girl's demoralized pose, tossed the steak into a pan, and lit a fire under it. "Looks like you bought the best hunk o' meat in the shop for supper tonight." She winked at Kohl. "And Carson's already spent the afternoon warmin' it up, so it won't take long at all to cook." She hugged Kohl and blew Carson a kiss. "I gotta run. See you in the

154

mornin' at my place for your first 'lady' lesson."

"But I can't . . ." She watched the woman prance from the room. ". . . go to your place." Carson finished her protest to Lily's disappearing back. Kohl was leaving the kitchen and she followed him out. "You know I can't go to such a place."

"You want to be accepted by those fine ladies, don't you?"

She watched him make himself comfortable on the couch and lean back with his hands behind his head. "How can you think they would even be seen on the same side of the street with me again if they see me going into such an . . . an establishment?" she cried.

He shrugged. "There are worse places you could be seen goin' into."

She threw up her hands. "Why can't you understand?"

"Carson, Lily entertains their powerful husbands. Many of those women know their husbands are Lily's customers. Those highfalutin women have no other means of support except their husbands, and I'm sure that if Lily dropped a word or two in the right places, not one of those women would ever turn her back on you again."

Carson rolled her eyes at the very idea. It was so outrageous that it just might be true. But it seemed almost too outlandish even for her.

As she continued to mull over what Kohl had said, black clouds of smoke suddenly started to issue from the kitchen. "Oh, no! The steak!" Carson screamed and ran into the kitchen, Kohl right behind her.

Kohl grabbed a towel, wrapped it around the frying pan and dumped it and the steak into the sink, furiously pumping water over it until the smoke quit billowing. Carson ran and opened a window, frantically fanning her hand. When she turned back to Kohl through the clearing smoke, he was holding the frazzled meat between his fingers, waving it at her with a half-smile half-frown on his face.

She forced a smile of defeat at Lily's attempts to teach her how to cook. He just shook his head, causing her to shrug. "I hope you like your meat well done."

Seated at the long dining table in the regal family mansion overlooking the city of San Francisco, Sinclair sucked in his cheeks at the sight of the overdone steak, which the family servant had dared to try to serve him. The rage within him built until he flung the dish against the sideboard.

"You know better than to try serving such garbage to me! That steak was not fit for the likes of dogs," he raged at the cowering servant. "Get that mess cleaned up before I have it deducted from your wages. And then send the cook in. I won't tolerate such sloppiness!" he bellowed. "And get me another steak. Properly prepared this time!"

"Sinclair, do calm down." Constance Westland picked up her fork and knife, and ignoring her son's red-faced outrage, sliced a corner off her skinned chicken breast. She took a dainty bite and savored the flavor while she watched for her son to comply meekly.

"I know you have not been yourself since it was necessary to send that Mueller girl away, but you really should not allow your temper to get the better of you in front of the servants. Our family is not to be set out as fodder for low class gossip."

Sinclair was immediately contrite. "Yes, Mother. But the servants know better, if they want to keep their jobs," Sinclair whined and glared down at the butler cleaning up the mess on the floor. The man did not even look up. He knew his proper place, Sinclair was sure of it.

Sinclair then stared at his mother. He was glad he had a reprieve from sweet, innocent Carson Mueller who his mother had picked out for him. "Mother, while I have no doubt the Carson Brewery would be a nice addition to the family coffers, don't you think that we could acquire one without my having to resort to marrying the girl?"

"Stop being so tiresome, Sinclair. A convent-bred girl is the best choice. By the time we have finished with her, she will come to you without the slightest hint of scandal attached to her name. You know how important it was to your dear departed father to keep the family name above such things. Furthermore, out of all the girls of marriageable age I had investigated by that dreary detective agency, the Mueller girl was the only one without living relatives to interfere with our future plans.

"Despite her . . . shall we say . . . propensity for acting rashly, she seems to be most pliable. I have no doubt that she can be molded and shaped into a proper Westland lady."

Constance picked the linen napkin from her lap and dabbed at the corner of her lips. Confidence surrounding her, she said, "Why, I am certain that she is most probably very hard at work on the task of becoming a proper lady this very moment, even as we speak."

Chapter Sixteen

Carson kept the largest bonnet she owned drawn down over her face all the way out to Lily's place in the brewery wagon. It wasn't the purpled eye which bothered her as much as where they were heading.

The wagon hit a rock and Carson's attention dropped to Kohl's leg, which pressed against hers and caused a gentle warm sensation to invade her breast. She couldn't help but smile to herself. Despite the fact that she had burned the steak to a crisp last night, she and Kohl had ended up laughing about it.

When they passed a well-dressed lady strolling along Fall Street, Carson turned back to crane her neck at the woman's proud carriage. That lady would never give consideration to going to a place such as Lily's.

"Kohl?"

"Yeah?" he answered without looking at her and moved his leg from against hers.

A strange disappointment surrounded her at his sudden withdrawal. "Don't you think I should help you make the deliveries today, instead of going to Lily's?"

"You're the one who wants to be a fine society lady," he grunted and snapped the reins over the team's rumps.

"Why can't I practice being a lady without going to a place like Lily's?"

He turned to look at her. His tight face was anything but benign, which caused those warm sensations to cool. He just did not understand about Lily's. If Sinclair ever discovered that she had visited a house of ill repute, he would never marry her.

"Lily can teach you everything you need to know to become a precious lady."

"Are you sure?"

"We've already had this conversation, Carson," he said as if he were speaking to a persistent child.

An idea flashed into her mind. "In that case, do you think that Lily and her girls would consider making house calls?"

Carson stood amongst the roses bursting with colorful blooms and filling the yard in front of Lily's house with their sweet fragrance. She was relieved that the house was located on the edge of town as she watched the wagon rumble away before she forced herself to go to the door.

Shock compelled her to swallow several times in rapid succession at the sight which greeted her in the parlor. And panic welled up her throat, threatening to cut off her wind.

Three strikingly beautiful women clad in no more

than scanty lace chemises and black silk stockings disappearing into naughty sheer pantaloons lounged around the room. One woman with jet black hair was tickling the piano keys with a bawdy song; one with orange-red hair was reclining on a red velvet settee eating chocolates and swigging from a beer bottle, which Carson recognized as Sierra beer.

The one with the bottle raised it in salute. "One of the best, right, honey? Lily said to expect you. Couldn't miss picking you out with that shiner you're sprouting."

Carson gave a self-conscious nod and trailed her vision to the last woman. The blonde was smoking a cigarette, and Carson almost smiled at that. For that had been the crime which had gotten her banished to this town, and Carson briefly wondered if the woman had ended up here for the very same infraction.

"Have you been smoking long?" she ventured.

The woman took a long drag on the cigarette, and blew smoke rings as she looked Carson up and down. "Oh . . . I'd say since I was about . . . eighteen."

The other women laughed and Carson was silently swearing never to go near another cigarette when Lily appeared dressed in a flowing red satin robe, dusted with ostrich feathers.

With a flourish Lily swept into the room. She gave Carson a big hug and inspected her eye, announcing it would soon heal. Then Lily boomed out, "Seasons, meet Carson. The young *lady* I told you about. She's going to spend the day as our protégée."

"Seasons?"

161

"I call my girls after the four Seasons since there ain't no time o' year we can't handle a customer's needs." She chuckled. "There's Winter, Spring, and Summer."

"Aren't you missing a season?" Carson asked.

"Honey, I'm Fall." Lily laughed. "Get it honey? Fall, as in fallen woman?"

Carson forced a smile, but she truly saw little amusing to such a distinction. She briefly wondered about their true given names but decided prudence dictated that she refrain from inquiring.

"Don't look so dumbfounded, honey. It's all in fun," Lily announced and proceeded to make individual introductions. "Winter, here, likes to snuggle, like when it's cold outside. Spring likes a good frolic, like all the young'uns born in spring." Lily dealt Carson a sly grin. "Only Spring's frolic's done in the hay."

Carson weakly smiled at Lily's reference to a roll in the hay and shifted her eyes to the last girl. "And this is Summer. She likes it hot and heavy. Fall rounds out the Seasons since you get a little bit of all kinds of weather. So you see, no matter what a man needs we got it."

Carson nodded. She could not believe her eyes as each one put on the superior airs of high society matrons. And despite her trepidation over Lily's crude introductions, Carson relaxed.

"Lily," the buxom blonde with the cigarette, called Spring, announced, "I don't understand what a big gorgeous hunk like Kohl Baron, who could have his pick of willing women, is doing bothering with the likes of her." She motioned to Carson.

"Hush up your mouth, Spring, and get yourself upstairs. It's obvious your heart ain't in helpin' the girl," Lily ordered.

"Pay her no mind, sweetie," Summer waved her dyed red hair, reminding Carson of her own nickname and natural hair color. "She's just jealous 'cause her drawers is hot for Kohl and he don't know she exists. Hell, he don't know none of us exists."

Carson blushed. But she was secretly pleased.

For the remainder of the day Carson walked back and forth in the parlor with a book on her head. She served the Seasons teacakes, and curtsied on the arm of one of the women as she pretended to be introduced at a fine charity ball. She made small talk and all the while marveled at Lily's vast knowledge.

"Well, I think you'll pass muster before the crown heads of Europe." Lily laughed and her ample breasts bounced. Carson wasn't smiling. Lily put her arm around Carson. "Honey, why so glum? You just proved you can be as good a lady as the best of 'em."

"To you and the Seasons, yes. But however am I going to have a chance to prove I am a lady when the good people of Carson City won't even give me a chance?"

"Stop that self-pityin', honey. From what I heard from Kohl, it ain't like you. You ain't goin' to give up now, are you?"

"You don't want to end up like us, do you? You can't quit, sweetie," Summer urged. "Not after we gave up our free time to coach you."

Carson looked around at the expectant painted faces, and she felt that in some way they were counting on her. Firming her original resolve, Carson stepped away from Lily and hugged each woman. "Thank you for all the help. Of course, I am not going to give up. I am going to be accepted into society if I have to attend their balls without an invitation."

"Did I come too soon?" Kohl said, entering the parlor. He was immediately surrounded by the Seasons.

Carson fought down the sprig of jealousy pricking her and, emulating the stiff walk she had learned earlier, went to greet him. She thrust out her hand. "How do you do, sir? I am so happy you could arrange your busy schedule to attend the festivities."

Kohl kept the grin from his face and took her hand, bowing over it. "I would not have missed it."

Carson giggled, but the warmth of his touch caused her cheeks to heat. "What do you think? Do you think I'll pass?"

Kohl shook his head while he continued to hold her hand longer than he knew he should. "There never was any doubt in my mind."

Lily wound her arm around Kohl's and leaned into him, edging out the other Seasons and causing Kohl to release Carson. "Carson, dear, why don't you go on and climb into the wagon while I finish up some business with Kohl."

Carson nodded. She put her big bonnet back on and left to wait for him outside, but she wondered what Lily could possibly have to say to him that she did not want her to overhear.

Lily waited until she heard the front door click shut behind Carson. Then as Spring was making her way back downstairs, Lily waved to her. "Go make sure the girl ain't eavesdroppin' at the keyhole."

164

Spring swung her hips suggestively as she went to check. "Carson's in the wagon," she announced upon her return and lit a cigarette.

Keeping her face sinless, Lily urged, "Kohl, we have to help Carson."

"I thought that was what you were doing today."

"We was. And the girl's a good student, too. But it ain't goin' to do no good for her to learn her lessons if she ain't got no one to practice on but a bunch of whores and a under-the-hill madame."

Kohl rolled his eyes. "Hell, she could practice on worse."

"You don't understand. That girl's desperate to have that fiancé of hers approve of her." At Kohl's tightening expression, Lily shooed all her Seasons from the parlor. Once she was alone with Kohl, she turned on him. "You ain't sweet on her yourself, are you?" Kohl's face tightened all the more. "I thought maybe you was having a change of heart over her."

"Don't be silly. Carson Mueller means nothing to me. I just don't like the sound of what that Sinclair fellow of hers expects her to do."

"Then with all the money you got saved up, why you livin' in that apartment over the brewery with her?"

"I am not livin' *with* her," he snapped. "She has her sleeping quarters and I have mine. Besides, there's a young girl livin' there with us. Furthermore, how I spend my money is none of your business."

Lily frowned. "Then you ain't developin' a hankerin' for Carson?"

"Hell, Lily, would I be 'developin' a hankerin',' as you put it, for Carson if I just assured her debut into polite society so that fiancé of hers won't be disappointed?"

Suspicious and anxious to learn Kohl's plans, Lily probed, "What've you done?"

"Let's just say that since I am now the proud owner of the *Tribune,* and I paid a little visit to Karl Heimerman's office today—"

"Not my Karl Heimerman?" Kohl gave a grinning nod. "Why he is one of my best customers."

"His wife was one of the old biddies who snubbed Carson yesterday during the fight."

Lily looked sympathetic. "Yes, the poor dear told me all about it."

"Well, she's not going to snub Carson again."

"I hope you know what you're doin'. Your success at helpin' the girl just might up and prove her own undoin'."

"I am not interested in Carson Mueller. She's not my type," he said with cold deliberation.

"You may be able to scare others into backin' off with that dangerous gunslinger routine of yours, but don't try to fool Lily. We go back too far, Kohl. I may be no-good. But I know what a deservin' man you are beneath that hard shell o' yours."

Kohl glared at the painted woman. "Just keep your nose out of my personal business from now on."

Lily was taken aback by the vehemence in his voice. "You've never talked that way to me before," she said in a strangled whisper.

"Never had to before," he said, plunked his hat on his head, and left Lily staring after him.

The door slammed behind Kohl, and Lily shook her head. "Honey, do you have it bad."

Kohl sat sullen on the wagon seat and sulked all the way back to the brewery while Carson did not even notice. She was too excited and babbled on all about the lessons Lily had taught her.

By the time they reached the brewery, Kohl wished he had never met the good-hearted whore. He ignored Carson when she offered her hand for him to help her from the wagon, and stalked inside the brewery.

"What the hell!" he roared, causing Carson to forget all about her annoyance at him and rush into the building.

Just inside the door, she gasped and slapped her hands over her mouth.

The room had been torn apart and ravaged. Someone had dumped the huge brewing kettle. Chairs lay broken amidst scattered papers soaking in the spilled malt. Sacks of barley had been ripped open and tar poured over everything that had not been smashed.

A barrel crashed to the floor on the other side of the room by the overturned desk.

"Get out of here," Kohl yelled. When Carson did not immediately move and stood there as if in a trance, Kohl shoved her back out the door and drew his gun before he returned to investigate.

Carson ignored his orders and quietly crept back inside. A moan issued from behind the overturned desk, and she rushed past Kohl. "Oh, my God, Horse!" she cried, cradling his bleeding head.

The old man had been savagely beaten. He was bruised and his plaid shirt torn, and he was bleeding from the mouth. His ear trumpet lay dented next to him. But thank God, he opened his eyes and looked up at Carson.

"I tried, but I couldn't stop 'em. Two of 'em there was. Wore masks. Come in here and just started wreckin' the place. I put up a good fight, though." With shaking fingers he touched his eyes. "Bet I'm gonna have a worse shiner than yours, Sunny."

Carson smiled through her tears at the old man's brave attempts at humor. She looked back at Kohl, standing behind her. His face was as dark and menacing as she had ever seen, and a cold chill ran through her heart. "Help me get him to his feet."

"I told you to get out of here and stay out," he said so coldly that Carson shivered. "You could have been hurt if it hadn't been Horse behind the desk." He pushed past her and helped the old man up. "You goin' to be all right, Horse?" Horse nodded, but flinched at the pain. "Help get him upstairs. Then stay with him."

"But shouldn't I return and help get this mess cleaned up?"

"No! It's about time you started listening for once or I am going to be forced to—"

"Wow! What happened here?" Addie questioned, joining them and interrupting Kohl's tirade. She looked around at the disaster. "Ain't never seed the like."

Kohl's temper had taken all he was going to take for one day. He grabbed the young girl by the elbow and escorted her from the brewery without ceremony.

Carson helped Horse outside. The old man was

still in a daze, but had been able to walk.

"Addie, go for Doc Harris over on Stewart Street. Be quick about it!" He watched the girl bolt down the street before returning his attention to Carson. "Get Horse upstairs, and stay with him until I get back."

Instead of immediately helping Horse up to the apartment, Carson watched Kohl go into the barn. He emerged atop a mighty stallion minutes later. "I thought I told you to take care of Horse."

"I'm just giving him a minute to catch his breath before having him climb the stairs," Carson retorted. She was not going to start cowering before him, despite the dangerous look on his face.

"Where are you going?" Carson probed, then swallowed the urge to shrink under his glare. She was worried about his safety.

"To find out who did this and why."

Chapter Seventeen

The fingers of light were receding by the time the doctor had seen to Horse after he'd collapsed in the yard. Horse had refused to attempt the stairs to the apartment, insisting he be taken home, and Carson had reluctantly agreed after he'd consented to allow Addie to stay with him and see to his care while he convalesced.

After Carson had gotten him settled in his house, Addie walked her out to the wagon. "Don't know why I have to take care of him. He lives in a barn. Besides, I got stuff to do."

"You are the logical one since I must help get the brewery back in operation." Carson shot the girl the same wintery look she recalled getting on the receiving end so many times at the convent. "Furthermore, don't you think it is about time you tell me where you keep disappearing to?"

Addie glared at Carson. "I'll take care of the old man, but I ain't got to account to you for nothin'."

Carson stiffened, wondering if she had made a mistake offering Addie a job while on the stage.

"No, you don't have to account to me. But you had better be there for Horse when he needs you, do you hear me young lady?"

Addie curled her lip. "I hear you."

"Good. I'll be back from time to time to check on Horse."

"I'll look forward to it," Addie sneered.

Carson burned driving back to the brewery. That girl was impossible! Then Carson broke out laughing; the very same thing had been said about her.

To her surprise when she entered the brewery, Lily was working alongside Kohl to put the brewery back in working order.

"What are you doing here? I thought I told you to stay with Horse," Kohl demanded.

Carson slapped her hands on her hips, daring him to try to evict her a second time. "Horse is settled at his place and I have Addie watching over him."

"I can see that I had best be gettin' back to my house. It's almost dark and time for business to start up," Lily announced. She knew when to make a timely exit. There was no doubt in her mind that those two did not need her presence to further complicate things. "Don't you worry none, Kohl. If any of my customers knows anything about this, my Seasons will finagle it out of 'em." She reached up on her tiptoes and gave Kohl a peck on the cheek. "Thanks for comin' to Lily, honey." Carson watched the madame fling a feather boa around her neck as she made a grand exit. She stopped at the doorway and winked at Carson. "See you around, Carson, honey."

"I thought you were going to find out who did

this?" Carson flipped her hand to demonstrate the mess. "Instead you rushed over to Lily's. Which Season did you go to see?" she charged.

They faced off. "What I do and where I go is none of your business. Or have you had second thoughts about that fiancé of yours and find yourself thinking about me instead?"

She was immediately sorry for making such an injudicious accusation. He was right; it was none of her business. Although it bothered her that he had gone to Lily's. "No. I am not thinking about you!" Yet that was not entirely true. He seemed to be entering her thoughts with added frequency all the time.

She threw out her chin. "I am going to marry Sinclair. And I am sorry. You were right. What you do is none of my business." She softened then. "I was worried about you, is all."

"Don't be," he said stiffly. Kohl relaxed his anger, but it had surprised him that she had been concerned about him. "I haven't had anyone worry about me since before my parents died over a claim dispute in the gold fields in California when I was fourteen."

Her heart out went to the boy he had once been, and she touched his arm. "Well, perhaps it is time someone started worrying about you."

"You haven't the time," he said gruffly. "Now come on, it's getting late. Let's get something to eat and get a good night's rest. There's going to be plenty to do here in the morning."

As he was escorting her up the stairs to the apartment, Carson suddenly became too aware of his touch. His fingers were curved around her elbow.

172

She stopped midway up the stairs. "Kohl, did you learn anything about why anyone would want to destroy the brewery?" she asked to change the unbidden thoughts she was having.

"I asked around at a few of the saloons, but no one seemed to know much. One bartender said some stranger had been through a week ago and mentioned some kind of trouble up at the Gold Hill brewery. But the man didn't know what. If any man in town knows what's going on, Lily's girls will be able to ferret it out."

"So that's why you went to Lily's," she whispered, relieved for some strange reason that caused her heart to race.

They finished taking the last few stairs and Kohl pushed open the door. He immediately drew his gun and shoved Carson behind him.

"What's the—"

"Hush! And stay behind me," he ordered in a harsh whisper.

"But I don't understand," she persisted.

He ignored her and cocked his gun. The window crashed and Kohl rushed past the overturned furniture to the window and threw it open. Leaning out, he fired off several rounds at a shadowy figure darting into the bushes. A second later two horses and riders lit out along King Street and Kohl fired off several more rounds.

Carson rushed into the apartment and leaned out the window next to Kohl. "Did you see who it was?"

"You might have asked whether I hit one of them or not."

"You couldn't possibly have hit anyone. It is too

dark out here," she said and ignored his disgruntled expression. "Well, did you see who they were?"

"Too dark," he said with a grunt. "Whoever ransacked the place got away. It's nice to know you have so much faith in my abilities." Kohl came out of the window and lit the lantern. He held it high, the warm light glowing gold across a pale face framed by big, frightened blue eyes. And an urge to protect her came over him. "Come on, let's have a look around." Carson nodded and made no reply. She did have faith in him. So why hadn't she said so?

Together they surveyed the damage. "By the looks of this mess they hadn't found what they were looking for."

"How do you know they were looking for anything?" She asked, glancing about with a sigh at the shredded chairs, the clothes strewn about, open cupboards with flour and other staples emptied and spilled from their containers.

"Look at the couch. They wouldn't have bothered to tear it apart the way they did if they hadn't been after something."

The events of the day suddenly seemed overwhelming and before she gave a second thought to her actions, Carson sagged against him.

"Oh, Kohl, this is so dreadful. Who could have done such a terrible thing?"

"Don't worry, I'll find out." It seemed natural to put his arm around her. He stroked the crimson satin of her hair, his body afire with awareness of her pressed against him. She smelled of honey and pine. Felt of warm velvet. And for an instant he wanted to whisk her into his arms.

Carson pulled back and looked into his face. She expected to see that same anger as she had noted earlier at the brewery. Instead, he looked back at her with an undefinable heated light in his eyes; a softer expression clung to the usual hard line of his lips.

"How 'bout some supper?" he suggested, breaking the spell which had held them.

Kohl made supper while Carson attempted to put some order back into the tiny apartment. She felt truly domestic, scurrying around tidying up. She stopped to peek at Kohl. He was amazing. By the time he stood frying potatoes, he had already made the kitchen somewhat presentable. Carson smiled to herself. He was just as much at home in a kitchen as he was behind a gun, facing someone. And she wondered if she could say the same for Sinclair.

Once they had eaten, Kohl announced that he would help her finish cleaning the kitchen. And Carson was delighted to find that they truly worked well together. He was not afraid to roll up his sleeves and get his hands dirty. Although she had always thought of such chores as distasteful women's work, she found she enjoyed working side by side with him.

"You about ready to turn in?" he asked, untying her apron and laying it over the back of the chair.

Her eyes went wide. "Turn in?"

"Bed."

"Bed?" she croaked.

"We've got to get an early start tomorrow putting the brewery back in order."

"Oh." She relaxed a trifle. "But . . . I mean, Addie is going to be staying with Horse, so we're—"

"Alone?"

175

"Well, yes. Alone."

"You afraid of being alone with me, Carson?"

His voice was a mere probing whisper and goose-bumps rose down her arms. She rubbed them. "No. Of course not."

"Well, then, what are you standing here for? Go do what females do while I make up your bed."

"You don't have to do that."

"I know I don't have to." He took her shoulders and turned her around. "Get going."

Fidgeting with her fingers, Carson pivoted around to face him. "Ah . . . Kohl?"

"Yeah?"

"Would you accompany me out to the . . . ?" Her voice trailed off. One did not discuss the needs of nature.

"You afraid of the dark?"

"What if there is someone lurking about outside?"

"I doubt if whoever did this is dumb enough to still be hanging around, but I'll be glad to offer my protection."

Despite Kohl's accompaniment, Carson imagined every shadow to be a man skulking, every bush took on a human form and every noise some foreign sound. She saw to her needs with all due haste and hurried back up the stairs, throwing the bolt on the door after Kohl.

"You still afraid?" he asked at her actions.

"I'll be fine. Good night, Kohl."

"Good night, Carson." She seemed so ill at ease, he asked, "Why don't I take the couch tonight. You can have the bed."

"No." She went and plunked down on the couch.

It was lumpy after it had been ripped apart. Kohl had done the best he could putting it back together. "I'll be fine. Good night."

"Suit yourself. Need the light?"

"No."

He took the lantern into the bedroom with him, leaving Carson in the dark room; the only light slivered through the lace curtains in foreign patterns, which Carson imagined to be men waiting outside the window. She hurriedly slipped into a thin cotton nightdress and jumped beneath the covers. She was being foolish. They were on the second floor; no one could be hiding outside the window.

But as time went by, she could not go to sleep. Each night sound was magnified. A light breeze tickled the tree limbs, swaying the leaves, and Carson's mind created fingers reaching out after her.

She stood it as long as she could, until an owl's hooting sent her scurrying into the bedroom. She did not stop to think of the propriety of her actions; she was too frightened.

She jumped into bed with Kohl.

Kohl's reactions were lightning quick. He grabbed the gun he kept holstered on the bedstead and had it cocked and aimed at the intruder before Carson could identify herself.

"Don't move a muscle or I'll blow your head off," he growled.

Carson did not blink an eye. She did not even dare to swallow, for his free hand was around her throat. The room was dark, so she could not see his face. But she felt the power in his fingers. Heard his slow even breathing, like a dangerous predator which has calmly stalked its prey and was ready to move in for the kill.

She opened her mouth to let him know he was about to squeeze the breath from her, but he increased the pressure of his hold.

"I said don't move a muscle until I can get a look-see at you," Kohl commanded.

Slowly, he removed his fingers and Carson was able to breathe. She was too glad to be away from all the strange, alarming sounds and shadows in the parlor to attempt to argue with him. She lay board-still, waiting.

Kohl chided himself for not paying more attention to Carson's concern that someone could be lurking outside when he'd escorted her to the necessary. He had thought she was just being female. But after being awakened from a deep sleep by someone trying to jump him, Kohl was sorry he hadn't checked out the yard while they were outside.

He kept his gun aimed at the intruder's gullet as he managed to fumble with a match and light the lantern.

Carson watched the light bounce off the walls in queer patterns as he lifted the lantern high and swung it over her head.

"Carson! What the devil are you doing in bed with me?"

Chapter Eighteen

"Didn't anyone ever teach you it isn't polite to point?" Carson croaked in a small voice, her eyes trailing to the gun barrel still pointed in her direction. "You might put that gun away before it accidently goes off."

Kohl was still sitting back on his haunches, holding the lantern high above her head. She was the last person he would've suspected to find lying in his bed. He stuffed the gun back in its holster. "And didn't anyone ever teach you that young ladies do not jump into bed with members of the opposite sex?" he retorted. "For heaven's sake, Carson, I might have killed you."

He stared down at her. Secretly the thoughts of how alluring she looked huddled in his bed crept into his mind. Her shiny red hair made a compelling contrast to the stark white sheets. Her blue eyes were the color of Lake Tahoe and nearly as big and inviting, the way she looked back at him. The peaks and valleys of her figure were hinted at through the sheet and Kohl had to fight to control his urges.

"I'm sorry. I guess I didn't think about you being a gunslinger," she said, forcing his thoughts to safer ground.

He shook his head and ran his fingers through his hair. "Sometimes I don't think you have enough sense to pour piss out of a boot."

Carson's first inclination was to whip out of his bed and march back into the parlor. But consideration of what had brought her running to him in the first place kept her where she was.

"Well, I had enough sense, as you put it, to come to you when I heard noises outside the window."

"You might have tried rousing me instead of jumping into my bed." He anticipated another round of excuses. When she made no reply, he added. "I'll have a look."

Carson waited, the sheet drawn up between her throat and chin while Kohl got up, grabbed his gun and went into the parlor. She was shocked to see that he was not wearing a thread of clothing. But the sight of a naked man did not repel her as the other girls at the convent had said it was supposed to. Instead, she found that she was fascinated by the male form.

His buttocks were slightly bronzed and she wondered how they had gotten that way. His thighs rippled with muscles beneath a light sprinkling of hairs. His back was wide, tapering into a slender waist. She had to admit she enjoyed the glimpse of him. But she was not at all prepared for his return.

"There's nothing outside the window," he announced, striding boldly back into the room. "Car-

180

son, didn't you ever learn not to stare?" he said with a chuckle from the side of the bed.

Carson's vision snapped from the maleness of him up to his face. He was grinning at her, but she was too intrigued by *that* part of him to make a retort. Without thinking about what his reaction might be, her eyes slid down to *that* part of him again as he returned his gun to its holster and climbed back on the bed.

"Do you find me interesting?" he asked, settling onto his side facing her.

She blinked. "What? Oh, Oh! I'm sorry. I-I mean. I-I didn't mean to stare," she flustered out. He was grinning at her and made no attempt to cover himself. "Don't you think you should put some clothes on?" she finally managed.

"I always sleep this way. And need I remind you that you barged into my bedroom?"

Belatedly realizing that she was not suppose to look at any man except the one she married, Carson flipped onto her side, facing away from him. She stared blankly at the wall, but visions of him appeared before her eyes.

Kohl had expected her to run out of the room, but she made no effort to get off the bed. "Carson, don't you think you should return to the parlor? Or would you prefer I sleep out there?"

She ventured a peek back at him, keeping her eyes averted from his lower half. "Would you mind terribly if I slept in here with you tonight?"

If there had been the slightest breeze in the room Kohl would have been blown off the bed, he was so surprised by her request. Of course, being convent reared she was ignorant to what occurred between a man and a woman and did not realize what such a suggestion conjured up in his mind.

"Carson, do you know what you are asking of me?" he said, starting to sweat.

"Yes, of course I do. I want to stay here until morning. I wouldn't ask, but I . . . I am afraid," she blurted out. "Please. I won't take up much room."

You won't need much room for what is going through my mind, Kohl thought as he climbed beneath the covers and lay on the bed with his arms behind his head. He stared up at the ceiling and wondered if he was going to continue to stare at the ceiling long after the light had been extinguished if she remained this close to him and he didn't touch her. Then the thought popped into his mind: Could he keep his hands off her if he did let her stay?

His contemplations intensified when she proceeded to do the unexpected again. She snuggled up against him and laid her head on his chest with her small hand resting next to her head.

"Thank you, Kohl. I was so frightened. But I feel perfectly safe now." She could feel his heart speed up its beats, and his chest rose and fell more rapidly beneath her hand, and she wondered at her own heart's racing.

"I'm glad you feel safe," he managed in a hoarse whisper. *I wonder how safe you would feel if you knew what I was thinking?*

"Kohl?"

"Yeah?" he answered in a strangled voice.

182

"Aren't you going to turn out the lantern?"

"If you'll move off me."

Carson drew back and watched the ripple of muscle across his back as he leaned over and choked out the light. Then she settled back in the crook of his arm despite the heat which suddenly had begun to radiate from her when he dropped his hand on her shoulder.

"Kohl?"

"Hmm?"

"Are you as hot as I am?"

"Hotter," came the gruff reply. If she only knew how hot!

"Isn't that strange since it doesn't seem to be particularly warm in here?"

"Not so strange," he grunted, amazed at her apparent total lack of knowledge concerning men and women.

"Kohl?"

"Hmm?"

"Would you teach me how to kiss? I mean because you seem to be so good at it."

I'd like to teach you more than that, with you against me, not separated by your thin nightgown. Instead, he snorted, "Carson—"

"Please, Kohl," she urged in a shaky voice.

If he managed to get through this night with only teaching her how to kiss, it would be a miracle, he thought in exasperation. Hell, with a woman so close to him in the past, he had not wasted a whole lot of time on kissing. He had always been more concerned with sating his own lust.

She placed an open palm along the length of his cheek. Her palm was as soft as a child's. Her fingertips brushed the contours of his lips and he gently took her hands in his and kissed her fingertips, longing to kiss much much more of her.

"Is that how you're supposed to begin teaching me?" she asked in that innocent voice that made him want to pull her beneath him and toss her out at the same time.

"Yes, that is how it often begins," he said, thinking of something entirely different than kissing.

Carson drew his fingers to her lips and fastened her mouth along his rough index finger. She felt his body quiver next to hers and she wondered if he were no longer hot. She suddenly wished the lantern still burned so she could see his face.

"You don't feel cold," she said, returning her palm to his chest; it was burning.

He did not deem to answer. Instead he removed her hand, rested his head on an elbow before leaning over and outlining her lips with his thumb. "You talk too much," he whispered thickly and touched her lips with his.

Waves of such sweet sensitivity flowed over Carson and she pressed herself closer against him. Her gown had ridden up high on her thigh and she felt his leg against hers. Her foot rode up and down his calf, mesmerizing her with the feel of him. Her arms naturally wound themselves around his neck, and she moaned at the deliriously powerful sensations squeezing inside her breast.

Kohl had not meant to deepen the kiss, but he was

losing control. His tongue entered her mouth and he tasted her eagerness. She was driving him beyond sense with her toes caressing his leg, her arms holding him to her. In response, his hands cradled her face before his fingers wound themselves in her silken hair and he kissed her with a gentle command.

Catching himself before his control had totally lapsed, Kohl drew back.

"Why did you stop?" she whispered in a hoarse voice, panting. "I didn't want you to."

"You don't know what you're saying," he grumbled and lay back against the pillow. His chest was rising and falling at an alarming rate and he was glad she could not see the effect she'd had on him.

"Would it surprise you if I said I know exactly what I am saying, and that I would very much like to have you kiss me again?"

"Not any more than the surprise you'd be in for if I did kiss you again."

"Then surprise me," she whispered.

She puckered her lips and closed her eyes. Nothing. She continued to wait. Still nothing. Growing impatient, her eyes flew open and she sat up to look at him. The moon had risen and dim golden light now illuminated his face. He was staring straight ahead, a solemn cast to his mouth.

"Kohl Baron, are you going to kiss me or not?"

"Don't let it be said that I didn't warn you," he growled and pulled her down on top of him.

This time his kiss bore little resemblance to the gentle way that he had cradled her face and pressed his lips to hers. His kiss held the urgency of long

185

pent-up desires, the savagery of lust. He grasped her to him, his tongue parrying with hers while his hands began roaming over her back, gathering her nightdress up until he made contact with the heated naked flesh of her nicely rounded buttocks.

Suddenly stunned, Carson pulled back, and Kohl could see the confusion mirrored in the blue depths as she stared down at him.

"I warned you that you might be in for a surprise."

Her hand shot out and before he could ward off an expected blow, she curled her fingers in the inky wave draped over his forehead. Her touch was tentative, causing him to push her over onto the mattress. "Dammit, Carson, I'm only human. What are you trying to do to me?"

"I'm not sure," she said in a cracking voice. "I only know what you do to me. Kissing you makes me feel . . . it makes me feel different than I ever have before."

"Chrissake, didn't your precious Sinclair ever kiss you?" he demanded in a rougher voice than intended.

"Not like you do. Kohl, when you kiss me I get butterflies in my stomach and my cheeks get hot, and I quiver inside. Like I felt you quiver when I touched your hand with my lips earlier. At first I thought you were cold, but you didn't feel cold. And I wasn't cold when I quivered either. What does it mean, Kohl?"

She was being so truthful and open with her feelings that Kohl wasn't quite sure how to react to her confession or such a question. But he did know that he wanted her more than he'd ever wanted a woman before in his entire life. Hell, he couldn't take her now when she lay next to him so trusting, so innocent, so virginal.

"It means nothing. It was just a reaction to kissing, that's all," he snapped. "Now go to sleep!" He rolled over and glared at the wall, wondering how he was going to get through the rest of the night with her so close to him.

She laid a hand on his shoulder. "But I don't want to go to sleep." Despite his grunt, she proceeded. "I want to understand. If nothing happens when I kiss Sinclair, does it mean that nothing is going to happen after I marry him? And if I get this strange quivering feeling in the pit of my stomach and it spreads through the rest of me every time I kiss you, what does it mean?"

"Probably's just indigestion from my cooking tonight," he grumbled.

"I don't think so. It was a most pleasant sensation, not upsetting."

She was driving him toward insanity with her reasoning. He swung back to face her. "Chrissake, didn't they teach you anything at that convent?"

She frowned into the darkness. "I told you I spent most of the time on my knees atoning for my misadventures."

"Well they should have spent some time teaching you about the birds and bees."

"I know all about nature's wildlife. What I want to know is about us!"

"Carson, there is no *us*. Now, will you go to sleep

187

before you force me out on the couch."

"If you go out on the couch, I'll just join you there," she said stubbornly. "Furthermore, what do the birds and bees have to do with anything?"

"Didn't you ever discuss anything about men and women with the other girls at the convent?"

"They used to giggle that holding hands made you get in a motherly way. I knew that isn't true. You have to be married first. And you didn't answer my question."

"What question?" He was getting truly frustrated and had the distinct feeling he was going to be sorry he'd asked.

"What do the birds and bees have to do with anything?"

"Nothing," he barked out. He'd never had to explain life to a female before. Of course he'd never been mixed up with some female who had been raised in the sterile atmosphere of a convent, totally isolated behind vine-covered convent walls before either.

"Then why did you bring them up?"

He rubbed his hand along his face. "Oh, for heaven's sake. Birds and bees is just another way of explaining how things are between a man and a woman. Now, does that satisfy that inquisitive mind of yours?"

"You mean mating?" she inquired without shame.

"I guess that is one way to put it. Yes. I mean mating."

"Why didn't you just say so. That is only something that occurs between a husband and wife."

"I've got news for you, darlin'," he said, exasperated with their conversation. "Those feelings you just had is what leads up to *mating* whether you're married or not." That should shut her up.

To his disbelief, she forged ahead. "Then you mean that if we hadn't stopped, we would have ended up mating?"

"Sweetheart, that is exactly what I meant."

"Oh."

Carson lay back on her side of the bed and said no more. But she did not sleep. There was too much on her mind. And mating with Kohl Baron was at the forefront.

Chapter Nineteen

As the moon traced a golden path against the black, star-studded sky, neither Carson nor Kohl slept. Both spent a sleepless night staring at the shadowed ceiling from each edge of the bed. By the time the first fingers of light crept into the room Carson was full of unanswered questions about men and women she did not know how to ask, but was determined to find out if she had to confer with Lily.

She peeked over in Kohl's direction. He appeared to be sound asleep. So she padded from the bed to the kitchen and put water on to boil. A knock at the door startled her. After last night she was afraid to answer it, but Kohl was up, into his trousers, a gun in his hand, before she had made a decision whether to go to the door or not.

He looked incredible with the hint of a beard shadowing his face, his tousled hair and naked chest. And his bare feet gave him a certain boyish charm.

"Miss Mueller?" a female voice inquired from the other side of the door just as Kohl reached it. The knock came again. "Miss Mueller?"

Carson rushed over to Kohl and grabbed his arm. "Please. Whoever it is, she can't see us here together," she implored in a whisper.

"Why not?"

"Don't be foolish, what would people think?"

He grinned down at her wide-eyed pleading and couldn't help himself. "That we have been mating?"

She gave him her most disapproving frown. "Kohl! Please!"

"Oh, all right," he relented. "I'll wait in the bedroom. But don't take too long to get rid of whoever it is, because I've got work to do in the brewery. And I have no intention of climbing out the window."

"Miss Mueller, are you home?" the scratchy voice asked again.

"Yes. I'll be right there," she called out and waited for Kohl to disappear before she opened the door.

Carson came up short. Before her stood the middle-aged woman to whom Carson had introduced herself during the fight out in front of the saloon.

The woman looked down her nose. "Miss Mueller?"

"Yes."

"I am Mrs. Beatrice Heimerman." She waited for the girl to be properly impressed. Although barely visible, she noticed the faint purple streak beneath the girl's eye and realized that the girl was the one from the fight. The gunslinger's lady from the articles in her husband's newspaper. She put a hand to her chest and fought to maintain the proper composure required of a lady. "You are going to invite me in, aren't you, my dear?"

191

"Oh, yes. Yes, of course," Carson stammered and stepped back, suddenly embarrassed by her cotton nightdress and bare feet. "Please, won't you be seated?"

Beatrice looked about the shoddy little hovel. She was appalled and tempted to leave without doing her duty. But she was a proper wife and her husband had specifically demanded that she present this girl to society at the request of her husband's new boss and owner of the newspaper. Despite her better judgment, she realized where her position in the community hailed from and she gingerly took a seat on a torn chair.

Carson smoothed her wild locks back. "I hope you will forgive the state of the apartment. You see, someone broke in last night."

Beatrice's hand flew to her throat. "Well, of course I understand. Perhaps some of the ladies would be willing to assist you to make it presentable."

"No!" she blurted, glancing at the door to the bedroom. Then she said more calmly, "I mean . . . I can manage."

"Very well. But I do hope you intend to report such an occurrence." Beatrice straightened her back. Her back always bothered her when she was forced to deal with such types. She rummaged through her reticule and pulled out an envelope.

"At any rate, the reason I am calling is to present you with this." She offered the pink stationery to Carson. "The ladies of the State Orphan Asylum Auxiliary are giving a tea for the town's businessmen in an effort to raise needed funds, and we would be honored if you would join us. And, if you would consent, we could use your help with the preparations."

Carson's heart beat faster and she touched her fingers to her eye. In spite of her misadventure she was being given another chance to become a member of society.

"I would be delighted." She was so excited, all concerns over the break-in and the woman's sudden appearance slipped from her mind.

A crash echoed from the bedroom.

Beatrice's attention snapped in that direction. "I hope I didn't come at a bad time," she said with a sly tilt to her lips.

Carson fidgeted. "No, not at all."

"But you do not seem to be alone." Beatrice rose and started for the door. "I do hope whoever untidied your apartment has not returned."

"Oh . . . no. Someone is staying with me," Carson blurted out without thinking.

"Perhaps whomever is staying with you has been hurt. We truly should check."

Carson flew past the nosy woman and blocked the door. "It is only the young girl I met on the stage on the way from San Francisco. She lost her family and I offered to care for her," Carson explain feebly.

Beatrice's brow lifted in distrust. "I see. Then perhaps we should check that *she* is all right."

"I'm sure Addie is fine. She is just at that clumsy age. You know how young girls can be."

"Addie?" Beatrice questioned, unconvinced.

"Yes. The homeless girl."

Beatrice was sure the young woman did not have a girl behind that door, the way she was so nervously standing with her arm across it. An idea came to Beatrice. "Since the girl is an orphan, why don't you bring her along to the tea?"

Addie's sheer independence and secretiveness, not to think about her lack of manners, flashed before Carson's eyes. "I'm not certain a tea for orphans would be the proper place for Addie."

Beatrice waved off such a notion. "Nonsense. The tea will be held in the rose garden of the Carson Theatre." She smiled benignly. "Of course, the invitation has all the information."

"Of course." Carson smiled weakly.

Beatrice started for the exit, then had another thought. "Your name, my dear. Isn't it an interesting coincidence that you should be named after our fair town."

"It isn't a coincidence at all. My parents christened me and my father's brewery in honor of the town." Carson escorted the woman to the door, relieved that she had stopped her from barging into the bedroom and seeing Kohl.

"Then your parents own the brewery?"

"They were killed during the Indian uprising at Pyramid Lake. I am half owner of the brewery."

Beatrice stopped at the door and looked down her nose at the young woman. "It is always unfortunate when one loses loved ones." She cleared her throat.

"While I have no doubt that you think you are engaged in an honest endeavor and your intentions are purely honorable, of course, I must tell you that there are many of us in this town who disapprove of drinking spirits. Well, good day to you, Miss Mueller."

"Good day, Mrs. Heimerman."

Carson stood in the doorway and watched the hefty woman move her bulk down the stairs.

"The snob," Kohl said and joined Carson at the door.

She quickly pushed him back and shut it for fear that Mrs. Heimerman would glance up and see that her "orphaned girl" was none other than Kohl Baron, notorious gunslinger. "Kohl, you promised to stay out of sight!"

"I did, didn't I?"

Carson glanced down before returning her gaze to his face. He had shaved and her fingers itched to feel his smooth chin. She held her hands, hoping the urge would wane. "I suppose you did. But did you have to make noise?"

"What did you expect me to do? Sit on the bed and hold me breath?"

"No. But you could have been more careful. I was forced to tell her that Addie was in the bedroom and now she expects me to bring Addie with me to the tea the ladies are giving."

"So she came to invite you to a tea?" he said, his face impassive.

Carson broke into a wide smile. "She invited me to join the ladies who are putting it on."

"I can see you're pleased."

She clasped her hands together. "Oh, yes. I am finally going to be the lady Sinclair and his mother expect to find when they arrive."

She went into the kitchen, completely missing Kohl's frown at her mention of Sinclair.

For the next three days Carson and Kohl worked side by side putting the brewery back in running order. Carson tried to ignore circling thoughts about what Mrs. Heimerman had said about the evil of spirits. But she was turning the brewery over to Kohl, she rationalized, and finally managed to force such contemplations out of her mind.

Each time Carson tried to lift one of the heavy sacks, Kohl was right there to take it from her. When she accidently dropped the copper yeast measurer on her foot, Kohl made her sit down, removed her shoe, and massaged her toes. He helped her in countless ways while he carried more than his share and went for fresh supplies.

By the time they were ready to light the fire under the malt, Carson had a totally different picture of Kohl Baron, and her thoughts were beginning to trouble her more and more. He had proved to be kind and considerate.

"Everything seems to be back to working order," he announced as the fire flared and the malt began to bubble. "Aren't you suppose to meet those society women this afternoon?"

"Yes. But if I am needed here I'll—"

Kohl turned her around and gently gave her a shove toward the door. "You're not needed. Go help out with preparations for the tea."

Help out was exactly what Carson did. It seemed that she was given every unpleasant task while the half dozen *ladies* sat in the shade, directing her efforts and fanning themselves. Carson held her tongue, but she began to question the importance of belonging to such a group.

"Put that chair over there . . . by the speaker's podium," Beatrice directed as she joined Carson. "My, but you appear to be rather done in. Why don't you forego the final preparations and run along and relax this evening so you will be bright and fresh for the tea tomorrow?"

Carson glanced at the assortment of fine-dressed ladies who had not lifted a finger. Of course, she was "done in." She had done all the work! She forced back a disparaging comment. "I think I shall."

"Good. We shall see you tomorrow."

Once the Mueller girl had left, Beatrice strolled over to the other women. "Well, I think that we shall have use for Carson Mueller after all."

"We wouldn't have to be subjected to that 'gunslinger's lady' at all if your husband hadn't insisted you include her," snipped Agnes Maplewitz, patting her brow with a delicate hankie. "I don't know why you refuse to tell us all about it."

The others nodded, and Beatrice could no longer hold her tongue. It was too juicy a tidbit. She took a chair and leaned forward. "Well, if you all promise not to breathe a word of this to anyone outside this circle, I'll explain."

All heads bobbed agreement. "Karl sold the *Tribune* to that gunslinger. That is why those delicious articles stopped. Anyway, the new owner demanded that Karl have me introduce the Mueller girl into society . . ."

The women listened attentively, relishing this latest bit of gossip. "So, you mean that part of the agreement to sell the paper was for your husband to force you to accept that young woman?" Agnes asked, appalled. "No one is going to accept her under such circumstances," Agnes announced to nodding heads.

"I never agreed to accept her," Beatrice divulged. "Just to introduce her. You have to admit she has her uses."

"Yes, but—"

"But we'll allow her to perform all the menial functions, and after Karl has the gunslinger's money, we'll publicly expose her."

"How deliciously naughty of you," Margaret Henderson said, toying with her blond chignon. "It would be the proper comeuppance for her; to think that she can force her way into a prominent social position. I like it. Tell us, Beatrice, how do you plan to unmask her . . . ?"

Carson stopped by Horse's place to plead with Addie to relent and attend the tea with her. The girl had held out until she'd gained two concessions for her agreement to go: She no longer was to be expected to remain with Horse at all hours, she could again come and go at her own discretion, and she no longer would be forced to sweep the brewery.

By the time Carson trudged up the stairs to the

apartment, she felt as if she had been dragged behind a spooked horse. The weather had turned quite warm and her face was streaked with perspiration.

"What have you been doing?" Kohl asked, greeting her from his position of lounging with his feet up on the couch. "Looks like becoming a lady is harder work than cleaning the brewery."

"It is." Carson plunked down on the chair next to the couch and dropped her arms between her legs with a sigh.

"Still determined to become a lady?" he inquired. He went to her and standing behind the chair, massaged her aching neck muscles.

Carson leaned her head from side to side, then back to look up at him. "I am going to be a lady if it kills me."

"From the looks of you, it just very well might."

He smoothed back an errant strand of hair from her forehead. "Why don't you lie down on the couch till supper time?"

She got to her feet, massaging her back. "I think I'll skip supper and take a nap. Wake me in time to attend the tea, will you?"

"Sure. Come on." He took her hand and against his better judgment led her to the bed. "You can have the bed tonight. I'll sleep on the couch."

He got her settled and turned to leave when she hailed him back. "Kohl?"

"Hmm?"

"Have you ever given thought to becoming one of the town's upstanding citizens, marrying and settling down?"

He stared at her, wondering if she was hinting at something in particular but not about to ask. "Me? The notorious gunslinger, Kohl Baron? Never."

"Kohl, be serious."

"I am, darlin'. Belonging to a group the likes of which you are trying to impress holds no draw for me. Besides, I like my life just the way it is."

Filled with disappointment, she watched him walk from the room. She laid her head back on the pillow, and as she was drifting off to sleep images of them getting married forced their way into her mind.

Chapter Twenty

Once he had eaten a supper of beans and ham, Kohl settled down on the couch. It had been a frustrating day. After Carson had left the brewery, he had gone back to the saloons he'd visited before and questioned the patrons to no avail. He had pressed Lily, but she'd vowed her Seasons had questioned all her customers without luck. No one seemed to be able to offer a reason as to why or who had broken into the brewery and apartment and ransacked them.

He couldn't understand it. It just didn't make sense that no one seemed to know anything. He had even wired Gold Hill, but had learned that the trouble at the brewery there had not been related, since it had stemmed from a worker pouring too much yeast into the kegs.

Kohl was still pondering over who could want the brewery to fail when he heard Carson moaning out his name from the bedroom. He was drawn from the couch toward her. She lay on the bed, her face pale, her full sensuous lips ready to be kissed.

He perched on the edge of the bed and stroked her

cheek with the back of his hand. "You are so beautiful," he whispered.

Carson smiled in her sleep and he wondered if somehow she had heard him.

Against his better judgment, Kohl lay down and gathered her into his arms. She felt so small, so vulnerable and he kissed her forehead. And when she turned her face up to his, he could not help himself. Her nearness was overpowering.

He kissed her, gently, intending to return to the parlor. But she moaned again and reached up to clasp her arms around his neck.

He knew he should go. But in her sleep she held him to her, and she pressed her lips to his.

"Heaven help me, I am going to be damned for this," he murmured against her eager mouth.

His lips edged hers open, and his tongue danced into her mouth in an age-old rhythm as tender as a lover's caress.

Carson was having a dream which seemed so real that it made her feel weak and breathless. In her dream Kohl was making love to her. She responded to him with a willingness, releasing a pent-up longing that she'd had for some time now. She arched against him as their tongues met and continued to duel with such an intensity that her entire being screamed for release.

Kohl pulled back and stared down at her. Her eyelids fluttered and she smiled up at him. "I knew you'd come to me," she said in a throaty whisper.

He could not believe it. It was if he had awakened a sleeping beauty. "I want to make love to you, Carson," he murmured, stroking her hair.

"Mmmm," she moaned.

She desired him as he desired her. A burning need exploded within him. He had to fight his hunger and remember to go slow, to be gentle, to temper his own needs as he introduced her to womanhood. "I promise not to hurt you, my love."

Carson's dream was reaching new heights as her conjured hero used his experienced fiery fingers to cradle her face. Then he moved down her neck and over her shoulders before dropping to the fullness of her breasts. She arched her breasts against the heat of his hands, moaning at the forbidden pleasures only allowed in dreams.

These new delicious sensations were overpowering through the fog of sleep. Her thirst for him, repressed from the first time he'd kissed her was no longer going to be withheld. In the dark veils of slumber, all the imaginings, all the longings would be quenched. Nothing would be held back. She could offer herself freely and willingly.

She dreamed his hand was igniting a trail of fire as he dipped beneath her nightgown and his hand rode up her leg to nudge her thighs apart. She moaned when long, slender fingers dipped into her most secret of places. She pressed herself against his hand, riding him in the sheer ecstasy of sensual pleasure awash with sensations so new, so strong, that in her sleep she begged, "It feels so good. So good. Make love to me."

Kohl withdrew his hand and shed his clothes. He could hardly believe that the Carson who lay open before him, entreating him to make love to her was the same girl he had parried words with.

He dipped his finger into her again. She was wet and hot for him and her muscles flexed around him as she rocked against his hand, moaning, "Faster."

He withdrew his hand and as he was positioning himself over her, her arms locked around him and he guided himself into her woman's sheath. She flinched and he lay still, holding her to him. "It's all right, baby, the pain will pass. It'll pass," he rasped into her ear.

She reached up and touched his back, the downy hairs curling over her fingers. The dream was so intense, so vivid that it seemed real. Then a profound urge overtook her and she began to move. Nothing she had ever experienced could compare with the sensations building within her.

"Oh, Kohl, it's so real," she whimpered. "It's so real."

She knew she was dreaming when she heard his deep voice answer, "It is real, baby. It is."

The sensations were hammering at her and she began to thrust herself against him in earnest. The heat building and building. Mushrooming until her eyes flew open and she gasped.

"It is real!"

Urges she hadn't known she possessed were in control, wiping out any consideration of protest. Her body ruled her mind. Heedless of the consequences, she reveled in sensation, holding him tighter, wrapping her legs around him and meeting his pounding thrusts with her own.

"Oh God, Carson," he groaned at the friction. "You're driving me wild."

Wild they both had become. Two human animals,

driven by passions so strong, so fierce that instinct ruled reason, urging them onward toward that ultimate pinnacle, that highest crest until Carson cried out and crushed herself to him in sheer raw ecstasy. Then Kohl, panting, groaned, his maleness throbbing as he poured himself into her.

"That was truly wonderful," she whispered as she tried to catch her breath.

"For me, too." He smoothed her drenched curls off her face.

"I've never experienced anything like it."

He kissed her neck. "Nor I. Open your eyes and look at me, Carson. I want you to look at me. I want you to see what you've done to me."

He lay atop her as she slowly fluttered open her eyes to gaze into incredible topaz blue eyes which gazed back at her. Only warmth and concern mirrored in the deep blue depths as she slowly drifted back to the cold hard reality of what they'd done.

She pushed at his shoulders. "Oh, Kohl, what have we done?"

He rolled off her and tried to pull her into his embrace, but she would have none of it. "What's gotten into you all of a sudden? One minute you are more loving and more incredible than I ever believed a woman could be. Then the next you push me away."

"You took advantage of me!" she cried, trying to cover her nakedness.

"I took advantage of you?" he said with such deliberation that if she hadn't known better, she would have sworn a stranger was in bed with her.

She stiffened her spine. "That's what I said."

"Well, I've got news for you, darlin'," he said in a

lazy drawl meant to irritate her. "You invited me into your bed."

"I invited you!"

"Darlin', you not only invited me, you practically attacked me when I came in to see what you needed after you called out my name."

Vague recollections of what she'd thought had been a dream materialized before her, and she blinked several times in an attempt to vanish them. Again she had acted on her impulses. Only this time she had been so sure those impulses were nothing more than an incredible dream. She dropped her head in her hands. Hurt by his insouciant treatment of what they'd just shared, she looked up. "Now what am I going to do when Sinclair finds out?"

Sinclair! It was like a knife in his gut that she was concerned what some man who had sent her away would think. His lips tightened before he was able to mask his feelings. A devil-may-care lift to his brow, he grabbed his shirt off the floor and began buttoning it.

"He need never find out unless you tell him, darlin'."

"But he'll find out on our wedding night."

"You still can't be seriously considering marrying the man."

"I am serious." *I think.*

"So you do plan to go through with marrying him."

Carson watched Kohl study his own reflection in the bureau mirror as he pulled her brush through his hair. His nonchalance got her dander up. She lifted her chin. "Of course I still plan to marry Sinclair."

206

She peeked at him from beneath her lashes. "Why do you ask?"

"Just protectin' my investment, is all."

Her heart sank. "Your investment?"

"The brewery is all mine once this Sinclair fellow claims his intended, remember?"

"You needn't concern yourself with that. If you'll recall, I agreed that the brewery is all yours whether I marry Sinclair or not. Now, if you would leave and close the door behind you, I must get my rest for the tea tomorrow."

Once she was alone in the room, Carson lay back against the pillow. Maybe if she were a true lady, she would be upset over losing her virginity in such a way. But secretly she was not sorry she had been with Kohl. She was only regretful that it had ended with him out on the couch and her left alone.

She felt so mixed up, so confused. She wished her mother could be with her now, so she'd have someone to talk to. She considered going to Lily. But that seemed out of the question now. Lily could not be objective; she was Kohl's friend. So, of course, she would be on his side.

An idea flashed into her head.

"Kohl?" she called out before she could stop herself.

No answer.

He was being obstinate. She padded to the door and squeaking it open a sliver, peeked out. In the moonlight she could see Kohl lying on the couch, an arm over his eyes.

"Kohl?"

He raised himself up on his elbow. "What do you

want, Carson?" he asked harshly.

"Are you sorry that you and I made love?"

"Darlin', I've never been sorry makin' love to a woman in my life."

"Oh." It was not the answer she had hoped for. "Kohl?"

"What now?"

"Have you made love to a lot of women?"

"More'n my share, I reckon," he answered and laid back, staring up at the ceiling. Chrissake, he was becoming an expert at ceilings!

"Kohl?"

"Hmm?"

"Did you enjoy making love with me?"

He sat up. "You know what they say." She shook her head. "Well, they say that there are only two kinds of lovemakin', darlin', good and better. A man's rarely disappointed when he's gettin' it. The worse I ever had was wonderful." But even as he was attempting to discourage her questions, he felt lousy.

"Oh." She had hoped he would have said that he'd never made *love* with anyone before her, and their experience had been the best. Her lips sagged.

"Carson, why are you asking me all these questions?"

"I'm not sure."

"Until you are, why don't you go back to bed. We both need to get some sleep," he said in a gruff voice.

He watched her close the door and shook his head. Damn, what had he done? She had been so naive before he'd taken her, and he had ignored his better judgment when he'd seen her, so desirable, on the bed. His heart constricted. Why hadn't he told her that he felt drawn to her, and it had upset him to learn that she still intended to marry that rich dandy. Filled with self-recriminations, he laid back and punched the air, wishing it were his own face.

Carson's lower lip trembled and she leaned against the door, unable to go back to the bed where she had allowed Kohl Baron to add her to the list of his willing women. *The worst I've ever had was wonderful.* His words echoed in her mind, recounting how foolish she had been to hope that it somehow had been different for them.

She slid down the length of the door until she sat on the floor, her knees curled against her chest, her arms circling them. *The worst I've ever had was wonderful* screamed at her again, and she rested her forehead on her knees, shutting her eyes.

She had been a fool. A complete, utter fool. The world was full of fools and she had proved one of the worst. Swallowing back a sob, she swiped at the tears trying to form on her lower lids. She was not going to cry! She had overcome much in her life, and she was going to overcome this. She was going to put Kohl Baron completely out of her mind and get on with becoming a proper lady!

Chapter Twenty-one

Carson awoke as stiff as the brim on a pasteboard bonnet. She had fallen asleep on the floor last night. Suddenly memories of what she'd done flooded back and she crawled to her feet.

She caught sight of the sheets, stained with the evidence that it was true; she had mated with Kohl. And everything that had happened afterward, the words they'd exchanged, it had all been real.

In an effort to deny the jumble of feelings barraging her, she started to strip the sheets from the bed.

"Here you are." Lily peeked her head through the door. "I knocked but no one answered. Since the door wasn't locked I let myself in. Hope you don't mind none."

Carson grabbed the sheets to her and swung around. Kohl had left without a word. Her heart ached, but she forced a cheerful, "Good morning, Lily."

"Heard you're goin' to be attendin' some fancy tea for the town's orphans today. So I brung you a dress

I had my dressmaker whip up special while I was out shoppin' for my Seasons."

"You didn't have to do that," Carson said feebly and tucked the sheets in a corner.

"Nonsense." She opened a drawer and flung out a fresh sheet. "And I can help you pick up and put things away while you try on the dress."

Carson was apprehensive over Lily's taste in clothing, considering the manner in which she dressed, but the dress couldn't have been more perfect if Carson had selected it herself. It was of the palest peach muslin with a darker peach sash. Carson held it to her and swirled around.

"Oh, Lily, it is perfect."

The impulse to ask Lily about the urges she had felt last night with Kohl came to the forefront of her mind. She forced it back. Lily would undoubtedly tell her it was normal. After all, Lily was in the business of appeasing those male urges and would no doubt defend Kohl.

"You look to be deep in thought, honey. Want to talk about it?"

"There's nothing to talk about," Carson said too quickly. She held the dress out, trying to ignore Lily's look of skepticism. "Would you help me with it?"

Lily came forward. " 'Course, honey. Pity Kohl ain't here to see the finished product. By the time Lily is through with you, you will be the most talked about young lady at that there tea."

"Carson Mueller is going to be the most talked about one here," Agnes Maplewitz whispered behind her hand to the other three women with her. "Just look at her, trying to make a grand entrance as if she were indeed a lady."

"I saw that fallen woman Lily at the dressmaker's shop purchasing a dress exactly like the one she is wearing," snickered the skinny wife of the mayor. "You don't think she is keeping company with the likes of the owner of that dreadful place, do you?"

"I shall find out," Beatrice announced and her vision caught on the young girl trailing behind Carson Mueller.

"So there really is an Addie," Beatrice said absently and fanned herself as she took in the whole picture.

The sweeping lawns, dotted with high-reaching poplars and punctuated by a magnificent rose garden, bursting with an array of perfumed colors were filled with the town's most important and best dressed citizenry. Ladies mulled near the refreshment table attired in lush silks and satins with flowering hats strung with gaily-colored ribbons. The gentlemen clustered near the podium, wearing pinstriped jackets and crisp white shirts bedecked in the latest neckwear.

"Agnes, you go see to the children while I must do my duty and greet the interloper." Beatrice left Agnes and the others staring after her and swished her gray striped skirt toward the Mueller girl.

Carson watched the overstuffed woman bustle in her direction. She looked to be overheated in her high-necked dress. Quickly, Carson advised, "Addie, now remember how I told you to act."

Addie yanked on her skirt, clutching her precious

box in her other hand. She rolled her eyes. "How long do I got to stay here?"

"Not long. Now, hush. Here she comes." Carson felt her burst of confidence droop. Kohl had joined the woman and was coming over with her. What was he doing here? Had he also been invited?

"Carson, we are so glad you are here," Beatrice said down her nose. "And this must be Addie. Hello, child. There are many other orphans your age here today, if you'd like to join them."

"Well, I wouldn't like," Addie hissed and hung on to her box.

"Of course, if you'd rather not it is perfectly all right I suppose."

Addie huffed out a breath. "Good."

"That is a nice box. Is it a family treasure?" Beatrice asked in a display of mock concern of the wretched child. Beatrice reached out to touch it. Addie swung to the side, holding on to her box for dear life.

Addie's eyes narrowed into mere slits. "Don't try to come near my box again!"

"It must be most important to you," Beatrice remarked and held her hands in a protective gesture.

"The box is all Addie has left from her family," Carson supplied in an effort to excuse Addie's gross breach of proper decorum. "Addie, why don't you go get yourself some refreshments?"

"Do I have to?"

"Yes." Carson kept her expression sweet. "Run along now, dear." She watched Addie kick at small pebbles on her way toward the long, linen-covered table. "Addie has not had a mother's guidance."

"Yes, well . . ." Turning her attention from the ill-mannered child, Beatrice recalled the information she needed to obtain for the others. "That is a lovely dress," she commented, picking at the skirt. "Isabelle was just remarking how lovely you look. I wish I could purchase gowns off the rack, but of course, Karl insists that I have my gowns specially made for me."

"This was specially made for me," Carson returned innocently, unknowingly playing into Beatrice's hands.

"Forgive me, my dear. Of course it was." Finding out what she had come for, she dropped a hand on Kohl's arm. Beatrice had been instructed by her husband to be polite to the gunslinger. She knew her duty. "You know our dear Mr. Baron, I presume." Again came that superior manner.

Of course she knows that I know Kohl; she witnessed the brawl out in front of the saloon. Carson looked, wide-eyed up at Kohl. He was easily the most handsome man in attendance. He towered over most of the men, and his double-breasted sack coat fit him like a glove. Whereas, many of the other men in attendance bore paunches.

"Carson, I do believe you are staring," snickered Beatrice.

Carson crashed back to reality. "I beg your pardon?"

"You were staring at Mr. Baron, my dear."

"I suppose it was simply because I've never seen someone of Mr. Baron's profession thus attired," Carson said sweetly, secretly wishing she could escape.

Beatrice looked askance. Kohl knew exactly what Carson had meant. "Mrs. Heimerman, I have no doubt that ladies such as Miss Mueller would expect me to be dressed in black and draped with six-shooters."

"Well, of course, I am sure those days must be behind you now that you own the *Tribune*, Mr. Baron." Beatrice lifted her chin ever so slightly, watching the girl. She didn't know about the newspaper, Beatrice thought smugly. "Why I would have thought you would be one of the first to hear the good news."

Not taking her eyes off Kohl, Carson gave Kohl a sugary smile. "I haven't had any good news in some time."

"Mr. Baron purchased the *Tribune* a week ago."

"About the time the articles stopped," Carson murmured.

Beatrice ignored the girl's babblings. "He has already begun making changes, and no doubt we shall see even more in the future."

"Tigers rarely change their stripes," Carson bit out acidly.

"I am afraid I do not understand," Beatrice said, secretly enjoying the exchange.

"Miss Mueller merely meant that I am a real tiger when I go after something."

"Why yes, that is exactly what I meant. Mr. Baron is unmerciful when he pounces on unsuspecting prey, isn't that right, Mr. Baron?"

Kohl's amused grin faded. "Why, Miss Mueller, I never would have suspected that you would be aware of tigers pouncing on prey, since they often do their

215

hunting at night, long after ladies such as yourself are safely cosseted behind locked doors."

"I hate to interrupt such an enlightening discussion, but since I am chairwoman, I must mingle. So, I do hope you two will excuse me. And Carson, I do hope you will join the other ladies and I for our sewing circle. We meet at the church on King Street Wednesday afternoons." Beatrice lifted her nose high in the air and sauntered toward more desirable company, feeling quite satisfied that she had managed, quite skillfully no less, to pair the gunslinger with his lady. That should provide plenty of gossip to fuel the fire of her plan.

Kohl took Carson's arm. She tried to pull away, but he held fast. "Smile, darlin', you don't want all those old biddies to have something else to talk about at their sewing circles, do you?"

Carson pasted a smile on her face. "What are you doing here?" she demanded between her teeth.

"Would you believe I couldn't bear to miss your debut into society?"

They strolled toward the other guests, who were beginning to take seats in front of the podium.

"I would believe that you came here to ruin things for me."

Kohl gave a bitter laugh. "My, but you have a high opinion of me."

Carson looked up at Kohl. Batting her lashes, she said sweetly, "Mr. Baron, I have no opinion of you."

Kohl would have liked nothing better than to have swept her away from all the staring eyes to get a few things straight between them. But he could not ruin her first big public appearance. "Smile, darlin', you

216

don't want the other guests to think that there is trouble in paradise."

"Being around you has been anything but paradise," she snapped.

"You didn't seem to think so last night. As a matter of fact, I'd 've thought we were both in paradise, the way you acted."

"That was a mistake!"

"I wouldn't call the time we spent together a mistake, Carson," he said more seriously.

"What's the matter, is your male pride wounded to find out that not all ladies are so eager to fall in bed with you?"

"Oh, I don't know. I'd say you were downright *eager* last night."

"But I didn't think it was real at first, I thought that I was . . ." Her voice trailed off, too embarrassed to continue.

"What? Dreaming?" At the slight tightening of her lips, he added, "Don't tell me that I am the man of your dreams."

"I would never think to tell you such a thing! Nightmares would be a more appropriate term."

"Since you seem to have trouble keeping me out of your mind, what do you plan to do, sit up all night from now on?"

"If I have to!"

"Mind if I offer my humble self to keep you company?" he suggested. "I could provide a diversion . . . just in case you're tempted to fall asleep."

"I have already been subjected to your kind of diversions, thank you."

"Ah, your manners are to be complimented. You

are the first woman to thank me."

Carson hissed in a breath. He was trying to goad her into doing something rash. She was not going to make a scene today. "Then I would like to thank you a second time."

Kohl looked suspicious. "A second time?"

"Yes. I would thank you to leave me alone."

"But what kind of gentleman would I be if I left you standing by yourself?"

"The kind one would expect to find owning a newspaper," she hissed.

"Carson, I'm not running it. I bought it to protect you."

"Me?"

"You wanted the articles stopped. I merely obliged."

"So you stopped them by buying the newspaper. And since you seem to have enough money to purchase the periodical, then I can assume that you have enough money to make other living arrangements. Now, please, just leave me alone," she said acidly, keeping her face a benign study of proper deportment.

Their talk had gotten out of hand. He had not meant for it to degenerate into a sparring match. And as they neared the others, he did not have any more time to straighten things out now. Reluctantly, he released her arm, gave a curt bow, and joined a group of men taking their seats on the other end of the podium.

He watched her glide over to those stuffy society matrons and exchange pleasantries. He still couldn't understand why someone like Carson Mueller, so full of life and curiosity, so able to hold her own with him, should want to imprison herself in such a staid existence in which those old biddies lived.

Hell, she was the only woman he had ever known who was able to parry words with him and come out ahead. And instead of being annoyed by her sharp wit, he smiled to himself. Life with Carson had proved to be anything but boring up to this point, and no doubt it never would.

Carson turned her back to Kohl, but she knew her cheeks still flamed. And although she tried to focus on what the tall lady in the lavender-ruffled dress was saying, all she could think about was Kohl Baron.

He had purchased the *Tribune* and suddenly the articles had stopped. Beatrice Heimerman's husband had owned the newspaper. Suddenly, Carson was very wary of the lady's seeming acceptance of her.

Carson straightened her back in line with the others. She would work doubly hard so they would have no excuse not to accept her by the time Sinclair and his mother arrived. Although, deep within her heart, Sinclair's arrival no longer held such an all-consuming importance to her.

As if she didn't have enough to worry about, her eyes caught on Addie. The girl was bent over the refreshment table stuffing the silverware into her pockets!

Chapter Twenty-two

The sun was sinking behind the mountains by the time Carson returned home. She had remained long after the last guest had left to help clean up. Beatrice had been most gracious and understanding over Addie's attempted thievery, despite the girl's refusal to apologize and then running off. All in all, notwithstanding Kohl's upsetting presence, it had been a successful day.

She entered the brewery and gasped.

Kohl was sitting on the floor, rubbing his head. Not about to be fooled by a sympathy ploy, she advanced on him, hands on hips.

"What are you trying to do, gain my empathy after the way you acted at the tea?"

Kohl looked up at her, a disgusted look on his face. "Yeah. Sure. I came back here after the tea, had three men jump me, render me unconscious, then waited for you to return so you could take pity on me and forgive me."

She knelt down and touched the bump on his head, immediately contrite. "Who did this to you?"

"Well, at least you no longer believe I hit myself over the head."

"Don't be smart. What happened?"

"That's what I'd like to know. I returned to surprise two masked men in the brewery. But just as I got the drop on them, I was hit from behind."

Carson glanced around. A frayed rope dangled from over the door. Behind Kohl an anvil, with the other portion of the rope tied around it, lay on its side.

Carson leaped to her feet. "My goodness, it appears that someone was trying to kill you. An inch more and you would have been killed. Look!"—she held up the rope—"It has been deliberately cut."

Despite his dizziness, Kohl examined the rope. "Strange. I thought it was a third man. But it seems that the thing was set up to trounce whoever came through that door." He settled a troubled gaze on Carson. "They may have been after you."

"Me?" she cried, slapping a hand to her chest. "Why would anyone want to kill me?"

"For that matter, why would anyone want to kill me?" he put in.

"You must have made more than a few enemies while you were a gunslinger. And just last week you got into a fight with three men."

"Over you," he reminded her. "Carson, why are we arguing over this? It's more important that we find out who and why this is happening, so we can put a stop to it. And until this is over, you are not going anywhere without me."

Carson could not conceive that it could have anything to do with her. But she had to admit she felt secure when Kohl was around. Of course, she was not going to admit it to him!

"I lived that type of life for fifteen years in the convent, if you'll recall. And I am not going to continue having someone watch over my every move!"

"Then why are you going to marry this Sinclair person? Seems to me he's already dictating your life and you're not even married yet."

Carson opened her mouth to protest, but closed it. There was a morsel of truth to what he'd just said. Sinclair had dictated her every move for the next two and a half months. Was that what her life with him would be like after they married as well?

"You look troubled. Thinking about what I said?"

Brought back from her uneasy musings, she snapped, "Certainly not! Sinclair is one of San Francisco's most eligible men, and he has chosen me out of all the beautiful girls he could have had. He will make a fine husband. Everyone at the convent thinks so."

"And is that what you think, too?"

She hesitated, dropping her eyes before she returned her gaze to him and said, "Of course!"

With a snort of disbelief he took her by the elbow and escorted her from the brewery. "What do you think you're doing!" she yelped at his overbearing methods.

"Since you are intent on marrying that man, you might as well get used to someone ruling your life. And starting right now that someone is me."

Outside, Carson stomped over to the stairs, Kohl on her heels. The men hidden in the bushes crouched low, watching through the leaves so as not to be detected. "You think he saw us?" the larger of the two said in a heavily whiskey-scented whisper once the skirt and pant legs were out of sight.

"Naw, he don't got eyes for nobody but that girl." The other one scratched his stubbly beard.

"Let's get back to the boss and report what happened."

"Report what? That we was surprised by that gunslinger and the only reason we got away was 'cause he got knocked out when somethin' fell on him? The boss ain't gonna like that we didn't find it."

"But hell, we already tore the place apart twice lookin' for it. It could be anywhere."

"The boss said it's got to be either 'n the brewery or in their digs on the second floor."

"What if the girl's got it on her? Ya know that gunslinger ain't got it since we already searched him while he was out cold. Maybe we oughtta grab her and have us a look-see. I wouldn't mind none at all searching the likes of her."

The other man's face split into a yellow-toothed grin. "Now you're thinkin', Slick. I ain't had me a good poke since nigh on six weeks and my pecker's itchin' to get outta my pants."

Saul nodded in agreement and scratched his crotch. "Mine, too."

"We'll stay put and wait our chance at her."

Settling back to wait for the gunslinger to leave the little gal alone, Slick and Saul kept their attention peeled on the second story light, which had just lent the tiny apartment a warm yellow glow.

Carson had calmed once she sighted the job Lily had done straightening up the apartment. The dear woman had stayed after she'd left for the tea just to help out in spite of her own responsibilities.

Carson pivoted to stare at Kohl. "Am I to assume that despite your money, you intend to remain here?"

"I thought I already made it clear to you; I'm not going anywhere."

"Well, you can cook supper then; I'm famished."

"Didn't you enjoy any of the refreshments at the tea? They were actually quite palatable," he announced, walking into the kitchen.

Carson followed him and took up a position at the table while he rustled around the cupboards and stove. "I spent most of the time trailing after Addie and returning the items she attempted to steal." Carson gave a mirthless laugh. "She stuffed her pockets with biscuits and meat, not to mention the auxiliary's silver."

"She's a real puzzle," he commented, dropping eggs into the spitting grease.

"Yes," Carson mused. "It is almost as if she is hiding some deep, dark secret she doesn't want anyone to know."

Kohl put the pan on the table and cut thick slices of bread before joining her. "Guess when she's ready she'll spill her gut. How is Horse getting along?" he asked, ripping apart a chunk of bread and slathering it with butter.

Carson finished chewing a bit of egg and swallowed. "He's feeling pretty feisty. Says he's coming back to work tomorrow."

"Good. It's time we got the brewery back in working order . . ."

Carson ate as she listened to Kohl relate all the

plans he had for building the brewery business. She could not help but get caught up in his enthusiasm. Despite their earlier disagreement, Carson discovered she was excited and wanted to be actively involved in the business.

She reached out and laid a hand on Kohl's. "Oh, Kohl, it sounds so exciting. When do we begin?"

"First thing in the morning." Kohl delved into her eyes. Excitement gleamed in the blue depths. The heat from her hand on his shot through him, and he ran his thumb along her palm. It was a rare woman who was interested in the daily operation of such a business. Carson was just such a woman.

Carson withdrew her hand at the sensations rippling through her. He was making her feel special again. That contemplation was dangerous to her already weakening resolve.

She left the table.

"Where are you going?"

She pivoted around. "To the necessary, if you must know." She needed some time alone. She couldn't think straight when he was near her, let alone when he touched her.

"Wait and I'll accompany you."

"Kohl, I know you mean well. But I think I can manage this by myself."

He watched her grab the lantern on the parlor table. "Don't be long, or I'm coming after you." She gave him a tart smile in return.

Outside, in the fresh night air, Carson inhaled the fragrance of late spring blossoms. Crickets squeaked and stars overhead winked. And Carson could not help herself. Nevada had surrounded her heart with its stark beauty, and she couldn't help but feel at home.

She saw to her body's needs and was strolling back toward the stairs, swinging the lantern, humming to herself. All of a sudden a hand shot out from the bushes and grabbed her. She opened her mouth to scream, but her breath was cut off by another hand over her mouth, and she was hefted off her feet. The lantern fell from her hand as she struggled.

"That's it, girlie, fight against me. Your wigglin' is just makin' my pecker sit up and take notice," Saul snickered.

Carson immediately stilled. Her eyes widened as another huge man stepped from the bushes. "See you got her. Quick. Pull her in here," Slick instructed.

Carson was roughly hauled into the bushes and slammed to the ground, tied and gagged before she could react.

"Now, ain't that a far sight better, girlie? Now you ain't gotta think about tryin' to kick old Saul." He struck a match. "Let's get us a look-see at what we got us here."

A meaty hand stroked her hair back off her face, ran down her cheek, and began fumbling with the buttons down the front of her dress.

"Quit wastin' time and search her first," Slick demanded from his position as lookout. "You can have your fun after we find out if she's got it on her or not."

"Aw, but look at her titties. They's goin' up and down underneath that there underdress in a mighty invitin' way." Saul put his hands on her chest and

226

Carson flipped her head to the side and looked away. She tried to think about anything other than the man's groping hands. "She ain't got it on the top of her."

"I'll check the bottom half," Slick announced.

"I grabbed her so I should get to have the first feel," Saul complained bitterly. " 'Sides, I'm always the one who gets your leftovers."

"Oh, all right. But get to it; we ain't got all night before that gunslinger comes lookin' for the little girlie."

Carson squeezed her eyes shut and silently screamed for Kohl. She struggled when she felt her skirt riding up her legs and the man's hand on the inside of her thigh.

"Come here and hold her down. She ain't cooperatin'," Saul sneered.

Slick left his position and clamped two hurting hands on Carson's ankles. She continued to struggle as she felt rough fingers make a quick search, then grab her around the flesh of her waist. "Gosh, she's got such a tiny little middle I can get my hands all the way around it." He sent a lewd glance over his shoulder at his partner. "Bet she ain't never had a man inside her before neither." His grinning gaze shifted back to her. "That right, girlie?"

She held her breath and kept her eyes clamped shut, refusing to answer. Her heart was riveting as her drawers were slowly being slipped down over her hip bones.

Suddenly, the torment stopped. There was a rustle of bushes. Then silence.

She waited. Nothing. She squinted open one eye.

She saw no one. Opening the other eye, she looked around. They were gone!

It was then she heard Kohl's voice calling her. "Carson! Carson!" She thrashed about in an attempt to give away her position as the light came closer.

Kohl picked up the fallen lantern and raised it high. Carson's shoe was sticking out from the shrubbery. Filled with dread, he split the branches.

Carson lay on the ground, bound, her dress pushed up past her waist, the top of her dress front unbuttoned. He dropped to his knees and ripped the gag from her mouth.

"My God, babe, are you all right?"

She gasped for breath. "Do I appear to be all right?"

Untying her hands and feet, he demanded, "Who did this to you?"

"Two men," she cried, trembling. "Oh, Kohl," — she vaulted into his arms — "at first they were looking for something. When they didn't find it, they . . . they . . . tried —" She couldn't force the word *rape* from her tongue. It was too ugly a word.

Kohl cupped the back of her head and held her to him until she calmed, crooning, "It's all right. You don't have to worry. I'm here for you." Then he adjusted her skirt down. He helped her to her feet, and while she stood before him, he rebuttoned her dress front.

Carson's breathing sped up as his fingers lightly brushed the inside of her breasts. Despite her fright, the electrifying sensations struck like lightning and buckled her legs.

Kohl lifted her up into his arms. "Their gone,

honey. It's all right. I won't leave your side again. And I'm going to put a gun in the wardrobe for you in case you ever need one."

Carson snaked her arms around his neck and leaned her head against his chest. His heart hammered against her ear as he took the stairs and laid her down on the bed. He perched on the edge and plumped the pillow. Returning to her senses and calming, she glared up into his face, a sudden thought hitting her.

"What took you so long to come looking for me?"

Chapter Twenty-three

Kohl threw up his hands in exasperation and stomped about the room. "What took me so long? If you hadn't insisted on going out back alone, this never would have happened." He turned on her. "Just don't try it again, do you hear me?"

"You make it sound as if I sneaked out!" she retorted.

His eyes narrowed. "If the shoe fits . . ."

In a fit of anger, she ripped off one of her shoes and hurtled it at the exasperating man. "Why, you!"

Kohl dodged it. "Don't ever do that again either."

Without thinking, she sent the other shoe spinning at him. He ducked, but it smashed into his shoulder.

"You little hellcat! I warned you."

With deliberate steps he stalked her. Carson scrambled to the far side of the bed, but wasn't quick enough.

Kohl pounced.

The wind was momentarily knocked out of her. She glowered up at him. But the sensations of his hard body lying the length of hers caused her scowl to fade and be replaced with a flourish of mesmerizing excitement.

Kohl had been angry when he'd launched himself. That vanished the instant he'd gazed down into those blue depths, and his anger was replaced by an urge to capture those full pouting lips not more than an inch from his. His breath mingled with hers. Her chest began to rise and fall at a faster pace against his.

"Oh God, Carson," he murmured, his lips swooping down on hers.

Carson responded, releasing all the pent-up tension within her. Grinding her lips hungrily against his, she tasted, sucked, and savored him. Her teeth played along the lower edge of his lip, taunting and nipping, daring him to quench the thirst that had risen in her, the longing to feel, touch, taste, in a unification of bodies into one being.

Kohl responded by tangling his fingers into the lustrous flaming tangle held by a comb at the back of her head. He broke the kiss and stared down at her while he unfastened the comb and slipped the pins, holding her mane in place. Not taking his eyes from hers, he spread the heavy layers of vermilion waves out like a garland around her face.

"I love your hair." He kissed her hairline. "I love your forehead." He dropped a kiss on her forehead. "I love your turned-up nose." He kissed the tip of her nose. "Your eyes." He kissed each eyelid, causing Carson to close her eyes and revel in the rich sound of his deep voice, the feel of his soft lips, and the security of his arms. "Your lips." He kissed her upper lip, then the lower. Continuing to murmur words of love, he moved to her throat and lower still.

Carson was having a difficult time lying still while her mind whirred at the word "love" on his lips. It sounded so real, so heavenly coming from Kohl.

He flopped off her when he reached her waist. He ran fiery fingers underneath her loosened clothing, along the curve of her stomach and twined his fingers in her woman's curls. "Your skin feels like heated satin," he breathed and continued to whisper each portion of her as he peeled away the layers separating them.

Swimming in mindblowing sensations, she reached out to unbutton his shirt, but he grabbed her hand and caressed it, running the inside of his bottom lip along each finger.

"Lie back and be still," he commanded. "I want this time to be very special." He kissed her throat. "I am going to make love to you."

Carson felt a hesitation. It was as if he were waiting for her to stop him. She couldn't, even if she had wanted to, which she didn't. Instead, she answered by rolling onto her side and winding her arms around his neck. "You know, I want y—"

"Shut up," he muttered. "No more talking. Only experiencing. Only feeling."

"Mmm," she moaned. Ignoring his order to be still, she fumbled with the buttons on his shirt, opening it to his waist. Her fingers threaded through the hair on his chest and her mouth dropped urgent kisses down the front of him.

He unbuttoned his trousers, and pulling her to him, guided her hand inside the waistband until she touched his fervid core.

"Yes," he moaned, emboldening Carson.

She pushed him onto his back and kneeling, tugged his boots off, then pulled on his pant legs. They did not give. She tried again, not wanting to break the raptured spell, but the trousers which molded to his muscled legs so well would not give way.

A sheepish twist to her lips, she looked up. "I don't seem to be as adept at this sort of thing as you."

Kohl grinned at her. "I wouldn't have you any other way. Allow me," he said and exchanged positions.

Carson now lay against the pillows, watching Kohl release himself. She gasped in a breath at the sight of him. He stood so proud, so engorged, so ready for her. She reached up with open arms to receive him.

Kohl needed no prompting. He had been thinking of little else than this exquisite woman since he had first taken her. He had been ready to kill the men who had tried to violate her, had they been anywhere in the vicinity because she was his.

"You're mine," he growled from deep in his throat. "All mine. I am going to possess all of you. Brand you with my love, so you'll want only me, Carson. Only me."

Carson was mesmerized at how suddenly his ardor had returned. And again the word love, spoken from his lips sent her senses soaring.

Her breasts rose in response to his touch. They formed craggy peaks, crying out to be conquered. In answer, he fastened his mouth on one rosy crest, suckling and demanding that she surrender. Her en-

233

tire being was suffused with such wanting, such pure utter longing that she gently guided his hand down, down, toward that part of her which had to have his touch.

She whimpered when first one, then two fingers dipped into the heat of her, and she thrust herself against his hand, panting. Just when she thought she could stand it no longer, his lips and tongue replaced his hand.

"Kohl, ohhhh," she cried, losing control, pounding herself against him. All that went through her mind as she closed her eyes was sensation, pure unadulterated sensation so powerful that all thought became blanked out and was replaced by surging ecstasy.

His mouth stilled. "Carson, open your eyes and look at me. I want you to see the man who makes you feel like a woman. I want you to know that that man is me. Only me," he murmured in a voice husky with passion. "I want you to know my body as I do yours, so I will be forever imprinted in your mind and heart. That's right, open your eyes, Carson."

Slowly, her eyes fluttered open and studied his face. His eyes had darkened to midnight blue; his cheeks were flushed and those lips—those lips which had tasted all of her, which had driven her beyond herself—they glistened with the heated dew of her. She raised up on her elbows and kissed him, tasting the musky wetness of herself. And she longed to taste him, to savor and know him the way he knew her.

Her fingers first encircled the silken head of his shaft. He was hot and smooth. Her hand embraced him and memorized the stiffened length of him, causing him to groan and arch toward her. With her other hand she fondled his groin in all its life-giving glory, exploring and offering him the same pleasure he had given her. She lightly pressed her lips to him and he throbbed against her. Emboldened, she increased the pressure with her mouth and fingers until he cried out.

"God, Carson, do you know what you're doing to me?"

"Look at me, Kohl," she murmured, following his lead.

But rather than look at her as she had him, Kohl reached up and pulled her to him in a frenzied kiss. Their mouths met, tasted, suckled, demanded, while arms searched and groped in a heated rush.

Unable to endure the urgency demanding release within her, she cried out for him to enter her, for he had already conquered her body. She gladly allowed him to take the lead.

All the while he kissed her mouth, her face, he pushed her onto her back. His fingers scorching their way up her inner thigh, he spread her legs and dipped into her.

"You are so ready for me. So hot. So wet. So sweet."

"Yes. Yes," she cried as the need nearly exploded within her.

He kneeled between her thighs and she guided him into her woman's depths. Her chest rose and fell at a rapid rate as he began long, slow thrusts, withdrawing and hesitating at her outer lips before plunging back into her.

She wrapped her legs around him, taking him in deeper and deeper until she had enveloped all of him. She held him with her women's muscles and he pulsed within her. He took her face between his hands and simulated the same thrusts with his tongue, increasing the rhythm. Over and over he plunged into her. Their cadence cumulative in its frenzy; the fury of their pounding taking them to heights higher than imaginable.

The feverish pitch which rocked Carson's body caused her to scream out her ecstasy as wave after wave so intense, so profound washed over her in drowning magnitude.

Kohl had held himself back with every ounce of will he'd possessed, and when he felt her release a flood gate opened within him and he followed her into total ecstasy, spurting forth his passion's spawn.

Once the contractions had eased, Kohl remained atop her, rocking his hips in slow, easy figure eights.

"What are you doing?" she panted.

"I'm not done yet."

Already waves of heat were building again within her. She answered his movements with her own, pulsing her woman's muscles around him, his responding in return.

"Kiss me," he ordered. He could not get enough of those luscious lips, her delectable body. He enshrouded her mouth with his. He wanted more of her nectared kisses, his naked flesh pressed against hers.

Carson ran her nails up and down his back, squirming beneath him as a luminous heat overtook her again. Although they had just made love, she still wanted him. She wrapped her legs around him and increased the beat of his rocking motions. An urgency overtook her and she drove herself against him mindlessly until the contractions broke over her again and again.

Slowing the arching of her hips, she gazed up at him. "Was it as incredible for you the second time as it was for me?" she asked, still wrapped in awe.

Kohl smoothed his palm down her cheek. "It's always incredible to know that I have pleased you," he murmured. He was not about to tell her that it usually took men a little longer to experience a second orgasm than it did a woman.

"Care to try for three?" she suggested.

He grinned down at his wanton lady. "My, but you are the greedy one, aren't you?"

"I guess you have created a monster, because if that is what it always feels like—"

Resting on his elbows, he caressed her face and kissed the tip of her nose. "Carson, it feels like that and better."

"Then I wouldn't mind doing it every night with you."

"You wouldn't, would you?" He chuckled at her candid spontaneity. "Well, my little monster, I hope I can live up to your expectations."

Never one not to speak her mind, Carson blurted, "You have done that and more."

"More?" he said, rolling off her. He tucked her against him.

An impish grin captured her love-bruised lips. "Actually, I didn't think much of you when we first met."

237

"Oh, you didn't, did you?"

"No, I didn't. You looked dangerous and forbidding the first time I saw you."

"At the stage depot in San Francisco?"

"Sinclair pointed you out and said you were the kind of man to stay away from. You know, the forgettable, unsavory kind?"

The irony of how close she actually was to the truth caused him to give a bitter laugh. "Yes, how well I know."

"But he was wrong. I don't think you are unsavory at all. And tonight you proved that by rescuing me."

Kohl lay cradling Carson in the crook of his arm, nuzzling her drenched hair. In a burst of emotion, he rasped, "Tonight I made you mine. Now, no matter how hard you try, you will never be able to put me out of your mind," he murmured. "You will never be able to forget me."

In her heart, Carson knew that what he had said was true. Kohl had left an indelible mark on her. She leaned on her elbow and delved into his eyes. "Kohl?"

"Mmm?"

"Did you truly mean what you said?"

"About what?"

"About me becoming yours tonight."

He rested his arm behind his head and did not think past the moment. "Of course I meant it."

"Then when are we going to be married?"

Chapter Twenty-four

Kohl bolted to his feet so fast that he knocked Carson off the bed. She hit the floor with a clunk. Startled, she struggled up on her elbows and stared at him in confusion. He was climbing into his clothes.

His shirt open, Kohl slid into his trousers, not bothering to button the fly. He plunked onto the edge of the bed next to where she now sat on the floor and tugged on his boots.

"What's the matter? Don't you believe in proposing without your clothes on?" she asked, confused by his strange behavior.

He did not answer.

Carson climbed to her feet. He threw her a blanket. "Cover yourself," he rasped. "I can't think straight when you look like that."

She wrapped the blanket around herself and tucked it in at the top of her breasts. "There. I'm dressed," she announced. "Shall I sit on the bed and you kneel before me, or would you prefer I sit on a chair in the parlor? That would be more traditional, I suppose."

Kohl got to his feet. He felt trapped and the room was suddenly stifling. He splayed his fingers through his hair, feeling awkward as a schoolboy. Hell, he'd made love to lots of women and never had one expected him to up and get hitched.

"Well?" she prompted. "What are you waiting for?"

Kohl paced back and forth, not attempting to glance in her direction. "Carson, what we shared tonight was special."

"Very special."

"Yes, it was. But a man like me—"

"Like you?" Suspicious, she inquired, "What are you trying to say, Kohl?"

"Oh hell, Carson, you don't want to marry a man like me," he blurted out.

She pinched her lips. "Of course, I do. We made love. You said so yourself. Furthermore, I lo—"

"No. You don't!" he cut in before she could say the word he knew was on the edge of her lips. "You only think you do. What you felt was passion. You can't build a life on that. A man like me isn't the marryin' kind."

She leaped off the bed and grabbed his arm. Although her heart felt as if it had shattered into a thousand pieces, she was not going to let him see how upset she was. "And just exactly what kind of man are you? Or does your kind tell every girl you've just made love to that she is yours?" She took a breath and continued. "Don't try to tell me that you didn't feel something for me, because I know you did."

He had felt something. It was true. And no, he had never told anyone the things he had said to Carson. But marriage! "I am not getting married and that's that!"

"All right," she burst out. "Then I'll just go ahead and marry Sinclair!"

"You can't marry a man who would ship you off to Nevada for three months to make yourself over for him!"

The pieces of her heart started to mend despite this latest imbroglio. He did love her; he just was afraid to admit it. She reached up on her tiptoes until they were nose to nose. "I not only can marry Sinclair, but if you continue to refuse to marry me, I will!"

He broke eye contact. "I'm going out on the couch."

Carson went to the chest of draws and with a vengeance gathered up the bedding and tossed it at him. "Go!" She was so angry at his obstinance, she slammed the door behind him. "I hope it's so lumpy you can't sleep!" she yelled through the door.

All night she stewed over Kohl's refusal to marry her. She tried to think of a way to change his mind. Nothing came to mind. She contemplated insisting that he seek other accommodations, yet she did not want him to leave. He was going to marry her; he just didn't realize it yet!

By dawn she had settled on acting as if nothing had happened and continuing with her plan to marry

Sinclair. Kohl had been adamant about her not marrying Sinclair, so she figured that if she went ahead with her plans, Kohl would have to relent. The only thing that troubled her was, what if he didn't!

Carson was in the kitchen heating water and measuring out coffee grounds when Kohl came in rubbing his eyes. "Mornin'," he grumbled. He turned a chair around and straddled it.

She sawed a loaf of bread into thick slices without looking up. "Morning."

"Carson, about last night—"

"What about last night?" she said with a cheery smile and handed him two plates filled with bread.

Kohl set the plates down. "I think we should talk."

She took a seat and with a shrug began buttering the bread. "There's nothing to talk about."

He grabbed her wrist. "Will you stop buttering that damned bread?" She looked up at him, her expression void of emotion. "Look, I know you were upset, but it is for the best that—"

She raised her chin. "I quite agree. Actually, after I had an opportunity to think about it last night, I realized that you and I are hardly suited. Sinclair is the much better choice." She rose and, using a potholder, grabbed the coffeepot, a complacent smile on her face. "Coffee?"

Kohl hauled a sack of barley over to the kettle for Horse. The old man was still a trifle stiff after the

242

beating he'd taken, but had insisted he was fine and raring to work again. As Kohl poured the grain his thoughts switched to Carson. He did not know what to make of the pose she was taking. She had seemed totally unaffected at breakfast, then had come down to the brewery and started working alongside him and Horse as if she didn't have a care in the world.

His gaze raked over her. She was standing next to Horse leaning on the end of a broom, chattering about the tea and yelling in the old man's dented ear trumpet so loud all about Sinclair that Kohl was ready to explode. Secretly, although Kohl had never met this Sinclair, he was coming to hate the man.

Unable to listen to Carson carol the man's praises any longer, Kohl announced, "I'm going for supplies."

Horse pointed the horn end of his ear trumpet at Kohl. "Eh?"

"I said, I'm going for supplies!"

"Got enough for a couple more days," Horse bellowed out. "Why don't you two young'uns get outta here 'n' let a old man do his job? Go fishin' or somethin'. Equipment's in the barn."

In disgust, Kohl waved off the old man's suggestion and headed for the door.

Horse scratched his head. "What's wrong with him?" he asked Carson.

"He's just afraid to be alone with me . . . even though I haven't the slightest interest in him any longer," she added for good measure, knowing Kohl could overhear.

Kohl stopped and pivoted around. "Is that some

243

sort of challenge?" he growled.

"Not at all. As a matter of fact, I had planned to spend the day visiting Lily and her Seasons. I'm sure they will be able to offer a few suggestions on how to please Sinclair once he arrives."

Kohl grabbed her hand. "You've already spent too much time with Lily. That woman's been filling your head with too many ideas. You're coming with me," he announced and dragged her out the door. But not before she glanced at Horse and winked.

Out in the warm sunshine Carson yanked her hand back. "Before I go anywhere with you I demand to know where we shall be going?"

"To drown a couple of hooks." Although spending the entire day with her was the last thing he needed to do, he had to keep her away from Lily filling her head with any more ideas. "Just don't go getting the wrong idea."

"I don't know what you're talking about."

"I am talking about us," he ground out, angry for being forced to bring up a subject which continued to weigh heavy on his mind.

"I have no further interest in you. I thought I made that clear earlier this morning."

"Humph!"

Kohl harnessed the team and stowed the fishing poles in the back of the wagon in silence. He did not even bother to offer her a hand into the wagon, waiting sullenly until she climbed aboard. He snapped the reins over the animals' rumps and turned west, heading along the main road toward Tahoe.

Carson did not attempt to make conversation as

244

the wagon slowly climbed the mountain. She sat back and inhaled the pine-scented air and watched the stellar jays flit from branch to branch. Gray squirrels scolded from their perches in trees high above them, and cottontails sprinted in front of the wagon wheels.

They traveled for hours before finally reaching the pearlized blue waters of the thirty-mile-long Lake Tahoe. Mighty boulders lined the shoreline where they parked the wagon and pines dipped down to the edge of the lake. Puffy clouds dotted a sky put to shame by the crystal-clear water.

"It's beautiful," Carson announced and leaped from the wagon.

Kohl did not answer. He had spent hours wondering what he was doing spending the day with her to no avail. Finally he had to admit to himself that he had wanted to be with her in spite of himself. Hell, what was wrong with him? He should be back at the brewery or at the newspaper office; anywhere but at a lake spending an entire day alone with Carson Mueller.

"I wonder how the lake got its name?" she mused.

"The owner of Lake House called it Tahoe. Before that it was called Lake Bigler after some governor until he lost his popularity because he was suspected of sympathizing with the South during the war."

"My, but you're a wealth of information," she said cutely.

"Humph!" He stomped around the wagon and yanked out the fishing poles, thrusting one into her hands.

"What am I supposed to do with this?"

"Fish," he grunted.

"But I don't know how."

"Then why'd you come?"

"Well, I like fish, and since we are so close to the lake I thought that since the opportunity presented itself I would learn. It will make Sinclair proud, I'm sure," she added for good measure.

"I'm sure," he echoed sarcastically and left her standing beside the wagon holding the pole.

"Where are you going?"

"To dig for worms." He ignored the face she pulled, located a damp spot, and starting shoveling dirt. In short order he had a half-dozen wiggling worms. "Here." He shoved out his hand, offering her one of the squirming creatures.

She stepped back, scrunching up her face. "What am I suppose to do with that?"

"Stick it on your hook."

"I will not!"

"You will if you want to learn to fish." He took her hand none too gently, dropped a worm into it, and went about setting up his own line. Perched on a huge boulder, he dropped the line into the lake.

Carson held the worm at arm's length and forced herself to impale it on the hook. Holding the pole far away from her, she rushed to the edge of the lake and dunked the worm not three feet off shore.

"What do you think you're doing?" Kohl boomed out, causing Carson to drop the pole and jump.

"I thought I was fishing until you scared me and made me lose my pole. Now, would you mind fetching it for me so I can get on with acquiring supper?"

"You want to fish?" She nodded. "Then retrieve your own pole." He turned his attention back to his pole, but watched her out of the corner of his eye. He had expected her to use common sense, but he should have remembered that Carson Mueller had a penchant for charging ahead without thinking.

Instead of climbing out onto the rocks and fishing it out of the lake, Carson leaned over as far as she could and reached for the pole, causing her to lose her balance and step, shoes and all, into the icy water.

Kohl shook his head. "You just proved my point."

She scowled at him. "And that is?"

"I said you didn't have enough sense to pour piss out of a boot."

Pole in hand, Carson narrowed her gaze at him. Without a word, she plopped down, untied her shoe and with great symbolic ceremony tipped it up and poured the water from it. That should wipe the smug look off your face, she thought and was pleased when it did.

To add insult to injury, an hour later Carson had four fat trout, whereas Kohl had only caught one so small he'd had to fling it back.

"Well, I think I have enough fish for my supper, and enough for you as well," she said innocently. But the look she'd cast him from underneath her lashes had been anything but innocent. He was perturbed which she found most gratifying, since it signified that he was anything but impervious to her. She headed for the wagon and called back over her

247

shoulder, "If we don't start back soon, it will be morning before we reach the brewery."

Kohl grumbled something unintelligible and caught up with her. He offered her his knife. "Aren't you going to clean your fish?"

Carson stared down at the huge weapon, gleaming in the sun. "What do I need that for?"

"To slit the bellies of your fish, dig out their guts, and cut their heads off."

Carson felt green around the gills herself as she looked from the knife to the fish. "Can't we just cook them whole?"

"If you want to fish you have to learn how to clean them." Carson headed back toward the lake. "Where are you going," he shouted.

"To throw them back."

"They're dead, Carson," he announced tonelessly.

She stomped back to where he stood and thrust out her hand, the fish dangling from a rope. "All right, I'll make a deal with you. You clean them and I'll cook them."

He gave a laugh at the irony. "You can't cook."

Less than an hour later, Carson sat around the campfire Kohl had built, a triumphant grin hidden beneath her placid expression as she licked her fingers. Kohl had relented. He not only had cleaned the fish, but cooked them as well.

She stood up and stretched, giving him a clear view of her shape beneath the form-fitting dress she had worn. "Well, after a successful day of fishing, I'm ready to head back now."

Kohl crossed his arms over his lap. "We aren't going back tonight. It's too late. We'll have to spend the night here."

Not about to give him the satisfaction of besting her today, Carson raised her chin. "Well, in that case, it looks as if it is going to be a long cold night."

Chapter Twenty-five

Kohl raked her with a carnal gaze. He ached to spend the night with her under the stars; out where no other human being would be within a mile. She was so desirable that it took all his strength not to pull her into his embrace and explore those full lips and curvaceous body. Within his grumpiness he realized she was his forbidden fruit, but he was a man starved for another taste of her.

He forced himself to tear his gaze away. "It's not going to be too cold tonight."

"Oh?" she said suspiciously, her arms crossed over her chest. She shot a glance at the scrawny blanket in the back of the wagon. "If you think we are going to share a blanket you are sorely mistaken."

He flashed his brows. He finally had the upper hand. It sweetened his sour disposition. "I think we'll manage just fine."

"If you think that I am going to—"

"I don't think anything of the sort."

"Than why didn't you wait for me to finish my sentence?" she accused.

A slow drawl to his words, he said, "Darlin', you started this whole line of thinkin'. Could it be that despite everything you have a hankerin' for me?"

"I have no such thing! Ohh!" she startled at the sudden feel of his hands on her waist. "What do you think you're doing?"

"Just helpin' you into the wagon. Or would you prefer to remain behind?"

She shot him daggers despite the heat radiating around her middle, and allowed him to assist her on board. Her back straight, she demanded, "Isn't it a trifle dangerous to travel down the mountain at night?"

"We aren't going down the mountain tonight," he said, joining her.

She averted her gaze. She was not going to give him the satisfaction of having to ask just where they would be spending the night.

The wagon bumped along the scenic road, which rivaled any of its kind found in Europe. The road was cut through the brow of a cliff and for a distance was supported by massive timbers. Maintaining her silence, Carson gazed over the edge toward the cobalt waters of the lake, glimmering through a forest of towering pines. Her head swiveled to the right and caught on a colossal keep of rocks, which appeared like a grand old fortress. And for an instant the thought of being imprisoned in such a keep assailed her before she set such nonsense aside.

Twilight was rapidly transforming the waters of the lake to indigo by the time they rounded a corner and the Lapham Hotel came into view. It was a delightful pitched-roofed structure with a swirl of smoke rising from the chimney. A porch skirted the front of the building, and guests lounged in chairs, chatting.

Carson ignored Kohl's scowl as she followed him onto the porch and inside the hotel. A kindly man with a pate long ago denuded greeted them. "You folks up from Carson City?"

"Yes," Carson answered for Kohl, who continued to sulk. "We spent the day fishing."

"This lake's a fisherman's paradise, it is. Why just the other day one of the hotel's guests pulled out a twenty-four-pounder. No one walks away without a boatful up here."

Carson grinned at Kohl. "I'm afraid he wasn't so lucky."

The man's eyes widened and settled on Kohl. "Don't tell me you didn't catch nothin'? Why, that's gotta be a record in these parts."

"You got any rooms?" Kohl growled.

The man fiddled with his suspenders at the stranger's ill temper. "Well, it's a good thing you two got here when you did. We just happen to have one left," he announced, sure it would soothe the stranger's dark mood. But he was sympathetic. He'd be grumpy, too, if he hadn't caught any fish.

"But we need tw—"

"We'll take it," Kohl barked out and shot Carson a warning to keep her tongue.

Puzzled, the man handed Kohl the key. "Upstairs to your right. We're still serving supper in the dining room," he called out.

252

Kohl had hold of Carson's arm, practically dragging her toward the stairs. She grabbed the corner of the wall and said over her shoulder, "Thank you, but we ate the fish I caught."

Kohl's fingers clamped tighter around her arm and his expression darkened as he stomped up the stairs.

In the rustic room, furnished with a quilted spread cast over a double bed and a rough hewn table set with a wash bowl and light, Kohl slammed the door and stood staring at her. "You like gloating, don't you?"

Carson raised her chin. "I was merely stating a fact. But you! You should have told that man we required two rooms!"

"You heard him, there was only one left," he said, ignoring her and surveying the room.

"We both can't stay here," she cried. "You are just going to have to sleep elsewhere tonight."

Kohl plunked down on the bed, a devilish smile on his face. "I paid for this room and I'm not leaving."

Carson's eyes widened. "You can't expect me to sleep downstairs!"

"I wouldn't think of it. You are perfectly welcome to stay in my room with me. I'll even allow you half the bed."

"Why you! You are no gentleman," she spat.

"Darlin', I never claimed to be."

In a fit of anger, Carson swung out of the room and stomped downstairs and across the lobby.

"Everything to your liking?" the clerk asked.

Carson pivoted around slowly to give herself time

253

to think. She couldn't tell the man she and Kohl weren't married. She had not said anything when Kohl accepted the key. Inspiration came to her. "Everything is fine. It is such a lovely night I thought I would go for a walk before I turn in."

The clerk scratched his ear. "But the temperature's dropped to nearly forty degrees."

Carson ignored him and went outside. She could see her breath, and wearing nothing more than a lightweight outfit a chill caused goosebumps to rise on her arms. She paced back and forth, trying to decide what to do.

Upstairs, Kohl parted the curtains and looked out to see Carson silhouetted by the full moon. She was rubbing her arms, obviously cold. Hell, he ought to leave her out there, the stubborn woman. But something inside him wouldn't allow it.

Kohl took the stairs two at a time and was striding out the door when the man behind the desk hailed him.

"Hope you got a wrap for your wife. It's getting mighty cold out and the little lady's been outside for some time."

Kohl did not answer, but he hadn't missed the man's referral to Carson as his wife. He had his hand around the door handle when the man called out again.

"Mr. Baron, your wife can use the shawl I got behind the counter. My wife ain't usin' it now."

"Thanks," Kohl said curtly. He took the shawl and strode out, looking for Carson.

He found her perched on a log, staring off into

254

the black waters lapping at the ebony shoreline. "Carson?"

She did not look up.

Against his better judgment, Kohl sat down next to her. "Here." He wrapped the shawl around her shoulders. "The man at the desk suggested I give this to my 'wife.' Said you were probably cold."

Carson's head snapped around at the mention of her as his wife. Her lips tightened. "And I suppose you didn't lose any time setting him straight, did you?"

"I didn't tell him a thing."

"Why not, Kohl? You are so adamant against such an idea, I would've thought you wouldn't waste a moment making sure everyone knows you are not married and have a woman in your room. Why, I bet all the men within earshot would've patted you on the back with envy." She bundled the shawl around her; she was cold despite the shame flaming her cheeks.

"I didn't tell anyone you aren't my wife, Carson," he said softly.

He took her hand and she tried to pull it back. But he held tight. Rubbing his thumb along the side of her index finger, he said, "I never meant to hurt you."

That was all it took. Carson leaped to her feet before he could see that tears had puddled in her eyes and were now spilling down her face. She turned her back toward him. But he was right behind her, grasping her shoulders and pulling her back against his hard chest.

"Carson," he whispered against her ear.

She swung on him, no longer caring whether he saw her shame or not. "Don't! Don't say another word. I am fine. So fine in fact that as soon as we return I am going to write to Sinclair and let him know that I have been accepted into the best social circles, and that I shall not need two more months to demonstrate to his mother that I am now an acceptable match for her only son," she snarled.

"Jesus Christ, you are the most single-minded female I have ever come across. Is marriage all you think about?"

"As a matter of fact it is—to Sinclair. Now, I am going to bed. I would very much appreciate it if you found other sleeping accommodations."

Taken back by the force of such a tirade, Kohl watched her storm into the hotel before he decided that she was not going to tongue lash him with the sole purpose of thinking such an invective would make him feel guilty enough to let her have the room. Furthermore, it was getting downright cold, and his days of sleeping out under the stars were past!

Determination surrounding him, Kohl stomped back into the hotel.

"Wait up there, son." Kohl eyed the man behind the desk suspiciously, wishing he would mind his own damned business. "The little woman looked to be mighty upset when she returned my wife's shawl—"

"Yeah, so?"

The man rubbed his chin. "Well, as I was gonna

256

say before you interrupted me, if you need a place to sleep tonight I can let you use the couch in the back corner over there." He motioned to a piece of furniture. "Slept there a time or two myself when my wife got a burr under her chin over something."

"I won't be needing it," Kohl announced and reached the first stair before the man's grating voice intruded on him again.

"In case you have a change of heart, I'll leave a blanket out."

Kohl snorted in reply and took the rest of the stairs resolved to sleep in the damned bed if he had to hogtie Carson and gag her!

He passed a couple returning to their room down the hall and nodded as he wrapped his hand around the doorknob.

The door would not budge.

The couple glanced back, apparently expecting him to go into his room. He tried the door again, his temper close to getting the better of him. Carson must have propped a chair under the knob. Feeling foolish, he nodded to the couple. "I'm sure you know how it is. Newlywed's quarrel," he said between his teeth.

They smirked and went into their room, finally leaving him alone in the hall. Hell, in the past he would have kicked the damned door in, guns drawn. For some reason he could not bring himself to do such a thing to Carson. He rattled the door. "Carson, let me in," he rasped against the portal.

"No!" echoed through the door.

"Carson," he said with more annoyance in his

voice. "If you don't open this damned door, I am going to—"

"You are going to what? Use your brute strength and force your way in?" came her reply.

"I'm warning you, if you don't open this door, you are going to be mighty sorry."

No response.

"Carson, open this damned door!" he barked and pounded against it. "If you don't, I am going to raise such a ruckus, you'll never be able to hold your head up in these parts again," he warned, growing exasperated with her refusal to cooperate. Despite an earlier decision, the thought of kicking in the door was becoming more appealing by the minute.

To his surprise the stubborn female finally gave in and the door swung open.

"It is about time," he rumbled, stomping into the room and slamming the door.

She was standing next to the bed as if to block any attempts to share it with her. "What do you want?" She raised her chin in that same annoying way those society biddies had of doing.

"What do you mean what do I want?" he echoed in disbelief.

"Well?"

"Dammit, Carson." He splayed his fingers through his hair. "You know damned well."

To his utter surprise, she strode past him as if he weren't there and swung open the door, standing to the side and holding it. "And I told you earlier that I have no intention of sharing this room with you tonight."

He stared at her in total disbelief. He had come up against some of the most dangerous outlaws west of the Mississippi and bested them without this much trouble. Hell, she didn't weigh much more than a hundred pounds soaking wet. He outweighed her by at least eighty pounds, yet she was standing her ground as if they were evenly matched. Christ, he could toss her over his shoulder and dump her on her side of the bed and climb in before she knew what happened, he thought sourly. But something held him back from physically forcing her to his will.

They stood glaring at each other as the minutes clicked off the clock until Kohl finally reached a solution. He plunked down on the bed and crossed his arms over his chest.

"We are sharing this room tonight and that is final."

Chapter Twenty-six

Kohl awoke at the first rays of light through the windows, feeling as rankled as a grizzly disturbed from hibernation and as stiff as a plank. He leaned up on his elbow and looked about for where the whooshing sounds were coming from.

"Mornin', son. I was tryin' not to wake you, but I got to get the lobby swept before the other guests start comin' down for vittles in a little while." The man smiled his understanding. "Guess the little woman was more peeved than you realized last night. I been married well on thirty years myself, and I can tell you that when a woman gets something in her craw, it's better to seek high ground before the storm hits. You was smart movin' down here and lettin' the little wife have time to simmer down."

"Just shut up!" Kohl barked out. He uncramped his legs from the too-short couch, forced his feet into his boots, and stomped outside among the far-reaching pines.

He broke off a branch and plucked out the pine

needles as his boots crunched through the trees. Hell, he was getting soft. Last night he had backed down under Carson's cold stare and stalked out of his own room. He'd never let a man, let alone a woman, do that to him before.

The faint sound of footfalls behind him broke into his reasoning and he swung around. Carson was heading in his direction.

"Good morning," she said, waving cheerily as she joined him.

"What's so good about it?"

"I had a perfectly marvelous rest. That bed was as soft as a cloud." Ignoring his grumpy demeanor, she went on. "I do hope you slept well, too."

Visions of that hard couch rose up before him and he arched a brow at her. "Oh yeah. Real well."

"Good. Ready to head back?" she asked, fighting to keep the triumphant grin from her face.

"You anxious to write that letter to what's his name—"

"Sinclair," she supplied with a dreamy smile for his benefit.

"Yeah. Sinclair."

"Actually, after you left last night I wrote the letter on the hotel's stationery and already gave it to that dear Mr. Timmons. He is going to post it for me." She waited for a response. When Kohl just stood there snapping the pine needles between his fingers, she grew impatient. He did not give her the response she had hoped for. The stubborn gunslinger was not cooperating at all! In an effort to hide her disappointment, she smiled brightly. "Well, I am ready to start back when you are."

By the time they returned to the brewery Kohl had added hunger to his list of gripes. Not only hadn't he had a decent night's rest, but he had not taken the time to fill his gut before they'd started back. The day was blistering hot in the valley, so unlike the pleasant days and clear crisp nights up on the mountain, which only added to his grouchy disposition.

Addie was just rounding the corner, but drew back where she could eavesdrop when she caught sight of the old man, all wound up over something. She'd spent days nosing around after running away from that stupid tea party, and had come up with some pretty interesting information. She just had to figure out exactly how it all went together. She peeked around the building to listen.

"Kohl!" Horse came running as fast as his old legs would carry him. "Boy, I'm glad you're back!"

Kohl rolled his eyes as Carson hastened to intercept the old man. Just what he needed: another problem with Carson right in the middle of it!

Carson was supporting the old codger by the time Kohl reached them. "What's happened now?"

"Eh?"

Kohl guided the tube of the ear trumpet into Horse's ear. "I said . . . what's going on?"

"Oh." He nodded his understanding. "We ran out

of supplies and our suppliers says they ain't gonna let us have no more."

Kohl leaned over the trumpet. "If it's a matter of money, I'll see to it."

"It ain't money. And we can't go nowheres else neither 'cause there ain't nobody else to go to," he offered before the question was asked.

"Then what could possibly be the reason no one will sell to us if it isn't money?" Carson interjected.

Kohl shot her an annoyed glance. That female was determined to get herself involved even where she wasn't wanted. "Carson, why don't you go up to the apartment and fix some dinner?"

"I'm not hungry."

"Well, I am!"

Carson stood her ground and glared at Kohl.

"If you twos done parryin' words, we got trouble," Horse butted in. "Seems that new preacher outta Kansas has been rilin' up folks to rise up against spirits of all kinds."

"But the suppliers are businessmen," Kohl announced. He could not fathom such reluctance. As a gunslinger he had worked for whoever paid him, and businessmen had always put the almighty dollar first.

"That's rightly so, but that preacher's got their wives makin' their lives a fiery hell if they agree to sell the fixin's to folks what's goin' to make liquor out of 'em."

Kohl ripped off his hat and rubbed his head in disbelief. "What!"

263

"That ain't the worst of it. I heard tell that the man's got those fine ladies of the community so het up they's plannin' to march against the brewery till we close down."

"No! That can't be," Carson cried. In a display of panic she grabbed Kohl's arm. "You've got to stop that letter I wrote to Sinclair."

"What do you expect me to do? Follow the mail back to San Francisco and snatch it out of the man's hand?" They had big trouble at the brewery and she was worried about that damned fiancé of hers. But the desperate look on her face made him say more softly, "Carson, even if I rode back up to Tahoe on the swiftest horse in town, by the time I got there your letter would be already well on its way."

"Perhaps you might be able to intercept the stage," she suggested, tightening her fingers around his arm.

"It's too late. You might try meeting with those fine society ladies you think of as your friends and try talking them out of such foolishness. Although I doubt you'd have much sway."

Secretly, Carson knew what he said was true, but she raised her chin in defiance. "It never hurts to try. They are reasonable ladies. I'm sure they will listen to reason," she announced and strode off.

Horse scratched his head. "What the devil's she up to now?"

Kohl watched her head off in the direction of the church down the street and shook his head. "God only knows. Come on," he yelled into the ear trumpet, "after I get me something to eat, we'll pay a few calls on those suppliers."

Addie smiled to herself. The gunslinger had trouble, which suited her just fine. Still wondering what the men she had seen sneaking around were up to, Addie left her position to follow Carson.

Addie was startled when she caught sight of the same two scraggly men who also were following Carson. Things were getting more complicated than she'd originally reasoned. Her box carefully clutched to her heart, the girl crept along from bush to bush, now keeping her eyes on Carson and the men following her.

Carson wasn't sure what she was going to say to Beatrice Heimerman to make her change her mind. But after what Kohl had said, Carson only knew that she had to try. Beatrice was the obvious spokeswoman, so Carson decided to approach her first. Carson opened the gate and strolled through the manicured yard of the church as if she hadn't a care in the world. It wouldn't do to let the women see how upset she was.

"Good day, pastor," she nodded to the tall preacher in the clerical collar coming out of the rectory.

"Ah, Miss Mueller," the pinched-faced man said, "have you come to repent?"

"Repent?"

"Yes. To stand before us and God as your witnesses and denounce your sins for making those evil spirits that are the ruination of so many lives."

"Sir, I—"

"Carson Mueller, do come in," Beatrice said, waving from the door of the rectory.

Saved from the man's tirade, Carson returned Beatrice's greeting. "If you'll excuse me," she quickly said to the preacher and hurried toward Beatrice relieved to be away from the fanatical man.

"I am so happy you have decided to join us," Beatrice announced, leading Carson into the rectory where a half dozen ladies sat in a circle sewing. "Aren't we pleased that Carson has chosen to desert her misguided path and join us, ladies?"

As the women applauded, Beatrice's mind swirled with how she could put the girl's unannounced presence to work. The girl had unwittingly fallen into her clutches and Beatrice intended to make use of it. Before she was done with Miss Carson Mueller, she would learn never to attempt to make a lady out of a little tramp again.

Feeling sick, Carson's gaze shot over the women. All head's were bobbing in agreement.

"Do come and sit down. We are helping the orphanage with mending." Before Carson could explain why she'd come, Beatrice escorted her to a chair and thrust a torn shirt and needle and thread into her hands. Feeling outflanked by the domineering woman, Carson dropped her gaze to her lap, staring at it.

She didn't know how to sew!

266

Beatrice disregarded the girl's apparent hesitation to help out and took up a position next to her. "We have the most exciting news to share with you now that you have decided to become one of us."

"One of you?" Carson rasped out haltingly.

"Why, yes. Your presence here today confirms that you have seen the light and come to realize that the evils of liquor are destroying this country. Reverend Linsey has told us that Kansas is rapidly becoming a dry state and we are going to start the push to have liquor outlawed in Nevada, too," Beatrice announced to another rousing round of applause.

"But, I don't think you realize—"

"We realize that we have been chosen to help with God's work," Beatrice proclaimed, cutting off Carson. "We have already enlisted our husbands. And with your help our voices will rise even further."

Carson swallowed back a retort. She felt like a captive in an enemy camp. She dropped her head and took a few stitches until she pricked her finger. "Ouch!" she cried out, then immediately looked around.

"My, but you've pierced your finger," Agnes observed, glancing up at the blood forming on Carson's index finger.

Beatrice seized an opportunity and jumped to her feet. "We shall declare that Carson Mueller has been the first to shed blood for our cause. Carson," Beatrice continued, taking Carson's hand and pulling her to her feet, "since you have been so brave as to join us, come." She dragged Carson to a corner of the rectory where three women were hunched on the floor working furiously over something Carson could not make out. "You can lend your hand—and blood—to our project."

Now that she and Beatrice stood out of earshot of the majority of women, Carson had to speak up. "Beatrice, the reason I came today was not to join any causes. If you have neglected to recall, I am half-owner of the Carson Brewery. Therefore—"

"Therefore, your support is all the more significant. It is essential," Beatrice said. "We need you, my dear. We need you!"

"But—"

Beatrice drew back, her face a troubled mask. "Don't tell me you believe in drunks?"

"No, of course not. It is just that—"

"Just that you never before realized that you share the responsibility for Man's fall from grace, isn't that right?"

"I never thought I had anything to do with men's souls before."

"But you do. Don't you see what an impression your joining us will make?" The girl was not as easily swayed as she had hoped, Beatrice reasoned by her continued resistance. Then inspiration came to her. "Carson, I think you will come to understand and embrace our position once you hear what I have to say . . ."

* * *

By the time he and Horse drove into the barn from a fruitless trip to the suppliers, Kohl was hot, tired, and enraged. Not one of the men had agreed to go against his wife's position and sell them supplies, stating that there would be no peace if he did. Almost as if the men had gotten together, Horse and Kohl had been told the same story; wait until the preacher moves on, then things will return to normal.

But Kohl could not afford to wait. He no longer had a lot of cash, after buying the newspaper. He had made the decision to settle down and give up the profession of hiring out his guns, and he could not afford to fail. He had never failed at anything he'd done since he'd left home. And he was not going to fail now!

He was in a black mood as he unhitched the team. What he needed was to put his feet up and relax, so he could plot out his next move. He was pitching the final throw of hay when he heard a ruckus out in the street.

"What now!" he spat and threw the pitch fork down to go investigate.

Outside, he stopped dead in his tracks. His hands balled into fists and his eyes narrowed with cold fury at the sight coming toward him.

A cluster of damned society women were carrying banners denouncing the brewery and heading straight for him. Six deep, their numbers seemed to be swelling as they swarmed toward him singing some jibberish about onward come the Christian soldiers engaged in war. And as mad as that made him, there was no comparison to the new heights his anger rose to when he spotted Carson.

She was leading the march!

Chapter Twenty-seven

Carson was at the forefront of the march, as big as you please, carrying a banner which read:

REPENT BEFORE IT'S TOO LATE
FOLLOW MY LEAD
CAST OFF ALL ALCOHOLIC SPIRITS FOR GOD

Kohl estimated there to be at least forty squawking women in the crowd, each one seemingly hellbent on causing such a scene that the sheriff, and no doubt the newspaper reporters, would be called in. Hell, that was just what he needed: His partner arrested for demonstrating against him and her own brewery!

He shot a quick glance back over his shoulder to make sure the door to the brewery was closed and caught sight of Horse peeking out the window. The coward! Left to face the oncoming horde alone, Kohl's hands slowly snaked toward his guns. Hell, he had broken up mob scenes before single-handedly. Only this time the onslaught was a mob of females!

As Carson drew nearer he swore to himself that if he could get his hands around her long, slender neck, he would gladly wring it, he was so mad. Once he took care of the mob, he was going to get to the bottom of Carson's participation if he had to wallop her rear end until she could not sit down for a week.

"Why don't you break it up and all go home?" he shouted, trying to be heard over the din of the crowd now not more than ten feet from him.

They were making such a fuss, hurtling censorious accusations at him, that he drew his Peacemakers, aimed them toward the sky and fired off three rounds. The commotion immediately ceased, the women clinging together as if he were going to shoot one of them and they thought he wouldn't be able to single one out if they knotted together.

"Now, that's a far sight better," he said and reholstered his guns.

"We demand that you close that evil place!" Beatrice roared, shaking her fist.

A buzz shot through the crowd and Kohl put up his hands for silence. "Now, ladies, I could more readily understand it if you were marching on Lily's or even a business where they distilled hard liquor, but I" — he motioned toward Carson, who hung her head — "and my partner brew nothing harder than beer. So, before I'm forced to call on my companions here" — he patted his revolvers — "I suggest you disperse."

"We demand to be heard!" Beatrice retorted.

"Even if more blood must be spilled!" She pointed to the smears of blood on the banner Carson carried. "Our leader has already lent her life's blood to the cause and we are ready to follow her!"

Kohl glanced at Carson's bandaged finger, then to Beatrice Heimerman. If that aging old hag had been a man, Kohl, at that moment, would have gladly obliged her thirst for blood and shot her. Instead, he suggested, "I am not going to stand out here and listen while you all try to talk at once. But I'll tell you what I am willing to do. I'll listen to your leader."

Beatrice conferred with several others, then stepped forward.

"Oh, no, not you, Mrs. Heimerman." Kohl waved her off. "I'll have a word with the one who was leading all you fine ladies down the street."

His dark gaze settled on Carson again, and she shrank back. She could tell by his deadly calm that he was livid. She had no desire to be anywhere near him when he unleashed his fury. She shook her head and stepped back further into the crowd, but to her chagrin, Beatrice pulled her forward and shoved her into the forefront again.

"All right, Mr. Baron. Talk to Miss Mueller alone. But I warn you, we expect results or we'll be back," she announced and herded the rest of the women back toward the church, from which they'd come. She was certain the girl's inability to sway the big gunslinger would only alienate the few women who had spoken out against Beatrice when she'd suggested the girl's comeuppance.

Kohl waited patiently until he was left alone with Carson. He took a threatening step toward her. Just then Horse came hurrying out of the brewery, slapping a hat on his head.

"Got to be gettin' on home." His disapproving gaze swung to Carson. "Don't cotton to violence none, even when it's well deserved." He nodded and was gone.

Carson put up her hands as if the gesture could ward Kohl off. "Now, Kohl, I know what you must be thinking."

"Then you must know that that pretty neck of yours is in jeopardy." Like a big cat stalking prey, he took a step closer, never taking his eyes off her.

She took another step back. "I can explain. It really wasn't the way it appeared."

"Oh, you mean that you weren't actually in the forefront of those foolish women marchers, carrying a banner? And that wasn't your blood streaked on that damned sign?"

"No. I mean . . . yes. I was in the front and I was carrying a banner. And that was my blood. But there is a simple explanation." She noticed his fists clench, and she took another step back. Her mind whirled with escape plans, but she had nowhere to run to accept to Lily's, and she surely would not offer her sanctuary when she heard what had happened.

Kohl took another step and Carson automatically bolted. He made a grab for her, but she was able to elude him. Spying the open door to the brewery, she sprinted into the building and managed to lock the door. Panting, she frantically looked about for a place to hide until his temper cooled.

"Carson Mueller, you come out here, you damned Judas. I'll teach you to lead a march against your own brewery!" he shouted.

Carson ignored his ranting as she scrambled up the ladder to the walkway next to the malt kettle. Sounds of Kohl battering against the door caused her to act without thinking. She slid into the kettle, her heart drumming, her pulse keeping beat between her ears. She heard him crash through the door and held her breath, hoping he would tire of looking for her and give up the chase.

Kohl stomped around the room, overturning crates as he searched for that little wildcat. "You can't hide from me," he announced. "I'm going to stay here all night, if that's what it takes to find you. Then I'm going to wring your neck for such a dumb stunt."

The briny water was cold and Carson shivered, causing the liquid to slosh over the edge. It splashed at Kohl's feet and his gaze trailed upward.

"So that's where you are," he murmured. The thought hit him that he ought to light the wood under the kettle. That would heat things up a bit. But, of course, he wouldn't go that far. He wanted to wring her neck, not roast it!

Carson heard the thud of his boots on the bottom wrung of the ladder and scrambled from her position. "Don't you come up here!"

He looked up. She was a comic sight, all wet and looking like a half-drowned kitten. "Then you had best come down."

"If you'll move away from the ladder."

A sly grin to his lips, Kohl got off the ladder and stepped back. "All right, Carson. Come down."

"Only if you promise to listen to what I have to say first," she bargained, wiping the clinging malt globs from her arms.

"I'll listen."

She had no other choice. She knew that. She put her foot on the ladder, her nerves so on edge that her heel slipped and she would have fallen if Kohl's reactions hadn't been honed so fine. He caught her before she hit the floor.

"Now I've got you, you brazen little idiot."

"You said you'd listen!" she hissed.

"Yeah. I'll listen to your wails while I'm beating your butt."

Carson struggled, but she was no match for his strength. To her terror he threw her over his shoulder and stomped to a bench against the wall. He plunked down and flipped her over his knee. For an instant her mighty appealing fanny gave him other thoughts, the way she was struggling against his lap. And his loins tightened.

But when she bit into his leg, all consideration he may have given her instantly died. "Why you little hellion!" At the same juncture that the flat of his hand made contact with her fanny, he said, "Bite me, will you!"

Whack! Whack! Whack!

"Stop!" she screamed. Although he was hurting her pride more than her person, she let out a whimper.

Kohl immediately halted and uprighted her. "Oh hell, I didn't mean to really hurt you. Are you all right?"

No! She wasn't all right! He had injured her pride. She'd fix him! She immediately started to cry harder, tears streaming down her face.

"Come on, darlin'," he cooed and dabbed at the briny tears. "It couldn't have hurt that much."

Before she thought through the consequences of her actions, she leaped to her feet and darted away, throwing back over her shoulder, "It didn't!" as she left the brewery.

Kohl was right behind her. "You're not only a Judas, you're a fraud, Carson Mueller!" he snarled, cursing as he chased after that little misleader.

Carson raced up the steps to the apartment, but Kohl was right behind her and pounced, tumbling them both down the stairs. They landed with a thud, Kohl on top.

"I've got you now," he gloated, his hands pinioning her wrists above her head. "And this time you are not going to get away!" He glared into the scared blue eyes which stared back at him, and his anger melted.

His face was merely inches from hers, her back

277

against the soft grass at the foot of the stairs. She was panting, her chest rising and falling against the rise and fall of his. The sensations were mindboggling.

"Kohl, I—"

"Damn you!" he growled as his mouth came crashing down on hers. It was a kiss filled with anger, punishing passion, and longing, seeking. His lips ground against hers and his tongue demanded entry to her mouth to take from her all he needed and more.

Carson fought her own urges against his invasion. But, despite the punishment of his kiss, her ardor rose up and she responded to him, moaning from the sheer hypnotic power his lips had over her. He released her wrists and her arms went around his neck.

Not breaking the unification of their mouths, Kohl's hand skimmed down to her breast. Her nipple rose in response, peaking against the cotton of her blouse. In answer, his experienced fingers made short work of the buttons and slipped inside her blouse to fasten on the puckered mound.

Electric sparks from his touch sent shock waves through Carson, and she came back to her senses. If she didn't stop now, she wouldn't be able to, and she wanted more than to be Kohl Baron's willing lover.

"No!" She shoved against his chest, grappling with all her strength. "Let me up! I am not going to be your whore," she hissed.

Stung by the very implication of her words, Kohl rolled from her without comment and climbed to his feet, splaying fingers through his hair. He offered her a hand. "Come on, get up," he said tonelessly. Although he kept his face impassive, silently he berated himself for losing control. But then, Carson Mueller had a way of bringing out his worse side. Carson wasn't like any of the other women he had known. And he'd never want her to consider herself in the same class as Lily's kind.

Not taking her eyes from him, she rose to her feet without his help. Panting, she stared at him warily.

"All right Carson, why were you leading that damned march?"

Carson brushed the grass from her skirt, annoyed with herself as much as she was with him for her near loss of control.

"If you'll recall, I went to the church to try to talk Beatrice Heimerman into convincing the others to change their position with their husbands so they would sell us supplies. But things just seemed to get out of hand once I arrived."

"My God, woman, you were picketing your own business! What the devil was wrong with you?"

"I had to!" she cried.

"You had to? Dammit, that's the dumbest stunt you've pulled yet. And all because you want to be accepted by those old biddies for your precious Sinclair's sake?"

"No! No, that's not the way it was at all. When

I saw what they were up to, I refused to be a part of it, but—"

"But, what?" he demanded. "What possibly could have driven you to such an unthinking act?"

Carson looked skyward and let out a huff of breath. "I only participated because some of the ladies had wanted to burn down the brewery during the demonstration. Beatrice convinced me if I joined them, the ladies would be less inclined to set any fires since they would not want to destroy the property of one of their own sisters."

"And the blood?"

"I pricked my finger trying to join their sewing circle, and Beatrice smeared the banner with the blood."

"That must have been some prick," he said, doubtful.

"If you must know, I can't sew."

The hard lines on his face softened, causing Carson to blurt out, "And now what am I going to do? You heard Beatrice before she left. If they don't get results they'll be back. What am I going to do?"

She looked so frightened that Kohl's anger totally dissolved and he gathered her into his embrace, this time crooning softly and stroking the silken threads of her hair. "You should have come to me."

"There wasn't time," came her words, muffled against his chest. "What am I going to do?" she repeated.

With the crook of his finger, Kohl lifted her face to his. Her eyes were filled with worry and concern.

"The first thing you are going to do is stop worrying and get you out of those wet clothes."

"And the second?" she asked, hopeful that he had a solution and feeling secure within his embrace.

"The second thing is to figure out what *we're* going to do."

Chapter Twenty-eight

From her position hidden behind a tree, Addie watched Carson go into the churchyard, stop to speak to some preacher, and then go into the rectory. Once Carson was out of sight, Addie's alert attention shifted to the two seedy men who had been following Carson. They whispered between themselves, then moved off.

Curious, Addie stealthily trailed the men to the section of Carson City known as Chinatown. Addie had seen the Chinese laborers working in the denuded forest hills on the flumes that carried wood and fuel down to the city. By the size of the area, she guessed there to be at least eight hundred Chinese.

The two men disappeared inside a shanty and Addie crept up to the open door and peeked in. The room was dark and dank with only a single bed, table, and three chairs for furniture. An oil lamp burned low in the middle of the table, illuminating the face of the shadowy figure she had seen the men meet a few nights ago.

"Gideon Farley, Carson's guardian!" Addie gasped and plastered herself against the outside of the shanty.

Gideon turned on Saul. "Did you hear something?"

"I didn't hear nothin'. You Slick?"

"Not me."

Gideon rolled his eyes in frustration. "Go check!"

At that, Addie scurried behind a stack of crates and waited while the unshaven man, his gun drawn, poked his head out the door, gave a cursory perusal, and went back inside. Careful, so as not to be heard, she crawled back to listen.

"Well, did you find it?" Gideon demanded.

"Hell, we's searched everywhere. There ain't no durned key on the girl, in the brewery, or those rooms she's stayin' in with that gunslinger," Slick complained.

Gideon pounded the table, causing Saul to jump. "I've got to have that key! The note Carson's father left in her safe deposit box states there is a key hidden and Carson will recall from childhood where to locate it."

"What's so all-fired important about a key?" Gideon glared at Slick, but did not answer. "Since that key ain't nowhere to be found, I think you outta jest let us bring the girl to you and you can find out from her where it is."

"You idiot!" Gideon's voice raised. "I'm not paying you to think."

"You ain't payin' us anyways. Your partner is.

283

Mabbe you outta ask whoever you're workin' fer what to do," Slick snarled.

"My partner is not your concern. Your job, for now, is only to watch the girl. Furthermore, I can't afford for her to see me. She thinks I left town, and I want to keep it that way."

"You mean she thinks you made off with her inheritance, ain't that right? Only her dead pa has outsmarted you and you got nothin', the way I figger it."

Addie noticed Gideon's face turn poison oak red with anger as the men continued to argue with him. She had heard enough for now, she decided, and slithered from the shanty, unsure what to do with another piece to the puzzle.

Addie found a quiet place in a meadow on the edge of town and folded her legs beneath her under a huge poplar tree. In the shade, she opened her box and laid its precious contents out before her. Folded papers, long since yellowed with age, lay with a rosary, a chunk of lead, a doll made of hair pins with a button skirt, a crinkled page torn from the Bible with the passage "an eye for an eye" circled, and a silver dollar, a hole shot clean through the center.

Addie fingered her treasures, heedfully unfolding the pages and reading the worn words printed there the best she could.

Her resolve reaffirmed to do what she'd originally set out to do, she carefully tucked away her treasures and headed back to the brewery.

Carson stared at Kohl. "Have you figured out what we're going to do about Beatrice's threat to return in force if you don't close the brewery?"

"Not yet."

Carson got up and paced the floor. She did not bother to inform him that she had gone to the rectory earlier to try to reason with the women. Now she was relieved that no one had been there. "We can't let them burn down the brewery if we don't shut down production."

"That's it!" he bolted to his feet and gave her a smacking kiss before she could react.

"What was that for?"

"For coming up with a way to stall those women while I figure out what our next move'll be."

"I'm only too glad to help," Carson answered, unaware of any helpful suggestion she could've made and still experiencing the tingling sensation his kiss had left on her lips. "What did I do?"

"Simple. We'll shut down production."

"But won't giving in to their demands ruin the business?" she questioned, disappointed to think that he could lose the brewery.

"We're not giving in to their demands. Only stalling them. Right now we don't have enough ingredients until the shipment arrives from Gold Hill in a couple of days."

"What shipment?"

"After visiting the suppliers yesterday, I sent a telegram to Gold Hill for supplies. So, in the meanwhile, we'll let them think they've won."

"What happens when they discover they haven't?"

"By then I'll have called in a few markers and diffuse those half-baked *ladies* so they go back to their kitchens where they belong."

Carson looked troubled. "They do have a valid point. Alcohol has ruined many families," she set out in the ladies' defense.

"Carson, it's not the alcohol that's ruined those families. It's the men who guzzle it. Outlawing it isn't going to solve the problem."

"Then what is?"

"Those men getting a hold of themselves and learning to take charge of their lives and not letting alcohol rule them. Furthermore, our brewery only bottles beer."

She didn't totally agree with him, but her mind had shifted to the word "our." It had a nice ring to it, and she had to admit to herself that she liked being involved in the business much more than spending time in the kitchen.

"Kohl, what can I do?"

He took her by the shoulders and swung her around facing the stairs. "Go inform that mob that our little talk was successful."

She nodded and left the apartment, feeling that their "little talk" had been quite successful. They were no longer at each other's throats. They now were allies, working toward a common goal, she thought as she closed the distance between the brewery and the church. She was feeling so good that she totally let the fact that she had written to

Sinclair and requested that he come to Carson City slip from her mind.

Kohl went to the window and watched Carson stroll along the street. His eyes caught on the gentle flare of her hips. Visions of those hips cradling his weight and lifting to meet his thrusts as they'd made love dominated his consciousness. She had been so uninhibited, so giving of herself that he felt a lump lodge in his throat.

He had taken her virginity, something that she had been saving as a gift to bring to her marriage bed, and then he'd stopped her when she had been about to pronounce her love for him. She had assumed he would marry her. But, hell, he'd never considered himself the marrying kind—that was until he watched her open the gate and enter the churchyard.

Despite her disappointment, she was helping him hang on to his business. She was bravely putting herself on the line for him. The least he could do would be to marry her.

Kohl's mind made up to make the great sacrifice, he set about cooking up a special supper before she returned.

It wasn't more than two hours later that Kohl heard the click of her heels on the stairs. Quickly, he settled onto the couch, grabbed an old newspaper, and pretended to be studying it as she came in.

Her eyes twinkling, she announced, "I did it! I made them believe that the march had the desired results!" She took off her hat. "You know, it was the strangest thing. Beatrice almost seemed disappointed when I told them that I had been successful. It was almost as if she had been hoping I'd fail. But, of course, that is silly."

"Of course," he muttered while he listened to all the details of her interview with the women. She was so excited about being accepted by the old biddies that he didn't have the heart to tell her he was suspicious of their motives. But she would no longer need those women's acceptance after he announced he was going to marry her.

"Hungry? I made supper."

"I'm starved," she answered, delighted that Kohl had gone to so much trouble for her. Her hopes buoyed that he might be weakening toward her, she followed him into the tiny kitchen.

Greeted by flickering candlelight when it wasn't even dark, Carson was enchanted. "What is the meaning of all this?" she squeaked as he took pains to seat her.

"I wanted you to enjoy a hearty meal first."

"First?" she inquired, suddenly suspicious.

"Eat first, then I'll explain."

Her eyes were wide with wonder as he served her with great pomp, then took a seat across from her. "This looks delicious," she said and took a spoonful of lumpy potatoes.

After a passable meal, Kohl was right behind her, pulling out her chair. She glanced back at him askance.

Kohl smiled widely, which warned Carson that she should be wary. Feeling strangely awkward, she made her way back into the parlor and was about to sit down on a chair when he ushered her to the couch instead.

"Here, sit here," he said.

Gingerly, she settled onto the couch. Her stomach was roiling, waiting for something to happen. She did not have long to wait.

Kohl sat next to her and took her hand in his. His thigh pressed against hers, he was so close. A hundred butterflies took wing in her stomach. She gazed into his eyes, expectantly waiting, hoping, praying.

Kohl cleared his throat. "Carson, I know we've had our difficulties in the past, but you have not let those problems get in the way. You are helping to save the brewery and I want you to know that I owe you."

"Y-you do?" Her voice cracked.

"Yes. And in order to save you from a man like your fiancé, I have decided to go ahead and marry you."

Her eyes went wide. "You what?" she rasped in disbelief.

"I have decided to marry you," he repeated with a grin, expecting her gratitude.

Carson ripped her hand back, she was so stunned. "Let me get this straight. You are going to sacrifice yourself to save me from Sinclair, since I am helping you save your brewery."

"Yes. That's right," he said.

She glared at him for a long moment, too astounded to answer as her hopes crashed. The pompous donkey's behind thought he was being noble by marrying her! When rational thought finally returned, Carson jumped to her feet and shook a fist at him.

"You . . . you ignoble, contemptible, swinish, beast!" she burst forth. "How dare you think, even for an instant, that I would even consider such a . . . an . . . asinine proposal!"

Kohl was on his feet in a flash, staring at her in a quandary. He could not understand the outburst or that she was turning him down. "I don't know what you're carrying on so about. It isn't every day I offer myself up to marriage!" he shot back.

"Well, then, I guess I am supposed to be flattered that I was selected for such an *honor!*" she screamed at him.

"I'd say so," he bellowed back.

"Well, I'm not!"

He glared at her. "Why the hell not?"

"Because when I marry, it is going to be for love. Mutually felt! Not because some gunslinger comes along and decides to save me from a fate he considers worse than death!" She continued to holler. "Especially when I consider your proposal only one step better than death!"

"Oh, I see. I guess I totally misunderstood. One minute you are angry because I don't ask you to marry me, the next you're angry because I do. And now it seems you'd rather marry what's-his-face and be some pretty little bauble to him. You'd rather be treated like some china doll, set on the shelf and gotten out when he wants to show you off. Is that this moment's accuracy?"

"That would be more agreeable than knowing you married me simply as a sacrifice!"

Finally realizing he had hurt her pride, Kohl lowered his voice in an attempt to smooth over the situation before it got completely out of hand. "It's not exactly as if I'd be a sacrificial lamb, Carson."

She narrowed her eyes at him. "Well, I've got news for you, Mr. Newspaper Owner. The only way I want a sacrificial lamb is barbecued!"

"Well, if that's the way you feel, I withdraw my offer! You can marry what's-his-face with my blessings!" he snarled, his ire rising again. "Sorry be it for me to try to save you from yourself again!"

"Save me from myself!" she hissed, incredulous. "Why you! No self-respecting woman in her right mind would have someone the likes of you!"

"Well, what's-his-face is in for a big surprise with you, too, darlin'," he shot back, his own pride now wounded.

"Sinclair!" she shouted. "His name is Sinclair!"

"All right. Sinclair," he echoed sarcastically.

Carson snorted and plunked down on the couch, grabbing the old newspaper and using it as a wall between them to put an end to such a disagreeable conversation.

Kohl also took a seat. But he glared at the newspaper, more agitated than he'd been the last time he'd faced a man in the street. Hell, he'd just offered himself to the ungrateful woman and she had turned him down!

Then he cooled as he stopped to think how his proposal could have been misjudged. But he wasn't an eloquent speaker. What did she expect? For him to get down on bended knee and proclaim his undying love? By offering marriage he had offered his love. And she had rejected it! Her loss, he grumped all over again. Silently he had to admit to himself that thoughts of spending the rest of his life with her was not all that unpleasant.

Considerations of heading to the nearest saloon filled him until the door swung open and Addie walked into the room.

"Evenin'," Addie greeted sullenly at the sight of Carson and Kohl seemingly enjoying quiet moments together. They may be happy now, but she had the perfect remedy to put a crimp to such a disgusting domestic scene such as them sitting near each other, Carson with newspaper in hand and Kohl gazing in her direction.

A smirk on her face, she queried, "Have you two seen the latest newspaper?"

Chapter Twenty-nine

In a rare moment of triumph, Addie snapped opened the front page of the newspaper and held it up for Kohl to read. Her heart sang when he jumped up, ripped the paper from her hands, and read it with a tight expression on his face.

"What is it?" Carson questioned, curious at what could make Kohl's face turn so murderous.

"Dammit! I knew the newspapers would get a hold of the story about that damned march you led. But my own damned newspaper! I am going to wring Heimerman's neck for printing this!" he snarled, wadding the paper into a crinkled ball.

Carson was still angry enough at him to smile sweetly and say, "Well, it is news."

"Trash! It makes both of us laughingstocks, so you can wipe that satisfied smirk off your face."

Carson had not thought of that. She grabbed up the newspaper, unwrinkled it, and read the headline story, describing in detail the event. Her heart sank. Again, she was in the headlines. Then it dawned on her. The only way the paper could have had so many intricate details was if Beatrice Heimerman had given her husband the story. She wondered why the woman, who had accepted her into their circle with open arms, would do such a thing. Then she realized that Beatrice's loyalty was to her husband. "I'm sure it will blow over," she offered.

"Like hell!" Kohl grabbed his hat and stomped toward the door.

"Where are you going?"

"To make sure Heimerman never prints another story like this one!"

Kohl pounded down the stairs, running into three Masons going to a Lodge meeting. One man cracked a joke about the march, asking Kohl if he were going to join the women next time they marched on his brewery, since his partner had already joined them. Kohl grumbled a string of curses and continued toward Heimerman's to set the man straight!

Addie could hear swatches of the muffled conversation Kohl had with the Masons. Secretly, she was delighted until she glanced up and saw the troubled expression on Carson's face. Despite a vow never to get close to another human being again, Addie liked Carson.

Addie went to Carson and laid a tentative hand on hers. "Anything I can do to help?"

Addie was only a child and yet she was offering comfort. "Thank you, Addie. But it's nothing, truly."

"Then why you actin' so aggrieved?"

Carson let out a breath. "I came here to prove to my fiancé's family that I could be a proper lady. All I've done so far is demonstrate the opposite."

"That's nonsense. Why, you're more a lady than all

them old hags at that dumb old tea party put together end to end," Addie insisted. A thought came to Addie and she was shamed. "Guess I didn't help much at that tea, did I?" Carson smiled weakly at Addie and she knew she had to do something to help. Addie leaped to her feet.

"Where are you going?" Carson called out. The girl was constantly disappearing.

"To help out."

"Addie, I could use your help here."

"I'll be back. But for now, I got a better idea of how to help," she said and flew down the stairs.

Addie headed straight back toward Chinatown to spy on Gideon Farley. If she helped Carson get her inheritance back, Carson would no longer be forced to live in that apartment with that murdering g n-slinger. She could buy back her family home and be ready when her fiancé came to fetch her. Whistling to herself, Addie was pleased that she could help Carson out and hurt Kohl Baron at the same time, since it was obvious that Kohl was sweet on Carson.

To Carson's relief life returned to some semblance of normalcy and settled into a routine. Yet to Carson's chagrin, after Kohl had returned from Heimerman's, he had acted as if nothing had happened between them. They suspended work at the brewery. Kohl went to the newspaper office daily while Carson joined the ladies.

To her surprise, the woman's group seemed content to return to their charitable functions. Even Beatrice was most cordial, considering the fact that Kohl had fired her husband from the newspaper and he was now at home under foot.

As days went by, Carson knew she should be pleased that she was finally becoming the lady Sinclair expected to find when he arrived, but the fact was being a society lady was proving to be downright boring! She missed the excitement that being in the middle of things with Kohl had brought, and she missed Kohl! He left for the office each day at dawn and did not return until midnight.

But worst of all was discovering that he intended to move from the apartment.

"I don't understand why it is necessary for you to move?" Carson demanded. She felt as if she were being abandoned. Addie was rarely around and now Kohl was leaving her. She had never lived alone and she did not want to start now!

"Carson, you have been lucky thus far. Those wagging tongues you hang out with haven't caught wind of us living here under the same roof together. But if they did they would cull you from their precious ranks faster than a Washoe Zephyr," Kohl said, his arms filled with his few possessions. "Besides, I'm not going far."

"But what about those two men who tried to to . . . ?" She still could not voice the intended deed.

"I'll be staying in the brewery for the time being to keep an eye on things. And I haven't seen hide nor hair of them since that night. They're probably long gone by now."

"Probably," she conceded halfheartedly. "You will let me know when you'll be resuming production, won't you?" she asked, hopeful. "I should be involved since I am still a partner."

"Carson, you have demonstrated that you can be a lady. Coming back to work at the brewery wouldn't be the wisest choice for you," he said, hating himself that he was letting her try her wings. But deep down he hoped that she would come to realize how ill-suited she was for shelf-sitting that he was certain her fancy fiancé would intend for her.

He tossed the newspaper on the table. "Here. You might be interested in last night's edition. Seems those stagecoach robbers we encountered escaped jail the day before their trial was to begin."

Carson picked up the paper without glancing at it. "Yes. Thank you."

"Sure. See you around."

Carson raised her hand into a halfhearted wave. "Yes. See you around."

Her lip was trembling and she had to fight back tears as he strode away from her. It was as if he had just walked out of her life. Unable to stand where she was and do nothing, she ran to the window and watched him traipse the distance to the brewery entrance. Her lips tightened, and she turned from the window.

Trying to concentrate on anything but Kohl Baron, she spread out the newspaper and forced her attention to the story about the stage robbers. They had sworn revenge on those responsible for their incarceration before they had managed to overpower a deputy and escape.

A sudden idea flashed into her head and she quickly skimmed the article again. Without giving debate to the consequence of her actions, she flew from the apartment.

Kohl Baron was not going to simply stroll out of her life!

She rushed and bought a newspaper, flipping through the pages for further news on the escape. Then, tucking it into her reticule, she joined the lady's sewing circle as if everything was normal. She endured another afternoon of listening to the preacher rant on about the need to rise up against spirits, then announce his planned departure for another town, while she politely smiled at the other ladies and futilely attempted to stitch a torn seam.

At the end of the meeting, while Beatrice was collecting the sewn articles, Carson turned and slipped a pair of scissors into her bag.

"Here you are, Beatrice." She smiled and handed the large woman her work of the day.

"I can see you still have a lot to learn," Beatrice commented of Carson's efforts.

Carson's face never wavered. "How true. But I can never be accused of not putting forth my most concerted efforts," she returned. But she was not thinking about sewing. She was about to put forth "her most concerted efforts" into forcing Kohl to realize he did indeed have feelings for her before it was too late! Kohl was as stubborn as a jackass, but he was worth a last ditch effort.

Carson forced herself to be patient as she lingered at the church, exchanging small talk and politely accepting recipes from well-meaning ladies. Then, as if she hadn't a care in the world, Carson excused herself and strolled back to the apartment.

Once inside, she spread the newspaper she had purchased out on the kitchen table. Using the scissors she'd snatched from the sewing circle, she began clipping. Grinning wickedly after the last word was trimmed, she laid a fire in the stove and tossed the newspaper into the flames. Then she set about making paste from the flour in the cupboard. Once finished, she carefully arranged the words on a sheet of paper and glued them down.

She held up the finished product. "There. That should stir things up a bit," she said, pleased with her work as she reread the note:

WE TEACH YOU TO PUT US BEHIND BARS

THE BABBITT BROTHERS

"Now all I have to do is slip this under the door." Kohl was still at the newspaper office when Carson finished packing the few things she would need to hide out for a few days. She hadn't the faintest idea where she was going or what she would do once he found her. But at least she would be constantly on his mind, and possibly he would come to realize that she meant too much to him to ignore.

After making a shambles of the rooms to make it appear there had been a struggle, Carson threw a wrap over her shoulders. Bag in one hand, note in the other, she crept out into the yard.

After making sure no one was present, she slipped the note under the door. She drew the hood of her wrap up, so as not to be spotted, and hastened away from the brewery.

It was already twilight as she headed along Nevada Street. Without consciously thinking about it, she turned toward Lily's, optimistic the big-hearted madam would take her in after she explained what she was about.

Carson was humming to herself, quite satisfied with her efforts to force Kohl to show his hand before Sinclair arrived, that she did not notice the shadowy figures following her from a safe distance.

"Shouldn't we oughtta grab her now?" Jake, the smallest of the three brothers, whined.

"Shut your puss," Avery Babbitt snarled. "We'll grab her as soon as there ain't nowheres she can run to."

"Sweet Thing's mine when we do take her," Bart reminded them.

Avery swung on his two brothers. "Quit belly-achin' and stay low."

The three remained behind a big flowering shrub as they waited, totally unaware that they were not the only ones watching Carson.

Slick and Saul hid across the street from her. They were getting impatient being forced to wait until whoever was masterminding the whole thing gave them the word to move on the little lady.

Saul scratched his crotch, rearranging his balls into a more comfortable position. "Where the hell is she goin' at this hour?"

"Don't know. But if she keeps on a goin', she's gonna be all by her lonesome in a few minutes. It shore does seem a shame not to grab her if we got us a chance," Saul said with a knowing grin.

"You know, Saul, that's one of the most interestin' notions you had in a long time," Slick concurred and rubbed his chin.

"We could snatch her up and force her to tell us where she hid the key," Saul reasoned.

"But she don't know nothin' about the key, or so

she said," Slick countered. "Mabbe she was jest fun-nin' us. Mabbe she's knows all about it. Ya know, Saul, if we was to get it outta o' her we wouldn't gotta put up with the likes of Farley or that mysteri-ous partner o' his. We could get whatever that there key opens all fer ourselves."

"Yeah," Saul enthusiastically agreed.

"Okay. We'll do it. Jest as soon as she's away from them houses over there" — Slick waved toward the thinning number of homes — "we'll grab the little lady."

Saul rubbed his hands together. "Then we can have us some fun."

Slick smirked. "Jest as soon as we get the key outta her you can have all the fun you want, and so can I."

Ignorant that they weren't the only ones tailing Carson, the two men waited the first opportunity to move in and kidnap the little lady.

Carson strolled past the last house for blocks be-fore Lily's place. She quickened her steps intent on reaching Lily's before the madam's usual swarm of customers started appearing. She could not take the chance of being seen by one of the men who might blab her whereabouts to Kohl once he frantically started combing the city for her.

Carson was so lost in her own thoughts that she was completely unheeding of two groups of men creeping closer, both prepared to take her against her will by whatever force necessary.

Chapter Thirty

Shadows lengthened, stretching black fingered branches across her path as Carson hurried toward Lily's. Coyotes howled and owls began their night calls, causing her to jump at the eerie sounds. She stepped up her pace, suddenly worried what she would do should Lily deny her refuge.

"You ready?" Slick asked his partner from their vantage point, spying on the girl.

"Shore enough," Saul replied and slithered closer behind her.

Across the street Avery waved for his brothers to make their move. As awkward and bumbling as Jake was as he crawled to his feet, his knee crunched down on a rock and he let out a howl.

Carson's head snapped over her shoulder at the unnatural bay and she broke into a run.

"You fool!" Avery sneered at Jake. "Come on, before she gets away."

Jake was momentarily taken aback by the girl's cape billowing out behind her. "But she looks like some kinda bat!"

"I don't care what she looks like! She's mine," Bart bellowed.

The three brothers bolted from the bushes, openly pursuing Carson.

Saul started, wide-eyed. "What the shit?" He scrambled to join in the pursuit, but Slick grabbed his arm.

"Wait!"

"Whaddya mean? Those three's gainin' on her. If we don't get a move on, they'll get her first!"

"Shut your face and wait," Slick hissed.

Despite his agitation at having to stand idly by and watch the chase, Saul almost laughed out loud at the comic scene unfolding before his blurry eyes.

The skinny one, despite his limp caught up with the girl. He made a grab for her, but came away with her cape, causing him to stumble and fall flat.

"You bitch! You better stop afore I get ta ya, or you'll be sorry," puffed Bart, his boot heels pounding the ground.

Carson's heart knew sheer panic as she raced toward Lily's, still some distance away. But she made the mistake of glancing back at her pursuers and stepped on some loose gravel, turning her ankle and tumbling her to the ground.

Avery was overtaking Bart, but Bart was not about to let his brother claim her first. He grabbed his brother's flapping jacket tails as they reached her and both fell flat, two feet short of their quarry.

Carson tried to scramble to her feet, only to have Bart clamp a meaty hand around her ankle.

"I got ya now, sweet thing," he crowed.

Carson screamed, but her cries were quickly muffled as the other two brothers joined in hog-tying their prey. They made quick work of wrapping her in her cape until she could barely breathe. Looking like nothing more than a bumpy bolt of fabric, two of the brothers carried her like a log, while the third pulled his gun in case anyone passed and got too inquisitive.

"Come on, Slick. If we don't go get her now we'll lose out."

Slick scratched his ear. "Naw. I don't rightly think so. Them's such a mess a stumble bums that I think we'll just tag along until the time is more right."

Saul sulked, he was so pissed at having missed out on all the fun. But Slick had the brains, so Saul reckoned he knew best. Saul returned his attention to the men, rapidly disappearing into a grouping of trees off the road.

"Come on, we'll follow them." Slick motioned to Saul and they left their position.

"Hell," Saul complained, "now we's tailin' four instead o' one."

"Just shut up!"

The two men trailed after the three men as they hauled the girl past the trees to an abandoned house. The big one broke a window and hoisted the skinny one inside. Moments later the door opened and they toted the girl into the house. Then light spilled from the curtained windows, and Saul and Slick crept up below the broken window and peered in.

Saul saw the one he heard called Bart by the one called Avery grab the end of the cape and yank, tumbling Carson out of the wrapper like a blowing tumbleweed. Saul twitched at the sight of the big man hauling the girl to her feet.

He held her at arms' distance. "Come on, sweet thing. Give ole Bart a big smooch," he said and puckered his lips.

Carson drew back in horror when she recognized the escaped outlaws. Her plan to fake her own kidnapping had backfired!

She had been kidnapped!

"What ya waitin' for?" Bart snarled.

Jake laughed. "She's just shy, is all." He elbowed his big brother. "Let me show ya how it's done."

Bart released Carson and punched Jake in the gut. "Nobody's gettin' first crack 'cept me."

The fight was on.

Avery stepped between his warring brothers and took his eyes off Carson long enough to break up the escalating battle.

Carson saw her chance and darted toward the door.

Out of the corner of his eyes, Avery noticed the girl trying to make a break for it and left his brothers to duke it out. With a roar, Avery launched himself in time to grab Carson's skirt. "No ya don't, girlie," he snarled.

The sight of another man about to get *his* due, really pissed off Saul. He drew his gun and leaped through the window, breaking the remaining slivers of glass and landing with a thud in the middle of the fracas between the two brothers.

"What the hell!" bellowed Avery. He gave Carson a shove into a nearby chair and whipped out his gun.

As he was advancing on the intruder, Slick crashed

through the door with his gun in hand to save his partner from himself. Avery wheeled around.

Both leaders faced off, guns cocked and aimed.

"Who the hell are you, the law?" Avery demanded, thinking the men must be two crazy lawmen.

"They aren't the law!" Carson cried, recognizing the man. "They are no better than you three."

For some reason, Carson's identification and explanation relaxed Avery and he let his eyes flick toward his brothers.

Following the other man's line of vision, Slick also settled a gaze on the fight. Only his interest was on Saul.

The fight continued, only now there were two against one, and Saul was taking the worst of it.

The two men with the guns returned their gazes to each other. In unison they shrugged, tossed their guns, and went to break up the melee.

Carson watched as the two obvious leaders tried to pull the three men away from one another. Then her sight caught on the guns carelessly flung aside. Her chest rising and falling at an alarming rate, she kept her eyes on the brawling men as she inched toward the two guns.

She was just about to lay her hand on one, but Avery and Slick noticed what she was about at the same time. They leaped for her, bellering their outrage and causing the others to stop and rub their wounds.

Avery ripped the gun from Carson's fingertips before she could get a good grip on it. He clamped down on her wrist. Slick grabbed her other arm.

Then the tug-of-war began.

"If you ain't no lawman, who are ya?" Avery hissed, pulling Carson toward him.

"My partner and me been watchin' and waitin' our chance at the girl," Slick retorted and yanked Carson back toward his side.

"We grabbed her, so she's ours," Avery growled, tugging.

"She's ours. We been watchin' her longer," Slick growled back, yanking.

Back and forth. Back and forth she went between the two outlaws. If she hadn't been so frightened they'd all join forces, Carson would have laughed at such blundering. She was getting dizzy and felt like a hapless hare caught between two coyotes, a rag between two dogs.

Then the three sitting on the floor, watching the tug-of-war started arguing among themselves.

"She's mine. I get her first," Bart insisted.

"Not on a bet," hissed Saul, prepared to fight for her.

The arguing went on until Jake pulled a gun and sent a shot echoing around the room and causing all contestants to cease the debate.

Carson no longer was so frightened. Her arms ached and she was mad! She snapped her wrists out of the men's grasps. "That is quite enough!" she spat with such force that all eyes went to her.

She threw up her hands. "What is wrong with you men? I will not be fought over like a piece of meat!"

To her surprise, the vehemence in her thoughtless outburst seemed to have a cowering effect on them and they hung their heads. Not one to waste an opportunity, she paced back and forth in front of

them, lamblasting each one in turn for such rude behavior toward a lady.

"Now, I want all five of you to go sit at the table
and reach an agreement in a gentlemanly fashion.
They all stood, planted to the floor, looking stupid.
"Well," she hissed, "what are you all waiting for? Get
moving!"

She could not believe her eyes as they all took up
positions around the table and looked to her as what
to do next. "All right, I want each of you to present
your argument why I should be your prize." She
took up a position in a chair near the splintered door
and crossed her arms over her chest. She raised her
chin. "I do not have all night to sit here!" she chas-
tised.

The two leaders both began to talk at once, arguing for the right to present his case first. Then the
three others jumped in. And the argument was on.
While they haggled, they seemingly had forgotten
about her. Taking the opportunity, Carson edged
from the chair and absconded with Slick's gun.

As she lifted her skirts and ran from the house,
she could hear the ensuing heated argument suddenly come to a halt, and a high-pitched male voice
let out a roar. She dove into a bush and flattened
herself against the ground, watching boots pound
back and forth past her.

Carson held her breath, not daring to breathe as
they seemed to join forces and fanned out to search
for her. She tried to think whether she should make a
run for it or stay put. If she ran she was sure to be
recaptured and this time there would be no outfoxing
them, despite their apparent lack of mental capacity.

If she remained hidden they were sure to find her when the sun came up if they didn't flush her out before then.

While she was still frantically trying to reach a decision, the tattoo of the outlaws' boots ceased, and was replaced with the pounding of horses' hooves against the ground.

"Help!" she screamed and dashed from her hiding place.

"Carson! Carson!" she heard the familiar voice holler, the horse illuminated by the dim flicker of lantern light.

Relieved that her rescuer was Kohl, she skittered toward the warm yellow glow and thrust herself into his arms, panting.

Kohl held her to him. Her heart hammered against his chest, and he stroked the back of her head until her muffled sobs into his jacket slowed.

He had been frantic after he'd returned to the brewery from the newspaper office and discovered the note. He had rushed out toward the sheriff's office and had run into Addie, who had suggested he'd find the sheriff at Lily's. It was only sheer luck that he had found Carson. Then his attention caught on Addie, and he wondered if she had anything to do with his being in the right place at the right moment.

He was brought out of his contemplations by Carson. "Oh, Kohl, I don't know what would have happened if you hadn't come along when you did. Those men . . . the ones who nearly . . . the ones who accosted me and those stagecoach robbers kidnapped me."

He held her from him. "It's all right, honey. I'm

here," he crooned in a soothing voice. "Let's get you back to the apartment.

Carson nodded and found herself being lifted into strong arms and placed before him on his horse. Riding slowly back to the brewery, she let her body relax and revel in the sensations of being held safely in his arms. She inhaled the scent of him. And she secretly swore she would never try anything so stupid again, for fear that it would come true.

Once he had safely settled her on the couch, he straightened the parlor. "How about a hot cup of tea?" he suggested.

"Sounds good," she said, watching his long strides into the tiny kitchen. She heard him clattering around, banging pots and opening cupboards. "Oh Kohl, you would not believe the harrowing experience I've had." *I hardly believe it myself,* she thought. Fact was stranger than the fictitious kidnapping she'd originally planned. "I don't know what I would have done if you hadn't come along. Those men might have killed me . . . or worse," she said, shuddering over what they'd had planned.

Kohl had pumped water into the kettle, set it on the stove, and had picked up a log to stoke the smoldering fire when his attention caught on the floor. Tiny shreds of newsprint lay scattered near the chair leg. He scooped up the scraps and examined them.

In three strides he was standing before Carson, his hand out palm up. An uneasy sensation swooped over her as she examined the contents of his hand. Forcing herself to lift her eyes to his face, she smiled weakly at his murderous mien.

"And if those men who supposedly kidnapped you

310

don't return and finish the job," he growled, considering her earlier remark about her feared fate, "I just might."

Chapter Thirty-one

Carson swallowed hard as she dropped her gaze from his murderous face and stared at his outstretched palm. She had been caught by her own heedlessness. But she truly had been kidnapped; it had actually happened. She was the victim, not the perpetrator . . . well sort of. She had originally fomented the plot, but she was ultimately innocent.

"I know what it looks like, but—"

"What does it look like, Carson?" he inquired much too calmly, crumbling the scraps of newspaper he'd found in the kitchen and letting them drift to the floor.

She watched them scatter before her. Lifting her gaze to fasten her eyes to his, she offered, "It looks like scraps from the kidnap note. But I can explain."

Kohl raked his fingers through his hair. "Dammit, I knew it! I knew it had to be another one of your stunts."

"But it wasn't. Or, rather, it was . . . at first. I mean . . . I pasted the note together, but then as I was going to Lily's—"

"You were going to involve Lily in your scheme?" he

said, incredulous at the lengths she would go.

She forced a weak smile. "Yes. But as I started to say, I was actually kidnapped. Oh Kohl, the Babbitt brothers did kidnap me. Then those other two men, who tried to accost me must have been spying on me. They burst into the house the Babbitts had taken me to and tried to force the Babbitts to let them have me."

Kohl cocked a brow and crossed his arms. "And how am I to assume you got away from five men?"

"They were arguing over me. It was the strangest thing. They were all fighting, and I just jumped up and demanded that they settle their dispute like gentlemen. Kohl, believe it or not, they agreed. And while they were all seated around a table debating, I managed to escape and hide until you came along."

Kohl scratched his head. Hell, he didn't believe a word of such a story for an instant. "Carson, if the Babbitts had a single brain among the three of them, they're long gone by now. And as for those other two—"

"They did kidnap me!" she exclaimed, jumping to her feet. "They did! And the other two were there as well! But if you want to know the truth. Yes! I thought up the whole kidnapping plot. I pasted the note together and slipped it under the door." She was so upset that she no longer cared what he believed. Her voice rising an octave, she cried out, "And if you must know, I did it so you would finally be forced to admit to yourself you love me! I thought that if I was in danger you would come to realize how much I meant to you."

Fighting to regain her composure, she clasped her hands and sucked on her lip before continuing in a calmer voice, although inside she proceeded to quake.

"But I can see that I was wrong once again. I apologize if I have inconvenienced you tonight. Now, I am most exhausted. So if you will please leave, I shall head for bed. Good night, Kohl."

Kohl wasn't quite sure how she'd managed it, but he found himself on the other side of the locked door. If he had not been so floored by her confession he would have kicked the door down and paddled her for taking ten years off his life with such a stunt.

"Dammit! I do love you, you crazy woman," he whispered to the door before he descended the stairs and made his way to the brewery. He lay down on his makeshift bed with his arms crossed behind his head and stared up at the ceiling illuminated by moonlight streaming through the windows.

For most of the night Kohl thought of little else but Carson. He remembered their first encounter at the stage depot back in San Francisco, how they'd clashed immediately. Her efforts to help capture the outlaws and her antics after discovering they were partners in the brewery.

Hell, she was a most unusual woman. She was zany, constantly getting herself into some crazy fix. But that was one of the things that set her apart from all the other women he had known. And he realized that Carson would never be considered ordinary.

But then the thought struck him. She had not been a woman until he had made her one. In bed she had been willing, giving as much as she received. She was a warm-hearted woman, caring and loving. Who could ask for more?

Hell, he came to Carson City to settle down. To hang up his guns and start fresh. Part of settling down meant getting married. And getting married to Carson certainly wouldn't be such a bad proposition. Trouble was, he had already asked her and she'd turned him down flat. Then his thoughts shifted to her last declaration. She had wanted him to proclaim his love when he asked her to be his wife. She probably wanted to be courted properlike. Suddenly, he realized that he never could let her go.

Kohl closed his eyes and finally drifted off to sleep once he determined to go to Carson in the morning and declare his love on bended knee and marry the wild, crazy woman, even if it meant courting her like some silly swain.

Kohl was in a fine mood the next morning as he washed up in preparation for declaring himself to Carson. He dressed in his finest jacket, white shirt, and string tie. After giving his boots a last swipe with a rag, he whistled as he left the brewery and bounded up the stairs to the apartment. Even Addie's usual nastiness did not dampen his mood.

"Where's Carson?" he asked the sullen girl.

Addie remained with her arms braced across the apartment door, barring his entrance. Her face was a study in ice. "She told me what happened last night. Told you the truth, she did."

"Yeah, no doubt you saw the whole thing," Kohl returned and removed her arm from the door. "Carson?"

Addie wiped off her arm where he had touched her and glared at him. "She's not home. And as a matter of fact, I did see enough to know what happened last night," she sneered.

"All right, Addie, since you obviously don't intend to tell me where Carson went until I ask what you know about last night, I'm askin'."

Addie gave him a sly grin and explained how after she had told him where to locate the sheriff, she had scurried after the lawman out of concern for Carson, and had seen what had transpired, but by the time she had returned with the sheriff the house had been vacated. She told of the sheriff bringing her home and taking Carson's story, careful to leave out further details. And she told how upset Carson had been. "You can check with the sheriff if you don't believe me," she sneered.

"Addie, I believe you and I believe Carson. Now, I don't know why we seemed to have gotten off on the wrong foot, but why don't you just tell me where Carson has gone. Then perhaps when I return you and I can have a long talk and start fresh, what do you say?"

Addie's face twisted into a wry grin. "If you really want to know, Carson has gone to the train depot to see that preacher off with the rest of those dumb old ladies." Then her eyes narrowed. "But as far as gettin' to like you, pigs'll grow wings first!" she snorted and skittered from the apartment.

Kohl just shook his head. It was quite apparent she disliked him, but he was dumbfounded if he could figure out why. He didn't have time to worry about Addie's childish antipathies now, he was going to fetch Carson and propose.

Kohl jammed his hands in his pockets and strolled through town. He stopped at the sheriff's office on his way to the train depot and learned that Addie had indeed fetched the lawman and the Babbitt brothers apparently were still in the area. Kohl thanked the man and continued toward the depot. Although it made no sense why those other shadowy men were after Carson, Kohl vowed to watch out for her.

A short distance from the station, described by a reporter as the finest depot between the Missouri River and Sacramento, Kohl stopped. That trouble-making preacher was standing in a carriage, waving his arms toward a crowd of what appeared to be twenty militant women. Kohl needed no part of that. He leaned against a post after singling Carson out among the crowd, prepared to wait until the crowd began to disperse before fetching her.

"My dear friends, you have risen to the cause of temperance and my family and I shall never forget your efforts. Now that the seed has be planted, I must travel on to the next town to continue spreading the word. I trust you shall carry on with this important work . . ."

A train pulled into the depot, its whistle drowning out the fanatic and the women's applause. Kohl smiled to himself. At least with that man leaving town, things should calm down a bit. He waited another five minutes while the women surrounded the man and his family and escorted him onto the train with great pomp. Then Kohl sauntered toward Carson, who was standing in the rear of the crowd.

"Mornin'." He tipped his hat.

Carson swung around, her face a mask. "What are you doing here?"

"Addie told me where to find you. Thought I'd just mosey on over and escort you back to the brewery."

"Oh, you did, did you?" she said, apparently still peeved with him after last night.

317

"Carson, about last night — I'm sorry I didn't believe you . . ." his words trailed off as Beatrice Heimerman emerged from the crowd and descended on him like a vulture after carrion.

"What are you doing here!" she demanded. "Look, ladies, the owner of that devil brewery dares to show his face here," she announced in a raised voice.

The women started crowding around him, chanting and carrying on so that it was impossible to speak in a normal voice. "Will you come with me?" he shouted at Carson, trying to be heard over the women as he ignored them.

"I think you should leave!" Carson hollered back. She was filled with warring emotions. On one hand she desperately wanted to accompany Kohl; on the other, she was annoyed at how easy it appeared for him to suddenly show up and apologize. She made the hasty decision to remain and force him to consider her in a different light.

Hell, she seemed intent to remain in spite of the escalating anger of the crowd. His patience waning rapidly, Kohl made a grab for her arm. "You are coming with me. I have something important I want to say," he yelled over the din.

Despite the women's raised brows and continued caterwauling over his presence, Kohl continued to attempt to convince Carson to leave with him. To his relief the train whistle sounded again, which seemed to draw the women's attention back to the passenger car and the preacher, waving from his compartment window. They surged toward the train, leaving him and Carson in the rear of the mob.

On the edge of the crowd, Carson slapped her hands

on her hips. "How dare you come here and try to make a scene in front of the ladies!"

"Carson, can I assume that you are still a little peeved at me?"

He looked almost boyish and contrite and wretched enough that if he hadn't so adamantly refused to believe her last night, she would have softened. "More than a little would be more in tune with my feelings," she said.

"If I apologize again for last night and promise to believe you from now on, will you forgive me?" he asked, silently swearing that if he weren't surrounded he would have pulled Carson into his arms and shown exactly what he was about.

Only sincerity shone in the deep blue depths of his eyes. He was a hard man, not used to atoning for his actions, so Carson knew it took a lot for him to seek her out in the middle of such a hostile group of women and offer an apology. She shrugged. "I'm not one to hold a grudge," she said. "What did you want to see me about?"

He took her hand, his heart swelling. He could recall his mother holding animosity for days, bearing her anger in strained silence toward his father. Silently he was thankful that Carson would never do such a thing. "Carson, I—"

His sentence broke off at the shouting of one of the women. "Look, ladies! That man is now accosting one of our sisters!"

Kohl looked about to see where he could be of help, but as his attention was averted, the next thing he knew a parasol crashed down on his shoulder.

"You unhand her!" the woman yelled at Kohl. She

raised her weapon to strike him again. Kohl put his hands up to protect himself, but Carson grabbed hold of the parasol.

The struggle was on.

More women converged on Kohl, keeping him from disengaging Carson from the other end of the woman's parasol. Carson was holding one end, the women the other. Neither one willing to relinquish her hold.

Women started screaming, arguing amongst themselves and verbally tongue-lashing poor, unsuspecting porters. The woman with the parasol wrenched the thing free and took a very unladylike swing at Carson. Carson, not one to stand idly by and turn the other cheek, landed a punch to the woman's jaw, causing her to stagger back and throw three others off balance.

Carson watched helplessly, shocked at what she'd so rashly done, as the women appeared as dominoes, one causing another to fall. "Oh no!" she screamed. But when she tried to help the first woman to her feet, the woman instead yanked Carson down on the ground with her.

The crowd of ladies had turned into a free-for-all complete with screaming, as Kohl managed to stave off the blows meant for him and reach Carson. He managed to help Carson to her feet. Then he pulled his gun and fired three shots into the air, which immediately put a halt to the burgeoning fray.

Everybody stopped in their tracks and seemed to calm, licking their wounds. Wide-eyed, the women whispered among themselves and slowly moved off, giving the gunslinger a wide berth. Kohl picked up Carson's flattened hat and was just setting it on the mess that was her red hair when a voice called out.

"Carson! Carson Mueller, there you are!"

A wave of utter dread washed over Carson as she slowly pivoted around to face the platform. She took a deep breath and prayed that she was wrong. Surely, she had mistaken the familiar sound of the deep voice hailing her. A scraggly strand of hair hung over her smudged face and she smoothed it back, holding it in place as she searched the faces of the crowd.

Kohl's attention was also drawn toward the platform and a sudden wave of unprecedented fear and ire threatened to engulf him. It was a first for the hard-bitten gunslinger who had faced notorious killers without the dread or sheer besetment he was experiencing now.

"Carson! There you are!"

Carson's heart nearly stopped when she caught sight of the man waving as he threaded his way through the crowd toward her. She quickly crossed herself, shaking her head. This was another of her doings. She had written that letter and posted it in a fit of anger and now Sinclair was here in Carson City, making his way toward her, accompanied by his most intolerant mother and the finely attired Annette.

Chapter Thirty-two

Although the morning was still cool, Carson's cheeks flamed to match her hair under the approaching chastisement of Sinclair's pale blond glare. His face was set in hard disapproving lines; his mouth a mere straight swash, matching eyes squinting with restrained rage.

Carson's white-eyed gaze moved next to Constance Westland and her breath caught. The regal older woman appeared to be utterly horrified in her perfect rose-colored silk traveling ensemble. But if having those two witness her latest fall from grace weren't bad enough, Annette Appleton's unexpected presence only added insult to Carson's injury.

Carson's gaze swung to Kohl for support, but she didn't know whether to be pleased or frightened. His face was as black as coal and filled with something she thought akin to sheer hatred. His fingers were resting on the butts of his guns and it seemed as if he could readily draw one of the pistols and kill. It was an expression she had never seen on him before. "Kohl, I—"

"Carson," Sinclair announced, reaching her and cutting off her planned entreaty. "What is the meaning of this?"

"Sinclair, what are you doing here?" Carson gulped, and Kohl had all he could do to stop from launching himself at the overdressed dandy.

"Mother and I came in answer to your letter. Carson, you stated that you had succeeded in meeting the goals set for you." He swung out his arm the length of her. "But look at you! I demand—"

"No, son. *We* demand an explanation, Carson." Constance stepped forward and her talonlike fingers fastened on Sinclair's arm, her eyes roving disapprovingly over Carson. Constance let out a long sigh of disappointment and clasped a gloved hand to her chest. "Just look at you!"

And look was exactly what Annette was doing. She raised her chin and looked down her nose at Carson. Carson's curls were out of control underneath a crushed hat sitting at a near ninety degree angle on her head, and the flower, a bright red rose, was mashed. A smudge of dirt ran down her cheek; her white blouse was covered with blotches and had inched out of her waistband; and the patterned flowers on her skirt seemed wilted, suffering from her apparent excursion on the ground. "She looks as if she has been rolling in the hay," Annette snipped and let her gaze shift to Kohl and then back to Carson.

Constance swung on the girl. "Annette! That is enough from you. You are staying with the Westland family in accordance with your parents' wishes and that does not entitle you to pass judgment. Remember, you are here as our guest."

Annette dropped her eyes, immediately abashed. "Yes, ma'am."

Constance noticed the local riffraff staring. She was not one to air the family business in front of strangers. Taking Carson's arm, the older woman escorted her from the train depot, leaving Sinclair and Annette no other choice but to follow.

Carson shot a glance back over her shoulder at Kohl, but he had already turned away. Carson's heart sank to her toes. Whatever he had come to the depot to say had been lost. But if he cared anything at all for her, he would not have allowed her to be led away like a prisoner.

"Sinclair, run along and hail a carriage," Constance ordered, diverting Carson's reverie.

Carson felt awkward in Constance's presence and she made a feeble attempt to straighten her hat. "I did not expect you," she said in an effort to make conversation and absolve herself before the woman passed sentence.

"Nonsense. Sinclair answered your letter and told you when to expect our arrival. Why, Annette mailed it herself, didn't you, my dear?" Constance said with an air of superiority that Carson had come to expect from Beatrice Heimerman. Those two women were poured from the same mold.

"Of course," Annette confirmed with the faintest wry twist to her lips.

"I never received it, I fear. I was at the station with the other ladies from the auxiliary, seeing one of the ministers off."

"A priest, you mean, of course."

Carson knew she was about to drop another notch in Constance's eyes. "Well, no. But I can explain," she said in a rush, feeling awkward and schoolgirlish. She drew in a breath. She had not felt this way since leaving the convent and San Francisco.

"We'll discuss it later. I see we still have an enormous undertaking ahead of us before you can be considered acceptable."

The carriage arrived and Constance directed its loading, then inquired, "Carson, what is the best hotel in this *city?*"

"The Ormsby House is quite nice."

"I suppose it will have to do. We have had a most long and tiring journey and need to rest and recuperate after your rather unconventional greeting, to say the least. Therefore, we shall get settled and rest. You may meet us in the hotel's dining room for a late supper. This Orsmby House does offer fine dining, I do hope?"

"I believe you will find it quite satisfactory," Carson offered.

"That remains to be seen. Be there at nine." At that she flipped her wrist toward the driver. "Take us to this Ormsby House."

Carson watched the carriage rumble from the station and felt thoroughly chastened. She was still standing, her esteem deflated, when Kohl rejoined her.

"So *that* is what you are engaged to?" he commented darkly. What he did not say was that he had

325

recognized the man from the more unsavory dens in San Francisco. Sinclair Westland had cut quite a figure with the town's sporting population.

"Sinclair is considered the catch of San Francisco, I'll have you know," she snapped. Kohl's unkind remark about her selection of a future mate got Carson's back up despite the sinking feeling she had experienced when she had seen him.

"San Francisco must be experiencing its first male shortage, if that's the case. You can't still be considering marrying that whiny pip-squeak, can you?"

Kohl's remark was all she could take. Her face red with anger, she turned full on toward him, her hands on her hips. "I not only can, but I am . . . for your information! I made a fool out of myself with you. But I see now that it was only a girlish infatuation. I grew up last night. I am glad Sinclair arrived. Now that I have finally come to my senses I can get on with my life. Good day to you, sir!" Carson headed away without looking back, although the urge was near overpowering. Everything she had just said was untrue. But Kohl had crushed the last ounce of her pride with his cruel remark about her abilities to make a proper selection of a mate.

Kohl realized he had managed to hurt her sensibilities again. She had not seemed too pleased when she'd first recognized Sinclair, but Kohl had put her on the defensive with his comments. Now she would never admit she had made a mistake accepting that dandy's proposal.

"Hell," Kohl swore softly. He had planned to propose himself before that entourage had descended on

Carson. She was so impetuous that he feared she would go through with marrying the dandy that Kohl had recognized as a whore's best customer down on the Coast if Kohl didn't do something. But to top everything off, Carson was now furious at him. She would never believe him if he simply told her about Sinclair Westland and offered himself in Sinclair's place; he had already tried that once. His emotions a jumble of self-disgust and determination, Kohl headed back to the brewery to meet the shipment of malt and barley coming in today from Gold Hill.

Carson's emotions were also a mixture of confusion and fear. The only sensation she had experienced when she'd sighted Sinclair had been panic. Her heart did not beat faster out of joy that he had finally come for her; it had sped up due to dread of what would come of her relationship with Kohl. And to make matters worse, he had just stood there and stared while she had impulsively tongue-lashed him. Not knowing what to do next, Carson decided to go to the one person who knew about matters of the heart.

She hastened to Lily's.

"Well, if the devil ain't tried to have his way with you," Lily said as she opened the door and surveyed Carson. "My God child, you look like you been dragged both ways through a knot hole and back again. Come on in and tell Lily about it."

After Lily had shooed the Seasons out of the parlor, ordered tea, and got Carson settled, the girl poured out the whole sordid tale of the last few weeks. She told of Beatrice and the preacher, the train depot, her fiancé and her feelings for Kohl, only leaving out the intimate details of her relationship with him. Lily took her hand.

"Honey child, looks like you got some serious choices to make."

"That's just it, Lily. I have already made my choice, only he hasn't cooperated."

Lily laughed. "You mean Kohl Baron, don't you?"

Carson gave Lily a sheepish grin. "Yes."

"Honey, Kohl's run free all his life. He's like a mighty wild stallion. It's only natural that he's gonna resist somebody trying to rope him."

"But what am I going to do?" Carson cried.

"What do you want to do?"

"I want to remain in Carson City and marry Kohl. But I don't want him to marry me merely out of some kind of duty. I want his love. And I want him to think it is his idea," Carson blurted out.

"That shouldn't be too tough."

The corner's of Carson's lips turned downward. "It's well on impossible so far."

"That's because you haven't learnt the most important lesson about being female, honey," Lily advised. "Child, most men fight being broke to the saddle; they just ain't as difficult to bust as Kohl. That one's one of a kind. But if you're willin' to follow Lily's advice, I think that you'll have him roped, bridled, and saddled with him thinkin' it was all his doin'. And before he realizes it, you'll have him fenced with the gate locked."

Carson sat up on the edge of her chair, hope reborn in her heart. "I'll do anything," she said rashly. "Just tell me what to do."

"Well, this is what you need to do first . . ."

Carson's concentration was so locked on Lily that she did not notice the red-tasseled draperies being pulled back.

Gideon had been as horny as a heifer in heat and decided to take a chance and visit Lily's despite the risks. He could have made use of one of the exotic Chinese girls, but Gideon'd had a hankering for the kind of sex served up at Lily's place.

His lips twisted into a self-pleased grin as he listened to Lily advise the girl on how to gentle Kohl Baron. If the girl followed Lily's advice she would have the gunslinger so busy that Gideon would be able to regain control of the brewery before either the gunslinger or little Miss Carson Mueller knew what hit them. Then he'd get that key he needed and resume the life he'd enjoyed before that priest in that San Francisco convent had forced the girl on him.

Fighting down his rising desire as he looked up Lily's half-open wrapper and enjoyed the peek of leg, Gideon sneaked out the back door and headed back to Chinatown to tell those two crooks he'd hired to watch the girl what he wanted them to do next.

Gideon waited at the shanty he'd been forced to endure since Carson Mueller came to town and ruined his life. He swatted at the buzzing flies thick around the light and stumped on a cockroach scurrying across the hard-packed dirt floor. "Damn you, Carson Mueller! If you'd only stayed in San Francisco and married that wealthy man. But no! You had to come back and wreck my plans. Well, now I'm going to wreck yours!"

"You startin' to talk to yerself, boss?" Slick said coming into the dim little hovel.

"Yeah," chorused Saul, who held his nose against the stench.

Gideon ignored their attempts at amusement at his expense; they'd pay after he got what he needed from them. "Where have you two been?"

"Around," Slick said. He was careful not to let on they had tried to take the girl themselves, but that their failure had resulted in their joining forces with the Babbitts, and now they no longer worked for Farley; they were here merely on the Babbitts' suggestion so Farley wouldn't get suspicious.

"I take it, the girl hasn't led you to the key yet."

"We told you; she don't know nothin' 'bout no key."

Gideon huffed out a breath. "And I told you to keep following her."

"We has been."

"Then where is she now?"

Saul and Slick exchanged guilty looks before Slick's gaze trailed back to Farley. "At the brewery?"

"No, you fools!" he yelled. "She's at Lily's. If you don't get back there and keep an eye on her, you won't get another cent out of me, you hear?"

"We hear," Slick said, forcing himself from just upping and shooting Farley.

"That's better. Now get over to Lily's and don't let Carson out of your sight again!"

Slick and Saul both bobbed their heads in agreement and left Farley to rot in that stinking shanty for all they cared. They reined their horses in the direction of Lily's place until they were far out of sight of Chinatown, then wheeled around and galloped south toward where the Babbitts were holed up. They were no longer doing Farley's bidding; the Babbitts had made them a proposition they could not refuse. There was a lot more money involved. They not only would reap a healthy share of the loot from the job the Babbitts were planning to pull at the U.S. Mint, but get their chance at Carson Mueller as well!

Chapter Thirty-three

Carson was more than a little perplexed as she made her way to Beatrice Heimerman's house. Lily's advice sounded more like some of the harebrained schemes she had hastily concocted in the past that had backfired on her. But Lily was worldly-wise, so Carson forced her fears from her mind and squared her shoulders as she approached the foreboding two-storied structure built with sandstone from the prison quarry.

As Carson entered the yard Beatrice came out onto the porch and shook her finger at Carson.

"Carson Mueller, you have a lot of nerve coming to my home after the disaster you caused at the railway station this morning!"

Carson halted her progress. "That is why I've come. I want to apologize and throw myself on the goodness in your heart that you will take pity on me and grant me your mercy."

Carson hung her head, but watched from beneath her lashes as the big woman's face underwent a regrouping of emotions. This was one of the most difficult portions of Lily's instructions, since Carson truly had come to believe that Beatrice Heimerman did not have a heart.

Finally, Beatrice raised her chin. "Well, never let it be said that I am not charitable," she said brusquely. "Come inside, young woman, where you can offer a proper apology."

Carson followed Beatrice into her opulent parlor jammed with collectables. "Do seat yourself." Beatrice motioned to a striped settee and turned from Carson. The older woman's eyes glittered as she joined Carson, sitting across from her with her back straight.

After Carson had presented a formal apology, Beatrice seemed to relax and leaned against the back of her chair. Confident that her atonement had been accepted, Carson forged ahead. "You may have noticed the arrival of my fiancé at the train depot this morning."

"How could anyone miss such goings-on," Beatrice sniffed. "Who do they think they are?"

"I apologize again. My fiancé's family is prominent in San Francisco and were quite distraught as well, I fear. It truly was nothing personal toward anyone other than myself. You see, they had expected to be greeted by a poised young woman." Carson hung her head again before returning her gaze to Beatrice. "Instead, I disgraced myself."

"You most certainly did," Beatrice pronounced haughtily.

"That is the other reason for my visit," Carson said in a humble voice.

Beatrice cocked a brow. "Yes?"

"Since you are so well versed in proper behavior, I was hoping you would aid me to redeem myself."

Beatrice puffed up with pleasure. "Well, of course, I do know a thing or two about proper etiquette," she answered with her nose in the air.

"Then will you help me?"

"What is it you have in mind?" Beatrice asked, her interest piqued.

It was working; Lily's suggestion that she pay a call on Beatrice and appeal to the woman's enormous ego was working better than Carson had hoped for. "I was hoping that you and the other ladies from the auxiliary might consider giving a reception in honor of my future in-laws, so I . . . ah . . . you could help me demonstrate that I will indeed make a proper wife for Sinclair—my fiancé."

At last! The girl had just given Beatrice the opportunity she had been waiting for. She would finally see that the girl had her proper comeuppance. Her lips drawn up into a calculating smile, Beatrice rose to her feet. "The other ladies and I shall be delighted. Now, you will excuse me? I must prepare a proper dinner for my husband." *Since he now is either underfoot or spending time at that dreadful Lily's place thanks to that gunslinger of yours first purchasing the newspaper, then having the nerve to fire him,* Beatrice thought malevolently.

"Of course." Carson rose. "Thank you for being so gracious and understanding."

"Don't mention it," Beatrice said, her eyes glittering. As Carson left, Beatrice stood at the door and waved. The girl had just played right into her hands, Beatrice thought gleefully.

By the time Carson returned to her tiny apartment, Kohl was sitting in the parlor just as big as you please with his boots propped up, his arms resting behind his head.

"It's about time you got back," he said with a big grin on his face.

"If I had been aware you were whiling away your precious time waiting for me, I would have come straight back," she said, her voice virtually dripping with sarcasm.

"Actually, I thought we might spend the rest of the day together."

Remember what Lily advised, Carson. Don't readily give in to him. Let the rope out and give him room to wear himself down before you try to saddle him. Let him work up a lather first.

Despite a longing to be with him, Carson said, "I am afraid that I've already made plans, thank you."

She went into the bedroom and closed the door so he wouldn't see the longing in her eyes. Hearing his boot heels pound across the room, she quickly moved to the wardrobe and was pulling one of her finest dresses from the rod when he entered.

"Didn't you ever learn to knock? Why, I might have been indecent," she said with surprise in her voice.

Kohl's face was dark. "What kind of plans?"

"I beg your pardon?" she returned, pretending not

to understand.

"I said, what kind of plans is it you have today?"

She hid a smile at his obvious jealousy. "Oh, this and that. You know, things ladies do," she hedged. She was enjoying his displeasure, since it meant he was not impervious to her as she had feared earlier.

"What kind of things do ladies do?" he demanded.

"Kohl, I simply do not understand you. What difference could it possibly make to you?" She went on, not giving him an opportunity to answer. "Why, now that Sinclair has arrived, you have become the proud owner of the brewery."

"I owned it before that dandy and his mother arrived," he reminded in a tight voice.

"Well, now you are the sole owner. And me? Well, I must get on with marrying Sinclair so I can take my place as his wife," she said innocently.

Kohl was so mad he couldn't see straight through the red haze of his anger. Just last night she was telling him she wanted to hear he loved her, and now when he had been about to declare himself, she stood before him talking about marrying that San Francisco bastard.

Suppressing the urge to grab her to him and show her that no matter how hard she tried she could never get him out of her blood, Kohl took a deep breath. "You still haven't told me what your plans are for the day."

"Well, if you must know, although I cannot for the life of me understand why, I am going to go shopping. I am meeting Sinclair and his mother for supper tonight at the Ormsby House and I simply must look my best."

"I'll go with you since I have nothing better to do today. I've been meaning to do a little shopping myself. Now's as good a time as any, I suppose. And who knows, I might find a new pair of boots."

"That is unheard of! How could I ever explain to Sinclair's mother should someone happen to mention you were seen accompanying me while I was shopping? No. I simply can not abide your going with me. No."

The weather had proved most uncooperative for strolling about town and browsing in shop windows. The afternoon sun glared down, intensifying the heat and a particularly strong Washoe Zephyr threatened to take up Carson's hat and skirts.

Kohl was ladened down with packages, feeling quite like a pack mule and as cranky as one. And now he understood why she had relented and allowed him to accompany her. She had dragged him through every store in town, and some twice. But he had kept his tongue despite the urge to toss the bundles, tote Carson over his shoulder, and whisk her away to the edge of the river and make love to her. Why he ever had made the decision to court her in a proper manner he could not fathom. But Kohl was going to be true to his plan if it killed him.

Carson stopped in front of a modiste shop and stood staring at a dress form draped in the latest fashion.

"Oh Kohl, wouldn't that gown look perfect on me tonight when I meet Sinclair and his mother for supper?" she enthused, eliciting an even darker scowl from the gunslinger. "Come on, let's go inside."

Kohl grunted, but followed her into the fashionable business decorated in the latest French decor.

"Good day, I am Miss Tandy, proprietor of this shop. May I be of assistance?" Nina Tandy asked.

"I would like to see that gown you have in the window," Carson said, eyeing the small shrivelled woman with the huge round eyes.

Nina went to the window and began taking the gown from the form. "You have excellent taste. It is one of my finest."

"That is what I need," Carson said, "your finest."

To Kohl's snort, Nina swung around, the gown draped over her arms. "Sir, there is a chair in the corner if you wish to rest while the lady is being fitted."

"Here, allow me to help you with those packages," Carson said to Kohl, suppressing a pleased grin at his annoyance. She was enjoying dragging him all over town. And although he did not complain, it was obvious he was not used to playing maid and he was fighting to maintain his temper.

Kohl ignored her offer and plunked down on the chair, dumping the bundles on the floor next to him. He stretched out his aching feet and crossed his arms over his chest.

"Mr. Baron has been kind enough to carry my purchases," Carson said to Miss Tandy.

Nina settled an appreciative gaze on the big man, guns slung low at his hips. "You are most fortunate indeed. My customers' husbands rarely accompany them."

"Oh dear me, I fear you misunderstand. Mr. Baron is not my husband, but merely a business acquaintance. I am meeting my fiancé tonight. That is what the gown is for."

Kohl gave an audible snort, causing Nina Tandy to fidget as she removed the last of the dressmaker pins she had inserted into the gown to keep it attached to the form. "I apologize. Naturally, I assumed—"

"Naturally," Kohl grunted.

"It was an honest mistake, you needn't be concerned."

Nina shot Mr. Baron a weak smile before returning her attention to the lady. Then it hit her who the pair was. "Oh, my, you are the 'Gunslinger's Lady' from those articles in the newspaper," she blurted out before she noticed the black glare the gunslinger gave her. "I am sorry. I didn't mean anything by it. It is just that it all seemed so romantic." She sighed and hugged the dress to her.

"Well, it wasn't," Carson corrected, annoyed, which caused Kohl to smile for the first time since he had accompanied her shopping.

"Oh, I don't know," Kohl put in with a pleased grin. "I think it had a rather *quixotic* ring to it."

"You didn't think so at the time," Carson reminded him. "Furthermore, that was in the past. Now I am to be wed into a most prominent family from San Francisco."

Nina Tandy's face dropped as if a romantic fantasy had suddenly died. "I am sorry."

"I beg your pardon!" Carson snapped as Kohl chuckled.

"I-I am sorry. Please, won't you step into the fitting room?" she quickly suggested, changing the topic before she lost a customer.

Carson ignored Kohl's pleasure over the woman's comments and followed Miss Tandy into the fitting room. Fifteen minutes later the modiste pulled aside the curtains, glowing with pride at her creation, and Carson glided before Kohl, parading the magnificent gown.

Kohl's breath caught at the vision of Carson in the pale blue silk. His gaze roved appreciatively over her. Beginning with the full skirt studded with crystals along a draped overskirt, his eyes moved to the fitted waist. Carson's waist was so tiny that his fingers itched to encircle it while he pulled her against him. He forced the vision into the back of his mind. That time would come if he had to tar and feather Sinclair Westland first. His eyes trailed up from the bow at her waist, lingering on her full breasts before they stopped at the exceedingly low neckline.

"You are not buying that gown," he barked out.

The puffed sleeves on the gown nearly touched Carson's ears as she slapped her hands on her hips. "Why ever not?" she hissed, although she already knew the answer from the way his appreciative gaze had stopped right above her bosom and his lips had tightened. "The gown is lovely and it is a perfect fit," she argued.

"It is too perfect a fit," he growled. "It leaves little to the imagination and I don't want that dandy getting any ideas he might come to regret."

Carson raised her chin, secretly enjoying his displeasure. "I haven't the slightest notion what you are talking about."

"You mean you have no idea that you are practically spilling out of the top of that infernal dress?"

Nina stepped forward, her hands clasped tightly in front of her. "I suppose I could raise the neckline, if you would prefer."

"No," Carson said.

"Yes," Kohl insisted. "You, Miss Mueller, are not leaving this shop with that gown the way it is, and that's final!"

Chapter Thirty-four

Carson checked the diamond-studded pendant watch, which had been her mother's, pinned at her bosom. It was precisely five minutes after nine. She took a buoying breath and peeked out from the lady's powder room door in the Ormsby House lobby. Not seeing Kohl anywhere, she quickly left her hiding place and dashed to the entrance of the luxurious dining room. There, she stopped and smoothed her flaming upswept tresses and took a deep breath.

She had made it!

She had eluded Kohl long enough to make a grand entrance. Although he had not been invited, she was pretty sure he would be along shortly. Her hand glided down the pale blue silk and her mind shifted to earlier in the day when Kohl had put his foot down and stated she could not purchase such a gown. After returning to the fitting room, she had informed Miss Tandy, in a whisper, that she would indeed purchase the gown. She had instructed the woman to wrap it up and she would be by later in the day, unaccompanied, to pick it up. Kohl had been so pleased with himself once they'd left the shop without the gown, that he'd promised to make it up to her. Carson had faked pique, but inside she had been most satisfied. She almost looked forward to his reaction when he saw her wearing the lowcut gown; he would be furious!

Carson blinked as a finely attired couple swept passed her and entered the dining room, bringing her back to the present. She sighted Sinclair and his mother at a far table. To her chagrin Annette sat regally next to Sinclair, a gloved hand resting possessively on his arm as she said something that made him smile.

Without giving a moment's thought to how the Westlands would react once Kohl made a furious appearance, which she was certain he would do, Carson strolled into the room amidst appreciative stares and whispers.

"Good evening," she greeted the trio. Sinclair immediately brushed off Annette's hand and rose to slide out a chair. "Why, thank you."

Sinclair was beaming at her, his face holding an entirely different gleam than she had ever noted before; it was something akin to hunger. "You look absolutely stunning tonight, my dear," he said, his eyes roving over her.

Constance cleared her throat, causing Sinclair to redden. "You certainly seem to have *matured* in the short time you have been in Nevada, Carson."

"Yes," grated Annette, who fidgeted with her own high-necked emerald satin. "I am surprised at your selection of gowns," she added cattily.

343

"I think Carson has chosen well," Sinclair piped up with a squeak in answer to Annette's affliction, his eyes openly fastening on her bosom.

"Yes, hasn't she?" came the dark foreboding deep voice from behind Carson. Sinclair blinked and he adjusted his line of vision to Carson's pendant watch. "If you were wondering what time it is, it's nine ten," Kohl added in a warning tone.

Sinclair's gaze immediately snapped from Carson to the tall stranger he had noticed at the train depot earlier in the day.

Recognizing the deep, disapproving inflection, Carson swiveled around to look up into blue eyes as icy and a face as dark as a stormy night. In spite of her trepidation over his response to her wearing the gown he had specifically forbid her to purchase, she was pleased with his reaction.

Yet her breath caught. He was even more handsome all dressed up in a finely tailored suit, crisp white shirt, and matching jabot. "Why, Mr. Baron, whatever are you doing here?"

"Sometimes I ask myself that same question," he said and took a chair. "Don't mind if I do."

Sinclair sputtered, outraged at the sudden intrusion by the dangerous-looking interloper. In Sinclair's estimation he would not stand a chance against the man in a physical contest. But, of course, he was sure the man could not match wits with him in a verbal competition. Therefore, Sinclair was about to mount a protest, but Annette placed her hand back on his arm.

"Are you a friend of Carson's?" Annette asked in

344

a flirtatious tone. "I couldn't help but notice you when we arrived this morning."

"Annette, I doubt this person could be considered a friend of Carson's," Constance announced, scandalized by the man's presumption to join them without proper invitation.

"Oh, I don't know. What would you consider our relationship, Carson?" Kohl asked with a wink.

Carson suddenly felt terribly ill at ease and the neckline of her gown now seemed much too low as all eyes swung in her direction, the women leaning forward and Sinclair cocking his head back, all waiting for her reply.

Kohl leaned an elbow on the table, resting his chin on his palm. "Well, aren't you going to inform these *fine* folks exactly what our association is, and then introduce me?"

To add outrage to mischief Carson noticed him flash his brows at her—the insufferable man!

"We are all waiting with baited breath, Carson," Annette inserted.

"This is Mr. Kohl Baron. He and I are merely business associates," she blurted. "We were discussing business at the depot this morning."

Constance grabbed her throat. "Business associates?"

Kohl's grin spread the breadth of his face. "We were partners in the Carson Brewery . . . among other things," he added under his breath.

Carson slashed him a frown while Constance's face turned ashen and Sinclair's lips drained of all color. "You *were?*" Constance inquired, evidently missing his added remark to Carson's relief.

Her comfort was short-lived as Constance's chafed expression turned in her direction. "Then can I assume that you had the good sense to buy this man out?" she probed, shooting a clandestine glance at her son.

"Not exactly," Carson gulped and forced a smile. She thought they would have been happy to hear that she was no longer Kohl's partner, but their reaction seemed rather strange and totally unexpected.

"What exactly, my dear?" Constance demanded.

While Carson explained about her guardian, and how Kohl had become her partner, Kohl noticed their faces undergo a rash of emotions, which made him wonder if they were up to something.

Constance's lips twitched. "Did you get such an agreement done legally? For your protection, of course," she added quickly.

"Of course," Kohl mimicked.

Carson shot him a daunting glance. "We had intended to, but I fear we never seemed to get around to it," Carson answered and Constance seemed to relax visibly.

"We were much too busy with other matters," Kohl inserted roguishly.

Carson disregarded the comment while Annette hid a smile, Sinclair frowned, and Constance looked down her nose in an uncomfortable moment of silence.

Finally, Constance broke the tense moment so pregnant with question. "Well, there's no need to discuss business matters any longer tonight. Shall we order?"

Sinclair snapped his fingers and the waiter appeared, offering fancy two-page menus to everyone. Then the short stocky man stood back, pad in hand, ready to take orders.

"Oysters sound good," Sinclair offered, scanning the menu. "They are one of my favorite dishes."

Kohl grinned like a Cheshire cat over his menu at the dandy. "I've heard some men eat oysters because they think it'll help them be more of a man. What is it, Sinclair, you need them to function normally?" Kohl raised his brows. "If you know what I mean."

Sinclair bristled back, his mother and Annette looked appalled, while Carson hid a smile behind her menu. It was quite apparent everyone at the table knew what Kohl had meant.

"I should say not!" Sinclair snapped. "I'll have the lamb chops."

Not content to let the dandy off the hook, Kohl's eyes openly slid to the older woman and back to Sinclair. "You know what's said about the leadership abilities of sheep, don't you?"

Sinclair let out a huff. "All right, make it chicken."

"Chicken, huh?" Kohl cocked a brow.

Sinclair snorted, his level of irritation reaching new heights as he again scanned the menu. He narrowed his eyes at Kohl and snapped the menu shut. Triumph lit his face. "Steak. I'll have the steak. And make it rare!"

"A man's choice, to be sure," Kohl remarked with a straight face.

The waiter took the other's orders, then looked to Kohl. "And what shall you be having this evening, sir?"

"Oysters," Kohl said with a wicked smile in his voice.

Sinclair looked positively aggrieved. Then an idea of how to slash the man with his wit entered Sinclair's mind. "It is true that some men ingest oysters to function normally," he offered, thinking that would put the big man in his proper place. He'd know better than to parry words with Sinclair Westland again, Sinclair thought.

Nonplussed, Kohl smirked. "Oh that. You should know that old wife's tale only pertains to raw oysters. These are cooked."

Carson dropped her eyes and made a sudden study of the linen tablecloth to keep from giggling. But she sneaked a peek around the table. Sinclair appeared as if smoke could come out of his collar, he was so angry. Constance and Annette seemed to be distressed. Kohl obviously was enjoying himself, which had not been what Carson had intended. She'd wanted him to be jealous!

Carson leaned over toward Sinclair. Sweetly, she said, "Ignore him, Sinclair. Perhaps he'll go away."

Kohl grinned even wider, if that were possible. "Not until after I have my oysters. After all," — he beamed with a smug lift to his lips — "they're one of my favorite dishes."

Sinclair nearly spilled his water, Constance cleared

her throat, disbelief that Sinclair had been bested held Annette's face still as a statue, and Carson glared at Kohl.

The rest of the evening went downhill from there. Constance tried without success to learn more about Kohl's ownership of the brewery. Annette hung on Sinclair's every word in his futile attempts to put Kohl in his place, which only ended up making Sinclair look even more foolish. And Carson was wrapped in a mixture of joy and botheration.

Kohl was supposed to have been jealous, not to enjoy himself so much. Sinclair, who had always seemed so debonair and worldly-wise, ended up looking like an utter fool as he attempted to escort Carson to her apartment door, only to discover Kohl leaning against a nearby post, his arms and ankles crossed, making a big production out of watching.

"Good night, Sinclair," Carson finally said when it became evident Kohl was not about to leave her alone with Sinclair.

Sinclair glanced back over his shoulder at the big man. His annoyance evident, he shook Carson's hand. "Good night, Carson. Mother and I shall be here tomorrow morning to tour the brewery."

"But why?"

"Well, since you are going to become my wife, and your business interests shall become mine, don't you think that we should see what it looks like?"

"But I already told you, Kohl . . . ah . . . Mr. Baron and I had an agreement. He now is the sole owner."

"That certainly is not legally binding. Now, we

shall be here at nine in the morning. Do be ready. And wear an appropriate gown to tour the city in a carriage afterward."

She opened her mouth to protest, but he pressed his index finger to her lips. "Remember that a Westland lady does not speak back. Good night."

Carson stood at the doorway and watched him saunter down the stairs and pass Kohl with his nose in the air. To Kohl's credit, despite the fact Sinclair had meant to slight Kohl, he tipped his hat to Sinclair.

"Good night, old man. Sure enjoyed those oysters tonight."

"Humph!"

Kohl waited until the dandy climbed in the coach he had engaged and was out of sight before Kohl took the stairs to Carson's tiny apartment two at a time. Not bothering to knock, he barged inside.

Carson had already removed her gown and stood just inside the bedroom, startled, in camisole and lacy underdrawers. Grabbing her gown and holding it up in front of her, she gasped, "What are you doing here?"

He plunked down on the couch where he had an unobstructed view. "You knew I'd come."

"I certainly did not!"

"Then why didn't you lock the door?"

"Because Addie is not home yet," she said with outrage.

Kohl's easy grin sagged. "Oh." Then it reappeared. "I'm glad you took that damned dress off. Should have known you'd go back and get it after I told you not to. Have to admit you looked lovely tonight though. Good thing I showed up or it would have been wasted on the likes of Westland."

Carson stiffened. "You didn't come to talk about my gown."

"No, I didn't," he said and went to her. "But since I'm here, why don't we make the best of it?"

He tried to hug her, but she batted at his hands and fled to the door, wrenching it open. "I have no intention of making the best of anything with you tonight, Kohl Baron! I am an engaged lady!"

"Yeah. But to the wrong man," he grumbled under his breath.

Carson heard his comment, but did not respond. Despite the way he was acting, so cavalier, Sinclair's presence was bothering him. She decided to make sure he was *bothered* even more.

"Sinclair and his mother will be here tomorrow morning at nine to inspect the brewery and I must be ready. So, if you will please leave?"

Kohl's easygoing grin disappeared and a frown sprang up across his face. "What do you mean they are going to inspect the brewery tomorrow?"

"Sinclair said that since our agreement isn't legally binding, they want to look it over."

She shrugged for his benefit, but the fact was she had no intention of reneging on their deal and she could not understand why Sinclair and his mother wanted to assess the brewery since it no longer belonged to her.

"Wait just a damned minute," he growled. "I—"

With a smile, she shut the door in his face and

threw the lock, effectively shutting him out.

She stood at the door for a moment expecting him to pound against it. But to her surprise the only thing she heard was the beating of bootheels against the wooden stairs. Then silence.

Carson got ready for bed with a dozen things on her mind. The evening had not gone as planned. And yet, Kohl had been jealous. Sinclair had turned out to be quite different than she had envisioned he'd be. A smile hovered around her lips as she went and unlocked the door for Addie before climbing into bed. Tomorrow was going to be anything but dull!

Chapter Thirty-five

Constance paced back and forth in front of the Ormsby House as she waited with Sinclair and Annette for a carriage to take them to the brewery. It was nearly nine o'clock and she abhorred being tardy. Her body was withered from age, but her mind was still as sharp as ever, and she expected punctuality.

She huffed out a breath. "What is keeping that driver?"

"I am certain he will be here shortly," Annette answered, standing beside Sinclair in all her silky gray finery.

Constance shot Annette a daunting frown and determined to send the girl back to San Francisco the next time she opened her mouth out of turn.

"At last!" Constance said as the open air coach rumbled to a halt in front of them. "It is about time," she grumbled while Sinclair helped her into the seat.

He handed a silent Annette up and joined the ladies. Constance leaned forward and instructed,

"Take us to the Carson Brewery. And do not waste any more of our valuable time."

The bearded driver leaned back, undaunted by the disagreeable woman. "You sure you want to go there, lady?"

"Of course I am sure! And if you want to earn your fee you will not question me again."

"It's your business, lady." The man shrugged and snapped a whip over the piebald's rump.

Constance leaned back against the seat, a triumphant smile on her usually tight lips. "There. That is how one deals with underlings."

Her victory was short-lived as they came to a sudden halt a short time later.

Sinclair put a staying hand on his mother's arm. "I'll handle it, Mother." He leaned forward. "What is the meaning of this, driver!" he snorted.

"I ain't gonna go no closer to that mob!" the driver announced.

"What mob?" Sinclair demanded and stretched his neck to see what the driver was carrying on about. There, a short distance before the coach, marching down the middle of King Street, was a cluster of about twenty-five women, chanting and toting signs.

"Well, go around them!" Sinclair ordered.

"Can't."

"Why not?" Constance interceded in a demanding voice.

" 'Cause those women's headed for the same place as you all."

Annette's eyes rounded. "To the brewery?"

"Yeah. This is the second time that bunch's gone

354

against it, although there ain't as many this time."

Constance sucked in a breath, dismissed the driver after announcing they would proceed on foot, and headed directly into the crowd. Sinclair and Annette were left with no other choice: He offered his arm and they followed after the older woman.

Used to dealing with unruly servants, Constance elbowed her way through the crowd. Nearly to the forefront, she stopped and moved off to the side. Deciding to wait and learn the outcome and if it could be used to her advantage, Constance stepped back into the shadows.

"Aren't we going to the brewery and stand by Carson's side?" Sinclair asked, confused by his mother's sudden halt.

"Hush up and listen, you fool."

Sinclair's cheeks reddened that Annette should be privy to his mother's ill-treatment of him. To his delighted surprise, Annette was looking up at him with adoring eyes, which took the sting out of his mother's sharp tongue. Feeling markedly better, he turned his attention to Kohl Baron standing out in front of the brewery ready to face the angry women.

Kohl stood with his feet apart, his arms crossed over his chest waiting to be descended upon again by those pious busybodies. He'd had the feeling something like this was going to take place when he had taken receipt of the supplies so he could start up production again.

At least this time Carson was not leading the women whose numbers had apparently shrunk dramatically. He put his hands up and the women stopped.

"You have begun making that evil brew again! And until you cease forever we are going to keep coming back daily," Beatrice yelled to the top of her lungs, "until we have eradicated the threat your spirits pose to our beloved city."

Horse came and stood beside Kohl. "Then maybe ya oughtta start by cleanin' up your own house first," he hollered back.

"What do you mean?" Agnes Maplewitz demanded.

"Eh?" Kohl directed Horse to put the ear trumpet to his ear and Agnes repeated her question.

"Your leader's husband's spendin' his days . . . and nights boozin' and livin' it up out at Lily's," he hollered. His eyes settled on a horrified Beatrice. "Seems to me ya oughtta be worryin' about what's goin' on there. No wonder your man ain't stayin' at home where he belongs."

"Horse! That's enough," Kohl called into the ear trumpet. "Go inside and let me handle this."

"I was just tryin' to help out," he said dejectedly, then shot a glare at Beatrice. "That old biddy. Tryin' to stir up trouble here again, humph!"

Kohl patted him on the shoulder. "I know. Now, go on inside."

"Is this true, Beatrice?" another woman queried. The women seemed to forget about the brewery, seizing on the latest juicy bit of gossip.

"Well, Mrs. Heimerman? What do you have to say for yourself?" Kohl asked. He was thankful that their attention had been so easily diverted from the brewery, although he did not have a mind to send trouble Lily's way.

The women crowded around Beatrice until she wanted to scream. They were unrelenting with their probing questions till she could stand it no longer. "All right! Yes! My husband has been spending time at that awful woman's place. And he has been imbibing. But it is his"—she pointed an accusing finger at Kohl—"fault," she cried and pushed her way back through the crowd. "If he hadn't fired my Karl he never would have gone there."

"Wait, Beatrice," Agnes called out but the woman kept going. Taking over Beatrice's leadership role, Agnes raised her hands for silence. "I think our cause could better be served if we support our sister. Beatrice needs our help." She raised a fist. "We'll return to the church and plan a march on that den of iniquity. We'll shut down that whore's place!"

Kohl watched in amazement as the crowd parted for the woman like the Red Sea, and she marched in the direction from which they'd come, singing something about Christian soldiers.

Shaking his head, Kohl rubbed his neck as he turned to go back inside the brewery and get on with earning a living.

"Good morning," Carson said, standing at the bottom of the stairs leading to the second floor apartment, smiling shyly.

She looked so beautiful that she took his breath away and he stopped and gaped. Outfitted in brilliant amber, flowered hat with matching ribbons and crisp white gloves, she was the picture of social propriety.

"You missed the latest march on the brewery," he said once he'd regained his senses. God, how he wanted to skip the awkward formalities and take her into his arms and kiss those luscious full lips.

"I saw it from my window. That was a good idea Horse had, although I pity Lily when those women turn their energies toward her place."

"I wouldn't worry about Lily. With that preacher gone it'll take those women some time to organize themselves. Furthermore, Lily can handle herself."

Carson wanted to go to him and tell him that Sinclair meant nothing to her any longer, but as she took a step toward Kohl, Sinclair and his mother joined her, Annette trailing meekly behind.

"You look passable this morning," Sinclair remarked. "Although you might have chosen a more demure gown in which to tour a brewery."

"It is obvious that you still require guidance," Constance said. "Look at Annette." She pulled the girl forward. "She is the perfect example of an appropriately attired young lady of breeding."

In her starched blouse, pale gray jacket, and matching skirt, Annette smiled sweetly at Carson. "Good morning, Carson."

"Well, if you're all done with your misplaced criticisms, why don't you two take your pretty little puppet and go tour the city or something," Kohl said. "Furthermore, there is nothing wrong with the way Miss Mueller's dressed."

Constance bristled back. "Well, I never! Carson, are you prepared to show us this brewery in which you are in partnership with this person?"

Feeling awkward under Constance's chastisement, Carson looked to Kohl, giving him a grateful smile. He shrugged. "Go ahead."

Carson followed the others inside and stopped, gasping. The brewery was in a shambles. Sacks were overturned, chairs broken and the place looked as if it would take a considerable investment to get the brewery functioning.

"Oh no! Those men haven't been back, have they?" she screamed at the disaster that was the room.

"Horse's working on getting the place in tip-top shape, I'd say," Kohl replied, his face straight. Horse kept his head down and pretended to be sweeping.

"What men?" Annette gasped, hanging on to Sinclair's arm.

"The workmen," Kohl answered. "They have been helping to clean up the place."

Fighting back a smile at Kohl's ruse, Carson sighed. "I'm afraid it isn't much."

Constance walked around the room fingering the broken equipment and picking up the spilled grain and letting it sift through her fingers. She raised her brows and sniffed. "My, but it appears this brewery will require a substantial investment before it can begin functioning at a profit."

Kohl suppressed a grin. His last minute plan was working better than he could have anticipated. His gaze swung to Carson. She could have exposed his charade, but she hadn't. It gave him even more to think about.

"I suppose we could visit an attorney . . . that is if you are willing to authorize the funds which will be required to get the business operational," Carson said.

"But what were those women doing here if this place isn't capable of producing?" Constance asked, suspicious.

"There was a preacher visiting from Kansas and he stirred things up a bit, I guess," Carson answered.

"But didn't you say you were seeing the man, who was not a priest, off at the train station?" It still galled her that Carson had sought out associations outside the church.

"Yes."

"Then why were those women here this morning?" Constance demanded again.

Carson thought fast. "Because Ko . . . ah . . . Mr. Baron fired the leader's husband and she is a vindictive and unhappy woman looking for someone to blame."

Carson watched the wheels spin in Constance's head as she digested what Carson had offered.

"Yes, well, that was mentioned. Sinclair, I suppose we should have toured this facility before your engagement. Come, let's at least make the best of the rest of the day by resting while we tour this quaint village since we are here."

"But what about the business? Aren't you still interested?" Carson posed the question in an innocent voice, her eyes wide.

"We certainly are going to have to give it further thought." Constance pointed her nose in the air and

360

marched toward the door, Sinclair and Annette following like sheep.

"Why don't you try the lamb chops for supper?" Kohl called out to their backs. "I'm sure you'll find they fit into your way of life."

Constance stiffened but did not turn around.

"What about me?" Carson called out. "Don't you want me to accompany you around town?"

Constance stopped at the door and pivoted around, her face an ugly mask of displeasure. "Not today. I feel an enormous headache coming on. After I have given the matter thorough consideration I shall inform you of the conclusion we have reached regarding your future as a Westland."

"But the ladies are preparing to give a reception in your honor," Carson said.

"Well, we certainly cannot disappoint the locals if they wish to entertain us. It is only fitting and proper. You will inform me as to when and where this function will be held?"

"Of course."

Constance placed the back of her hand to her forehead. "Good day, Carson. I hope you will use the intervening time to your advantage and"—her eyes trailed to Kohl—"surround yourself with a more acceptable element of society."

Carson gave a half-nod, holding her face impassive until they had gone. She then strolled back and forth in front of Kohl, imitating Constance's walk. Then she doubled over, her face crumbling into a roaring giggle. To her further joy, Kohl chuckled as well.

"I do hope you 'surround yourself with a more acceptable element of society,' " Kohl mimicked.

They stood side by side laughing. Kohl grasped her around the waist and swung her around, then stopped, letting her slide down him. The mood instantly changed. For a long moment their eyes met and held, each delving, searching, suppressing a hunger to speak openly, for their pasts had been void of unconditional love and family acceptance and support of youth's forays into the courtship ritual and its accompanying disappointments.

Carson let out a sigh. Then catching herself before she threw her arms around his neck and kissed him, she pulled away and swallowed her urges. "Oh Kohl, I would never renege on our deal. The brewery is yours."

"I know," he said softly. "Thanks for not giving me away with the Westlands."

"They had no right to demand a tour of the brewery like they did."

"Jesus Christ, Carson, you aren't still considering marrying that pathetic shadow of his mother, are you? Hell, that proper dandy haunts some of San Francisco's lowest saloons."

"And how would you know?" she demanded.

"Because I recognized him."

"That doesn't exactly speak well for you either."

"I've never claimed to be a saint." His palms suddenly damp, he wiped them down his trousers. "But if I was a woman I'd rather be a spinster than be tied to that poor excuse for a man."

"Are you saying that I should forego my chance to

become a proper lady?" she said, stung that he could have suggested she remain unmarried, which in her mind meant that he needed another push in order to declare himself. He had offered to sacrifice himself on the matrimonial altar, but she had to have more than that. "Why, I would have to be crazy to give up Sinclair to Annette.

"You know, we were raised in the convent together and Annette has always wanted Sinclair. She is the one I told you about. The one who actually lit that cigarette on the vigil candles."

"What you were blamed for?"

"Yes."

She waited for him to tell her that he loved her more than Sinclair ever could and to let Annette have him. But he just stood there. Well, she wasn't giving up yet! Somehow she was going to get Kohl Baron to save her from herself — one way or another!

Chapter Thirty-six

Carson still could not believe it! Despite Beatrice Heimerman's embarrassment at the brewery earlier in the day, she had gone ahead with arrangements for a reception. A myriad of emotions warred in Carson. She cared nothing for stuffy social obligations, but then she realized her best chance to get Kohl to declare himself would be at the reception. All she had to do was to make sure everything went right.

"What are you doing here at this hour?" Addie asked, coming into the parlor of the tiny apartment.

"I live here," Carson answered. "You might try explaining what you have been up to lately. I hardly ever see you." Carson kept her face straight, although she almost had to laugh; it had not been that long ago that Mother Jude had said practically the same thing to her. The thought made her realize she was no longer a child.

Addie shrugged. "Oh, that. I been busy. What about you?" Addie asked quickly to deflect the conversation away from herself. She had been following

Gideon Farley, but hadn't yet decided what to do with the information she had gathered.

"My fiancé, his mother, and a girl I grew up with at the convent are in town," Carson said casually. "The ladies from the sewing circle are giving them a reception tomorrow afternoon at Beatrice Heimerman's home."

Addie frowned. "You don't seem real pleased. Ain't he what you want anymore?"

"Oh, Addie, you are wise beyond your years." Carson sighed.

Addie's face fell. "You ain't got your eyes set on that stupid old gunslinger, do you?"

Carson put her arm around the girl's thin shoulders. "If you promise not to tell anyone yet, yes, I do."

Addie flung herself away from Carson and stood trembling, her young face filled with rage. "You can't love him! You can't!"

Carson was taken back by the girl's virulence. "Addie, Kohl is a good man."

"But he's a gunslinger. He's kilt people. Innocent people!" she hissed. "He's a no good murderer!"

Carson knew the two hadn't seemed to hit it off, but the girl's outburst was totally unexpected. "Kohl has lived by his guns. But he isn't the type to kill innocent people. And he is not a murderer," Carson said softly. "Addie, if something is bothering you, why don't we sit down and talk it over?"

Addie held her box to her chest with white knuckles. "There ain't nothin' to talk over. He's a murderer and you can't love him! You can't!" Her little chest was heaving and she blurted out, "If you got your money back you wouldn't have to marry anyone, would you?"

"Well, I suppose if I had money of my own, it might make my choices less complicated." Carson paused. "But, Addie, it wouldn't change the way I feel toward Kohl."

Addie was only half listening and heard only what she wanted to hear. If she somehow managed to get that man Farley to confess and return Carson's money, then she could live with Carson, and Carson wouldn't have to think about marrying either one of those dumb good-for-nothing men.

"I hope you will come to the reception," Carson called out as the girl rushed toward the door. "Where are you going this time?"

"To get your inheritance back!" Addie flung over her shoulder and was gone.

Carson shook her head as she went to get her hat. She didn't understand that girl at all. But it was becoming more and more apparent that she was greatly troubled. The next time Addie made an appearance they would have that talk, Carson vowed. She plunked the straw creation on her head and hurried along to inform Sinclair's mother of the reception, and to invite Kohl.

Addie crept back to the shack in Chinatown determined to flush Gideon Farley out into the open, using herself as bait. Not bothering to conceal herself as she had been, Addie took a buoying breath and barged into the shack.

Gideon's head snapped up at the intruder. "What the hell?"

To Addie's surprise, the man was not alone. Her eyes registered five other big ugly men sitting around the crude table. To her horror, she recognized them as the ones who had tried to kidnap Carson and had stopped the stagecoach. "Sorry. Guess I got the wrong place," she gulped and started backing out of the dank room.

A heinous grin came to the skinny one's lips and he drew his gun. Pointing it at her, he said, "Stop right there, little darlin'."

"I got in the wrong place. I got to go," she insisted.

For his size, Slick was pretty quick. He reached out, caught her by the arm, and jerked her onto a chair. "Sit right down, young'un."

"What's you doin' sneakin' around here?" Avery demanded, taking over as leader.

"Now, just a minute," Gideon objected. "I am the boss, so I should be the one questioning the girl."

Avery snickered, a calculating grin on his face. "Shut your puss, Farley. We's been lettin' you act like the boss . . . up to now. Now, I'm takin' over this here operation. So, unless you want to be carried outta this here little hole feet first, go find a corner to crawl into and keep your teeth clamped together."

Gideon skulked into the far corner and plopped down on the narrow bed. His whole scheme to regain control of the brewery as well as getting the rest of Carson Mueller's money was turning sour since the two men he'd hired had brought those damned Babbitts into it.

Avery toyed with one of Addie's braids. "How 'bout tellin' us what you're doin' here?"

She glared at the huge man. "Nothin'. I told you, it was a mistake, is all." Avery gave the braid a yank and drew his knife, running the flat edge of it along the length of the woven hair. "Ouch! What you do that for?"

" 'Cause, if you don't up and spill your gut true I'm gonna start by cuttin' both them pretty little piggy tails clear off your head."

Addie drew back, her eyes wide, her heart hammering against her box. "I'm just a poor little kid," she wailed.

Slick hovered over her. "Cut the crap. You been stayin' with that there sweet little lady we's been watchin'."

"So what!" Addie hissed. Slick ripped the box out of her hands. "Give that back or I'll kill you!"

"You ain't gonna be killin' nobody. Now, let's just have a lil' look-see inside your precious box."

Addie let out a wail as Slick emptied the contents of her treasured possessions onto the table and sorted through it. He looked up, his face a study in disappointment. "There ain't nothin' here worth nothin'." He held up the silver dollar, putting it to his eye. "Why I can see plumb through it." He chuckled and tossed it onto the table.

Avery's interest in the girl heightened. "You think if we send a little note to Miss Carson Mueller and tell her that you got yourself into a heap o' trouble that she'd come a runnin' to your rescue?"

"No!"

"How 'bout that gunslinger Kohl Baron? You think he'd come right along with that friend o' yours if we was to send him a invite, too?"

"No!" she screeched out so bitterly that the others' heads snapped up.

"Oh, so you don't think much of this Kohl Baron, huh?"

"I hate him!"

"Whaddya know fellers, looks like we just may o' found us a little helper." Avery laughed and the others nodded their agreement. All accept Gideon, who sulked in the corner, worrying about what his partner was going to say about the sudden turn of events, and hoping he'd have an opportunity to show his expertise with a gun when the odds were in his favor.

"I ain't gonna help you," Addie scoffed despite her fear for her braids.

Avery shrugged. "Guess I'll have to keep this here little box then. It'll make a good place to stash them piggy tails o' yours."

"No!"

"What do you say, boys? Think this is fair payment for the young'un's stickin' her nose into where it don't belong?"

Addie was trembling as she noted the heads bobbing their agreement. Her ma had given her the box before she'd died and it hadn't been out of her possession since. She made a grab for it, but the huge man clamped a meaty hand down on hers.

"What'll it be? We can let you go without the box and that fine hair o' yours, or you can keep your scalp and the box . . . in exchange for a little help, that is."

Addie swallowed hard, thinking to get her box and run to the sheriff. "What do I got to do?"

"Good girl. She's a smart one, ain't she, boys?" They all nodded, grinning at her. "What's your name, since we're gonna be partners?"

"Addie," she said tonelessly.

"Oh, and by the way, Addie girl, just in case you might be thinkin' you'll get this here box back and then not keep your part of the bargain, and maybe run and tell somebody, I'll keep it right here, nice 'n' safe for you till you've fulfilled your part." Avery took a seat across from Addie. He flung the contents back inside her box, then tossed it to Bart before he returned his attention to the girl. "Now, here's exactly what I expect you to do . . ."

Carson sighed as she strolled from the Ormsby House after informing Sinclair's mother of the reception. The woman had announced they would meet her there and then dismissed her as if she were a mere annoyance. Carson shrugged, at least Kohl had been more receptive. Then an inner smile materialized on her lips; he had insisted on escorting her.

"Carson! Carson, wait!"

Brought back from her thoughts about Kohl and the Westlands, Carson stopped and pivoted around. She was surprised to see Annette hurrying along the boardwalk in her direction.

"Oh, I am so glad I caught you," the girl puffed, holding her midriff. "I was afraid I'd have to wait too long before Mrs. Westland wouldn't get suspicious."

"What do you want, Annette?" Carson asked stiffly, recalling her expulsion from the convent and Annette's part in it.

Annette's face fell. "I hope you aren't annoyed with me for accompanying Sinclair and his mother here," she said and her face took on a hopeful tinge.

Carson sighed. "No, I suppose not."

"Oh, thank you. And I want you to know how sorry I am about that cigarette and you getting sent from the convent. When I return to San Francisco I'll tell Father O'Clanahan I was responsible, if it will make you feel any better."

Carson stared at Annette. She seemed to have changed; she was more compliant and docile now. "That's in the past. Let's leave it there."

"But Sinclair and his mother—don't you want them to know you weren't responsible? Gosh Carson, if it were me, I wouldn't want the Westlands to think . . ." Annette's voice trailed off and she dropped her head before raising wide eyes to Carson. "I'm sorry, Carson, truly I am. About everything—not mailing the letter telling you we were coming, all the terrible things I've said and done—everything."

Carson placed a 'hand on Annette's arm. "You really are in love with Sinclair, aren't you?"

A floodgate broke inside Annette and she started

371

to sob as if her heart was breaking. "Oh, Carson, I have always loved Sinclair." She snuffled, trying to regain her lost composure. "Sometimes it seems as if he returns my feelings, although he is engaged to you. His mother picked you out two years ago when he turned from me, you know." She went on unaware of what she was divulging. "Sinclair said that his mother thought you would be the perfect choice of a mate since you owned that brewery, which could increase their fortunes, since Mrs. Westland did not want to continue to pay the cost of a middleman to stock some of their properties.

"Mrs. Westland thought you would be perfect, too, because you have no relatives, so they could control your entire fortune without outside interference. And, of course, they thought they would find you had truly become a lady when they arrived. Can you imagine their surprise?"

"Yes, I'm afraid I can," Carson muttered.

Annette was immediately contrite. "Oh, Carson, I'm sorry. I didn't mean—"

"No, of course you didn't."

"Then you truly love Sinclair despite all the trouble you've caused him?"

The trouble I've caused him, Carson thought bitterly before she realized it didn't verily matter what Annette had exposed. She had no intention of actually marrying Sinclair Westland anyway.

"Annette, the only one who truly loves Sinclair is you," Carson said, wondering why Annette would want someone so under his mother's influence. And wondering why she ever had wanted someone like

Sinclair Westland in the first place.

"Then why are you going to marry him? He deserves someone who is going to love him."

"Like you," Carson answered, skirting Annette's question.

"Well . . . yes. Like me."

"You are precisely correct. Sinclair does deserve you. You two deserve each other," Carson said, a little ashamed for her uncharitable thoughts toward the pair. But happy that she had discovered there was so much more to life and love than Sinclair Westland could have ever offered.

Annette's intake of breath was clearly audible. "Do you truly believe that?"

"Yes, I do."

"Then how can you marry him?"

"Annette, I can't."

Annette clasped her hands together. "Truly?" Then her excitement suddenly waned and suspicion sparked into her eyes. "If you truly aren't planning on marrying Sinclair, why haven't you told him so?"

"I suppose I just haven't found the right moment yet." A conspiratorial smile crept onto Carson's lips. "Besides, Sinclair's sudden unannounced appearance has managed to force a certain gentleman that I am interested in to stop and think." *I hope.*

Annette's eyes went wide. "You mean that gorgeous Kohl Baron? But isn't he a notorious gunslinger?"

"He was," Carson said staunchly. But she suddenly realized that it didn't matter what Kohl did to earn a living, she would love him anyway.

Hope glittered into Annette's eyes. "Do you love him?"

"If you promise not to say anything to anyone . . ." Annette hurriedly made an "x" across her heart. ". . . yes. I love Kohl Baron."

"He sure does seem to be protective of you. Do you think he feels the same way?"

"Yes."

"Has he told you he loves you?"

"Not exactly. But if he truly thinks he is going to lose me to Sinclair, he will declare himself. I just know it."

Annette's face looked trouble. "I sure hope you know what you're doing, and it doesn't backfire on you."

Despite the niggling fear that had been surrounding Carson that that very thing could happen, she raised her chin to demonstrate her assuredness. "Don't worry. Nothing can go wrong. Once Kohl sees how close he is coming to losing me tomorrow at the reception, he'll declare himself. There is not a doubt in my mind."

Chapter Thirty-seven

Kohl stood with his heel up on a keg, swiping a rag back and forth across his boot with a vengeance. He was so engrossed in thoughts of Carson and that dandy that he didn't hear Horse come up behind him and set the copper measure down.

"You keep at it the way you're doin' and you won't have no boot left pretty soon," Horse hollered.

Kohl ignored the old man and kept on buffing his boot.

"What you gettin' all spruced up fer?"

Kohl tossed the rag aside and faced the old man. "You're a persistent old coot. If you must know, I'm escorting Carson to a reception for her fiancé."

Horse scrunched up his face and plugged the funnel end of the ear trumpet into his ear. "I hear ya right? You gonna escort our little Sunny instead of that Westland feller she's plannin' on gettin' hitched up with?"

"You heard right, old man."

Horse scratched his head. "Can't rightly figger it. Sunny's suppose to marry that mama's boy. Yet she's got such a hankerin' fer you that anybody with eyes in his sockets can reckon it. And you! You stand by and allow it, and yet you're no better off than Sunny. No. It just don't figger none atoll. Why don't ya just stand up and let her know she ain't gonna marry nobody but you. It's what ya both want."

"And why don't you just up and mind your own damn business?"

Horse ignored the big man's scowl. " 'Cause o' your pigheaded pride, ain't it?"

Kohl's face turned dark and he fingered his guns. "Be careful, old man."

"You ain't gonna scare me. Past gunslinger or not, you ain't the sort to go after a old geezer like me."

"Oh, hell," Kohl swore. "Why don't you get out of here and leave me in peace."

"Boy, you ain't gonna have no peace till you make that little gal your own." A wide grin split his lips and he chuckled. " 'Course, with Sunny, can't rightly say that life'll ever be peaceful."

Kohl rubbed his mouth to keep the old man from seeing the smile lurking about his lips. For despite his irritation with Horse over the old man's too close observation, Kohl had already admitted to himself that life with Carson would no doubt always be interesting, to say the least.

"I've said my piece. Guess I'll be leavin' ya to chaw on them little words o' wisdom." He shook his finger at Kohl. "Just don't let your pride get stuck in your throat or it's likely to choke ya."

Kohl rolled his eyes as he watched the old man

hobble from the brewery. But inside what Horse had said gave him something to consider while he brushed his thick black curls and slid his long arms into his best jacket.

Hell, he had planned to ask her to marry him, went to meet her, in fact. Then, before he could get her aside and tell her what was in his heart, she nearly caused a riot and then that dandy and his mother showed up to further complicate things.

He was straightening his tie when Horse's words echoed in his ears. *Don't let that pride get stuck in your throat or it's likely to choke ya.* But hell, he had to know that Carson wanted him, only him. He had been waiting, hoping she would come to him after he'd showed her exactly what a dandy Sinclair Westland was. Instead, she seemed to be clinging to that damned notion about being a fine lady.

Carson's voice jerked him back to the reality of their situation when she called out, "Kohl? I couldn't wait for you any longer. Are you ready? We're late. Sinclair and his mother are probably already there."

For an instant Kohl thought his own fantasy had just come true; Carson had come to him. Then he heard the name Sinclair and his hope crashed in flames the color of her glorious hair.

"I'm coming," he answered less than enthusiastically.

Carson looped her arm with Kohl's. The fresh scent of early summer roses encircled her, and he had all he could do not to crush her to him. As they strolled to the barn the pressure of her hand on his arm, coupled with the heat of her nearness built inside him until all the pent-up feelings exploded.

His arm shot out and he whipped her into his embrace, his warm, moist breath hot on her neck. Carson could feel the uneven rhythm of his heart drumming against her, and her breast filled with longing and anticipation. She squeezed her eyes shut and waited, afraid she would cry if he didn't come through.

The next thing she knew, she felt herself being lifted in strong arms. Her eyes flew open. He was striding with her into the barn. "W-what are you doing?" she ventured.

"Don't talk. This time I want you to listen," he said and set her on a bale of hay.

To her secret delight, he turned from her and shut the barn doors. Returning to her, he pulled her to her feet with "Oh God, Carson," and crushed her against his hard chest again and held her to him for a long moment as if he were melding them together for all time. Then he took a half step back.

Searching her face, his hands tossed her hat aside and unpinned her hair, letting the heavy carmine waves drape over his fingers. Lifting a handful of the spun vermilion, he stroked it along his cheek before he bent his head and nuzzled his nose against her ear. "You are so beautiful," he murmured.

It was now or never, she thought, her heart slamming against her chest. "Shouldn't we be going?"

He cradled her face between his palms. "I can't take you to him."

She fought for a breath to ask, "Why not?"

He started raining kisses all over her face with an urgency before unknown to him. He had always been the patient predator, cautiously waiting until his opponent was thrown off balance in his rush to emerge the victor. And now, here he was unable to wait any longer for her to come to him and make this his victory.

He kissed her eyelids, her nose. "Because you are mine." He kissed her cheeks, her chin. "You will never belong to another." He kissed her mouth, long and hard. "Not as long as I draw breath. Do you hear me?"

Despite a determination to force a proposal from him before responding, her arms snaked up along his chest and wound around his neck. She tried to swallow down the question burning on her tongue, and managed, "I hear you."

"And you are going to be my wife just as soon as I can round up a preacher to make it legal," he rushed forth.

To his dread she pulled out of his arms and stepped back, dropping fists on her hips.

Keeping her face irresolute, she said, "Kohl Baron, that is the darnedest proposal a girl ever had."

He couldn't believe his ears. Here he was declaring himself, baring his heart and soul to the woman, and she was annoyed with the way he was proposing! He threw up his hands. "What do you mean that is the darnedest proposal a girl ever had?"

"That isn't exactly the way I had envisioned being

proposed to," she announced, discounting the first time he had offered himself. He was acting like a wounded bear! And after all the time she had been waiting for him to finally get around to proposing properly!

"I haven't exactly made a habit out of offering my name to women before."

"I should hope not!"

He narrowed his eyes, his jealousy threatening to get the better of him. "And I suppose that dandy Westland got down on bended knee and took your hand in his and slobbered all over it."

Carson blinked at the memory of Sinclair's proposal. "That is not exactly how it happened," she said weakly, her lip trembled. "If you truly must know, Sinclair came to me and announced that he and his mother had discussed it and decided that we should marry."

Hearing her confession, Kohl's anger abated and he got down on bended knee and took her hand. "I'm not too good at this, and I don't promise to always do the right thing. But this do I promise you, if you'll consent to marry me . . ." He swallowed the lump, making such a proposal so difficult. ". . . I'll protect you with my life; I'll—"

Carson threw herself into his arms, knocking him backward into the hay scattered over the ground and cutting off the rest of his declaration with her lips on his.

Kohl's eyes were wide and his arms went around the crazy, wonderful young woman. He was reveling in the taste of her lips on his when she suddenly pulled back and propped herself up on her hands. "You'll never let me go, will you?"

"I think I already said that."

She smiled down at him. "Well, say it again. I love to hear it."

He ran his fingers through her hair. "You'll always be mine."

"Then what are you waiting for? Kiss me and make love to me."

Kohl needed no further invitation. His lips captured hers in a grinding, searing kiss. His hands roved over her back, down, down, until he held her buttocks tight against his rising desire. With finesse, he laid her on her back in the soft straw and kissed the long column of her neck. Then he sat back.

Carson leaned up on her elbows. "Why did you stop?" she crooned in a saucy voice.

He winked. "Don't worry, I haven't even begun yet. But first I'm going to make this engagement official."

Carson watched him remove the plain gold band he wore on his little finger. Her breath caught as his lips took her ring finger into his mouth and he kissed the tip of it. He slowly slid the ring down the length of her finger and she shivered with emotion.

"There. Now it is official," he murmured.

Carson's vision was pinned to the ring and she touched it with reverence. "It is beautiful."

"It was my grandmother's. My grandfather gave it

to her the night he proposed. So it should become yours."

Nearly overcome with emotion, Carson cupped his face and kissed him. "Thank you. Now make love to me before I'm forced to attack you."

A hearty chuckle escaped him and he shook his head. "You are full of surprises."

Not wasting another minute, Kohl slowly undid the buttons of her ruffled blouse and bared her to his heated gaze while he murmured how silken her skin felt beneath his touch.

A gasp escaped her when she felt his lips fasten on a peaked nipple, and she arched her back, wanting him to devour her. Not taking his mouth from her, he managed to slip her blouse from her waistband and slide the garment off her shoulders.

Carson's senses heightened as his tongue swirled around the rose-colored nipples and she tore at his shirt, nearly severing the buttons from the fabric.

Kohl sat up. "You really are a little wildcat," he said and shed the near-ruined shirt. "Never had a woman rip the shirt off my back before."

She smiled up at him. "I'll make a note to see to it regularly from now on."

"Mmm. Very regularly."

He angled his body along hers and she pressed a hand against his arousal, eliciting a groan from deep within his throat.

"Don't stop with your shirt," she whispered, her voice thick with excitement.

"Never let it be said that I don't follow your dictates," he answered and removed the remainder of his clothing. "And never let it be said that you don't follow mine. Take off your skirt and stockings for me."

His voice held a command which brooked no other response. Her lids heavy with awareness of his strong, corded masculine body, her craving was so deep within the center of her being, so overwhelming, that Carson did not hesitate. She raised up on her knees, unhooked the waistband and let the pale green skirt slip down her thighs. Then she lay back and raising one thigh at a time, rolled her stockings down her legs, and cast off her drawers. She opened her arms to Kohl who had been watching her closely.

He was so near to exploding just watching her disrobe for him that he had to make a conscious effort to prolong their mating ritual. He wanted this time to be memorable.

"Spread your thighs for me, Carson. I want to know all of you."

Carson watched his blue eyes deepened to near indigo as she opened for him and she gasped when he bent over her and kissed his way from the hollow of her stomach through her woman's curls to bury his face in her woman's core. She writhed against such a sensuous onslaught, captured by sensations so strong, so convulsing that she whimpered, straining against him.

"That's right, baby, let me know what I do to you," he murmured and returned his attentions to driving her wildly beyond herself.

"Oh, please, please, stop; it feels so incredible that I can hardly stand it," she begged.

His hand replaced his lips and he crooned. "Then let yourself go."

She cried out as the spasms grabbed her and she clawed at him, panting and clamping her legs together. His possession was nearly complete and she grasped at him. "I need to have you inside me. Please, now," she moaned.

"Carson . . ." Her name came out heavy and raspy from his need.

Kohl positioned himself between her thighs, bent over and kissed her. Carson closed her eyes and reveled in the pure sensations. She could taste herself on his mouth and felt him part her woman's lips and ease his length into her. He throbbed within her. Potent, mind-bending sensations imprinted the power of his total possession of her in her heart.

She wrapped her thighs around his waist and moved against him, their rhythm building, expanding, spreading, burgeoning forth through her consciousness until she was no longer aware of anything but the intense heat thrusting her toward that all-consuming precipice. Then suddenly she tumbled over the edge and wave after convulsing wave grasped her and she cried out her release.

Then and only then did Kohl allow his own release and he poured himself into her, holding her to him with all his strength.

"I love you," he murmured and flopped onto his side, cradling her drenched body against his. "I'll love you for all time and eternity."

Before Carson could reveal all that was in her heart the barn door slammed open with such force that their heads snapped toward the swinging door.

Chapter Thirty-eight

A dust devil fiercely danced into the barn through the swinging doors, and Carson and Kohl both let out a sigh of relief and laughed.

"It's only a Washoe Zephyr," he announced.

"Yes." She reached for her clothing. "Oh, Kohl, we're terribly late."

He rose up on his elbow, watching her don all those feminine underthings. "For what?" he asked, suggestion ripe in his voice.

Carson forced herself to ignore the urge to rejoin him. "We must attend the reception."

Kohl's easy grin disappeared. "There's no longer any reason to go appear before those old biddies."

"But there is. I want everyone to know how happy I am." Then her smile faded. "And I must tell Sinclair that I can't marry him."

"He'll get the message when you don't show up," Kohl argued.

"I know. But you are a prominent member of the community now whether you like it or not. Furthermore, you don't want all those women picketing the brewery again." Her face brightened and a gleam sparked into her eyes. "I have an idea which will help keep them from coming back."

"Oh?" Kohl rose and yanked on his clothes. He was disappointed, but had to admit she was right about attending that damned reception.

"I was thinking that we could open a restaurant and brew beer to serve to our customers."

He looked skeptical. "I don't know the first thing about serving food, and I doubt that you do either, the way you cook."

She sat down and tugged on her shoes. "But don't you see, a restaurant will bring in people from all over the community . . . families, not merely men. The women object to their men leaving them at home while they go out. So a nice restaurant that serves beef from neighboring ranches and at the same time serves our brewed beer will satisfy the men and the women."

Kohl fussed with his tie. "You might just have a point. I'll consider it."

A big grin came to her lips. She had set out her idea without first trying to rashly implement it and he had listened and responded favorably. It gave her something to mull over, and she decided that she would try to talk things over with him from now on.

"Are you ready?"

"Not really, but let's go get this over with."

Carson heard giggles coming from inside Beatrice Heimerman's home as they approached the front

387

gate. "It seems rather unusual to hear laughter at one of Beatrice Heimerman's functions," she said to Kohl.

"Maybe she couldn't attend."

Carson batted at his hand. "Oh, Kohl, do try to be serious."

Kohl reluctantly let her pull away. "Who says I'm not?"

She cast him a cute frown and pranced to the door ahead of him. But as she reached the entrance and the door opened, Carson's spirits plummeted. She clasped a hand to her mouth, her eyes as big as shattered dinner plates.

She turned away from the door and Kohl caught her in his arms. She was trembling. He searched her distraught face. "What's wrong?"

Kohl's head snapped up at the smug sound of Beatrice's voice. "Aren't you coming inside? After all, this reception is being given in your honor to allow your future mother-in-law to see the type of daughter-in-law she will be getting."

Kohl gazed into Carson's troubled face. "If you don't want to go in, we can leave."

Carson gathered herself together. "No." Raising her chin, she walked through the door to face all the vulturous eyes watching her.

When Kohl followed Carson inside he was tempted to shoot that rotten Beatrice Heimerman, who stood off to the side next to Constance Westland, grinning like a triumphant predator. But Carson shook her head, her eyes beseeching him to allow her to handle it.

Reluctantly remaining where he was, Kohl fought down the urge to intercede and perused the parlor. It was decorated in large red tassels with red paper wrapped around the lamps to give the room a crimson glow. Red velvet had been hastily draped over the furniture and empty beer bottles adorned the refreshment table.

"Carson Mueller, I demand an explanation!" Constance's voice boomed out and the woman, although tiny, bore down on Carson like the wrath of creation. "I demand to be told what is going on here?" She flipped her wrist toward Beatrice. "That person said you would be able to explain such a lurid display."

Carson's gaze trailed to the ugly twist on Beatrice's lips before returning to settle on Constance. "I believe Mrs. Heimerman has prepared a reception for you in hope that you would find me utterly lacking," Carson announced, not about to let any of the horrid women see how close to tears she was.

"And I fear that Mrs. Heimerman is correct, in that regard," Constance said stiffly. Then her superior, daunting glare bore into Beatrice Heimerman. "Although, with this . . . display . . . the hostess has shown that she is the one totally lacking in social etiquette herself and has done no more than reflect on her own inadequacies. Even the most common individual would know better." Constance stuck her nose in the air and moved back to rejoin Sinclair and Annette, established quietly in the corner.

Carson felt like a specimen under glass, left standing in the middle of the floor alone. The other women whispered behind their hands, then hung their heads, seemingly ashamed for going along with Beatrice's plans. For once Carson was grateful to the overbearing Constance, for she had seemed to daunt the undauntable Beatrice. Carson's gaze caught on Kohl. He had grabbed Mr. Heimerman and was hauling the poor wretch out of the house by the collar.

Agnes Maplewitz stepped forward and offered her hand, swinging Carson's attention back to her own plight. "Carson, I want you to know the rest of us had nothing to do with the decorations, and we realize how ashamed we all should be for allowing Beatrice's personal vendetta to blind us. I hope you will accept our apologies."

"Of course." Buoyed by the success that had risen out of the ashes of disaster, Carson smiled brightly. To her surprise the women started applauding and red-faced Beatrice slammed from the room.

Carson raised her hands for silence. "Thank you. Now, since I am surrounded by friends, I would like to make an important announcement." Constance immediately started to make her way back to Carson's side, but Carson ignored the silent glare that she remain quiescent. "I am proud to announce my engagement to Mr. Kohl Baron."

Constance led the round of gasps. Annette tightened her hold on Sinclair and he patted her hand. Then all the women began crowding around Carson to offer congratulations. She accepted their well-wishes, but she kept watch on the door until Kohl reappeared, and Mr. Heimerman scurried in the direction that Beatrice had gone.

When he reappeared, he had Beatrice in tow and she begrudgingly offered her apologies and explained that she'd had personal reasons for picketing the brewery. The women turned away from her, seemingly aghast at being used, although Carson heard their concerns about their men leaving them at night to go drinking.

Kohl moved to Carson's side. "And I am proud to announce that in accordance with many of your wishes, Carson and I shall be turning a portion of the brewery into a restaurant to meet the needs of families. Not only will men be able to enjoy Sierra beer at our restaurant, but the entire family will be able to enjoy a fine meal at their sides."

The women cheered and Carson's pride swelled with his announcement until Constance clasped a hand on her arm. "Carson, dear, we need to talk . . . outside."

Kohl narrowed his eyes on the petite woman. "It is all right, Kohl. I shall only be a minute."

Carson followed the woman outside and discovered that Sinclair and Annette were already waiting. Constance swung on her. "What is the meaning of you announcing your engagement to that . . . that gunslinger? You are engaged to Sinclair!"

"Not anymore," came the deep male voice from the door.

Carson's head snapped up as Kohl joined her and dropped a possessive arm around her shoulders. Carson straightened her stance, feeling buoyed and totally supported without reservation for the first time

391

in her life. Having someone stand beside her was a heady feeling, and for the first time in her life since her parents died, Carson knew the true meaning of unconditional love.

"You are merely after her brewery!" accused Constance, who sputtered a string of indictments.

"Maybe you forget, but I'm already sole owner of the brewery, so—"

"So you wouldn't have been able to get your hands on it even if I had married Sinclair," Carson finished. "Oh yes, I know all about your scheme to marry me off to Sinclair so you could control the brewery since I have no other relatives. Well, your scheme didn't work. You sent me here to mature . . . and luckily I did."

"Well!" Constance huffed, outraged. "Come Sinclair. I am certainly glad I found out before you married *that* girl. We shall return to San Francisco and discuss betrothal plans with the Appletons."

Carson stopped a laugh behind her hand while she watched Annette's startled but pleased expression as Sinclair dragged her off behind Constance.

"Good riddance," Kohl said and swung Carson into his arms.

Despite the public place, Carson placed a peck on Kohl's lips, then craned her neck for one final glimpse of the three marching down the street. "Poor Annette. I pity her future."

Kohl raised her chin toward him. "I wouldn't. From all you told me about Miss Annette Appleton, she is going to get exactly what she's been bargaining for."

"Mr. Baron. Miss Mueller," a scratchy voice called from the house.

Carson and Kohl pivoted around to see Karl Heimerman grasping a sour-faced Beatrice's arm. "My wife has something more to say to both of you." He shook her arm. "All right, Bea."

Her scowl did not change and she huffed out, "I-I am truly sorry for all the trouble I caused." Her face twisted into the pretention of repentance.

"I suppose only time will tell whether you sincerely mean it or not," Kohl said on a skeptical note.

"She means it, Mr. Baron. And again, thank you for your kindness. We both greatly appreciate it." His fingers tightened on his wife's arm and she gave a curt nod. "Truly we do," Karl Heimerman said and pulled Beatrice back inside.

"What did you say to Mr. Heimerman to get him to force Beatrice to apologize?" Carson questioned, astounded.

Kohl winked at her. "I gave him a chance to put his life back together. I rehired him at the paper. But I didn't do it just for him. Now that I am going to have to focus my attention on getting our new business off the ground, I'm not going to have time to spend riding herd on a newspaper."

"I like the sound of that. *Our* business," Carson said and hugged him despite the eyes peeking at them through the curtains.

"For the rest of our lives everything I own is going to be ours. Want to go back inside and enjoy that old bag's comeuppance?"

Carson giggled and nodded. Beatrice had meant

to show her up at this reception and ended up losing her own position in the process. Carson almost could have pitied the woman if she hadn't been so vicious.

Inside, Beatrice was sitting on the couch alone. The other ladies were busy whisking away all the remnants of the decorations meant to crush Carson. One of the ladies noticed Carson and rushed over to her, a red tassel still in her hand.

"I want you to know I am happy to see Beatrice's fall. She's held too much sway for way too long. Although, honestly, I can't say that marching against that den of transgression was such a bad idea."

Carson did not comment since she considered Lily a friend. Quietly, Carson vowed to visit Lily and tell her the good news about her and Kohl at the first opportunity.

Carson basked in the glow of acceptance, still unable to believe her good fortune. Out of the ashes of her life the pieces had miraculously come together, making her stronger for the adversity. Her life was so full. Soon she would marry Kohl and they would build a wonderful life together. He liked her idea about the restaurant and the ladies of the town were in support.

She clasped her hands together. She glanced over at Kohl, who had been captured by a group of ladies and was patiently listening, although he kept looking her way no doubt hoping she would rescue him. That was a novel thought and she winked at him as she sauntered over to join the ladies.

"We were just telling Mr. Baron what a wonderful

idea you have for a restaurant, dear," Agnes enthused.

"Yes. I'm sure Mr. Maplewitz will be equally as excited to learn that soon he will be able to enjoy a libation now and then away from home still surrounded by his family."

"I'm sure he will," Kohl said tonelessly. If he were lucky he'd only be tarred and feathered when the other men heard how his future wife planned to rob them of a little solace.

Carson ringed her arm through Kohl's. "Will you please excuse us, ladies?" she said and pulled Kohl away from the cluster.

Once they were alone, he sighed. "I didn't think you were ever going to save me from those women."

They strolled toward the refreshment table. "Oh Kohl, it is all so wonderful. Nothing can happen, not even having to listen to those women, to mar my happiness today."

Carson had no more than got the words out of her mouth when Addie entered the parlor. The girl's wide eyes were set in a pasty white face.

Chapter Thirty-nine

Addie frowned. She could hardly believe her eyes as she elbowed her way through the crowd. Carson and Kohl seemed to be enjoying themselves. Glasses were tinkling and she heard one woman mention how much she'd always liked Carson. It was not what Addie had expected to find. She'd thought that Carson would be happy to get away from the reception, which would have made her job easier. But Carson and Kohl seemed to be perfectly relaxed. Trying to think fast, Addie made her way to Carson.

Before Addie could put the Babbitt brothers' plan into action, Carson reached out and took hold of Addie's hands. "Oh Addie, have you heard the good news?" Carson virtually bubbled.

Misgivings filled her big eyes. "What good news you talkin' about?"

Carson hugged the troubled child, then held her at arm's length, in her happiness missing the girl's apprehensive expression. "Oh Addie, I am so happy! Kohl and I are engaged. We are going to be married and open a restaurant at the brewery. And you can be part of our family, if you'd like."

Carson's euphoria waned as she watched the jumble of emotions flit across the girl's face. Carson knew that Kohl was not one of Addie's favorite people, but she thought that the girl would at least be glad for her. "What's wrong, Addie? Aren't you happy for Kohl and me?"

Addie tugged on her braid, which reminded her of how that dumb outlaw had done the same thing and threatened her. Her face drained of all color, she curled her lip. "If you're happy, guess I am, too."

It was then that Carson realized for the first time that something was bothering the girl other than her dislike for Kohl. "Are you okay? You look positively ghostly."

Addie shot Kohl a furious frown from under her sparse lashes, then made an effort to appear frightened. "I need to talk to you without him. Please, Carson. Please."

Kohl's face was filled with suspicion but he gave a curt nod. "I'll be nearby if you need me," he said and moved off.

Carson waited until they were out of his earshot. "All right, Addie, what is it?"

"I can't tell you here, not with him nearby starin' at us. But it's mighty important. Will you come away from here with me? Please, Carson."

Carson glanced back over her shoulder at Kohl. He was staring, cynicism on his face. Then she searched Addie's young face; it was filled with fear.

Those two did not get along, so Carson could understand Addie's reluctance to speak with Kohl around.

"All right, Addie, we can speak over by the door."

"No! I mean . . . can't we talk outside? I-I don't want any of these women to overhear either," she stuttered.

"I suppose it would be okay."

Carson followed the girl from the house and out into the yard. The day was warming and Carson fanned herself. "Okay, Addie, I want you to tell me what is troubling you?"

"Over here, let's talk in the shade. It's heatin' up pretty good out here," Addie said and scampered over to a thick clump of bushes at the far edge of the yard.

Carson sighed and followed after the girl. She had been constantly running off and acting rather strange, so her behavior now did not do more than annoy Carson. She stepped into the patch of shade beneath a spreading poplar tree and placed her hands on her hips.

"All right, Addie, what is this all abou—"

Carson's sentence was suddenly cut off and she found herself whisked off her feet and plucked hard into the bushes. Flashes of the men who had attacked her before grasped her and she struggled with all her might, trying to cry out. To her horror Addie stepped in beside the masked men and just stood calmly by while the four men gagged her, tied her ankles and her hands behind her back.

"Don't hurt her. You promised," Addie hissed,

dashing Carson's hopes that Addie would go hail Kohl and bring help.

It did not take long before Carson found herself tossed into the back of a wagon and a canvas cover thrown over her. She heard the sharp snap of a whip and the wagon gave a jerk. It was hot under the canvas and salty perspiration dripped into her eyes, causing them to sting. Carson could hear muffled voices, but could not discern what was being said as the wagon rumbled away from Kohl and help.

It seemed like an eternity before the wagon came to a halt and the canvas was thrust aside. The bright sun caused her to blink. As she was able to focus, the ugly faces of the men came into clear view. She had been kidnapped by the Babbitts and those two awful men who had attacked her!

"You're gonna smother her," Addie cried and pulled the gag off Carson.

"Why, Addie?" Carson rasped, gasping air into her lungs. The girl refused to meet her gaze, instead she hung her head and stepped back.

"You don't need to know why yet," Avery Babbitt sneered and cut the ropes binding her ankles. He gave her a shove. "Get inside, little altar girlie." His grin was lewd. "Once we get the information outta ya what we need, we're gonna have us our own little sacrifice. Then we're gonna rob the mint in town 'n' show ever'body that we're no fools."

"Don't forget, I getta be first," Bart whined and hovered near Carson. "You excite me more'n the thought of all them shiny new coins we's gonna get us."

Carson stumbled and Bart caught her up, lifting her into his arms. He tried to kiss her, but she bit his lip. He pushed her back and tasted blood. "Well, sweet thing, you're goin' pay for that."

"Don't you come near me again!"

"I'm goin' to do more than come near you." Bart smirked and dipped his head as they entered the dimly lit shack.

Carson blinked to adjust her eyes to the dark room when a shadowy figure in the far corner moved into the light of the flickering candle. "Gideon!" Carson cried, relief flooding through her. "I knew there was a reason why you left so suddenly. I knew you hadn't taken my inheritance and run off. I just knew it! Oh, Gideon, how long have they held you here?"

Slick gave a vicious chuckle. "She thinks that we're holdin' you captive, Farley. Don't that beat all."

All five men threw back their heads and laughed. Then Jake pulled out a chair and Carson found herself flung into it and securely tied. She looked to Gideon. "What are they laughing for?"

Slick grabbed a lock of Carson's hair and twirled it around his dirty fingers. "How do you suppose we come to be watchin' you, girlie?"

Carson jerked her head, effectively pulling her hair out of his hand. "I don't understand."

"Don't you?" Jake snickered, having to get his two cents in. "Your precious guardian sicked those two on you and we merely joined forces with 'em after you escaped us. You do recall that little fun we had, don't you?"

Carson shook her head in disbelief. "Gideon? It isn't true, is it?"

Gideon shrugged and took a seat across from her. "Afraid it is, my dear."

"But why? I don't understand."

"Couldn't live on only half the income from the brewery. I spent your portion that I was supposed to be saving for you, and then you had to get yourself banished here. I had hoped you would marry that rich man and forget all about your inheritance since you'd have all the money you needed. 'Fraid that once you arrived I had no choice. I cleaned out the safe deposit box and planned to leave the area. But a note wrote to you by your father before he died kept me here. My partner and I hoped the two boys here"—he motioned to Slick and Saul leaning against the wall with lurid smirks on their faces—"would force you to tell them where the key was hidden and not make this untidy business necessary. But I am afraid you've been a naughty girl. You haven't been very cooperative."

"I don't know anything about a key. The only key I have is the one you gave me to the safe deposit box."

"You can quit the innocent act, girlie," Slick said.

Carson sighed and deigned not to answer the man. Although she hadn't the slightest idea what Gideon was talking about. Then her gaze trailed to Addie. "What does she have to do with this?"

"The fool girl has been spying on us. We merely caught her and then were able to reach a mutual agreement," Gideon offered, careful not to mention that the girl's part was thought up by Avery.

"Addie, I don't understand you," Carson blurted out. "This is where you have been disappearing to all this time?"

Unable to tolerate Carson's disappointment in her and stand idly by any longer, Addie jumped forward and hissed at Avery. "Where's my box? You promised to return it, and you promised not to harm Carson."

Avery grasped her arm. "You stupid kid. Get the hell outta my sight and I might think on returnin' your dumb box—if 'n' when I get 'round to it." He thrust her so hard that she fell.

"Don't hurt her. She's just a child," Carson screamed.

Addie's eyes registered disbelief. Carson was still trying to protect her after what she'd caused. She had never meant for Carson to come to harm. "You fat donkey's rear end! You wart hog!" she screamed at Avery, scrambled to her feet, and bolted from the shack.

Jake started after her, but Avery's hand shot out and stayed his brother. "Forget about the brat. She's just got her tail singed, is all. She'll come back when she cools off since she wants that box o' hers back."

"Kohl will come after all of you now," Carson yelled, her heart praying that Addie would realize what she had done and do the right thing.

"I wouldn't be so smug, little altar girlie. That young'un hated your gunslinger enough to get you brung here. She ain't gonna risk nothin' to help you now," Avery said, confident of his words.

Carson sagged in her chair, fear rising anew as she looked around the dank room. She was trapped like a bird in a cage of cats. The man she had called uncle had betrayed her. Trying to keep her spirits up, she fingered the plain gold band despite the fact that her hands were tied behind her back. It had been Kohl's and she hoped it would give her courage to endure what she feared lay ahead.

Addie cursed under her breath and kicked at rocks littering her path as she trudged aimlessly out of Chinatown. That dumb old Avery Babbitt was going to pay for not returning her treasured box. And he had gone back on his promise. Now Addie feared that those men were going to hurt Carson. She didn't want that to happen. An idea sparked into her head and she started to run toward the apartment. She'd get her box back and free Carson. Then she'd kill Kohl Baron all by herself!

Addie reached the brewery and ignored Horse, who was leaning against the door frame, fanning himself. "What you in such a all-fired hurry fer, girl?"

Addie rushed up the stairs. The door was locked. She tried pounding her shoulder against it, but it wouldn't give. In a panic, she rushed back to Horse.

"You got a key to the upstairs?"

"Eh?"

Fighting to hold her temper, the girl grabbed the funnel out of his hand and jammed it into his ear. She yelled, "You got a key to upstairs?"

Horse patted his hip pocket. "What you need it fer? Nobody's home."

Addie watched his reactions and despite the fact that she liked the old man she grabbed at his pocket, ripping it from his hip.

The key clattered to the ground.

A horrified look dropped over the old man's lined face. "Sorry," she mumbled as she fumbled for the key. "Don't try to follow me," she warned.

Horse sadly shook his head and watched the girl rush back upstairs. Glumly, he admitted he didn't have the strength to stop her.

Addie burst through the door and went right to the wardrobe in the bedroom. "It has to be here," she snarled and tore the clothes from their places. "At last!" she cried out when her fingers touched cold, smooth metal.

"At last what?" came an enraged male voice.

Addie's intake of breath was clearly audible from across the room.

"Well?"

"Nothin', I ain't doin' nothin'," she mumbled as her fingers inched along the barrel, groping for the handle.

"Nothing! You nearly knocked Horse over, steal the key to the apartment from that old man who

404

cares for you, and then you try to say nothing. And where is Carson?"

When the girl did not turn around and look at him or attempt to answer Kohl strode toward her, determined to find out what was going on.

Addie tensed at the pounding footfalls thudding in her direction. Frantic, she scrambled to get a good grip on the gun that Carson had told her Kohl had stashed in the wardrobe after Carson had been attacked by those awful men.

Addie's hand had just settled around the grip when she felt Kohl grab her shoulder. Her hand closed around the butt, one finger ringed the trigger, her thumb cocked the hammer.

Trembling, she spun around and fired.

Chapter Forty

An instant before the girl pulled the trigger Kohl saw the glint of metal in her hand and managed to leap out of the way. The bullet whizzed by his head, just missing him. If his reflexes had not been honed sharp by years of living by his guns, she might have killed him.

Kohl did not have a moment to spare; Addie was cocking the gun again. He leaped up and pounced on the girl, which sent the gun skidding across the floor. He grabbed her by the arm, and as he was hauling her to her feet she bit his hand and kicked him in the shins.

Suddenly another blast from a gun stopped the struggle. Still panting from his arduous climb up the stairs, gun in hand, Horse hollered, "That's enough. Addie, you get yourself on the bed and settle down. Kohl, I want you to explain what's goin' on here."

"I don't know what's going on. I came looking for Carson and the first thing I know Addie shoots at me."

Horse swung on the cowering girl. "All right, young'un, you stole the key to this here place, nearly knockin' me flat in the process, then run on up here and end up takin' a potshot at Kohl. I think it's 'bout time you start talkin'."

"Where's Carson?" Kohl demanded. "If you've done anything to harm her . . ."

Addie's lip trembled as she looked from man to man. She was cornered. There was no way out, no escaping. Neither man's face held sympathy for her. "I didn't mean for nothin' to happen to Carson. They promised!" she blurted out and started to cry.

His heart pounding with fear for Carson, Kohl ignored Horse and grabbed Addie's shoulders. "Who? Who promised?"

"I didn't mean for nothin' to happen to her," she repeated in sobs. "I didn't."

Kohl grabbed her shoulders tighter. Slowly, his words precise, he questioned her. "Addie, you've got to tell me about Carson. Do you understand me? You've got to help Carson."

"They said they'd take care of you." She sobbed harder. Tears streaming down her face, she managed between sobs, "Carson's uncle, those men who tried to rob the stage, and those other two, they took my box and wouldn't give it back unless I helped them. I didn't want nothin' to happen to Carson. Honest. They made me."

"You know where they stashed her?" Horse barked out and leaned his ear trumpet closer.

"Horse, I'm awful sorry."

"It's all right little one, you didn't hurt me none. But if you know where Sunny is you'd best fess up."

"They-they took her to Chinatown." She sniffled. "A shack on one of them back streets, in back of the Wong store."

Fighting to hold his temper under tight rein, Kohl demanded, "Do you think you can find it?"

"Y-yes."

"Good girl. Horse, you fetch the sheriff and direct him to that store. Okay, Addie, let's go."

Kohl saddled his horse and put Addie up in front of him just in case she had a change of heart. Driving the animal for all it was worth, they raced toward Chinatown. Around the corner from the shack Kohl gave Addie instructions and warned that she could put Carson's life in jeopardy should she waver.

Addie nodded and hurried to the shack. She gave a last look back toward where Kohl waited for her signal and then ducked inside the building.

"What you doin' back?" Avery growled.

"Came for my box," she snapped and surveyed the room. Gideon was sitting across the table from Carson, staring blankly at a crumpled paper in his hand. All the others but Avery were lounging in a circle playing cards. Avery took a threatening step toward Addie and grabbed her arm. She'd been grabbed so many times that her arm was throbbing. Next thing she knew she was plunked into a chair next to Carson.

"You stay put while I think," Avery ordered and went to confer with his brothers.

Addie leaned over to Carson. "They didn't hurt you none, did they?"

Carson shook her head and did not speak to the girl. Instead her eyes trailed to the far end of the table. A knife with its point imbedded into the wood gleamed in the candlelight. She had been working the ropes all the while they had been questioning her. Now, with the men seemingly ignoring her, she let the ropes binding her hands slip off her wrists and lunged for the knife.

Gideon's head snapped up. He started for her until the other five joined the pursuit. Then he moved into a far corner out of the action.

"Nobody move any closer," Carson ordered, brandishing the knife as she backed toward the door. "Addie, get over here by me."

Avery threw back his head and laughed. "Now you know you don't want to go tryin' to cut any one o' us, little altar girlie."

Carson was quaking, fear threatening to overcome her as the men slowly advanced on her. She took another step backward, her heel coming down on the edge of a tin cup. Her ankle twisted and she went down.

It was then all hell broke loose. Carson screamed. Addie launched herself on her hands and knees in front of the men, screeching for Carson to run as the men tumbled over her like dominoes. Carson managed to scramble to her feet and dashed from the shanty, only to run headlong into a hard chest.

"No!" she shrilled. She pummeled against the

chest, fighting for all her might.

"Carson, it's me," Kohl said and quickly lifted the hysterical woman off her feet and carried her behind a stack of crates.

Suddenly realizing it was Kohl, Carson ringed her arms around his neck so tight that Kohl started to choke. "Thought you'd be glad to see me," he rasped in a strangled voice. "But you're trying to suffocate me."

Reason finally returned and she loosened her grip. "Oh, I'm sorry. Are you all right?"

"Other than knowing what a noose now feels like, I'm fine. And you're safe now."

"Oh, Kohl, Addie's still in there," she cried.

"Stay here." He handed her a gun. "Use it if you have to." With his other one drawn he crept toward the shanty.

Carson watched in fright as the Babbitt brothers burst from the building, followed by the other two and Addie. Kohl leaped in front of them.

"Hold it right where you are unless you want a hole blown clean through your guts."

Avery gave an evil grin and raised his gun. Before he could aim it at Kohl, Kohl fired and Avery fell to his knees, the gun falling from his hand into the dust. The others immediately dropped their weapons, raising their hands in surrender without a fight. Jake kneeled down and cradled his groaning brother, who was holding his gut.

"Whaddya go and shoot him fer?" Jake cried.

"You're lucky I didn't kill him," Kohl returned and

410

waved the others against the wall. "The rest of you kneel down with your hands against the back of your filthy necks. Addie, go collect their guns."

"Nobody move," the sheriff called out from behind them. He was in the lead of four lanky deputies with Horse bringing up the rear.

"I've got everything under control," Kohl returned. The sheriff holstered his gun and directed his deputies to cuff the kneeling men.

"Looks like you didn't need any help, Baron. I'll be damned if you don't already have them down on their knees repenting their dirty deeds," the sheriff said with a chuckle at his own attempts at humor. He took off his hat and rubbed his forehead. "The way old Horse was carrying on I was sure we'd find a bloody massacre on our hands. You must be changing, Baron. Only one wounded.

"There's a healthy reward for those Babbitts. Come on over to the office when you get a chance and I'll have the necessary paperwork ready so you can collect it." The sheriff turned away to help the deputies, then stopped and pivoted around. "And . . . ah . . . thanks, Baron. Guess I was wrong about you. Welcome to Carson City."

Kohl gave a nod. "Glad to hear it."

Kohl watched the sheriff head toward the outlaws until Carson joined him. "Oh, Kohl, where are Addie and Gideon? Addie must have gone back inside," Carson cried. "Gideon could harm her!"

"Wait here." Kohl rushed back into the shanty. He looked around. Gideon was nowhere in the room.

Then his gaze caught on Addie. She was sitting on the floor, her box open, sorting through her treasures. He went over to the child and kneeled down.

"No!" she yelled and tried to hide her possessions from him.

But Kohl had noticed the silver dollar shot through the center. He grabbed it up.

"Leave it alone! It's mine." She made a grab for it, and when she did the yellowed newspaper clippings fell open onto the ground.

Kohl read the headlines:

BYSTANDER KILLED BY GUNSLINGER'S WILD SHOT

She jumped up and beat at his chest. "You murderer. You killed my pa! You kilt him, and I'm gonna kill you!" She grabbed for a gun lying at her side, but Kohl was quicker. He got the gun and tossed it away. Then Addie seemed to crumble into his arms, her chest wracked with sobs.

With one hand Kohl read the rest of the article. It described the demise of Addie's father at Kohl's hand. His heart went out to the child and it suddenly dawned on him that Addie was the one behind the anvil that had trounced him. "Oh God, Addie. No wonder you hate me."

She pulled away and grasped the piece of lead from her box, shaking it at him. "This is the lead what kilt him; I saved it. It's from your gun! Why'd you kill my pa?" She half screamed, half cried. "Why?"

Kohl grabbed her wrist, took the lead, and examined it. Then relief coloring his face, he glanced back up at the shaking girl. "Addie, I am sorry about your pa. But this lead didn't come from one of my guns." Her expression still showed disbelief, so Kohl emptied a cartridge from his gun and held it out to the girl.

Reluctantly, she took the bullet from his hand and compared it with the one that had been taken out of her pa. Tears befogging her eyes, she looked up at Kohl. "It doesn't match."

He laid a comforting hand on her quaking shoulder. "No, Addie, it doesn't match."

"Then you really didn't kill my pa?"

"No."

"But you were there, the newspaper said so," she cried, not sure what to believe. She had held the hate locked inside her for two years, and she wasn't sure she could let go of it.

Kohl gave a bitter laugh. "Yes, I was there. I'll always remember that day in Bodie. I was leading my horse down the street when two of the men I'd been trailing burst out of a saloon, their guns blazing. There was another one in the alley. He grabbed a woman hostage, wildly shooting at anything that moved. There was an exchange of gunfire. I got the two from the saloon, but the third one got away with the hostage. I left town after the third one before the sheriff had a chance to question me.

"Addie, most sheriffs have no use for gunslingers. So he must've assumed I shot your pa and closed the case."

"W-what happened to the third man . . . the one who really kilt my pa?" she ventured, finally believing him.

"I caught up with him five days later. I killed him," Kohl said without emotion.

"And the hostage?"

"He had killed her." What he didn't tell the child was that the woman had been raped and horribly abused before she'd died.

A scream was torn from her trembling lips and she thrust herself against him crying her heart out. Not knowing what else to do, Kohl cradled the terribly distraught child while she wept. "I almost kilt you," she wailed.

"But you didn't, Addie. You didn't," he crooned softly.

"And all those awful articles in the newspaper about you and Carson; they were my fault. And the anvil, too. I'm sorry," she cried.

"All is forgiven, Addie," he murmured in a calming voice and decided not to press her further. Some things were best buried.

When her flow of tears seemed to stem, Kohl looked about for Carson, suddenly realizing she had obeyed him and had not followed him into the shack.

"Why don't we go outside and rejoin Carson?" he suggested.

Exhausted from the lifting of such a heavy burden, Addie meekly nodded her agreement. "Then

414

you don't hate me?"

"No, kid. I could never hate family." He smiled down at the child. "Don't you want your box?"

Love pouring into the place in her heart vacated by hatred, Addie looked down at the box. "Maybe the box, the rosary, and the doll. My ma gived them to me. But none of the other things. Don't need the other stuff no more."

"Good girl," Kohl said and waited while she tore up the page on vengeance she'd saved from the Bible and scooped up the box.

A big grin on her face, she announced, "I'm gonna look up 'turn the other cheek' and put that page in my box."

Kohl sagely decided not to ask her what she meant. He was just glad that they had worked out their problems. And he knew that that would make Carson happy, since she had taken such a liking to the girl.

They walked arm in arm out into the hot sun. The sheriff and deputies had already hauled off the men. Only Horse was leaning heavily on a nearby wagon wheel, puffing.

"Where's Carson?" Kohl questioned loud enough for the old man to hear.

Horse scratched his head. "Sunny?" he echoed. "Oh. She mumbled something 'bout goin' to Lily's to warn her 'cause that Farley man's escaped and she said he had mentioned Lily's name while he was questionin' her 'bout some key."

Kohl's fists clenched. "That crazy little fool. I

thought she had obeyed me and stayed outside, but she must have looked in and discovered Farley was gone. And now she's impetuously rushed headlong into calamity . . . again."

He swung around and headed for his horse. It was gone. Carson. He cursed under his breath and unharnessed one of the wagon horses. Addie was right on his heels. "I'll go with you," she insisted.

"No! You help Horse back to the brewery, and you can tell him the good news about Carson and me." She hesitated. "Mind me! Now git!"

He watched the girl reluctantly scamper over to a confused Horse. Explaining the situation to him, she helped him into the wagon before Kohl mounted the horse bareback and wheeled it toward Lily's.

As he spurred the animal to the limits of its endurance, he could not understand why Farley would go to Lily's. But of one thing he was certain: If there was going to be trouble, Carson would be right in the middle of it.

Chapter Forty-one

Worry over Lily's well-being in face of Gideon's desperation spurred Carson into a gallop as she hurried to Lily's place on the north edge of town. She reined in Kohl's horse in back of the neat house. Everything looked peaceful. The Seasons were filing into a buggy.

Carson joined them. "Are you all leaving?" she questioned.

Spring leaned out of the buggy. "Yeah. Lily gived us the rest of the afternoon off. We heared from one of the customers that you're about to snag Kohl Baron." The girls giggled and Carson blushed.

"Yes," she answered. "He's a lucky man," she added since she knew they all thought she was the lucky one. Then a thought came to her. "Where's Lily?"

Summer shrugged. "Inside." She cracked the whip over the horse's rump. It was rare that Lily allowed them all the whole afternoon and she wanted to leave before Carson engaged them in any more conversation, which would give Lily time to have a change of heart.

Winter leaned out of the buggy and called back, "Giddy's with her, so you might not want to disturb them."

Her heart increased its beats when she heard Gideon's name. And without giving thought to her own safety or what Gideon's state of mind had been to come and try to harm Lily, Carson whirled into the house.

Hearty sounds of laughter danced down the stairs, drawing Carson's attention. Taking the gun Kohl had given her from her skirt pocket, Carson carefully made her way upstairs to the door left ajar. She listened for signs of duress.

A moan issued from the other side of the door and Carson burst into the room. She came to a dead halt. Her mouth dropped open with a gasp and she lowered the gun.

Gideon and Lily were lying in bed, Lily's dress front open. "Why, honey, can't you see Lily's workin'?"

Gideon leaped off the bed, his trousers unfastened. He cursed under his breath; he'd never dreamed she'd show up here. He took a threatening step toward Carson, but she raised the gun.

"Take one more step and I'll shoot."

Gideon stopped.

"Oh, Lily, I'm so glad I was able to get here in time to save you from him. Get a rope so we can tie him up until we can call the sheriff."

Lily's fingers worked the buttons down the front

of her dress as she climbed off the bed. "But honey, there ain't no law against a man payin' a call to Lily in the afternoon."

Carson hurriedly poured out the story of her kidnapping since Lily already knew about his thievery.

Her eyes huge, Lily answered, "You mean Giddy's a fugitive?"

"Yes. Hurry. Get a rope." Carson's hand was trembling and Gideon did not take his eyes off the gun.

Lily moved to Carson's side. "Better let me handle the gun, honey. You look near spooked, and we wouldn't want it to go off accidentally."

Grateful for Lily's great presence of mind, Carson gave over the gun. "Don't take it off him. Where's the rope?"

"Take the silk cords off my wrappers in the wardrobe in the next room. We can use them."

Carson hurriedly obtained the cords, but as she rejoined Lily the cords were suddenly yanked out of her hands and twisted around her own wrists, and she found herself tossed onto the bed.

"Lily, I don't understand," she cried.

Lily was standing behind Gideon repinning her mussed tresses, and he now had possession of the gun.

"It's very simple, really," Gideon smirked. "Lily's my partner."

Carson's eyes shot to Lily. "I don't believe it!"

" 'Fraid it's true, honey. Your presence here has complicated things a tad, though." She leaned an arm on Gideon's shoulder. "I had hoped that you and Kohl would keep each other busy, so we'd be long gone before anybody figured it out." She let out a sigh. "Pity."

"You're the partner Gideon mentioned at the shanty?" Carson mumbled, still having a hard time believing that the good-hearted Lily could be so diabolical. Then she remembered how Lily had offered to help in the apartment, and she had known which drawer had held the sheets when she had helped her change them. Realization hit her that Lily must have been hiding behind a facade of big-hearted kindness as a ploy to search for the key Gideon had been after.

Gideon laughed. "It was Lily's idea to start stealing your inheritance little by little years ago when I ran into financial trouble."

Lily cast him an annoyed frown. "What're we gonna do with her, Giddy? She's Kohl's woman, so we can't just kill her. He's been too good to me in the past. Besides, if we did kill her Kohl would hunt us down no matter how long it took him."

"Okay, okay. Finish tying her up so she can't warn anyone until we're long gone."

Carson opened her mouth to protest, but found herself gagged. "Sorry, honey. But I told you a gal's got to make a living."

Lily had just begun securing Carson's ankles when the door downstairs slammed. Her head snapped up. "What's that?"

"It's probably one of your Seasons come back to retrieve something she forgot," Gideon offered. It couldn't be anyone come after him since he did not think anyone would be so foolish as to slam the door

420

and alert them. "Finish with the girl while I go check."

"Be careful, Giddy."

Gideon had barely closed the door behind him when a thud echoed from the hallway. Her mouth dry, Lily picked up Kohl's gun and crept to the door. She was slowly opening it when all of a sudden it was thrust open, throwing her off balance.

Kohl rushed into the room and Carson watched helplessly as Lily threw herself into Kohl's arms. "Oh Kohl, I knew you'd come," she sobbed. "I was so frightened."

"Everything's fine now."

"What about Gideon Farley?" Lily asked to Kohl's back as he went to Carson's side.

"He's all taken care of." Kohl stood over Carson, a smile on his face, his hands on his hips. "It's tempting to leave you that way, you little troublemaker. All trussed up like that would keep you out of trouble."

Carson narrowed her eyes and tried to speak from behind the gag. To her relief despite the fact he hadn't removed the gag, he untied her ankles, then worked the ropes on her wrists. She had been glaring at him, but out of the corner of her eyes she noticed Lily creeping slowly toward Kohl, the butt of the gun raised.

With a muffled roar, Carson launched herself from the bed and vaulted onto Lily, sending them both flying backward, Lily landing on her back with a clunk. The gun was knocked out of her hand and the two women struggled.

Kohl jumped into the female fray and grabbed

Lily. He was just about to pull her off Carson when Carson bunched up her fist and let fly with a right upper cross, smacking Lily square in the jaw. Lily slumped in Kohl's arms.

Carson gained her feet, removed the gag, and brushed her hands. "Glass jaw."

Kohl put Lily on the bed, then turned on Carson. "Would you mind explaining your latest rash exhibition?"

"She was working with Gideon, Kohl. If I hadn't just put on that 'rash exhibition,' as you call it, she could have killed you with your own gun."

Kohl's gaze swung to Lily, who was just coming around. She sat up and rubbed her jaw. She shrank under his glare of disappointment and dealt him a guilty shrug. "As I told Carson, a gal's got to look out for herself."

Suddenly it all became clear why Lily and the Seasons had not been able to learn anything about the trouble at the brewery. Kohl shook his head in disgust. How could he have been so wrong about her? "Tie her up."

Carson nodded and made short work of the woman. Then she returned to Kohl. "I'm sorry, Kohl. I know you two were friends."

Kohl took Carson into his arms and smoothed back her flaming mass of hair. "Nothing to be sorry about. The only important thing is that you weren't harmed." Then he winked. "Only problem is now that bunch of women may return to march against the brewery since they won't have to worry about Lily's place anymore."

Carson's giggle was abruptly cut short.

"Baron! Kohl Baron! Come out here and face me like a man!" an enraged voice hollered from out in the street.

Carson watched in horror as Kohl's hand left her shoulder and drifted down to his gun. "No!" she cried as Kohl broke away from her. She rushed to the window.

Standing out in the street, his shirttails flapping in the wind underneath his suitcoat and waving a gun, Gideon stared back at her. "Gunslinger's lady," he sneered up at Carson. "Tell that man of yours to quit hiding behind your petticoats and come down here and face me like a man."

Carson swung back from the window to find Kohl casually checking his gun. "You can't go down there! He could kill you!"

"Gideon does consider himself to be an expert with a gun, Kohl," Lily said quietly. "Why don't you just let us go and save ever'body a whole lot o' trouble?"

Kohl ignored Lily's entreaty, picked up the gun on the floor, and gave it to Carson. "Keep an eye on her. I won't be long."

"No! You can't go out there and face him. You're done with that life, Kohl. Just let me go fetch the sheriff. Please!" she pleaded.

Kohl looked down at Carson. Fear was reflected in her eyes. "There are some things in life a man can't ignore. That man down there could have killed you —"

"But he didn't," she interjected.

Kohl cradled her face in his hands and ever so gently pressed his lips to hers. It was a tender kiss, filled with love. His lips were soft and warm, moist and reassuring. "I love you," he whispered against her lips. "Always remember that."

Carson fought down the urge to beg him not to go and clung to him. "I love you, too. Come back to me," she murmured in a raspy voice dry with fear.

"I will. But do me a favor."

"Anything, my love."

"Don't look out the window. Promise me you won't. And this time I want you to keep your promise."

Her eyes filled with tears, Carson nodded her head. He kissed her hard and long, holding her to him as if he never intended to let her go. Then he was gone and Carson heard Gideon's voice spike through the window.

"What's the matter, Baron? You yellow?"

A stifling quiet fell over the room. Fearing her legs would not hold her, Carson forced herself to sit in a chair away from the window. Somehow she was going to keep her promise this time. Her gaze caught on Lily. The pathetic woman was slumped down on the bed sullenly staring at the wall.

Eternal minutes passed and Carson held her breath as she waited, afraid to breathe.

Suddenly two shots in quick succession rang out.

Her hand went to her trembling lips. One of the men was dead. It couldn't be Kohl! Unable to endure the wait any longer, Carson rose to her feet on unsteady legs and stumbled down the stairs and out into the street.

A half dozen spectators milled around the two men. Gideon sat on the ground, pressing a hand to his shoulder, a sour expression on his face. Carson's eyes frantically searched for Kohl. He was quietly talking to two men, one of which was the sheriff. It took all the strength she could muster not to go to him and interrupt them.

Carson noticed the sheriff say something to Kohl, which caused him to turn in her direction. He nodded to the sheriff and started toward her. That was all it took. She ran to him and locked her arms around his waist.

"I was so frightened you'd be killed."

He took her face in his hands. "My crazy, wonderful, impetuous woman. If you ever followed my dictates, I wouldn't know how to act." He snaked an arm around her waist. "Let's go home. The sheriff'll take care of Lily and Farley."

Kohl helped Carson up onto his horse in front of him and they rode slowly back to the apartment while he told her all about the secret Addie had finally relinquished.

Horse and Addie were there waiting for them when they arrived. Before they had barely closed the door, Addie rushed to explain herself and apologized again to Kohl. Once they were all seated, Addie readied refreshments and passed them around while Kohl poured out the story of Lily and Gideon. Addie was amazed to hear about the key which had been Gideon's downfall.

"You mean that the key your pa was talkin' 'bout

in that note your guardian kidnapped you for was love?"

Carson sat on the worn couch, holding Kohl's hand. "Yes. My father told me from the time I was old enough to understand that love was the key to happiness. In the note Gideon had, my father had written that he hoped I'd find the key he'd told me about since it would open the door which would fulfill my dreams. Gideon thought it was riches. I suppose it is." She squeezed Kohl's hand and he sent her an adoring smile. "Only not the kind Gideon thought."

Horse took a sip from his glass. "Well, I'll be."

All heads swung to Horse. Carson laughed. "You loveable old scoundrel, you can hear better than you let on."

"Must just be from the dent those fellows put in my trumpet." Horse shrugged his shoulders at the disbelieving faces and took another sip of lemonade. Then he gathered himself to his feet. "I think it's time Addie and I mosey along home," he announced.

"But I live here," Addie protested.

Horse winked at Carson. Then he took hold of Addie's hand. "Not tonight you don't, young'un."

"Why?" she demanded.

Kohl ringed his arm around Carson and pulled her in close to him. "Carson and I have some things to talk over."

"What you gonna talk about that I can't be here for?" she demanded, suspicious.

Horse fought back a knowing grin and gave the

426

girl's arm a yank. "When you're growed you'll understand."

Kohl waited until they were alone and lifted Carson into his arms. "Now that we're finally alone, how about going into the bedroom for a little *talk?*"

"I thought you'd never ask." She giggled and kissed his neck as he strode into the bedroom and laid her down on the bed.

Crooning words of love, Kohl had just begun unbuttoning her shirtfront when an insistent knock at the door echoed into the room. They tried to ignore it, but the hammering kept up. Kohl muttered a string of curses and went to the door while Carson sat up, hurriedly refastened her buttons, and joined him.

Addie was standing at the door, a huge box straining her arms. "Horse said I could bring this up, since it just arrived and it's to both of you. But he said I can't stay. Here." She thrust it into Kohl's arms and skipped down the stairs.

Carson closed the door and threw the lock while Kohl set the box in the middle of the floor and tore into it. "What is it?"

A Cheshire grin spread his lips when he pulled an iron kettle out of the box. They broke into a round of laughter and Kohl removed a note tucked inside the pot and read it out loud.

Thought that by now you two would need a complete set of my cookware to set up house with, since I knowed from the first you two were destined. Surprised since I haven't been

427

nearby, aren't you? Please accept the cookware as thanks for saving my money from those robbers. Hope you enjoy many good meals with them.

— Mortimer South
(Pots)

"Oh Kohl, he knew all along we would fall in love," Carson cried.

Kohl dropped the pot back into the box and gathered Carson into his arms. "There's no doubt," he murmured with a wink. Cutting off her protest, he kissed her long and hard. With deft fingers he began unbuttoning her shirtfront again as he whispered against her lips. "Now, where were we before we were so rudely interrupted?"

Epilogue

November 1885

Carson sat at her rosewood secretary, dipping a quill pen into the inkpot. She placed a long envelope in front of her on the shiny surface of the desk and scrawled the San Francisco address in swirling letters. Outside the nearby window, snowflakes drifted onto the branches of the old pine at their home on Robinson Street. She and Kohl had selected the spacious two-story together after she'd declined his offer to repurchase her parents' old home, stating that they needed a place to start their own family and build memories.

As she finished circling the last "i" on the address, Kohl came into the room and stood behind his beloved wife. He dropped a hand gently onto her shoulder. "What are you doing?"

"Addressing a letter to Mother Jude at the convent in San Francisco."

"Mother Jude? Isn't she the one who caught you

with that cigarette and was responsible for sending you to me?"

Carson placed her hand over her husband's, and gazed up at him with adoring eyes. "One and the same."

He chuckled. "I hope you thanked her for me."

"Actually, I'm sending her a copy of the family portrait we had taken with the three children and Addie in front of our successful restaurant."

"Why are you writing her after all this time?" Kohl wondered out loud.

"Because she predicted I'd come to ruin within five years. And since our fifth anniversary recently passed, I thought it fitting. One of these days I'd like to pay her a visit and personally show off my family." She picked up the photograph and Kohl took it out of her hand.

"Pity Mother Jude can't see how much Samantha looks like her mommy with those red curls of hers."

"And how much Nathan looks like his daddy, as does the baby."

"I think George looks like you," Kohl said.

Carson didn't argue because secretly she also thought George would have her fine features. Kohl handed her the photograph and she carefully slipped it into the envelope and sealed it.

Kohl took her hand and pulled her up into his arms. "Have I told you today how much I love you?" he whispered against her lips.

She leaned back and sent him a conspiratorial wink. "About seven times before the children got us out of bed to tattle that Addie was going for a sleigh ride with her first beau. But you can say it again. I love hearing it."

He hugged her. "Mrs. Baron, you are shameless. I lo—"

"Mama! Mama!" four-year-old Nathan bellowed, bursting into the room.

Carson and Kohl broke apart, and Carson went to the red-faced little boy, half-dressed, half-tangled in his snow outfit. "What is it, Nathan?"

"It's Sam'tha," he wailed as he struggled with the heavy coat.

Kohl kept a serious face and bent down to help his wife ready their son to go outside. "What did Samantha do this time?" Kohl asked. For an instant his thoughts shifted to some of Carson's infamous antics as a child and he wondered if the old nun could survive a visit with their precocious daughter.

Nathan screwed up his chubby face into a pout, forcing Kohl's attention back to the child. "She rushed outside without her coat. You told her not to. She's always doing no-no's."

With a groan Kohl rolled his eyes. "Just like her mama."